Star-Crossed:
The Confounding Calamities of Byron the Cad and Marietta the Zombie

To Margo Walsh

And oatmeal

Table of Contents

Part One

Part Two

Part One

In Which Our Heroes Make an Introductory Appearance, Or: Rose Water and Bile

"And so I held his little fluffy white body in my hands, feeling his racing pulse underneath my thumb—"

"It was your own pulse that you felt, if it was your thumb," the barkeep interjected between scrubs of the grungy wooden counter. The man telling the story with the enraptured attention of at least three serving wenches shot him an angry look. The barkeep took another glance at the dapper raconteur before going to retrieve more glasses. He was going to lose money on that one, all right.

"Then I leaned over its little head and opened my mouth as wide as it could go—"

"You didn't!" one of the serving girls squealed, oblivious to her other customer banging away for more beer.

If one word could be used to describe the bar, it would be sticky. The barkeep continued to wipe at the sticky silverware, the sticky windows, and the sticky tables—all ten of them—with three sticky people scattered among them like patches of scum floating on an otherwise clear lake. In this small, sluggish town, his bar was the only source of entertainment, and it tended to attract a certain clientele. One man looked as if, with any more liquor, dirt, and time, he could be the primogenitor of a new kind of alcohol-based plant life. The second was a grizzled man with a long, frazzled beard of wiry grey hairs everywhere but the top of his head. The third had a jacket made out of what could reasonably be construed as human flesh, if one were so inclined to ask the musket-wielding madman underneath it—but as none had dared approach, the barkeep had yet to learn the true answer. He reasoned with himself, however, that as sticky as his patrons could be, at least theirs was the honest, human filth, not the undeathly kind that too often hung around these parts. And even the well-kept yet annoying man, an obvious outsider who disrupted the temperate alkalinity of the bar, was better than a single Star-Crosser.

The churlish barkeep watched, still wiping at the same brown, sticky spot, as the young man levelled his gaze at the squeamish girl—whose customer was now so thirsty that dust was pouring out of his mouth—and pulled her close with an arm around her waist. His lip curled when his hand strayed too far south and found a clockwork leg meeting silky white flesh at her hipbone. But the girl, intrigued by the denouement of the story, was oblivious to its teller's disgust.

"I assure you, miss, every bit of this story is true. As true as Queen Victoria's illustrious and long-winded reign, as the Great Sailor as my witness." He clipped the consonants so that, even across the room, the barkeep could hear the air hitting his too-white teeth. Obviously, this man's blood was far bluer than that of the local clientele. "I opened my mouth and bit down, cracking the creature's skull with my teeth, and began eating its brains as I had seen my mother do hundreds of times before. My father, you see, Sir Reginald Llewelyn-Cave, had kept my mother after she turned. She was chained up in her boudoir and fed every day precisely at three, when everyone else was taking their tea. I would sneak in, young delinquent that I was, and more often than not, her repast would consist of several baby bunnies that we had ensnared from the grounds. I was merely imitating my mother; I could not possibly hope to understand her condition at my young age."

"That's disgusting!" another serving girl, a brunette, intoned. "What did it taste like?"

He let go of the girl with the clockwork leg, put his thin, white fingers around the brunette's jaw, and pulled her close as if to kiss her. "Rather having the consistency of scrambled eggs." The girl made a face, but he drew her closer until her pink skin began to blanch under his fingers. "If said eggs were, of course, the foetid, rotten corpses of half-drowned snakes. What did you think they would taste like? Frog's legs? Goose liver?" He threw her face away and dismissed her with a slight wave of his hand.

"Greta," the barkeep barked. The brunette shot up like hand from a grave and straightened her apron. "Why don't you check on those potatoes?" The girl, trying to compose herself and wiping the corners of her eyes with her sleeve, nodded and disappeared into the kitchen with a dull thump of its wooden door. He eyed the young stranger, still narrating in a nasal drone, and grumbled to himself again, wiping the same worn spot on the bar and shielding his eyes from the setting sun. There weren't too many fops like him around, not this far away from the order of the Guard and their protection. How did he get this far without any sort of weaponry? The only thing the barkeep could see that could potentially be a defensive tool was the young man's outlandish bowler, which dangled from the chair's edge.

The girl with the clockwork limb was now sitting on the storyteller's lap, idly picking at his coiffed hair and pressing herself up against his chest. There was a slight hiss from the machinery as she moved, puffing her skirt up mid-thigh. The barkeep thought that he might start paying the girls more if they stopped throwing themselves at every halfway decent-looking man—though this man was more than halfway decent, even handsome in a dilapidated, ruined kind of way, as copper becomes handsome with a slight patina—in the hopes of getting enough money to move away from this town and the Swarm of Crossers that congregated near the edge of its forest. Too often those stories ended with heartbreak and bruises, not fairytales and tiaras.

He realised with a bit of a shock that the sun was slowly sinking into the nearby hills. He had been far too distracted with the young stranger—a characteristic he never thought he would share with the likes of Greta. One of the sticky clientele was eyeing him, urging him to secure the place before the night descended fully.

"I'm locking the doors!" he yelled across the room. Only the grizzled man looked up from his foamy beer. The brass keys at his waist jangled as he walked towards the two heavy, reinforced wooden doors. Their magic locks, which shone when anything without a pulse approached, were intricate pieces of work, interlocking such that a stray finger could be pinched off if its owner wasn't careful. They hadn't had an attack for a few months, but the Swarm had been unusually active the night before, and that a full two days before the zenith of the Homunculus Star.

"—was killed by my ruthless Uncle Archibald for his money, leaving me bereft," the man continued, oblivious to the loud thumps of the lock's tumblers engaging. He reached into the right rear of his mouth and seemed to adjust something back there before droning on with his story. The man couldn't even pick his teeth like a normal person. The barkeep placed the last key on the ring into the final lock. But as he began to turn the last tumbler, a bright blue light began pulsing from the gears that littered the door like the opened back of a clock.

"Liza!" the barkeep yelled, backing away from the door until he ran into the bar and cried out at the pinch on his hipbone. Gooseflesh began to crawl up his legs as the last serving wench jumped up, lifted her skirt, and pulled out the two small hatchets she had been hiding. She twirled them in her fingers, tensing every muscle along her back as she took her place by the door to face the walking dead. The nightly rush of adrenalin soaked with slow terror grew a familiar knot in the base of his stomach.

"How did…?" the young man asked, now trying to shed the girl who desperately clung around his neck as the blue light grew brighter. Pulling her away by her upper arm, he checked a gold-plated pocket watch whose face bore far too many markings, frowned, and replaced it into his right trousers pocket. Still frowning, he walked towards the barkeep and Liza. The other girl trailed behind, trying to catch a piece of his clothing as if it would protect her from the approaching threat. "Imbecilic girl!" he whispered to no one in particular.

The clockwork-limbed girl merely pouted, and as the man tried to wave her away, pulled herself close to whisper in his ear.

"My sister—they took her a week ago. Do you think she's returned?"

"As rousing and captivating as your inane ramblings are, my dear, please do shut your mouth and allow me to save you," the man replied, pulling out of that same seemingly endless pocket a set of brass knuckles and a small dagger with a flintlock revolver welded to the side of the hilt. He cocked the trigger with his left hand, pointing the dagger towards the ceiling, and slipped his right hand into the knuckles. The barkeep scratched his head, wondering how so many things could fit in such a wee space as a dandy's front pocket. And how such things had stayed in said dandy's possession, given his preening demeanour and the rough, highwaymen-ridden roads. The barkeep was no thief, but such an easy target made even his calloused hands itchy.

"We wouldn't want you to lose your other leg, would we?" the dandy continued and the grin he left the girl with showed too many teeth and didn't even reach halfway up his face, let alone his eyes. She shivered, colour draining from her cheeks, as the bright blue lights began to flicker. The barkeep watched the girl hunch her shoulders against the cold, and he couldn't help but think that her chill had more to do with the man than the steadily crescendoing creatures outside.

Nevertheless, she stayed behind him and continued to hold onto the back of his brown tweed jacket while reaching for his bowler hat on the chair to shield herself. Without her noticing—her eyes were fastened on the glowing door, her ears primed to every groan that issued from beyond the wall—he plucked the black silk plush from her grubby fingers, dusted it, readjusted the goggles sitting on its rim, and popped it atop his own crown.

"These goggles, I'll have you know," he said, looking down his long nose at the girl, "are capable of looking through the human body itself—and can thereby distinguish between the hummingbird-esque beats of a nervous prevaricator and the slow, honest plod of an unruffled truth-teller. However, the calibration alone takes at least thirteen hours, twice that on Sundays, and requires absolute silence, so I'd rather you didn't touch them. Or anything else I have bodily upon me. Or, for that matter, my body."

She jumped as the door buckled with a grating groan of creaking wood.

They had arrived.

"Seeker or Stumbler?" Liza asked, balancing the twin hatchets in her strong grip. The three others behind them were quietly pulling out weapons—bats, revolvers, daggers, anything even remotely useful for defence—and taking up positions around windows and doors. The room became silent, save for the occasional shuffle of rumpled fabric or a nervous cough.

"I knew that Swarm was too active last night," he murmured. "Should have called the Guard."

There was another pound at the door.

"Bloody Star-Crossers," the one-legged girl muttered. "I hate them all."

"I'm quite assured, milady, that they love you. Or rather, now that they have a taste of you," the storyteller said, eyeing her clockwork leg, "they'll be wanting more. So I would save your vitriol for more physical help, as your morale-boosting quips are shockingly empty. Otherwise, I shall remove your tongue and throw it to them to use for better purposes." The young man's low tone was quite different from the tenor he had been using to tell his convoluted story. Such a substantial voice was better suited to one of the usual sticky clientele than a narcissistic crooner. The barkeep knew that spirits could draw out a wicked, degenerate creature in the most austere of men, but such a change set him even more on edge. It was almost preternatural, how badly he had misjudged the lad.

There was a quiet gasp from the girl; the dandy rolled his eyes as she began to sniffle and tears sprung to her wide eyes. He searched his suit for a handkerchief—again, the barkeep furrowed his brows and eyed the material, shape, and fit of the younger man's trousers—and eventually found one in the seemingly bottomless pit of his right pocket. It was faded with age and latticed at the edges with care. A precise hand had stitched the monogram ML into the corner in dark, glossy ribbon. He held it between two fingers, as if it were slowly burning him, and snatched his empty hand back when she took it. She dabbed at the corner of her eyes with what she thought was a sense of propriety. To the young man, however, it was just another display of her lowliness as a giant honk came from her nose with an accompanying splatter of yellowy mucus into the centre as she blew her nose.

Then her eyeballs rolled back into her head. He tucked the

revolver into his belt, handling it as if it were an egg, and barely missed catching her before her head hit the hard floor. The brass knuckles rang out against a chair he had scuffed and the wood began to crackle as the ringing noise grew in pitch. With tears in his eyes, he quickly stifled the vibrating brass by pushing his hand into a breast pocket.

There were a few more eyes on the young man now. On its own, nothing the barkeep had seen would have been enough for him to intervene, but the young man's overall behaviour was slowly approaching that line. He smiled as he dragged her body to a chair and lay her like a ragdoll with her limbs at awkward angles.

"Fainted from the stress," he said to the gruff, bearded man holding what looked like a large tree branch with a spike on its edge. "Poor thing lost a sister and it was too much for her, I'm afraid." He winked, pulled the handkerchief from her clutched hand, wiped most of her mucus off onto the edge of her dress when the bearded man had looked away, and then stuffed it back into his bottomless pocket. He adjusted his trousers and stalked back to the front door, gripping the revolver once again in his left hand. Either he was oblivious enough not to know the barkeep had been eyeing him the whole time, or—and what he felt was closer to the unpleasant truth—the man simply didn't care.

"Where did you last see the Swarm?" the storyteller asked, sidling up next to the barkeep. The older man could see the faint line of sweat against the top of his cleanly shaven lip and the stark blue veins standing out against his too-tight grip on the revolver. A subtle, but cloying smell of perspiration was covered up by incense and cologne. He looked to be in his early thirties, with still a boyish look about his cheeks and scarcely a wrinkle around his eyes. This was a man, just out of adolescence, who had little reason to smile through the bright green of his eyes and the dull salmon of his lips. His slick black coif, now losing its shape, fell into his eyes and lay stark against his olive skin. Nervously he slicked it back with a salt-stained hand and gulped, causing his prominent Adam's apple to jump.

"Boy," the bartender said, clearing his throat and then spitting the remnants into the corner, "I don't need someone behind me who's going to run at the first sight of a Star-Crosser, especially if it's a Seeker. Why don't you go back—"

The large door finally buckled, raining splinters that clouded the air with dust. A slender, half-rotten arm punched through the jagged hole in the door and began clawing at the edges, groping for anything it could drag back outside with it. Liza, a scream tearing from her throat, raised her axe high and sliced it down parallel to the door in an effort to chop the arm off. But the hand grabbed her own and began to pull Liza through.

She struggled, dropping her other axe to brace the crumpling door. Its jagged jaw, full of splintered teeth, looked as if it was digesting the girl a few joints at a time—up to her wrist, then her elbow, then her shoulder—before the barkeep rushed over to sling his arms around her waist and pull backwards. Even their combined effort was not enough to prevent Liza from slipping through the cracked wood, splinters pulling at the delicate skin of her ribs and the underside of her arms through the cheap fabric of her dress. The barkeep's grip shook with exertion against a creature who could not feel pain, who did not care that it was tearing itself apart to reach its prey. When Liza finally slipped from his grasp and disappeared into the darkening abyss of the outside, he crossed himself and uttered a prayer to whomever was listening in the starkness of his universe.

"By the Great Sailor's sandy tits!" the barkeep spat.

The young man next to him fired his flintlock into the darkness. For a brief second, in the brackish orange glow of the powder, the barkeep saw a single female Star-Crosser digging into the stomach of Liza. Her hand extended back towards the door in anguished pain before she was again enveloped in the acherontic light, as if a torch had been doused in ink. He swallowed before realising the boy was climbing out through the blood-stained crevice with Liza's other axe stuffed in the waistband of his trousers. He tried to pull him back with a hand on his shoulder.

"She's gone, lad, and what you're about to do is suicide. It may look like she's the only one, but one drop and you're wet, wait a few minutes and you're soaked. More'll be coming, I'll swear by the Great Sailor himself. You won't get back in time if you go after to retrieve her body. We'll try to find her tomorrow to burn them out, but it's best to just come back and let us barricade the door until dayfall."

The young man paused, both of his hands against the crevice where Liza's had been seconds before, and began speaking into the fading light as if he were talking to the sun itself instead of the barkeep. "The most humane way to kill one of them is to sever the spine. The night my sisters came home, begging to be let into the glass doors from our garden, I watched as my father cut off the eldest's head with the machete—given to him for his troubles as a missionary in India—that he kept on our family crest over the fireplace. As her head flopped down and began bleeding the brackish swill what passes for Star-Crosser blood into the cooling ashes of the pit, I knew that she had been released. The youngest reeled away in terror and is, to this day, such as is the extent of my meagre knowledge, still roaming the countryside, stuffing her face with the undue rotten leftovers of human flesh. That day I vowed, my good sir, never to allow such a travesty to happen in my presence again, even to a woman I have barely just met—yet with whom I had hoped to become more than mere acquaintances. There is no deeper connection than releasing one's soul back to the Great Sailor in the sky."

He then pushed through the door and walked into the darkness. The older man squinted his clouded eyes, but only glimpsed a few more powder burns shattering the calm of the night, each one a different portrait of two bodies struggling for survival. The young man's last cartridge pierced the gloom before the gruff man with the grizzled beard stepped in front of the barkeep and pushed an upended table against the hole.

"We'll get his body in the morning," he wheezed through half-rotten, yellowed teeth, before sitting down with a few others against the table to brace it with their backs against any ravaging Star-Crossers. Then he added, with a malicious smirk: "If there's anything left. And if it doesn't crawl away from us when we try."

The barkeep went back behind the counter and began pouring drinks for the men stationed at the windows and door, to keep morale up and prevent a riot from the mix of hot tempers and the sudden letdown of inaction.

"Anything about the young man?" he asked to another man with a large, curling moustache who looked out a window, pistol primed. He received a solemn shake of the head in response. Greta came from the kitchen with a small plate of bread and cheese and began circling the room, offering it to anyone who could stomach the dry crust and spots of mould. At last she bit her lip, breathed a sigh to steel herself, and approached the barricaded door to serve the grizzled man and his companions. She had just dipped her wrist to lower the plate when three loud knocks on the other side of the door expelled a cloud of dust.

"What should we do?" she asked, staring at the door with wide eyes. "Star-Crossers don't knock, do they?"

"It's just a bloody trick, is what it is," the bearded man replied, closing his eyes and leaning further back against the table, as if fighting for his life was as normal as the stale bread lining his mouth; he gave as much thought to shooting what had hours ago been a good friend as he did to chewing. "We'll wait for day, as we always do."

There were three more knocks and then a distinctly upper-class voice: "Hello?"

"It's the boy. Open it up! Open it up!" The barkeep rushed from behind the counter and rolled the table from beneath the other men, spilling their half-drunken bodies on the floor.

"No, don't! You'll let them in!" another panicked voice screamed.

"We'll not leave him out there to be attacked. Not after what he did for Liza," the barkeep said, using all of his near-exhausted strength to move the heavy wooden table out of the way. Before he had even gotten it halfway past the door, the young man's arm stuck through the hole, much like the Star-Crosser's had before. Someone screamed at the sight. His face came into view and he winked at the brunette, still frozen with the food half-slipping off the tray. Then his face disappeared, only to be replaced by the half-decayed one of a young girl, her lip oozing black, briny blood and her cataract-covered eyes rolling back into the depths of her forehead. He pushed the head through the opening and it hit the ground, staining the floor like a grimy ink-blot before trundling into the centre of the room, where it settled on its eye socket, showing off the hacked stump of the neck.

One of the young man's long, lanky legs stepped inside before he sucked in his breath and pushed the rest of his body through. The last part of him to appear was his right hand, which held a half-rotten heart dripping congealed black blood onto the floor. The barkeep quickly rolled the table back and wiped the sweat off his brow. The part of him that had become immune to the walking dead, to dismembering those he once considered friends and family, laboured under the thought of how much time he would have to spend scrubbing his tavern clean again before marvelling at his own callousness. He slapped the young man's back, causing him to start forwards half a step.

The young man returned the gesture by giving the barkeep a smart look and adjusting his hat. He then slapped the sticky heart into his hand and nodded solemnly, brushing off the imaginary strings of gristle that clung to the foetid organ with a distasteful look.

"I believe the customs here for a proper burial include the heart of the Crosser? You'll find Liza's remains—or as much as I could salvage from the beast—near the oak tree. It was only a Scouting Bunch, not a Swarm, and that's the head of the leader," he said, pointing towards the seeping trophy. "I suspect that by the morrow you'll be close to the Swarm. The Homunculus Star is almost at its zenith come the setting sun." He squinted as if he could see it through the roof of the tavern. "You should have enough time to avoid a grisly death if you call the Guard in the morning."

"Greta!" the barkeep yelled. The stunned brunette snapped to attention. "Get out our best stuff from the back!" He turned back to their saviour. "Thank you, sir. You've done us a great service. I have to admit, I didn't think you was much to look at, but you've proved me wrong. How can we ever repay—"

"Free room and board," he replied, rubbing his hands together and then pulling a rag out of the barkeep's apron to wipe them upon, "as much liquor as my measly stomach can hold after eating nothing but greasy turkey legs and gruel for the past three days—" Here he leaned in to speak directly into the barkeep's ear: "—and some warm company, if you'd be so kind." He gestured with his head to Greta as she came back holding a large dark bottle sloshing with a sulphurous liquid. "That one is a little skinny for my refined tastes, but she'll do in a pinch. Ahh, thank you." He pulled a mug out of her hand, kept on motioning for her to fill it until it was almost splashing over the rim, and drank in large, raucous slurps intermixed with equally raucous coughing.

"I'm not sure if—"

"Nonsense!" he cried. He wiped his mouth and gestured for another glass. Halfway through Greta's pouring he coughed, cleared his throat, then coughed again, splashing the alcohol all over the floor. "Strong stuff, eh? Almost as strong as my Uncle's servant's bootleg whiskey! Used to call it the Tongue-Stomper when I was a lad...I'd sneak into the cellar for a taste before the barrels were ready. Lost my virginity that way to a one-eyed gypsy fortuneteller, but that's another story! I'll take this," he said, picking up the head and walking down the hallway and into the rooms, opening the doors to each, startling the occupants inside until he found an empty one. Each time the young man unbolted a door, the barkeep opened his mouth like a dying guppy to protest and wonder at the young man's seamless ability to open locked doors. By the time he expelled a warning grumble, the supposed hero had disappeared, his voice echoing down the hall: "I'll be here. Send her in half an hour." The door slammed and the barkeep was left holding the slowly dripping heart. A misjudgement of character, indeed.

The sun barely wriggled above the horizon, but already Marietta could feel it sapping all life from her stiffening limbs. With a disgustingly large amount of effort, she persuaded her arm to knock at the boarded-up third window of the building. She waited, heard nothing, and letting the impatience get the best of her, let out a raspy cry. "Byron! Open the damn window!"

Through the thin walls—how did they ever think these shambling excuses for plaster and wood could ever stop a truly determined Crosser?—she heard a dramatic yawn. It was then accompanied by a groan that she could only assume was him stretching. At least, that's what she hoped.

"Byron!" she yelled again, growing more nervous as the sun began to tidy up the countryside. She stuck her fingers into a poorly hammered beam and began to free the window from its bindings. Holding half of the rotten wood in her hands, she stuck an eyeball into the opening. If there was one thing to get Byron moving, it would be an audience.

She saw him, groggily smacking his lips and popping all of the joints in his back. Arms spread wide, he stretched until his hand met soft flesh. He squinted down at the naked back of the girl lying next to him, as if noticing that her face was familiar, but not quite remembering where he had seen it before.

"Byron!"

How she hated that name. She hated the fact that she was always saying it even more.

He put his ear to the girl's face to hear if it was her voice calling to him, smelling instead the slow puff of her rancid breath. As Byron pulled the girl's mouth open, even Marietta could see a set of rotten teeth with green slime where pink gums should have been. He curled his lip in disgust.

"Why is it so hard to find a specimen of feminine beauty anymore?"

"I have a smoke bomb. I am not above making the entire tavern think you have drunkenly set fire to your room. Now open the window before the sun comes up!" she hissed through the opening.

"Speaking of feminine specimens…" Yawning again, he plodded over to the window, squinting in the half-light from behind the boards. He slid open the window and pretended to jump in horror as he saw her.

She smiled, pushing every last ounce of malice between her teeth, and knew that he had somewhat of a point. She was now decayed enough that patches of her skeleton showed through her cheek and her left hand was nothing more than bones held together by cartilage. There was a large hole in her chest and every once in a while a detached vein would squirt something resembling mucus. It had been so long since she saw her true hair colour that even she didn't know if it was once red that had been browned by caked-on mud or brown reddened by her victims' blood. Even her violet eyes, the only pristine thing about her, were ruined by the putrescence of her fair, freckled skin. Around her waist was a large belt that held all manner of weapons and jingled as she walked.

She held out her good right hand and flicked her fingers towards herself. She could get his attention by acting coy.

"Oh, yes, your accoutrements," Byron responded, disappearing from her view as he bent over to fetch his trousers. When he straightened up, he was rifling through them for the correct pocket. "Now where did that blasted thing move to now? I know it was in my right pocket last night, but it seems to have migrated."

"Please don't tell me you're naked." Then she caught a glimpse of Greta's backside. "Your reward?"

"One of many. Also, I'm going to convince her to come with us today as we head for the Swarm."

"And by 'convince,' you mean…"

"Threaten her with consummate violence. But by the way she was chattering while we were—"

"Don't give me any details my mind hasn't already forced upon me."

"—eating dinner," he finished, now digging through his vest pocket, "she is completely enamoured with me. I'm sure that once I make you look a bit more…" She felt his eyes examine her from the top of her head and slither all the way to her toes; the gesture was one that she was familiar with, but the expression that accompanied such a perusal was jarring. Byron looked as if he might vomit. "Alive, she'll come to accept you as my servant." She scoffed, but he ignored her. "But no fighting over me like with the last one. I could barely stand all of the attention."

"Kara was the only one who wanted anything to do with you. I would rather fight over who gets to castrate you—"

"Ah ha!" he cried, finally pulling out the flintlock dagger and brass knuckles from his right breast pocket. He handed them over. As she placed them amid the various guns, knives, liquid-filled bottles, and dust-filled pouches on her belt, the hole in her chest started emitting a steady stream of blood.

"How's the condition of that head?" she asked, looking at the grimy remainder of a Star-Crosser they had found a few weeks ago. It had been useful in their deceit; Byron could prove that he had slain the beast and she got to keep her head. Marietta had told him many times that she doubted the villagers in their panic even cared if the Star-Crosser head looked anything like her, but he needed the pretence in order to "fulfil his motivations as the dutiful hero."

"One more week and then it'll really begin to smell. Not unlike the mildew between my Uncle's toes. Nastiest smell I've ever had the pleasure to sniff in my life, and that includes the distinctive combination of rose-water perfume and bile."

"I don't care what your Uncle's feet smell like, Byron," she sighed, rubbing the bridge of her nose with skeletal fingers. "But did you really have to take my heart?"

"I wanted to add some flair this time. Keep the routine fresh. I get tired of playing the dashing hero, so I thought I'd try something new. Besides, you'll get a new one as soon as we're done with Greta."

"You remembered a name this time."

"As easily as I wish to forget yours, Marietta. If you weren't so useful, I'd have let you decay into nothingness long ago. So when you get a new heart, you'll have to name it Greta. Didn't you name your left foot after Lucretia? And your eyes after Blanche?"

"Couldn't you at least do something about the gaping hole? It's distracting."

"Only if you want to give me an initial of the man who hired you."

"No."

"I see there is more than one gaping hole. Or else the one in your chest is migrating towards your head. Now..." he said, putting on his trousers with some difficulty. His overindulgence in the tavern's cheap liquor was showing. "It would be best to get going." He started pulling the sheets into his pack while at the same time trying to button his shirt with thick fingers and an even thicker brain. His hand was halfway to the pillow when Marietta stopped him.

"Free room and board, remember? You don't need to sneak out like you usually do. And it would be rude to steal the linens, given that you're the dashing hero—or at least the bringer and breaker of hearts—of this little township."

As she put her hand on his, he jerked back, stumbling into

a nightstand and falling backwards. Greta barely stirred in her sleep at the crash. He got up, brushing dust from the floor off the shoulders of his shirt.

"Jumpy?" she asked. She had to hide the smile that came unbidden to her lips.

"Yes. A condition brought upon by the fifth time you tried to kill me," he responded, rubbing at the stubble on his chin. He adjusted the tooth at the back of his mouth and grunted. "Poison in my tea, wasn't it? Excruciating curare, if I remember correctly. Meant to make me vomit uncontrollably until my internal organs liquefied."

"That was the third. The fifth time, I tried to eat your eyeballs while you slept."

Byron picked up Greta's shirt and threw it at Marietta before continuing to pack.

"For the hole in your chest. I don't believe I'll be able to patch it up completely this close to the Zenith."

"She won't notice? I have spare clothes next to the oak tree with the rest of our supplies. I just need you to dig it up."

"The sun's just barely risen. You'll be able to make it back there before its rays stupefy you too much. No, I simply have too much to do here before we leave. Use that for now, then get the rest of our gear and come back. I'll be eating breakfast by then, so don't be late. I don't think that this one—" He pointed to the sleeping girl, "—will be coherent within the next week. I trust you fed well on our friend with the double hatchets?" Before she could respond, he said, "Good," and dismissed her with a subtle wave of his hand.

She cleared her throat. Then cleared it again when he ignored her to rifle through his breast pocket for a small metal flask, from which he took a swig. Marietta could smell the graveyard earth mixed in with the two-bit whiskey, and as he pulled the flask away from his lips, she could just see the tail of a worm between his front teeth. She cleared her throat for the third time; Byron finally capped the flask and looked at her with an overwhelming hatred barely masked by civility. She made a note that he wasn't nearly as hungover as she had first assumed.

"I'm going to get shot at looking like this, regardless of the state of my blouse."

The hatred was replaced slowly with confusion. Then a carnivorous smile appeared at the corners of his mouth.

"Ah, yes," he replied. "Enjoy it. It'll only last a day."

"What? Tonight I'll turn into a pumpkin?"

"If we're playing fairy tales, my ashen Cinderella, then I'm Prince Charming. Or perhaps the Fairy Godmother, given my powers and prowess over you."

He closed his eyes and started moving his lips like he was saying a prayer underneath his breath. Marietta could only catch the low vowels and the hissing sibilants. The most decayed parts of herself began to burn, as if hovering over an open flame—but since it was the only sensation that visited her since her death over a year ago, she enjoyed even the pain of it. Invisible needles pierced her skin and pulled as ghostly hands sewed her ragdoll body back together. The ruined skin at her cheek paled from deathly green to beige; the exposed ribs at her side knitted together and then were clothed in flesh. If she was a little too emaciated for a healthy girl, at least she didn't look like a Star-Crosser.

The burning faded and she took one last look at her newly regenerated body—still with a gaping hole in the chest, which she covered up with the loose-fitting blouse from Greta—before looking back at Byron. He was clutching his left arm and Marietta watched as it started to rot before her eyes. He swept her aside, found a glove in his breast pocket, and quickly put it on before she could see any more. By the time he looked back at her, wearing an impatient expression that told her she should leave before he reversed the process, there was barely any pain left in his chiselled features.

She turned to the window, glad to feel that her joints moved without any terrible creaking and her strength had returned. She winced as she stepped into the rising sunlight and made a beeline for the tree where the remnants of Liza's body were strewn about, waiting to be collected for a proper burial. Marietta bowed her head to the woman she had killed and eaten the night before as she began to dig up the hidden pack at the base of the tree. She had long since learned not to curse the tenets of her new existence as a Star-Crosser, albeit a very different one from the fumbling, mindless Swarm they were going to be pursuing later that day. She had kept her faculties, remembering who and what she was, fully existing in the horror of undeath, because of the strange influence Byron had over her. What she regretted most, however, was not the state she found herself in, but allowing the insufferable Byron to continue his own filthy existence using her as a tool. She would have rather become one of the roving, feral corpses than a sentient being enslaved to Byron's capricious whims.

She started digging up the pack with her bare hands, thankful that her fingernails were no longer in danger of tearing free. It was a shallow pit and the burlap covering scratched her fingertips after just a few scoops of dirt. Brushing off the pack, she ransacked it, making sure all of their possessions were still there when she noticed a glint off a piece of metal from what used to be Liza's torso. It was one of the double hatchets Liza had taken into the scuffle the night before; Marietta had been too hungry to notice them before. She wiped them on the grass to get rid of the ichor and found a place for them on her belt. Perhaps, after the Star had ascended, she would ask Byron to give her a bottomless pocket of her own so she could store all of her weapons and not have people wonder why a Star-Crosser was so armed. But she would need hers to be pinned down, and since Byron's was always wandering all over his clothes, she'd have to get a second opinion on the magic. Maybe she'd ask Ferret when they found him amid the Mephistopheles Market.

With the pack slung around her shoulder and most of her weapons secured so she wouldn't attract too much attention, she gave herself the once-over to make sure that she wouldn't be executed on sight, then made for the tavern. The sun was above the horizon now and as she walked towards the door, she fished out a heavy cloak that would protect her until noon, when she would have to rest. She would look strange, but that would be nothing new, given the clientele this place usually attracted.

A flimsy piece of wood had been half-heartedly nailed over the hole she had made the night before. She pushed on the doors and they opened with loud squeaks of protesting hinges. A few gazes drifted towards her, either deciding whether she was a threat or pondering what she looked like without her clothes. Not a one would be able to stomach what she could show them; the thought made her smile as she walked up to the barkeep. He had dark bags underneath his eyes and clearly hadn't slept well after the attack. He was leaning over a butcher block and cutting up the last ventricle of her heart into small pieces, which were then being hung out to dry. She felt a pang of regret before she noticed that he was staring at her.

"Awful early for you to be travelling, ain't it? There's no place around here close enough with the sun just coming up. So you're either crazy or got nothing to lose. And if it's the latter," he said, leaning over the bar so only she could hear, "I don't want you anywhere near here when you turn. So I'm giving you fair warning now."

"I'm here for Byron. We're travelling together and got separated," she said, unwilling to let servant pass her lips. "Can you tell me what room he's in, please?"

"Him?" A deluge of emotions flashed over his face: first relief, followed by anger and then by compassion. "Saved us last night from a Scouting Bunch, he did. Still sleeping off his reward." The way he said the last word, Marietta knew that he approved as much as she did about how Byron spent his time when he wasn't plotting revenge or lying through his perfect teeth. "He's through there, third door on the left. I was just about to bring his breakfast."

"Oh, let me, please," she replied and took the tray from a small, vacant-eyed boy. "Looks like you need some help."

"Lost two girls last night. One to the Seekers and one from shock. Found her dead, over there by the corner," he said, pointing. "I can probably get a good amount of money from her clockwork leg, bad as it was, to find another serving girl. That is, if you're not interested in the position." He winked. With a false smile, she hefted the tray onto her shoulder and started down the hallway. "Or maybe even just the leg?"

"Mine work very well, thank you."

"Can I take a look to make sure?" a half-passed out drunkard grumbled, raising his head to glance at her sideways, his cheek peeling audibly off the sticky table.

She ignored him and continued to walk down the hallway. Before she reached the third door, she balanced the tray on her hip, bracing it with the wall, and pulled a small green flask out of one of the pockets on her belt. From the flask she sprinkled a dark green powder into both mugs of what could have been considered tea; she sniffed the acrid liquid and decided to add a little more of the powder just to make it taste better. Then she stirred with her finger and licked off the excess, pulling a face at the taste of the poison, and made sure to close her eyes before entering. And for good reason—there was a shriek, a clatter of dishes as the washbowl of warm water shattered on the floor, and a loud curse from Byron.

"Breakfast is served," she said, squinting out of one eye to make sure that she wasn't going to see anything she later wouldn't be able to get out of her head. After living with Byron for more than a year now, she had learned that knocking was useless; one generally had to burst through the door to get anything accomplished, which carried some understandably unpleasant side effects. Greta sat up in bed half-naked, sheets thrown haphazardly around her, and Byron sat at the desk, browsing through an old tattered book. His hands were careful with the delicate pages, but he looked for all the world like he was going to throw it out the window because it had personally and vigorously insulted his mother.

Greta clumsily got dressed, using the sheet as a dressing curtain until she let it fall, a Venus stepping out of stained linens instead of sea foam, and started looking for her shirt to go over her underclothes. Marietta dug through her pack, pulled out a crumpled blouse, and threw it at the girl, who caught it with a question between her lips but then shrugged it off. Not asking too many questions was a good sign; the ones who were always wondering and asking things tended to taste a little stringier, like half of their energy went into churning their brains, leaving the bodies to turn to gristle.

She set the tray down on the table and watched as Greta, half of the blouse over her head, reached blindly for a stale sandwich with a gooey egg stuck somewhere in the massive slabs of mysterious fried meat. Then, pulling the shirt down, she greedily drank half the cup of dishwater tea. Byron pecked at the oatmeal with disinterest, still absorbed in the book until Greta asked if he was going to finish his part of the breakfast. He declined, waving all of it towards her with an absent air. She made noises like a small animal as she devoured the last crumbs of food and drank even the dregs of the tea without so much as a thought to taste.

Meanwhile Marietta had started stashing Byron's things away in their packs, loading herself up more like a mule than a human being.

When the two girls had finished with their respective duties—the tavern wench eating like a rapacious thief and the Star-Crosser consuming supplies and tools instead of flesh and brains—Marietta went over to Byron and declared them ready to travel. He stood up, tucking the book into his right breast pocket, and pulled on Greta's wrist.

"You are coming with us," he said, gripping harder as she started to resist. There was little emotion to his voice.

"I have to stay here, honey. Most of my money goes back for my little sister," she replied, slipping her dainty wrist out of his grip. She gathered up the bedclothes to have them washed and began stacking the dishes onto the tray to take back with her. Her movements were as nervous as those of a caged bird—waiting for the door to open, wondering whether it was safe to go outside.

"Tact," Marietta whispered to Byron, stepping between him and Greta so she wouldn't hear their conversation. "Use that charm that worked so well last night. We don't want any loose ties that can be traced...like carrying a hysteric girl out with us."

He coughed into his left, gloved hand, then straightened his clothes and slicked back his hair with his right before approaching Greta. He rested a hand on her shoulder to make her sit down on the bed with him.

"I don't want you to get the wrong impression," he said, his voice softer than any linen sheet the girl had likely felt before. "I don't know how often you find yourself in a position like this—" He had to pinch himself in order not to smile, "—but what we had last night was something that defies explanation or words or even human existence. I want you to come with me, not out of some malicious avarice or gormandising, but because without you, my road would be as lonely as that of a wolf in love with the moon. I would always feel the glow of our time well spent together, but I would never be able to touch it, to luxuriate in it." He twisted his hands around hers. "I had two sisters once, and Dorcas lost her twin to the Pox when they were children. She was never the same after that; she was always pining underneath the tree they used to climb when they were girls, tying ribbons in its branches as she used to do with Birdie's hair. I would be like Dorcas if you were to stay here—always trying to reach back for our connection, as a blind man yearns for sight."

Her lips had parted in anticipation for a kiss as he leaned into her.

"I...I cannot..." she whispered.

He stood up so abruptly that she had to catch herself. When she opened her eyes, she was staring down the twinned ends of a dagger welded to a flintlock. Marietta had barely seen him move and wondered at the empty holster on her belt.

"You will come with us one way or another. And if you make any noise, it shall be awfully painful." Sensing that she was about to bolt, he took a few steps closer. "Have you ever seen anyone lose a limb to a Stumbler's bite? The gangrenous flesh peeling off bit by bit, sensation still left in those perishing, decaying nerves, fizzling out like dogs dying in heat? My best friend succumbed to injuries such as those, squealing out in pain, the light fading from his eyes as I held him in my arms. If you do not come with us hale, Marietta will bite you and you shall come with us in pieces, for surely no one here will be able—or willing—to treat your injuries as well as I."

"You would have had her if you had just played along," Marietta sighed, looking up at the ceiling and trimming the split ends of her hair with a small, sharp dagger.

"I have had enough of his wench's lips to last me millennia," he said, turning his head to Marietta. Greta knocked the flintlock dagger out of his hand and started to run for the door, screaming as loudly as she could, until Marietta dove in front of her, spun her around, and began crushing her windpipe with her fingers. The scream went out of her throat like a fading bell.

"The tea you drank this morning was dosed with Flowering Gu, a poison specifically designed to kill within three hours if the victim is not administered an antidote every day for three weeks. Your internal organs will liquefy; you will choke them up in bloody vomitus and breathe them out in noxious foam. You will die a horrible death if you don't come with us."

"What she said," Byron replied, uncocking the gun and holstering it in the waist of his trousers.

"Shut up. I figured you'd have trouble persuading her, so I took an extra step."

"Why do you think I didn't drink the tea? But please, darling, let us not argue in front of the children." He pulled out a red flask from Marietta's pouch and waved it in front of Greta. She was crying now, her snot running down Marietta's fingers. When she began to wheeze from the tight hold and her own sputum, the assassin let go of her. She crumpled to the floor. Byron pulled up his trousers and knelt, bringing him face-level with the sobbing girl, and pushed her head up with a hand under her jaw. The touch was tender against her abused flesh; Marietta knew that now they had her. Byron would treat her with the utmost care, tending her as one would fatten up a particularly lovely lamb.

"My love and this antidote are really the same thing: red, dangerous, and able to sustain young ladies for lifetimes. Now, how does that offer sound?"

"What do you want from me?" she asked. "I'm poor. I have nothing to give you."

"Oh, duckling," Byron said, chuckling softly. "You have exactly what we need." He knocked his knuckles against her head. "This time tomorrow night, you shall not have to worry about feeling the pain of death, for we fully intend to eat you come the rise of the Homunculus Star. But as we have learned a great deal about painless deaths—it makes the flesh taste sweeter, you see, if you don't struggle into the afterlife—you shan't feel a thing."

In Which the Theoretical Existence of a Queen is Discussed, Or: The Charred Thickets

"How doth Greta beat within thy barren chest on this, a most breath-taking night? Reminds me of when I was seven and I looked out at the stars from underneath my parents' gazebo, where my father had found my mother after she crawled through three days' worth of swamp mud, only to die on the steps and come back as a Star-Crosser. It was my last night in that house. The stars shone brightly, the Homunculus Star brightest of all, and by the next morning, my father was dead, killed in a horrible cricket accident involving a soggy wicket and an even soggier bowler, and my Uncle was shipping me off to the nearest orphanage so he could begin courting Lady de Leon."

"I am dead, Byron. So she beats poorly in that she doesn't beat at all. Besides, I thought your Uncle disowned you when you were ten because you had displayed, and I quote, 'a nervous tendency to ritualistically slaughter the neighbourhood pets?'" Byron scoffed and Marietta continued, "And I find your fascination with naming my body parts after dead girls somewhat disturbing."

"Some would call that romantic. Not unlike Shakespeare comparing women to seasons and goddesses, I compare you to the most beautiful thing of all: the truth."

"I call that a nervous tendency to criminal insanity."

"It seems your chest, lacking your actual heart, is not the only thing that is barren."

"You came close to sleeping with me once and I'm sure you've never forgotten the experience."

"Ah, yes! The all-consuming night of earthly passions that led thusly to our current predicament! How different things would be if we had just kept our hands off of each other! Or, rather, your hands off of me, since they were the ones fingernailing me all night."

The bar was five days, two dead bodies, and one Homunculus Star away. They had gotten enough rest—and for Marietta, human flesh—to set out towards the next town to do very much the same thing there.

The moon peeked from beneath thin clouds as they walked down their weed-covered path, outside of the smallish village that Marietta was eyeing as a potential target. Dust kicked up into the air from their boots and glittered in the white luminescence so that it looked like the trees had a rather bad case of dandruff. It had rained earlier, but the water had evaporated to leave everything flaky and mildewed. The overpowering smell of rot that usually drifted from large Swarms after a downpour clung only faintly to their bodies as they walked. Byron patted down his waterlogged ensemble, then began digging through each pocket specifically. He finally settled on his left coat pocket and pulled out two pairs of human canines, followed by two small jars filled with dark liquid in which floated, respectively, an eyeball and a uvula.

"Damn," he muttered. Marietta looked over to him with a questioning expression.

"Forget something?" she asked, her hands free but itching to wield the double hatchets again. She felt restless this night as they walked along the deserted road. It wasn't the rambling Star-Crossers she feared—their hunger for flesh was not a concern for either her or Byron, as they had long since discovered that neither the fast, quick-witted Seekers or the bumbling, barely conscious Stumblers had a taste for their corrupted meat—or even human highwaymen. But something uneasy was transmitting itself through the sparse trees.

"Forgot the spleen," he said, sticking his arm halfway to the elbow in his jacket, digging to see if it was lost somewhere within his bottomless pocket.

"None of them had an intact one, remember?"

"I thought we found a Stumbler amongst them, remarkably preserved."

"You're thinking of the last time we went on a raid for The Hawktopus. That was three weeks ago."

"Ah, yes," he replied, stuffing the jars back into his pocket but continuing to examine the teeth as they walked. He held one up to the moonlight and squinted at it as the tension began to crawl up Marietta's back and take up permanent residence somewhere around her collarbone. She wouldn't have noticed otherwise, but she had decayed badly in the fortnight since the zenith of the Homunculus Star and Byron hadn't felt the need to make her look more human. She knew she looked horrible—she had taken a bite to her back from one particularly voracious Seeker—and the skin had continued to peel off until most of her back was flayed. Her right leg was little more than bone below the knee, though her foot was still intact.

"What are you so damned nervous about?" He began throwing the teeth into the air, only to catch them with a deft hand before they hit the ground.

"There's something not right about this forest," she replied, her hands inching closer to the hatchets on her belt. Violence made her feel comfortable, especially when directed against others. She pulled one out of its leather loop, enjoying the heaviness of the smooth wooden handle in her grasp, the perfect balance that allowed her to throw it with precise accuracy. "Something is watching us."

"Is this your beginning to an epistemological conversation? I must say, I didn't expect such far-reaching thoughts from you—"

"There," she said, pointing into the deeper forest. The main part of the path meandered through thin, skeletal tree branches far above their heads, letting moonlight splash through. But the forest thickened considerably even a few steps off the trodden grooves; it could easily become a labyrinth if one was not accustomed to its twisting ways. In the darkest parts were the Charred Thickets, beastly trees scarred by time and hardened into blackened stone. "Do you remember the stories about the first Star-Crossers?" Her voice was barely a whisper.

"No," Byron responded, his voice loud and echoing through the stillness. "I care not for your silly superstitions. I am tired and irritable and these measly few parts simply aren't going to get the information we need from the rather exacting and parsimonious Ferret. The errant thought that I should just give them you, as a specimen of unique disposition, has been running through my head for the hundredth time since entering the Smoke Forest—and your chittering away does nothing to hinder such contemplations."

"They came from the trees. From deep within, you remember."

"Does this have anything to do with what I've just said?" he whined.

"The first ones," she said, taking a few steps off the path and hearing the crunch of the undergrowth under her shoes. A few spooked birds took to the air with biting caws. She winced, hating how much noise she made when her body was decayed; she couldn't even control how lightly she set her foot down. If only the apprentice assassins could see her now. "What if there's still something there? No one goes into the Thickets. Or if they do, they rarely come out, and even then, usually they're missing tongues. What if there's something like what the rumours say, like what your book says." She pointed to his pocket. "I'm getting the same teeth-rattling feeling now as when I'm around a big Swarm, but there's nothing."

"Stupid," he said under his breath, then louder when she asked what he had said. "I would feel it more than you. Or did you forget?"

"I didn't forget. But it got stronger once I got off the path. Just come here for a few seconds—"

"I will not indulge in your scared little-girl fantasies. There is nothing in that forest. The Charred Thickets are nothing more than trees warped by volcanic activity thousands of years ago, as I traversed them many years ago to prove my manhood for the most desirous creature in the known cosmos. And my book, I'll have you know," he replied, getting angrier with each passing word until he was stalking towards Marietta with his arm raised, "is more than just idle chit-chat from toothless rumourmongers!" His left foot hit the same patch of bristle-covered undergrowth that Marietta stood upon, and she watched as a chill moved up his leg and spread across his shoulders in a visible shudder. Deep within the reptilian part of her brain—the part that could be controlled by Byron—a stirring began, sinking hooks into the side of her head and pulling itself out of her unconscious, so that she became acutely aware of Byron standing next to her. But it was even more than that. She travelled along the sloping paths being created within her that reached out for him, like a man buried alive, struggling for air, and received a single clear thought: turn around. And without knowing why, she rotated until her back was facing him.

Something larger, more primitive, further from life than even Marietta, responded in such a loud, shaking voice that Byron jumped back onto the path with a gasp. A sheen of sweat covered his entire face and Marietta saw an encroaching dampness along his chest and around his armpits.

"I knew you could control Star-Crossers if you were close enough to them," Marietta breathed, doubled over not in pain, but in reassurance that she was still in her own body, controlling her own movements. "But you've never been able to affect me like that."

"And that other thing out there…" he said, gazing off into the Thicket. Marietta followed his line of sight. "It responded. It's dead, like you—"

"Like us."

"—and it responded and I've never felt that before. Do you think…?" Marietta saw another idea forming within his brain that took over the first. His mouth curled into that rapacious smile that she knew meant he had figured out another way to use somebody else for his own nefarious gain. "This is what we need. For Ferret. He'll give us everything about Archibald if we give him this."

"We don't even know what 'this' is."

"It's a Queen," he said in a breathless whisper and started running into the forest. It always astonished Marietta to see the collected Byron, always worried about the pristine condition of his shiny fingernails and even shinier hair, always smoothing wrinkles and primping hair, take off with such alarmingly careless speed, like a small boy running after the promise of a surprise gift. It was moments like these that she knew he was telling the truth—not stunted, twisted half-lies and deliberate manipulation. It was in moments like these that she almost forgot how badly she wanted to kill him.

"Byron!" she yelled after him, running as fast as her desiccated body would allow. (Which was comparable to a Star-Crossed horse leg trying to hoof it on its own without any of the rest of the horse.) "You'll need to create a path or we'll get lost! Byron!"

"I know where I'm going! It's directing me!" he yelled as he jumped over fallen trees and sprinted into the grimy gloom of the Thickets.

"But what's going to help me?" she asked, stopping as his silhouette was eaten by the fog-covered trees. She put down her pack and started going through it, hoping that Byron had put the candlestick back in and it wasn't lost somewhere in his bottomless pocket. While she was digging with her left hand, she pulled the brass knuckles off her belt and slipped them over her right hand. As soon as she felt soft wax beneath her fingers, she let out a sigh of relief. The ball of twine was still wound around the base of the candle from the last time she had to go chasing after him, when he had gotten lost in the Critterskeep looking for pickled spiders' legs to construct a giant web for catching Cronenberg Flies.

She felt around her belt for matches and found a single one left in the second-to-last leather pocket. She let out her breath, held it for longer than she should have been able to, and struck the match against her gun holster, smelling the ignition of the sulphur tip. A small bright light flared so that she had to look away, seeing greenish-purple spots over her eyes in the darkness, as she brought the match to light the candle. The blob in front of her left eye remained and she knew that she had blown out the pupil. She sighed and dug a finger into the left socket to remove the now-useless eye. She put the dangling thing, nerves trailing behind it, into a pocket and wondered if she would rather throw it away than see it in Ferret's tumultuous collection.

The flame burned orange, let out a few sparks that spooked a few more large crows, then turned a deep purple that burned hotter than any mere candle. She blew out the match and left it to litter the forest floor. She waited a minute while the wax grew hot, then tipped the candle so that the drips ran down the side in rivulets to collect on the brown twine. The wax glowed the same phosphorescent purple and spread its colour everywhere it touched the twine. It began to levitate, casting eerie maroon shadows that caged Marietta within the undulating trees.

"Now for the scent," she said to herself, and punched the side of a nearby tree with the brass knuckles. A small ringing pitched upwards as the tree began to splinter, until the entire trunk exploded into chunks of sap-globbed bark and there was only a slight, fading squeal within her ears. "Come on, come on!" She waited as the twine stopped trembling and started to curl like a snake readying its strike. Byron had been the last to use the knuckles, so the vibrational frequency was still in tune with his astral scent; she hoped the twine could follow it. It was winding in on itself, almost ready to tie a knot, when it sprang out into the forest, a purplish glow emanating from its buzzing fibres. Hopefully the twine wouldn't run out before she found him.

She picked up her pack, held the candle firm in her hand as the cord continued to unravel, and set off in the direction it had gone, keeping one hand over the flame. If it went out, the magic would be broken and she wouldn't be able to start it up again. Her legs creaked and a few maggots leaked out, but she kept her focus on the twine and moved as fast as she was able.

The trees became thicker and thicker, their trunks blacker and blacker. Branches gnarled and twisted like the arthritic hands of an octogenarian. The bark, instead of flaking off as she brushed past trees, became hard and smooth as she began to enter the Charred Thickets. The petrified giants loomed above her, their branches bare, but so many of them criss-crossing each other that only motes of light could penetrate the timbered blackness. Her sense of unease grew, but she didn't know if it was because of the woods' association with Star-Crossers or because she was getting closer to whatever Byron wanted to discover.

She tried to think of how many targets she had tracked down using a similar system and how gifted she felt each time she completed an assignment. She wondered at the fleetness of the last two years, and how, once—her assignment before this one—she had tracked the bastard son of the King of Calderia in order to extract the family sigil that he had stolen, trying to impersonate the legitimate Prince Tully. She had repossessed the sigil and given it to the King, still attached to the unfortunate boy's hand. The coin she had palmed would have been enough for the rest of her life, but she had taken one last job: the easy assassination of a fatalist troublemaker by the name of Byron Ulysses Llewellyn-Cave.

Now she was dead, half rotted away, and tracking him through what could be a decently haunted forest—and for what? She wondered if she should just let him die of exposure in the elements and be free of him…

…and forever remain the way she was. And who knew? Without him, her mind could degenerate until she was nothing more than one of the thousands of mindless Stumblers that roamed the countryside. She wasn't even technically a Seeker, one of the fast, robust dead that had not yet decayed into Stumblers. She was something else, and being that way was the reason that she had sabotaged all of the murder attempts, save for the first one—well, two—before he had killed her and turned her into a Star-Crosser. She had to find some way to get out of this decaying Hell before taking his life with her own hands, lest her condition remain permanent. And how sweet the smell of his last breath would be in her perfectly pink, fleshy nostrils...

Lost in grotesque thought, she hadn't been paying enough attention to the forest around her. The rain from the previous days had made a puddle and she thought it only a few fingers thick. It wasn't until she was mid-thigh in brackish water with eels and water snakes swimming around her sopping skirts that she realised she had made a miscalculation. With a small splash, she wiped off mud from her face before she understood that the mottled red-and-yellow snake was more dangerous than her stuck leg. The leg could potentially be replaced, especially since they were on their way to see Ferret—not to mention that Ferret's encampment now neighboured Shropshire, a town with as many raven-haired, leggy, instantly-forgettable named girls as there were Crossers, and replacement parts could be easily snagged. But snakes and eels were only one step below spider nests in terms of infestation problems. She began struggling, pulling at her leg with both hands, feeling the skin peeling off between her fingers until finally she was able to wrench it free. By that time, though, a few eels had slithered their way into her back and were now roosting somewhere within her torso. She could hear them sloshing around inside of her and she bit her lip in frustration as she climbed out of the ditch to continue after the purple twine. She locked her arm, keeping the flame up above her head to avoid dunking it into the sludge.

Water began dribbling out of her sides as she walked along. One eel squirmed out of a hole by her ribs and fell into the mud, twisting itself into panicked knots. Byron was going to owe her a complete revitalisation by the time she found him. The bones in her left ankle ground against each other; she didn't know how long she was going to be able to continue walking before the damn thing fell off. Another eel slithered out of her back right before the twine completely unwound itself from the candle and shot out into the darkness. The stunted trees quickly ate the light of its twinkling purple spark.

Now she could only hope that she would eventually find Byron by travelling straight after the last coordinates given to her by the magic. He would owe her some new Binding Twine when they reached Ferret's too. And a new candle, she thought, beginning to mumble a list of all the things Byron was going to do for her before realising that all of the sounds in the forest had stopped. Even the eels inside of her quieted. Nothing moved save for the twisted branches and the small circle of flickering light from the candle.

Cold dread clawed from her feet to her hands until she found herself shaking so hard that she almost dropped her only source of light. There was something pulling at her, taking over her body, dulling her thoughts until there was nothing left but the awful yearning for live flesh. Something infecting her, possessing her—not unlike the stilted, overwhelming presence of Byron when he had made her turn around earlier, but even more powerful. A voice inside her head, commanding her to find victims and bring back their pieces.

"What?" she yelled into the darkness. "What do you want? Who are you?" She clutched her head, unearthing the part of her who had been the fearsome Marietta Margot-Pierre Lapine, master assassin, knower of the fifty ways to kill a soul with a teabag, possessing an encyclopaedic knowledge of every weapon made by mankind and still others not made by man, and not just the undead servant of a pompous, foolish, sadistic rapscallion.

"Marietta?" She heard Byron's voice a few yards off. "Stop making all of that racket and come here!"

"There's something else here," she replied, still clutching at her temples, trying not to pull out her hair in an effort to excavate the entity from within her skull. "Don't you feel it?" Talking was helping her focus, but she couldn't walk at the same time. She didn't even realise that Byron was next to her until he put a hand on her arm and everything suddenly stopped. She was the only one left within her mind.

"It was a residual psychic force...left here by her," he replied, breathing the last word in such a reverential tone that he could have been talking about his saintly mother. He started pulling her along, then stopped when he realised that he had pulled her shoulder out of its socket. He popped it back in and started dragging her again until she stumbled along. "It's...beautiful."

They reached a copse of trees, all of their branches bowed and intertwining to create an eye-level hammock. The smooth blackness of their bark was loose and blowing in the faint wind so that black ash rained down to stain Byron and Marietta's clothes and faces. In the middle of the hammock lay a cocoon, burst open and dripping a greyish jelly. The smell would have knocked out a small boy accustomed to smelling his own sweat-drenched armpits. Marietta could imagine that, had the sac been complete, it would have throbbed and gasped like the last fitful push of air through a dead man's chest. Another tremor passed through her thoughts, filling her with decrepit humours.

"Again, we need to work on your ability to differentiate between appropriate and inappropriate verbal responses," she replied, trying even harder to dislodge the remaining water snakes now that she had found Byron. It was strange that she felt better now that she was with him. But when Byron looked back with a blank expression, she continued: "That is an inappropriate outburst. An appropriate one would be, 'It's horrible. In fact, maybe the most horrible thing I've ever seen, and I'm a former assassin who now regularly consumes human organs and used to study Inquisitorial methods for the torturing arts and primate methods for the love-making arts. And I have six toes.'"

"Don't you understand? It's finally the proof I need."

"No, still inappropriate. An appropriate response would be: 'But I'm not an assassin,' or 'But I make love like a salt-ridden slug trying to cross a patch of burst tomatoes,' or even, and I would begrudgingly accept, 'You have six toes?' In which case, I would respond that I used to have six toes on my left foot when it was my real left foot. This leg belongs to Lola. She, fortunately, has five extremely dainty little piggies. Though they are hairy, which was always somewhat disconcerting to me—"

"It's a Queen," he replied, stepping closer to the cocoon and examining the goo inside without actually touching it. "In Ikkaku-san's Stumbling Against the High Tides of Star-Crossers Consuming Your Brains, he postulates that Star-Crosser Queens need time to pupate in a cocoon before gaining their considerable powers. By feeding only on the brains brought to them by the Stumblers," he said, taking a jar out of his bottomless pocket and scooping up some of the jelly, "they become what they are."

Marietta limped a few steps closer and looked inside the jar. There were floating pieces of brain, crushed up and pureed, and cerebral fluid that lent a thickness that gave the entire mess the consistency of coagulated blood. She stuck a finger in the mixture and licked it off. "They're all human. How many people died for this?" The entire cocoon, longer than a tall man, was half filled; excess jelly had leaked out onto the ground in a gelatinous mass, splotched with black ash and quivering in the wind. "Delicious, though." She took another taste and Byron slapped her hand away. "Don't judge until you've tried it yourself." He curled his lip in disgust. "Oh," Marietta responded, "I forgot. You're too good for eating flesh until the Homunculus Star. And since it's another month until its zenith, you're even too cultured for my crass cravings."

"Not that, my little flowering Rafflesia," he said, sucking on his teeth. "Though you are correct in that I am able to restrain my baser lusts, unlike the way I've seen you staring at my backside—don't try to deny it, just try to correct it. I am taking this to Ferret. He will appreciate it, and perhaps even help to corroborate my story for Queen Victoria."

"How did we start talking about Queen Victoria? I know I'm missing an eye, but I don't remember misplacing my ear anywhere."

"Great Sailor! Woman, you're missing an eyeball! That'll take more energy than I have in order to be presentable for Ferret. Do you happen to have an eyepatch upon you?"

"No," she replied flatly. "Why don't you look in that pocket of yours?"

"Good idea," he said, searching all of his pockets and mumbling under his breath. "Moved again...I will find the Incomparable Lord Bartholomew who taught me this magic and cut his...blasted thing is as useful as a third eyeball on my ass—which, coincidentally, I met a tribe of pygmy head-shrinkers in my pursuit of my Uncle through Africa and encountered just such a person—ah! Yes!" He pulled out an eyepatch and flung it at Marietta, who tied it around her head with a sigh, already knowing that she was going to be scratching at it in a few short hours. She wouldn't be surprised if the last person to wear it were some sort of flea-ridden pirate. That would certainly explain the skull and crossbones.

Byron had gone back to scooping as much of the jelly into a jar that he could, acting as if she weren't there, not answering her repeated question about Queen Victoria. It was almost worse than when he patronised her. She wanted to push him into the burst cocoon and see him flounder in the congealed mass of brains for a few seconds, but she knew how quickly even his best moods could turn to destructive rage. Better to be ignored than be locked in a closet and left to rot into a skeleton. She shuddered at the memory of her internment—had it only been days? Time had stretched like a greasy ligament pulled by rotting teeth—but placed a cautious hand on Byron's shoulder. Using his hatred of her touch was the quickest way to get him to focus.

Then she was wondering if the Incomparable Lord Bartholomew had also taught him how to move faster than even she could see. He had pulled out a small, gold-plated instrument that looked like a cross between a pair of scissors and a leather glove fitted with small, sharpened blades. It was one of the weapons she had been trained in (and Byron had stolen from her), meant to create small, precise cuts with any deft movement of the fingers. He stopped it right at her stomach, close enough that any slight movement would give her a hole in her torso to match the one over her—well, Greta's—heart.

"What did I tell you about touching me? It reminds me of the most unpleasant time of my life, barring the incident with the Fishbone Weavers and their slobbering hounds. Lost my best friend that way to the horrible smell of the Weaver's nets; his eyeballs melted and his nose collapsed and blocked off his airway." As he put the finger-scissors away into a normal pocket, he watched with fascination as another eel wriggled out of a small hole in the side of her stomach. "At least we'll have dinner for a few days." He went back to collecting the gelatinous mess.

"I only meant to tell you that we should get back on the road. Ferret moves camp incessantly and we have no way of knowing how long he'll stay outside of Shropshire. Besides, you can't bring back all of that," she said, pointing to the cocoon. "And it'll begin to start smelling even worse than us soon. The Charred Thickets are wearing at me, and we have no idea how far away the thing that burst out of the cocoon is. I'd rather not meet it."

"No, don't you see?" he said, putting at least three jars of the jelly into his pocket and then pulling out his flask and filling it to the brim. "If we find her, everyone will have to believe me. And then I can finally be done with this tireless quest and your less-than-pleasing face."

"Byron," she said quietly, taking a few steps back and hearing the bones in her ankle grinding, "Crosser Queens don't exist. Whatever burst out of that cocoon is—"

Pain bit into her stomach and she doubled over. The flesh began to wrinkle and shrink onto her bones and whatever pink was left in her skin began to grey as gravity and Byron's power tore at each other for dominance. Her back jerked in small spasms as muscles dried out and snapped. The hole in her torso grew bigger; the eels that couldn't squirm free began drying out as quickly as she was, decaying at the touch of her flesh.

"Please," she whispered, her vocal cords straining before they dried up completely, "you need me to see Ferret. You'll just have to reverse this all—" There was a sharp pop and her voice gave out; all she could do was wheeze through the rapidly forming holes in her throat that exposed cartilage and bone alike. She could only plead with her remaining eyeball before that too began to soften.

It would surely have rotted out of her skull if, at that moment, the silence had not been broken by hundreds of small feet padding through the underbrush. The forest around them was suddenly littered with as many small red eyes as there were stars in the sky.

They both froze, moving only the three eyes between them to look back.

"How many aerial bursts do you have left?" Byron whispered before realising that Marietta could no longer talk. He cursed under his breath and closed his eyes. She sighed with relief as her holes knitted themselves up and her body parts filled out, regaining their pinkness. He groaned, gritting his teeth but not moving, as his left arm began to shrink underneath the glove.

"Maybe three. You took a few when we were fighting the Dreamscroungers." It took all of her concentration and training not to grab the double hatchets. They would be attacked en masse if either of them moved, and if that happened, their teeth would be the only things the beasts left intact.

"I did not—" he yelled curtly. All of the red eyes swerved to them in the darkness. "I did not," he continued, his voice humming low. Marietta was just thankful that the story was cut off before the denouement. The last thing she wanted echoing into her afterlife was Byron's tenor droning on over the abyss.

"But I used the last of the matches to find you. So unless you have a source of ignition upon your person—and not in that damnable pocket of yours—we won't be able to use them anyway."

"Hurricane Harvey once told me about the time he was flanked by these creatures. He had to throw fifty of his best men in their way even to escape. And they still started on his left foot first, for revenge. When I arm-wrestled with his first mate—"

"This is no time for one of your stories, Byron. Unless Hurricane Harvey came up with a better way of escape, I think you should save your breath for screaming as they eat you from the leg up."

"As I was going to say," he replied, dignified and presumptuous, "when I won the arm-wrestling contest against his tattooed first mate—who, by the way, had the very vulgar tattoo of a topless mermaid doing unspeakable things with a dolphin on his forearm that I had a chance to study intimately as I bested him—"

"Byron!" The eyes moved again. One of them plopped out of the shadows and began to stalk towards them. Its long ears circled around its head until they lay flat against its neck, and it bared its small, sharp, buck-toothed grin. The red eyes glowed brighter.

"Allow me to finish!" he hissed. "I was told that one of these was the only hope for survival if one ever found oneself in such a predicament. I stole it from Ol' Hurricane meself." He slowly pulled out of his right coat pocket a small rabbit's foot that was so brilliantly white it looked translucent under the moon.

"What are you doing? Don't make them even angrier!"

Byron spat on the rabbit's foot and the throng seethed again.

She began praying. "Great Sailor in the sky, bless me for I have sinned. I have committed murder, adultery—"

He began rubbing the spittle into the foot with his thumb.

"—robbery, cannibalism—"

A strange red light began to glow from the foot that was altogether too similar to the beasts' eyes.

"—robbery whilst dressed like Queen Elizabeth, the latter whilst engaged with the former—"

The creature closest to them snarled. Marietta could see its features clearly now. The small, red-eyed rabbit was just one of many in the Star-Crossed Long-Eared Legion that could eat an entire village within the span of a few seconds. They had once come across the ruins of such a place, finding only teeth in otherwise unscathed homes. Teeth scattered in teacups in a perfectly set service, in shoes as shiny as the day they were made, in fireplaces that could have been lit with a single spark from a dying match, and, as impossible as it was for Marietta to wrap her head around, teeth stacked into an exact replica of the Eiffel Tower.

"—blasphemy, incest, the latter whilst engaged with the former—"

The rest of the rabbits in the thicket churned, filling the skies with unbearable chatter. Marietta closed her eyes, certain that the horde was going to come down upon them. Her last sight would be the three-day stubble upon Byron's cheek instead of a large pile of gold, upon which she'd always assumed she would succumb to the death of old age. She sneezed, noticing a curious scent on the wind.

Certain that she would see the dire afterlife of her childhood as proclaimed by the Lighthouse orphanage, she opened her eyes and saw a small, live bunny sniffing at Byron's hand, trying to find a piece of grass to nibble. The scent was coming from it. She also noticed that the entire Legion had quieted. Byron dropped the small rabbit and it darted off, taking the Legion with it in hot pursuit.

"Even the undead and the fluffy are drawn to the allure of a woman, especially one with a beating heart." He wiped his hands together and started walking back into the forest, in the opposite direction of the retreating Legion.

"The rabbit's foot was magicked?" Marietta had yet to move, still stunned that she had survived the encounter.

"Gives off the smell of a sexually maturing female rabbit, but is made of nothing more than spit and fog. How so very much like our own elusive searches for love, don't you agree? Now come on. Back to the road. I've wasted enough time trying to find you in this damn labyrinth."

One Year, Four Months, Thirteen Days and Eleven Hours Ago, Or: A Fishy Flashback

Her sea legs wobbled beneath her as she stepped onto the dock. It was always more jarring, she thought, to step back onto land than to take those first few steps onto a tossing ship. She was used to the world turning upside down; it was stability that made her nervous.

She had been called into the Lighthouse's Keep almost as soon as her feet touched the half-rotten pier at the port city of Shipshallow. Lighthouse Foster's spies, little urchin boys who had more stolen coin in their pockets than teeth in their heads, had kept an eye out for her along the docks. She had just flipped a coin to the captain, thanking him and his considerable seaside manner, when she saw three small, hunchbacked shapes clad in bleached potato sacks. She hefted her bag around her shoulder, ignoring the captain's doe-eyed offer to carry it for her, and quickly immersed herself in shadows when the three boys began fighting over who would pick the pocket of a wealthy man who had gotten off the boat with her.

They were triplets, their features barely indistinguishable from each other. Then again, they were also barely indistinguishable from all of the other scruffy, prickly boys and girls who roamed the streets to look for meals and avoid becoming meals themselves. These rapscallions, however, were beady-eyed with hooked noses and shockingly blonde hair. Marietta only knew as much, however, because of the customary bath that all orphans were given when the Regional Inspector for Parentless Foundlings came around. Otherwise, their hair was as brown as the unwashed skin of a squash—and just as infested. It was appropriate, then, that the merchant ship had already left, lest it confuse these three with scurvy, vertically challenged pirates.

Once she saw their confused looks, she swam out of the darkness and dragged one of them into the alleyway by his mangy collar, leaving the other two clueless. She pushed him up against the wall and pulled out a small, sharp dagger encrusted with jewels—a new acquisition from her last assignment in Calderia's capital of Tephra—and placed it at the boy's bellybutton.

"Haven't gone soft as everyone says you have," he replied, showing off three teeth and a bit of brown dribble that stained his shirt. Everyone at the Lighthouse had a habit of chewing blackened Star-Crosser tongues; it turned saliva slightly acidic, a good defence mechanism for the uncouth underclasses. But it also had the unfortunate side-effects of eating through teeth and oesophagi and creating ulcers that resulted, more often than not, in chronic nightmares wherein sufferers were turned into mud puddles and repeatedly run over by carriages. Marietta had stopped chewing when she was nine. These boys were now thirteen, six years older than she had been when the Lighthouse had adopted her. She wondered at their downfall of standards for their recruits in the past five years.

"Scab?"

"Spider, actually," he said.

"Spider I know. He has a large mole on his left buttock. So then you must be Spittle. Wasp's angry, huh?"

He looked behind him to check his backside, back at Marietta, and then back again at his bum. "How did—?"

"Answer the question." She knocked him about the head again. A dab of spit landed on her hand and she wiped it onto his shirt before it began to burn.

"Wasp has some venom-mouth letters for you," he replied, rubbing the side of his head. "Says you should hear it before you go lapping up some other shore and teething with the goonies. The job's hot and he doesn't want someone else to buff the nails up, but if the merch's moving, then we have to play with the squirmies in the shallows, eh?"

"No, no 'eh.' All I got was Wasp, job, incomprehensible nonsense, and something about getting a venereal disease. You should have that examined." She folded the dagger, placing it in her pocket, and started rubbing the bridge of her nose. Spittle shifted from one foot to the other as she sighed. It seemed like she wasn't the only one hating the rooted feeling of standing around. "Tell it to me straight: Rumours reached the White Cliffs about my going 'soft,' so Foster's angry. Thus, by referring to him as Wasp, you're telling me that he's going to sting when I enter the Keep. The goonies are my parents, and he's finally going to tell them that I'm not an ornithologist and that all of the money actually comes from killing people. The merch means that there's now a price out on my head, and the squirmies are the maggots that are going to be feasting on my body because he's sent the Warbler after me. And everyone knows you can't escape the Warbler's flightpath once he's sat on your branch and—"

"Actually, Miss Lapin, we were just told to escort you to the Keep," Spittle said in a proper accent. He wiped his mouth and smoothed his hair down. "Wasp's not angry at all. He just told me to tell you that he has a job for you and that he wanted to tell you first because you have some history with the target, is all. Do you get these moments of irrationality all the time, or just when you're coming off of a boat? You're as nervous as a rapist in the stocks."

She smacked him over the head again and whistled so that the other two could find them. Once Spittle saw his brothers coming over, he hunched his back again, messed up his hair, and spat at their shoes so that were forced to jump back.

"That's for unfishing me in the darky, you arrow droopers," he said.

"You're the girl-thrower for getting rope-tied like an eyepatch!" Spider yelled.

"Barrel it, you mankey-nosed scale-hole!" responded the remaining one, whom Marietta could now recognise as Scab as he pushed his hair back for a fight.

All of them starting spitting at each other until there were three dirty boys roughhousing in the slightly-steaming mud pile at Marietta's feet.

"Boys!" She tried to pry them apart without touching them with more than her fingertips. "Boys!" They continued to scuffle.

"Carriage-licker!"

"Finger-noodles!"

"Comb-over!"

"I guess I'll get to the Keep without you boys and tell Wasp how, instead of escorting me, you three decided to draw attention to yourselves until the Constable over there was forced to make note of your faces and dress, rendering you unfit to work anywhere—"

"At your service, milady," Spider said, bowing while the other two began brushing off their clothes and parting her way through the crowd of people. Before she knew it, she had entered the Keep and the urchins had scuttled away back into the great sea of people walking down the cobbled street in front of the crumbling orphanage. Cockroaches would have been better escorts than those three, but Wasp got more information out of them than most of his spies, so Marietta would just have to live with them.

Besides, underneath all of the dirt and the acidic slaver and the parentlessness and even the beady eyes, they reminded her of herself at that precious age. All three of them together, of course; they were no match for her prowess at assassination and would never hope to be. But there was just enough fondness there that she didn't use them for target practise.

A small cough echoed off the stone walls. She passed the rows upon rows of pews and incense carriers until she reached the confessional box. Stepping in, she straightened her dress and patted down her hair, feeling for all the world like a street urchin meeting a lord for the first time. She clasped her hands together to keep from showing the Lighthouse how anxious she was.

"Bless me, Great Sailor's Lighthouse, for I have sinned."

"Yes, my child?" said the scratchy voice from behind the patterned screen of the confessional. "How long has it been since your last confession?"

"Two weeks," she replied, hanging her head in shame. "I've been away. In Calderia. I stayed longer than I intended, trying to find a bit of solace, Lighthouse Foster."

"Troubled thoughts haunting your faith? I would not worry so much, Marietta. We all have thoughts like these. And all of your hard work with the Tullys has opened another avenue for your life. It is not blasphemous that you have these inklings."

"But it would be blasphemous for me to act upon them?"

"That is between you and the Great Sailor."

She tapped on the screen between them. Her anxiety was quickly being replaced with indignation. "Has your light gone out? For a Lighthouse, you have a funny way of guiding me. I feel more in the dark now than ever."

A few moments of silence ticked by as she looked through the tightly patterned screen. The light behind it cast small, octagon-shaped patches onto her hand. Marietta moved around so that her mottled skin changed with the angle from the flickering candles, reminding her of the play of light on the open sea that she had left not hours before. How clear her thoughts had been while under the halcyon, full sky of the sea, as blue as a dead man's liver. She was going to retire from the bird-watching business, take her gold, and live out the rest of her days on an island. She was going to tell Foster in clear, succinct sentences and not allow him to sway her. As the minutes ticked by, she felt her resolve weakening. She knew the words that were sitting on his tongue, but her mind was making them harsher than he would ever say.

"I don't want you to think I'm ungrateful for everything that you've done for me—how you taught me everything you know. But I just want to say that I'm growing tired of doing the same thing over and over. N-not that it's always the same, because I get to go to exotic places and talk to different people and it's sandy or it's wet or it's swampy or it's a city and that's fun, telling people what we do before I watch their lifesblood come pouring out of their nostrils, but it's just...I-I'm tired, and I want to take the money I got from the Tullys and build an island out of it—'c-cause I can do that you know, with how much I got—and I want to roll around in it like it's silk and I want to be naked in it and I can't do that here because the door locks are faulty and no doubt—"

"Do you remember your only failure, child?"

"Scab will want to know why I have six toes—my—my failure?" Her face darkened. "Lighthouse, I don't see what that has to do with anything."

The only time she had failed in her duties as a Ward of the Lighthouse Keep was the darkest period in her life. Foster had punished her for it, scourged her flesh, so that she still had the marks on her flank where he had carved the word ONE. Most of the Wards had failures, and the numbers racked up along their ribs—if they survived the thrashing at all. But Marietta was one of the few with just a single number carved on her body. She put a hand against her side and felt the small bump of raised flesh underneath her shirt.

"You had been sent after a boy, not much older than you, and told to make it look like an accident."

Fourteen Years, Eleven Months, Twenty-Three Days and Seven Hours Before That, Or: The Wormy Woes of Butlerkind

She shivered in the cold rain, trying to find a spot underneath the branches of an elderly oak tree where she could be sopping instead of absolutely drenched. Her target was inside a mansion across from the hill upon which she sat, sleeping comfortably in a warm bed, a crackling fire mere feet away from him, oblivious to the drowned girl slavering with jealous rage at his dream-drenched paradise.

It was the third day she had been watching him and everyone else in the mansion, learning their habits, their routines, their way of life, so that she might infiltrate it and kill the boy in the last day before her deadline. She had already placed the razors, sanded the butler's shoes, and stockpiled the Sanskritian Death Worms that buzzed in a flask in her pocket. All she needed was for the Frilled Man to fall asleep before instigating the entire plan. She dreamed with open eyes about the clockwork-legged Doctor, with his spill of lacy coverings, and the last time she had felt warm.

The confessional had been cold in the middle of the night when she was woken by a cloaked Lighthouse—one she hadn't seen before, or merely unrecognisable underneath the heavy hood. She held her candle in her right hand while rubbing at her eyes with her left. The floor was even colder and she hopped from tile slab to tile slab until she found the confessional and saw the whites of another Lighthouse's eyes through the star-patterned holes. They were bloodshot from the early-morning hour.

"Rabbit," he said. She had bitten another Ward's finger off with her sharp teeth not two months earlier and the nickname, which had only been slightly sticky before, had solidified, as labouriously as she tried to scrub herself of it. "I've got a mission for you." His voice was grave and he rubbed at the bridge between his eyes. He was never like this when he was handing out missions, especially not to her.

She looked underneath the slats at knee-level in the confessional and saw the strange, hooded Lighthouse talking to another man, who was wearing so much lace around his neck that his chin seemed to be comprised entirely of white fluff. He wore more rings than most men had fingers and they all glinted, even in the half-light swallowed by the pews. He laughed and it rang through the stone walls. A shiver went up Marietta's spine. After the laugh was a spurt of air, a little gush of oil, and then Mr. Lacy cursed loud enough to stop Foster from speaking.

Marietta watched with fascination as the ringed man snapped his fingers and the cloaked Lighthouse bent to one knee, pulled out a small, multi-faced tool, and began rolling up the high-born's trouser leg. From ankle to knee, all Marietta could see was an intricate pattern of gears, brass knobs, and chains that moved together like muscle rippling underneath a cat's fur. She had seen people with clockwork limbs before, but nothing so intricate. The Lighthouse had unscrewed a panel and started tinkering inside before Foster rapped against the panel that separated them.

"Rabbit, pay attention. This is very important. You'll be all by yourself this time and I've been instructed to tell you that the consequences will be severe if we do not succeed."

"Instructed by who?"

"'Whom,' dear child. It's an object of the clause. By whom."

"What I wanted to know," she said, rolling her eyes, "is why you—the great Lighthouse Foster, more commonly known as The Wasp, striker of fear into the hearts of those targeted with others' hatred and gold, punisher of those who would threaten your Keep and its Wards, deadliest assassin in the known Empire—is taking assignments from a fop with more frills around his neck than Queen Elizabeth and probably just as many male lovers. Have you seen how many times he's been at the snuff in the last three minutes? I'm surprised he still has a nose. Or is he waiting for the syphilis to take it? I've heard that's very—"

"Such is not for a child to discuss. We take money, we kill targets, and then we collect more money. Nowhere in that equation is any question about the identity of the hirer, why he wants his target dead, or even how long he's had syphilis and if he's tried taking Red-Lined Bottlersbreaker Elixir for it. And there is little time to discuss even the necessities. Your target is a young boy, black hair, green eyes—no, I don't know his name, and neither shall you, but the address of his location will be given to you. You will have four days to complete your mission. And it must— Marietta, this is important—absolutely must not be tied to us. If any suspicion arises as to the nature of his death, our money will be forfeit and you shall have a nice cell with exposure to the Star when it rises next week."

She gulped, the sound muffled by the thin wood of the confessional, but still loud enough to make Lighthouse Foster eye her through the patterned screen. It was the thirty-first rule of the Keep: show no fear, or be mistaken for a craven and left legless among the Star-Crossers. There was nothing that motivated Marietta more than the decaying Seekers that moved as quickly as a man and devoured everything in their path with migrating teeth and long, lean throats that led to bottomless stomachs. She had suffered many a nightmare in which their long arms and biting mouths ate her up, bit by bit, and she was still alive to feel every indentation of their incisors.

"A girl?" the lacy man exploded. Marietta didn't even need to look to know that the angry footsteps crowding the small, pew-lined halls were coming for her. "They're sending a useless, poodle-faced, dripping green girl? What am I going to do with her? I might as well hire a Seeker to kill the boy, for all the good a gamine guttersnipe will do me!"

"Go now. Follow Lighthouse Frederick. He'll take you to the mark."

"The Warbler?" Marietta squeaked. Maybe there were things more upsetting than the quick Star-Crossers. The deft-handed Lighthouse Frederick had an entire stained-glass triptych depicting his success with assignments—in a code that made him look more saintly than sinister—but Marietta knew the reputation of his prowess, and how quickly that type of skill could turn on a young apprentice such as herself.

Another bloodshot eyeball stared at her.

"I mean, of course, Lighthouse Foster. I shall not disappoint you. May the Star-Crossers fade away before I fail in my duties."

"She is my best assassin, Doctor L..." she heard Foster explaining before a heavy, scarred hand settled on her shoulder. The cloaked Lighthouse—whom she now knew was the dreaded Warbler—pulled her outside and into a black carriage. Without a word, he shut the door, leaving her to rumble down the pockmarked streets to the assignment location.

All of which left her in her current predicament. The Frilled Man—the Doctor, as others had called him during her spying—paced in front of the smoking-room hearth, a floor beneath her young target, as he thought about something of grave importance. The pacing, methodic and staccato, began to lull Marietta to sleep as she tumbled through her thoughts. She had figured out that the boy was somehow related to the Doctor, but why he wanted said relation dead still baffled her. The words of Foster came back to her—as did the heavy feel of the Warbler's hand on her bony shoulder—and she disregarded any more curiosity.

"Go to sleep, go to sleep!" she whispered like a mantra, staring through the water-streaked lens of her telescope. She rested her eyes, collapsing the device and stuffing it back into her pocket, causing the Death Worms to squeal as she jarred their flask. She wouldn't need it to see when the Doctor turned off his light and she could begin the intricate first step crucial to her plan. "For someone who wants this boy killed so badly, you sure do like to stall when the moment comes. Quit thinking about whatever it is you're thinking about and go to sleep!" She pulled the front of her clothes and wrung them out, watching with annoyance as water streamed out of them like she was a raincloud herself. She was certainly in a grey enough mood.

Finally, the Doctor began to blow out the candles one by one until he got to a picture frame lit by a single beeswax candle on the mantel. She quickly opened up the telescope again, eager, despite what she had just told herself, to learn more about the mysterious Doctor. The telescope began to tick, clocklike, and its lens burned a bright blue. The long shadows and dim shapes in her view were thrown into a sharp, ghostly relief as the telescope illuminated the night. Any oncoming Star-Crossers would be enveloped in a blue aura, as if by gaslight. She had added that extra precaution in case she were ever too focused on a target to recognise the unsteadiness of their gait.

The Doctor stroked the glass of the picture frame before extinguishing the nearby candle with a gold snuffer, breathing in the latent smoke. By the flicker of the dying fire that the butler now started attending, Marietta could just make out the curly, leonine mop of a woman's hair in the photograph. Its style—a cascading mane of curls that framed her face—suited a woman in her middle thirties, but belonged to ten years ago. (Foster had trained them in the fine points of upper-class fashion so that they would be able to tell a person's station simply by glancing at their shoes, their pocket watches, or even their handkerchiefs. Marietta had been especially fascinated with the intricacies of hairstyles over the past few years.)

As Marietta continued to think upon the young woman in the daguerreotype, the lights began to dim and she noticed that the butler had left. In fact, he was already on his way to the stairs. Her plan wasn't going to work if she didn't get it in motion before the butler reached the second floor. She shimmied down the tree quickly and ran for the side of the house. She slipped in the wet gravel that covered the hillside, recovered, and began climbing up the footholds and handholds she had carved with the backside of the telescope. It had been one of the first things she had done upon arriving at the Manor House; she had since been in and out of the servants' entrance half a dozen times.

"Mary!" a kitchen girl said, her arms covered to the elbow in flour. Marietta was out of breath and hunched over in the servants' entrance to the kitchen, but she snapped to attention when she heard the scalding voice. "What are you doing out so late? I thought you'd heard Master tell everyone to be in by nine tonight. The Guard said there's a Swarm just outside the gates this evening. There's been soldiers going back and forth all night."

"Yes'm," she mumbled, letting all of the consonants run together. Mary had been a soft-headed serving girl before Marietta slit her throat and took her place. It hadn't been hard—all she had to do was scruff up her cheeks with some dirt and blacken her hair with shoe polish. No one gave much notice to the switch. In fact, no one gave much notice to Mary at all, which was why she had chosen the girl in the first place. Even Foster's domesticated pack of Boar-Eared Weathertusks would care only that she was too stringy, with not nearly as much meat as they were used to. "I'm to make sure the young master's room is warm enough, mum."

"I doubt that!" the girl said, spraying spit into the batter she was beating with a spoon. "He doesn't need the likes of you in his room, messing up his stuff with your dirty hands. Tumble back into the cellar and keep peeling those potatoes, will you? We have to get all of this food prepared for the Master's guests tomorrow."

"But, Bertha, I—" she said, trying to think of something clever to say. "I just...I wanted to say goodnight to him, that's all. I'll be real quick about it." Pretending as if she'd been promised a new Bloodstinger Dagger for her birthday, she quavered her voice and looked up into Bertha's eyes with hope.

"Oh! Has Little Miss Mary got a little crush on the boy?" Bertha responded, clapping her hands and puffing flour everywhere to settle on Marietta's shoulders. Bertha smacked her upside the head, sending another plume of white dust into the air. "How long do you think you'd last here if the Doctor heard you? You best be mindful of what you say, girl. Even what you think. Who knows what the Doctor can do with that clockwork limb of his?"

"A metal limb is supposed to read minds? Should I also be wary of its ability to eat my unborn children, or is that a clockwork arm?" she said. Regretting the words immediately, she beamed like the dull-witted girl she was supposed to be and received another smack on her ear that made her wince in pain.

"That's it!" Bertha shouted. She pinched that same ear, making Marietta cry out, and started dragging her towards a closed door. "I'll have Quincy take care of you when he returns from doing his rounds in the smoking room. It's been awhile since he's gotten to use the rod, so I'm sure he'll be excited to try it out on your hide."

"No! No, Bertha, I promise I'll be good. Please, Bertha!"

The older woman wouldn't hear any of it. She threw the girl into the small closet that served as the butler's pantry—Marietta braced herself just as a corner of the silverware cabinet hit her in the ribs—and locked the door behind her. Marietta struggled up and began pounding on the door

"You best be quieter'n that, if you don't want me to double what's coming to you!" Bertha's screeching voice could carry through the intestinal tract of a whale.

With a hand on her side, mouth opened as if to protest further, she slunk back into the corner and sat down on a small chair that was as comfortable as a rather large toothpick.

After a few minutes, she pulled the worm flask out of her rags and shook the bottle again. They buzzed inside and she could hear a faint clinking as their tiny sucker mouths tried to eat through the glass. She pulled out the stopper with her teeth and ran a finger around the inside edge of the rim until it had gathered a pea-sized smear of their excretions.

She had brought in Tungstun Firepowder and sprinkled it on all of the fireplaces to make the Manor unbearably hot. In her three days' reconnaissance, she had noticed that Quincy often took off his jacket and hung it in the very room she was in (unless he was speaking to the Doctor directly, in which case his shoes shone, his hair was parted correctly, and his dress was nothing short of impeccable). Otherwise, he would sweat like a wild-eyed dingo about to devour a baby and stain his neat white shirts with yellow perspiration. She rubbed the greasy build-up on the back of his jacket, then blew on it to make it fade until there was only a slight sheen when the light hit it just right.

She had just finished when the door swung open. She jumped backwards; hopefully he'd attribute her guilty look to her smart tongue and nothing else.

The butler glanced at her, shrugged into his jacket, and pressed his lips together.

"I swear, Mary, every time I see you, you become uglier. By the time you reach maidenhood, you'll resemble a thrice-decayed Stumbler. Whatever you've done now, girl, it'll have to wait until I make my rounds. Then I'll deal out your punishment swiftly."

He brushed off the dust from his jacket, straightened his hair, then slipped out of the room and locked the door behind him. She counted to five in her head, leaning her ear against the door to hear if he was coming back, then slipped a pin out of her hair and worked it into the lock. It clicked open and she slunk out, closing the door behind her. She left her shoes in the butler's alcove. She could take the risk that someone would wonder why it hadn't been locked; if she needed to get back to the room in hurry, it wouldn't do to have it barred.

Quincy was headed towards the smoking room on the first floor. She quietly moved upstairs, jumping over the third stair from the top that squeaked horribly at the slightest pressure, and found a dark corner along the hallway that ran past the master bedroom, a guest room, and the young master's room. The latter was dark, but the master bedroom was still lit; the Doctor often stayed up late into the night reading books and making notes. She only had a few minutes to start the plan before Quincy reached the stairs.

When no one called out at her presence, she began digging through the fibres of the multi-hued Persian carpet outside the Doctor's room until she found the razor blade she had sewed into it, edge down, the day before. The pile was so thick that someone could have walked over the blade barefoot without feeling a thing. Pulling at the fragile strings broke the carpet's grip. She scooted over to the hardwood floor outside the boy's door and slid the razor between two slats of wood, standing it upright. It glinted in the flickering light. She put the slightest pressure against it and smiled when a small red drop rose on the pad of her thumb.

She licked the wound, stood up, and tilted a painting on the wall next to the door; Quincy wouldn't be able to help straightening it when he walked past. Then she crouched, face next to the crack at the bottom of the door, and whistled a low note three times.

From inside the room came the sound of crinkling paper, faint and whispery. She had left an origami rabbit outside in the gazebo next to the small garden where the boy liked to walk and smell the dozens of different types of flowers. He had picked it up with a small gasp, amazed by its simple elegance, and taken the small treasure to his room. Now it crinkled and stretched its paper legs and shook off its inanimateness, hopping around like its real-life counterpart and twitching its little paper nose. The young boy shifted in his sleep and opened his eyes, only to see nothing but the shadows thrown against the wall and fall back asleep.

She whistled another note, higher this time and wavering with vibrato. The paper rabbit shivered in the draught from the open window, then twisted its body so that it took to the air, landing on his nightstand. She flinched at the sound of Quincy coming up the stairs. She whistled one last short note, hoping the command would get through to the magic paper, before running back into the darkened corner and holding her breath.

The third stair from the top squealed like it was getting an axe to the skull. Quincy appeared on the second floor landing and began walking down the hallway. Marietta was hidden in the corner opposite the master bedroom; she slitted her eyes so the whites wouldn't give her away when he knocked on the Doctor's door and received a grunt in response. With utmost propriety and concern, he opened the door, remarked how he would finally get a carpenter out to fix the rotten wood underneath the staircase, then asked—in the distinguished timbre he adopted when speaking with the high-born—if there was anything else Sir needed for the night.

Something fell over inside the boy's room and Marietta smiled. The Firepowder not only encouraged Quincy to shed his coat, but made the boy so thirsty that he had started keeping a glass of water on his nightstand.

There was a brusque cough; Marietta caught a small glimpse of the Doctor tweaking his clockwork limb again, and as Quincy closed the door, she could hear the gears grinding against each other. She strained to see if the boy's water had spread over his floor and into the hallway yet, but it was too dark and she was too far away. She exhaled slowly and waited. And waited.

Until the hallway burst into pandemonium.

Quincy had walked towards the catawampus painting and gone sprawling into the air, frozen in an aerial ballet doomed to fail as soon as gravity took hold of him. He landed on his back and cried out in pain. She had buffed his shoes so that he would slip on the water knocked over by the origami rabbit, land on the razor blade embedded in the floor, and bleed onto the Death Worm larvae smeared inside his jacket.

She slunk back further into the shadows to watch as blood leaked from his back and small black squiggles started growing, like darkened clouds building into a thunderstorm. They squirmed and danced in the redness until they were the size of the first knuckle of a large man's thumb. Marietta took out her small flask and shook it so its inhabitants buzzed. The free ones crawling over Quincy started wriggling upwards. One, then two made it onto his shoulder before he could stand up. The rest fell off. She watched as the first two slithered up his neck, his wits still too scrambled by the painful fall to swipe them off, and wormed their way into his ear.

The young boy opened his bedroom door, rubbing his eyes at the light in the hallway. Evidently the ruckus had woken him up. With a great yawn, he stretched, then stopped with his arms above his head as he saw the injured Quincy. He bent down to help, though he wasn't much taller than the man's stomach.

"Quincy? Are you all right?" the timid boy asked in a trembling voice. He wiped his brow from the heat in the hall and looked around nervously, as if he could sense something watching him. Marietta curled herself smaller and shut her eyes, listening as well as she could for any sign of discovery. "Quincy?" This time his voice was barely audible and contained a tremor of fear, as if his frequent nightmares were beginning to come true.

The first signs, Marietta knew, of infection by Sanskritian Death Worms were red blotches on the face—

"Quincy, did you lean too close to the fire?"

—reddish-tinged tears and mucus leaking from the nose—

"Do you need a handkerchief?"

—and red-ringed eyes as the Worms infiltrated the spinal column. There, they would induce a state of such ferocious rage that the host couldn't help but kill the very first thing he laid eyes upon.

"Quincy?" the boy mouthed, his voice almost silent, wrung out by a deluge of fear.

A roar of inhuman rage tore through the otherwise distinguished butler's mouth. The Doctor opened his door, his hair at odd angles and his frills gone, so that he looked like an emaciated madman. His leg lay in pieces in the room. He hobbled, using the wall to help balance himself; his nightgown barely reaching past his good knee, allowing the boy to see the dead space where the other leg was supposed to be. A hand, so much larger now that it was free of its lacy frills, stretched an almost impossible length to try to help, only to be hampered by the length of the hallway.

Quincy's hands had just reached around the boy's throat when the family dog came running out of the Doctor's room and launched itself at Quincy, biting down on one arm and dragging the half-wit away from the traumatised boy. As he swung around, the body of the dog hit the boy square in the face and he went down, clutching his jaw and spitting tufts of fur out of his mouth.

Horrified, Marietta watched as all of her plans, the entirety of the four days she had spent infiltrating the Manor House, came to ruin—all because they had let the dog in out of the rain. She could have screamed in frustration, save for the fact that she needed to escape from the hallway in order to try again before the day was over.

As Quincy and the corgi wrestled, Marietta shook the flask again in a swirling motion and then pulled the cork out, leaving the adult Death Worms to pick up their young from Quincy's jacket and fly out of the open window in the boy's room. They would die in the cold, leaving no trace of evidence.

Had it actually worked, her crime would have been perfect. She would have run back to the closet, crying and hysteric, until someone found her. She would have accused Quincy of threatening to kill the young master and raving about her being the last piece of gristle to hold the bones together. She had even gone as far as to mail letters written in Quincy's own hand to his relatives explaining just how angry he was and how, given the smallest provocation, he might snap at any moment.

But now, she just had to salvage the situation as best she could.

With her eyes on the boy and the thrashing butler, she started to back up in the shadows until she reached the first stair and felt the rest of the way with her feet. It wasn't until she had put most of her weight on the third one that she remembered.

The squeak wasn't loud compared to the other noises in the room. But it was enough to draw the attention of the Doctor, who glared in her direction.

"I paid you to kill him, you whore," he hissed so that only she could hear. "I told the old fool that sending a girl was ridiculous! You get out, and if there is any trace of you, I'll make sure they pull all of your teeth and nails out before they kill you."

She didn't wait to be told twice. By the time she had run down the stairs and back into the butler's pantry, she was shaking so badly that it took her three times to open the door and make it look as if she had burst out in the panic now spreading throughout the house. Bertha eyed her as she slipped out the back door, but was soon distracted as the body of the corgi landed in the foyer with a sickening thud. Marietta ran off into the dark, rainy night, sweat steaming off her body in the cold air.

There was the same black carriage waiting to take her back to the Lighthouse when she reached the cobbled street. The temptation to bolt, to run past the carriage and into the spiralling night, held her for a few seconds. But she knew that Foster would find her anywhere. His arm was longer than her knowledge of just exactly how big the world was. She would be swatted away no matter where she went.

This time, the hand that led her into the compartment gripped her like a vise; her insides froze as the Warbler gave a wan smile and a chuckle that could crack teeth. She hung her head, knowing the punishment that awaited her when word of her failure reached Wasp. His sting was a more enduring and frightening legend than even the Star-Crossed Triple-Nosed Bogeyman. Marietta had spent many a late at night at the Keep, as orphans whispered across their beds the horrors they had heard about those who failed their mentor. Those rumours swam in her head—images of flayed men, of being roasted in a large pot, of cracked toenails and bloodied tongues—until she found herself in the common room, the rows of pews taller than she had ever remembered them being.

She moved towards the confessional, but she was tugged aside by a hooded man. Not even the curiosity to see who he was remained in her. She went along willingly, staring at her feet as they scuffled past the hard slate slabs in the common room, the hardwood of the hallway that led to the dormitories, and finally the carpeted finery of the offices. She had never been this far into the sanctum of the Keep since her first paradigm-shifting visit, but she didn't care. These would be the last things she saw before her eyeballs were plucked out, pan-fried, and fed to her.

The cloaked Lighthouse sat her down in a large chair that didn't allow her feet to touch the ground and closed the door behind her. She slid as far back as she could and waited, eyes barely adjusting to the gloom. She wasn't even sure if she wanted to see the bottled creatures and pin-stuck bugs that Foster liked to keep in his shelves—including, it was rumoured, the head of the first person he had ever assassinated.

When he walked into the room, she gulped loud enough that she thought all of the sleeping dormitory must have heard.

"Marietta," he said softly.

"I planned for everything, just like you've always taught me, and I had at least three exit strategies—one would have burned down half the west wing, but that was nearest the kitchen and could always be blamed on a scullion—and then I also got rid of much as I could while still leaving our calling card so that your brothers would know, but it was raining, and I hadn't counted on their dog being there and he ruined—"

"Rabbit, you failed. We did get more than half of the money upfront, and that's nonrefundable, but I'm still very disappointed in you. You know better than to try to execute a Lucius Garrett mechanism without the proper backup! Especially in such delicate positioning."

"I just wanted to make an impression. The Doctor was so dead-set against me that I thought if I could give him something spectacular, something that no one would ever be able to trace back to us—I mean, butlers go insane and kill their wards practically every day, especially when they're as snotty as this one—I could make him sorry for ever doubting us."

"And what have we learned, then, Marietta?"

She began speaking the words she had learned long ago, that had become almost a daily repetition: "That if your brothers ever come in, especially Ladybird, we're to spit on their feet and kick them in the shins and, if possible, try to drill their eyes out with our fingernails—"

"No, not that. What have we learned about your failure?"

"Oh." She sat and thought for a bit, screwing up her face, more to make Foster think that she was contemplative rather than actually contemplating. In fact, she was thinking so hard about how hard she wanted him to think she was thinking, that she wasn't thinking very much about what she should be thinking about at all. "That...this is going to hurt?"

"Yes," he sighed, standing up. He went to a small bar that held fifty-year-old cognac and poured himself a glass. To it, he added a fingerful of what looked to be common dirt, then pulled from his pocket a squirming worm. He crushed its muddy viscera into the shining gold liquor and knocked the concoction back. He poured another glassful and added a pinch of black powder, releasing a small cloud of smoke that formed itself into a dragon before dissipating into his nostrils. They grew cavernous as he downed the second glass. As he sat back down, tendrils of black smoke slipped out of his mouth and nose. When he began to speak again, he wore a moustache of smog. "But you also need to learn that we are killers. We aren't in this for glory, or for revenge, or even for money."

"But you made a bet with your brothers about who could profit the most from their orphanage, and because of that, you made us all into assassins, so aren't you in it for the—?" She stopped when he gave her an eye whose pupil gleamed softly with fire. It was another aftereffect of the Dragonscale Powder that helped the user to focus on a specific task for exactly forty-three minutes, after which they would have to either sleep upon at least one gold coin or gaze upon at least one virgin, lest their fingernails turn black and curly.

"We kill because we are meant to. All of us are here for a reason, you most of all. And so..." he said, taking out a small knife from somewhere upon his person. Marietta couldn't see from where, but the Wasp was known to have more stingers than most street urchins had stolen wallets. He gestured that she lie down on a stark chaise lounge. "While I mark your failure, I want you to tell me about the time we met. And every time you scream instead of talk, I'll make the cut that much deeper."

She nodded and sat down on the couch, lifting her shirt over her ribs. "I was six or seven. I don't remember. Years ago, however, my mother had sent me out for a cup of flour..."

Five Years, Two Months, Six Days and Three and a Half Hours Before That, Or: A Flouring Assassin

Marietta stood in the middle of an empty street in the late afternoon with an empty cup. Her feet were dirty, as were her face and hair. She had just moved with her parents into a hovel somewhere in the Nightslane District, away from the hustle and bustle of their previous house. Her mother had sent her out after discovering that their last few cupfuls of flour had been overrun by rotworms that turned it black and mushy, not unlike the pulped carcasses of feral cats hit by steamcar wheels. If they wanted to eat that night, Marietta would have to go begging for bread flour. It wasn't the first time, but her father had assured both her and her mother that it would be the last.

His new job as an ink-maker for the Undersecretary to the Department of Ancillary Extremities and Supernumerary Quanta had allowed them to move from their parochial backwater village surrounded by Swarms and into a somewhat less decrepit town. Now, however, they never saw poor Prentiss.

"Perfunctory Prentiss" was the indelible nickname that Marietta's half-blind, boil-ridden Grandmother Oculus had bestowed upon her father, even though every time she used it, Marietta's mother hushed her with another swig from her hip flask. Clarice had learned to bootleg vodka as a young girl growing up on the Russian steppe with a nomadic bunch of runaway bank robbers. Since the banks were few and far between, they had to hit the same ones over and over again, necessitating the constant invention of new, innovative robbing methods—until, eventually, they were just offered employment as property protectors. It became their jobs to rob the robbers and split the profits with the bank, which, in turn, gave them credit lines unseen outside of Odessa. With all the excitement taken out of the robbing business, her mother turned to criminal housewifery. Clarice knew how to do three things well: open a safe, make a getaway, and win a drinking contest. All of which, of course, translated perfectly into domesticity, but did not necessarily allow one to make money in more legal arenas of commerce. This left Prentiss as the sole proprietor of domiciliary remuneration.

In the six months since their move, Marietta had seen her father twice. But her stomach had been fuller than she had ever remembered, allowing Clarice to finally put her bank-robbing skills to use in the kitchen. Grandmother Oculus was sucking on a piece of rock sugar when a flour-covered Clarice puffed her hair up with her breath, sending white dust through the air.

"Marietta!" she yelled, bent over with her head in a cabinet full of brass pots. "What happened to the rest of the flour?"

"I don't know," the small child replied, looking at her mother's backside and wondering if one day she would be that wide.

"It's not in there?"

"No. And now I won't have enough for the molasses cakes. Marietta!" she cried again, not remembering that her daughter was standing next to her. "Take this," she said, putting a measuring cup in the girl's hand without even looking at her, still digging through the pantry, "and go find some flour from our neighbours."

The street was dusty. A ravaging Swarm had decimated the area a month ago, opening up new homes for families such as theirs. Marietta glanced over her shoulder to the phalanx of patrolling Guards, their various weapons gleaming in the afternoon sun, their march a metronome-like crunching in her ears. Some carried Whirring Turret Shredders that exuded small puffs of smoke as their steam-powered engines churned whirring blades for grinding up stray bits and pieces of Star-Crossers; even fragments no longer connected to a body would attack on their own. Others carried pristine Brassery Blunderbusses that made horrible grinding sounds as the gears churned to shoot incendiary, exploding grapeshot meant to stick into the fleshy bodies and light the victim on fire, leaving him more concerned with his rapidly charring body than finding brains. The last few, somewhere in the middle, were carrying what looked to be steam-powered cricket bats. Marietta had no clue as to their purpose, other than the obvious blunt-impact brutality of them. She would have to consult Weapons for Killing the Already Killed: A Compendium of Shooting Stars. Grandmother Oculus had gotten it for her instead of a book about princesses like she had wanted for her fifth birthday, but after careful perusal, she had welcomed the manual and read it every night before she went to sleep.

With the empty metal cup still in her hand, she began walking to the houses next door and knocking. After she received no response, she tiptoed around and tried to look into the windows to see what was inside. Spider webs and dust stared back at her through the grimy windows. In one house, she found a nest of scorpions that scattered as soon as her boot hit the wrong floorboard. She moved on, checking every house within four doors of hers each way, until she started running into closed shops and military outposts.

Finally, she turned around and started looking across from her house. In an awkward corner between two angled streets was a cramped building whose grounds were full of children, running around and screaming at each other in imaginary games of Guards versus Seekers. Wary, Marietta approached, trying her best to ignore the stares of the children. Eventually she reached the door and knocked.

Nothing happened. She knocked again, quieter this time,

as the children were gathering at the gates around their play area to yell or stare at her—this strange young girl going into the orphanage alone, without someone dragging her in spitting and biting. Grandmother Oculus liked to tell her stories about children orphaned by Star-Crossers; sometimes they would even infect them, so that when they finally found a new home, they would turn and kill their new families by eating their pocketbooks first. It was really a jibe at her father and his nose-to-the-grindstone ways, but Marietta had taken away an unnerving fear of both Star-Crossers and orphans.

Just as she was about to throw her metal cup to the ravaging beasts that the children had become in her mind and run away, the door creaked open. A young man appeared, his hands full of scrolls and books and papers, and bumped into her. Squealing, she dropped the measuring cup and would have scrambled away if one of the books had not plopped open in front of her. She knelt for a better look.

"You have the second edition of Hackenbusche's Compendium? When did it come out? Is the glossary updated to include the recent Star Legume Shooter with a special trifold that allows the bullets to travel through more than one target? What about the additions to Eli's Steamer Propulsion system? I mean—" she said, gulping loudly as she looked up at the towering young man. She searched for her cup with one hand and proffered it to him. "Can I borrow a cup of flour?"

Another book trickled out of his fingers and Marietta caught it, stacking it on top of the second edition, trying to shuffle the heavy leather-bound books and her empty cup. The young man tried to push up a pair of glasses with his elbow and looked her over once, twice. Then he dropped his books on the threshold and disappeared, his back fading into the darkness of the room, leaving

Marietta to chase stray papers as the wind caught and blew them haphazardly through the courtyard.

After deciding that there were too many loose pieces of paper, she sat down on the steps and pulled the second edition of her book into her lap. She had become immersed in the pictures when a small cough behind her jarred her concentration. She craned her neck around her shoulder and saw the bespectacled man waiting in the building, a long set of pews running behind him. The sun glinted off his round glasses, making it look as if his eyeballs were made of phosphorescence rather than tissue. She snuffled, wiping her nose on her sleeve, and picked up her flour cup again.

"Please, sir. My mother needs it and I've been gone far too long already and you're the only other people on the street other than the Guard and I doubt they have anything to spare—"

"A cup of flour, dear child! Oh, of course!" he replied, pulling his arms in a way meant to invite her in, but also reminding her of the stance one should take while arming a Trigger-Hared Longbow. (A highly accurate crossbow built from the skeleton of a young rabbit.) "Wouldn't you like a cup of tea first, though? It's awfully chilly out there," he said. Marietta looked behind her to see three tumbleweeds and two dust-devils play in the street. "We can chat while Wasp fetches your flour. Wasp!"

A man of equal height to her host limped up to the door, collected all of the books within seconds, and shooed away the children, who had by now gathered around the gates to see what was happening. The man was wearing a dark brown leather mask that hid his lower face and a pair of goggles that hid everything else but his ears and forehead. There was a small wasp worked into the left side of the mask and several layers of lenses dangling above his right cheek. The way he watched her through the darkened eyepieces gave Marietta the chills. He walked stiffly, not bending his left knee, as if it hurt him to do so.

"Oh! She's just what we expected they'd send!" the man in glasses said.

"I'm...sorry?" Marietta responded, looking around. There was no one else he could have been addressing.

"I didn't say anything, darling," the man in glasses responded. He looked at the masked man. "Wasp, go get this precious childling a cup of flour! And make sure the tea is hot in the sitting room." He turned his attention back to Marietta when Wasp started towards the door. "Oh, excuse me! Please allow me to introduce myself: My name is Meriwether Foster, youngest of the Brothers Foster, proprietor of this fine establishment, at least for the last three months, and your host for the evening. Wasp!" The masked man stopped, then clicked his heels and listened for the next order. "Make sure there are those little crumbly biscuits I like, yes?"

Another heel-click sufficed for an answer and Wasp disappeared into what Marietta assumed was the hallway. Foster had moved a few feet away from her and was apparently talking to a bust of a stern-looking man with a very large moustache and an oversized top hat.

"The dirt she has on her face disguises her identity perfectly! How clever to send one exactly like I've been making after Foster—I mean, me!"

"Mister...Foster? Who are you talking to?"

"No one, pet! Now follow me." He started walking down the hallway. After a few steps, he looked over his shoulder and motioned for her to follow.

"I just want some flour!" Marietta wailed, throwing her head back and stomping down the hallway after him. They turned into a sitting room with a large carved mahogany desk, dark Persian rugs, and various animals frozen in dark umber liquids that, when they caught the light, made the whole room look like it was underwater. Marietta began to feel sick to her stomach; she avoided looking at the grotesque figures smashed up against the insides of the glass jars, but their petrified faces and slimy appendages seemed to reach out for her as she passed.

Then a deformed squirrel moved to look at her.

Squealing, she jumped back and bumped into the table where the tea had been set. There was an assortment of biscuits and scones, clotted cream and butter and some condiments Marietta had never seen before in her life. It was hard to understand how a man could be fascinated with such horrible creatures and still have an immaculate table set.

"Oh, don't worry about Renaldo. He's harmless in there. They all are."

"But it—he—it moved."

"Yes, he would. After all, he is a Star-Crosser, just of the Sciuridae variety." He sat down and motioned for her to do the same.

After some effort, she crawled up into the velveted chair and found herself two feet from the table. Trying to scoot herself forwards, she strained with small popping noises until two large hands gripped the armrests and carried her the rest of the way. She looked up, only to see the cleft chin of Wasp and the bottom of his mask.

"I'll be interested to see what she tries to do!" Foster squealed. He steepled his fingers and looked at her through them, as if constructing a place for her in his imagination.

Wasp shot a glance at Foster through the goggles, lowered a

lens so that he could presumably see something that Marietta could not, then backed silently out of the room.

"What do you think I'm going to do?" Marietta asked. The man certainly had a strange habit of talking as if no one else were present.

"What? She can read minds, too! Most interesting! Most interesting, indeed! Have some tea, dear." He poured a cup for her and placed a few biscuits on his own plate. "Sugar?"

"No." She took a sip, then remembered her manners and added: "Thank you."

There was a crash, followed by a muffled curse. Marietta looked to her right, at the large portrait occupying most of the wall. The sounds seemed to be coming from behind it. But Foster quickly poured more tea into the cup she was already holding and started talking about the latest Swarm that had ravaged the town just a few weeks prior. Just before she looked back towards her host, she thought she saw the portrait's eyes move. After seeing the monstrosities trapped in the bottles, she wasn't going to be quick to dismiss this painting as a trick of her imagination. She sipped her tea again, hoping to escape somehow through politeness before resorting to shin-kicking and biting. It was bitter and astringent, but so far, it was the most normal thing of the entire afternoon.

She didn't know what else to do or say, other than hope that Wasp would come back with her flour soon so that she could leave—and that her mother wouldn't use the caviar-covered paddle she had gotten from the nomadic bank robbers on her backside when she got home. Already feeling her bottom tingle at the thought, she looked down at the table, only to see a scorpion crawling across the wood grain. She must have picked it up going through one of the abandoned houses. Her mouth opened to warn Foster, but he had started talking to himself again.

"She sips her tea, waiting to strike, just like a practised assassin! I wonder if there are techniques we can try with the children here to make them so calm in the face of danger? I wonder if she'll try to poison me? I'm allergic to scorpion venom. I wonder if she'll try that. Or perhaps just strangle me with her small, yet deceptively strong hands? My windpipe is rather fragile. Or maybe even stab me with all of the knives hidden over her body, piercing my most vulnerable soft parts in quick succession so that I can neither breathe nor see nor cry out for help! Ooh, I can't wait!"

The scorpion by this time had crawled onto his sleeve and plopped down into his tea. Before Marietta could say anything, Foster brought the fatal cup close for a sip. The creature stung him repeatedly on the lips. His eyes opened wide, a faint line of foam trickling out of the corner of his mouth. Then he fell over backwards, taking the chair with him, its legs sticking out to point at Marietta like accusatory fingers.

She jumped out of her chair and knelt beside him, noticing as she did that the scorpion had crawled into his open mouth and disappeared. His face was purple, his glasses askew and one of the lenses broken. She realised that there was nothing she could do for him.

The door swung open to reveal Wasp, his chest heaving. He flicked a succession of lenses across his right eye and, presumably finding nothing, started to move towards her with his hands outstretched. She screamed, jumped backwards, and hit one of the shelves that housed the preserved Crossed animals. A jar containing a small rabbit rolled on its side—Marietta could hear the glass edge grinding against the wood of the shelf—and her stomach dropped just as it hit her on the head and exploded, spewing its stagnant liquid everywhere.

She blacked out—whether from the concussion or from the

horrid thought of what the Star-Crossed vermin would do to her, she couldn't say. When she awoke, she was sitting on a chaise lounge that had been shoved into the corner of the sitting room. There were several children cleaning up the spilled liquid, but no sign of the preserved rabbit. Her entire body shuddered and she began brushing off the imagined dead rabbits tickling the hairs on her arms and the back of her neck. She began to recite the glossary of the Compendium in order to calm herself down.

"Backscratcher, page fifty-two, capable of firing thirteen rounds per minute and bringing down Stumblers at a rate of six to one, given if it's used on a Tuesday and the weather is somewhere between partly cloudy and mostly sunny. Potted Flower Puncher, page one-oh-four, spans the width of four natural hands, assuming that your hand width is the same size as King Henry the Eighth's at the time of his third wife, and capable of bringing down a Cluster of Seekers within twenty minutes of their appearance by exploiting their presumed fear of leafy green stalks..." she mumbled. She struggled for more and realised she couldn't remember anything else.

She knew her name and the fact that she had gotten hit on the head by an undead rabbit. Pictures flashed through her head of people whom she must have loved and cared about, but where she lived or what she did or even how she had gotten to this place was a mystery. All she knew were the entire contents of the Compendium and how to use every single one of the deadly weapons detailed in the pages of Hackenbusche's opus.

"You are the greatest assassin that has ever lived!"

She perked up to see a masked man slithering from the dark corner of the opposite side of the room. He wore goggles, but the rest of his face was bare—something that seemed incongruous to Marietta, though she couldn't explain why. There was a blue tattoo of a wasp on his left cheek, over a scar that mangled the flesh to the left of his nose and along his jawline. Her young and paranoid mind wondered if he had a matching wound on his leg that caused his limp. "I will pay you double, no, triple what you were being paid before, if only you come work for me and help me train the other fledgling assassins in this orphanage!"

Marietta blinked. There were three lenses over the man's right eye that magnified the blue of his iris. His face was so enthusiastic and his eyes so wide with wonder that Marietta, without thinking about who this man was or why he seemed familiar, began to think about his words. Yes...that was why she could only remember deadly weapons used to mangle and kill and re-kill. If she were the greatest assassin, then of course such knowledge would be ingrained within her. This man with the wasp tattoo was offering to hire her, to protect her, and to allow her to hone her craft.

"I'm sorry for my previous subterfuge," he continued. "I am the true Meriwether Foster. The man you assassinated was my assistant—I've become so paranoid within the last three months that I've had him pretend to be me, just in case something like today were to happen! As I'm sure you've noticed, I was injured from just such an attempt a few days ago." He gestured to his leg and then to the dead host. "Poor fellow...he was a bit daft, always speaking out loud what he presumed to be his innermost thoughts, but a good man nonetheless. I had been hiding behind the painting." He pointed to the large portrait of a man with a beard that made him look like a congested walrus and three small boys, crowded around him more like furniture than sons. "I only looked down for a brief second when my candle wax dripped on my hand. When I looked up, Geoffrey was dead and you were leaning over him, without so much as a weapon in hand. No, don't tell me how you did it! If you work for me, I will give you anything to continue your living legacy, but I also realise the need to take some trade secrets to the grave. Will you please consider my offer?" There were tears in his eyes and he had gone down on one knee to meet her gaze.

"Of course," Marietta replied, a smile breaking out over her uneven teeth, despite a nagging feeling that there was something else she needed to do.

Five Years, Two Months, Six Days and Four Hours Later, Or: A Pourtent of Tea

"And then you handed me my cup of flour and winked, mumbling something about trade secrets again and how flour must be an important ingredient in however I managed to kill Geoffrey, and sent me on my way," Marietta finished through gritted teeth. Foster was almost done carving into her ribs, sweat dripping down the wasp tattoo on his cheek, as if the insect itself was crying. "I quickly came back, however, when the drought we had been going through turned into a torrential downpour that threatened to flood. My shoes were really nothing more than thin pieces of leather strapped to the bottom of my soles."

Parts of her memory had come back to her within the next few months, when she hit her head again during a routine training exercise involving a carriage wheel, a gallon of milk, and a Roman candle. But until now, she had neglected to tell Foster that she had ever lost it at all.

She had eventually gone back to her mother four months later, once she remembered where she lived, with a cup of flour. She had gotten a hug, a beating, a months-stale molasses cake—Clarice had refused to throw them out until she had found her lost daughter— and then another hug when she opened her pockets to reveal them loaded with gold bars and jewels and money. She had told her mother that an ornithologist had apprenticed her, as his hands were too large to dig through the holes in the nearby forest to extract nests and record the contents therein. Furthermore, they had had to set off immediately to camp in the forest for the entire four months of the Blue-Tailed Hobnosed Spindly Seagret's reproductive cycle— which could not be disturbed, lest the crunching of their boots in the dried mud upset the male's delicate mating call.

When she remembered that she was not the world's greatest assassin, she feared that she would now lose the purpose in her life that the tattooed gentleman had given her. But by then, it made no difference anyway. Her savant-like knowledge of the Compendium had only been a sign telling her that the deadly arts were her true path—and what did it matter if her life began with a lie? It was only the first of thousands to come, and not even the most life-changing at that.

She had only cried out twice during her carving; thus, the down-stroke to the N and the second horizontal stroke of the E were the deepest cuts. Foster straightened out his back, wiped his razor blade, and gave her a patch of gauze to press against the wound. She watched as the word ONE seeped through the white cloth in squiggly red lines. There was a twisted sense of pride in having kept her calm while he had scarred her body; she beamed as Foster stood up. When she tried to do the same, blood rushed to her head and she had to sit back down so that she wouldn't faint.

"Here," Foster said, handing her a glass of sugar water. "This will help."

There was a light knock and an orphan came in with a silver tray containing a teapot, fine porcelain cups that tinkled against each other as his hands shook, and dried seaweed in stacked slices so thin that they would melt as soon as they hit saliva. Foster poured himself a cup of tea, took a sip, then placed three dark green, crinkled pieces in his mouth and made a face at their saltiness.

"I would offer you a cup, but your story has made me somewhat uncomfortable, given the fact that it was me you meant to kill that day." He continued eating the seaweed and drinking the milky tea in silence. Only his chewing could be heard across the room, accompanying the soft ticking of the large clock mounted in the stuffed head of a snaggle-toothed alligator that hung next to the portrait of the young Wasp and his family. The goggles that Foster had worn at their first meeting were slung over the reptile's glass eyes.

Growing restless, Marietta started counting how many times he had chewed. At fifty-two she decided that, by the time he hit sixty, she would cough or otherwise do something to get his attention. Blood had almost soaked through the gauze and she wasn't sure if this was still part of her punishment or not.

"Ah, yes," he said suddenly, watching his fingers as the nails began to blacken and start to curl. He pulled a gold coin out of his pocket and licked it three times, after which they returned to their normal pinkish-purple colour and he buffed them against the tweed of his jacket. His pupils returned to normal, their fire dissipating, as the blood drying in the gauze began to feel tacky against her fingertips. "And for you," he continued, flipping her the coin, which she caught.

He then instructed her on how to dress her wound. As she was leaving, a tight bandage wrapped around her side, Foster stopped her at the threshold.

"The Doctor wanted your head, you know." He drained the last of the tea, swirled the cup around three times counter-clockwise, turned the cup over brusquely, and stared at the remaining tea leaves. "I'm going to be killed by a Seeker when lightning that doesn't come from the sky burns my home to the ground," he mumbled, as if to himself.

"You got all that from the tea leaves?" Marietta wondered whether those two thoughts were correlated and whether the latter had anything to do with her.

"Good heavens, no, child!" Foster responded, wiping the tea leaves away and then brushing his hand onto the front of his shirt.

"The tea leaves were for you, even though you didn't drink any tea. The Warbler is a most fantastic palm-reader and he was most gracious enough to read my fortune earlier this morning."

"Then what did the leaves say?"

"Those? Oh. Well, I told the Doctor that he couldn't have your head, of course, and that his next assassination would be free on us, since we failed him this time. The tea leaves just confirmed what I suspected." He took another piece of seaweed and worried it in his mouth before swallowing.

"Well?" Marietta asked, impatient.

"You haven't seen the last of the Doctor. In fact, you're going to die because of him. But that won't be for years, dear. Well, at least two."

Fourteen Years, Eleven Months, Twenty-Three Days and Seven and a Half Hours After That (In Other Words, At Least Two Years Later), Or: The Oldest Profession in the World

"This isn't about that tea-leaf thing, is it? Because it's been a lot longer than two years, and I haven't died because of that stupid Doctor and his stupid nephew and his stupid assassination assignment. And I don't care how good of a palm-reader the Warbler is, there is no such thing as fake lightning."

"What are you talking about, Rabbit?" Foster said through the confessional.

"Well, I mean, we were talking about the only time I failed, and then I remembered how you told me your stupid tea leaves predicted that the Doctor would kill me."

"Obtuse, doltish, imbecilic, puerile," Foster replied, putting out a finger each time he said a word.

"Now what are you talking about?"

"Other words for stupid, dear. Maybe you'd be better off if you had memorised the contents of a thesaurus over the Compendium," he responded.

"Yes, because knowing that consanguineous is just a fancy word for 'related by blood' is helpful when eviscerating someone."

"Not necessarily for evisceration, no. But I did once kill someone solely with the knowledge that a florilegium was different than florimania—and that, in fact, the words have little to do with each other, despite the common root. In fact, the Warbler was once challenged to a contest in which the first one to correctly pronounce pneumonoultramicroscopicsilicovolcanoconiosis would live. Ha! I guess that means that I would have lived!"

"Well, then why isn't the Warbler here, recounting all of his greatest moments in a series of exacerbating yet strangely intriguing flashbacks?"

"Because he isn't the one who has a chance to redeem himself," Foster said, now leaning closer to the confessional so that Marietta could see that he hadn't shaved in a week. "And you actually believed that I could read tea leaves? Rabbit! Though I am very talented, I have never shown any inkling for the clairvoyant arts. I am as dark about the future as others are about how many feet of entrails you can remove from a man before he loses consciousness. I just wanted to give you extra incentive never to leave any unfinished business, knowing how gullible eleven-year-olds are about such things."

"Because cutting into my ribs wasn't lesson enough?"

"You always have to reinforce good behaviour! Besides, I understand your want to retire, but I thought first that you should know: The good Doctor is once again trying to kill his nephew, and he's come back to us. Apparently he's fallen on hard times indeed and needs to call in his complimentary assassination."

"I guess even a rich man like that would be hit by the recent recession."

"What? No. He fell and broke his clockwork hip on, strangely enough, a stone clock. And since he's so vain, he wanted the most state-of-the-art advancements in technological body parts. He commissioned the Department of Ancillary Extremities and Supernumerary Quanta, but when your father found out that he'd tried to bribe his way into a higher spot on the list—ridiculous, you'd think that the very creator of the things of which they are the department would be given preferential treatment—I told him in no uncertain terms that I'd make the entire matter disappear if only he'd reconsider my offer."

"So by 'complimentary,' you mean—"

"I made him pay out the Star-Crossing sphincter. And he also admitted that he may have been a bit rash in his judgement of your talents the first time around, so he's willing to allow you onto this case."

"And by that, you mean—"

"I threatened him with the destruction of all that he holds holy, up to and including the ruination of his collection of porcelain unicorns. Worth millions, if not tens of millions." Marietta gave him a disbelieving look. "Some people take their earthenware memorabilia very seriously, Rabbit, and just because you are not part of that select coterie does not mean that you can judge. A little culture would round out your rather rough edges, I think. Besides, I do believe that the target will interest you."

"What's more interesting than the bastard son of royalty who's worth more than ten times his weight in gold? Which, given that he probably weighs ten times as much as me, means I can build an island out of gold? Not just build an island because of my gold, but actually with the gold. Did you forget that?"

"The same boy—well, he's a man now, I presume, excluding any unforeseeable accidents—that you failed to assassinate the first time around. The Doctor is just as angry with him, but had, up until this point, been content to merely disinherit him from his will and kick him to the curb. Something has triggered his murderous and somewhat malodorous intent again, and nothing puts things more into perspective than being drenched in the splattered gore of a long-hated enemy." He cleared his throat. "I hope that this time, Marietta, you've learned your lesson about—"

"Now that I'm taller than Ladybird, I should not only go for his eyes, but to also try to pull out his teeth? Yes, I remember."

"I meant—"

"I know what you meant. Don't worry, Lighthouse...I have something that will work so much better than a Lucius Garrett mechanism."

She hefted her corset higher, leaving only the cleavage showing. She knew that it was as distracting as she could possibly get without going stark naked. Testing it out, she had whistled over to a few of the Guards, whom she knew were absolutely terrified of her, and they had all but fallen over themselves to talk to her. As the corset was very tight, however, she was unable to reply with more than a few words before needing to lean against something and catch her breath.

It was well after dark, with practically no one abroad who wasn't a street walker, a street sweeper, or a street surveyor, so she stuck a hand into her skirts and found the hidden pocket. She pulled the set of goggles Foster had given her onto her head, then flipped down a few lenses, casting the dank blackness of the Catscratcher District into an eerie purple glow. Red lanterns seemed to glow an off-colour blue from her right eye, but the rest of the street looked the same as any other, save for the prostitutes clustered around the scant sources of gaslight for a chance to glimpse their customers before deciding on proffered jobs.

All of the other girls on the street were dressed much like her: corsets, bustles, lacy shirts, fingerless gloves, colourful cheeks and eyes. But each one had a different colour wrapped around her right arm and her face covered by a mask more suited to masquerades than cheap doxies. Marietta's many informants upon the corner of Hooker and Moll had told her of the need to disguise their identities—oftentimes the Guard would memorise their faces and, if a girl didn't give good enough service, refuse to help during the day if she ever ran into a Crosser problem—and wear bands to let them know which particular flesh-peddler the girl belonged to. Gang wars and petty disputes between Green Gilt Gideon and

Purple Paul the Pilgrim had sometimes even splashed over into the Assassination Guilds and wreaked havoc.

Assassins and prostitutes weren't really all that different, she thought as she walked through the cobbled streets, avoiding the steam exuded by the various tenant houses and places of business. She did a dirty job for money—anywhere between a cheap, quick off and an expensive, high-class, drawn-out conclusion. Hers was a toe-to-toe relationship, dealing with the various bodily functions of her client (sometimes with as many as twenty-one or as few as eleven toes) which oftentimes involved a rather deft hand. And last, but certainly not least, they were both hallowed occupations with rather Biblical leanings, thereby creating mixed emotions with which only a very few people were equipped to deal.

The band around Marietta's arm was a deep blue studded with white marks to resemble the night sky. She figured she was a woman of the night for only as long as she needed to fool her target, so why not wear something more appropriate for the occasion than the obvious trollop fare? If anyone asked—and there were sure to be a few questions from the prostitutes who didn't know her—she would just say that she was a transfer from the Fishitcher, the maritime version of the Catscratcher's dim alleyways and smoky bars, filled with desperate sailors and melancholy pirates instead of repressed dandies and drunken silver-spooners looking for the excitement denied them in daytime hours. Marietta had even heard rumours that the Catscratcher streets, if you knew where to look, would cater to those whose tastes ran into Star-Crossing territory, though the motivation or even the mechanics behind such a prospect baffled her. She put such thoughts away as she began to get closer to a group of motley-dressed girls, their tasselled hair strewn over pouting lips to hide faces that were otherwise plain or ruined by time and profession.

Green Gilt Gideon's girls were flamboyantly dressed as

celestial objects tonight, with pieces of broken mirror glued to their clothes and persons to make them shimmer more brightly than all their true personalities put together. Pinkterton's Pansies lauded the entirety of Parliament, with their cut-up robes and powdered wigs that had been tressed to make them more feminine, and a few of the more hirsute men with as many pocket watches as walrus moustaches flocked to either dominate a hated politician or canoodle with their favourite. Jasper's Jade Jezebels were at once luxurious and cruel, giving icy rebuffs to anyone who even looked at them. Heaven forbid one even try to talk to a Jade Jezebel without having more than twice the typical going rate stuffed somewhere within guilt-sewn pockets.

Marietta flipped the lenses on the right side of her mask and found that she could see various auras surrounding all those around her: men and women, the unwanted gits whose brood mothers tried to placate them, the children who had snuck from their homes to watch the girls strut around like so many coloured birds in the harsh red flicker of the swaying lanterns.

Foster had told her that the goggles were slightly out of this time and showed the intentions of those observed, circa three seconds into the future. He had worn them on their very first meeting in order to understand her emotions, hoping to catch her before she could initiate her fatal plan; what had been remarkable about her was that she had betrayed nothing of her true objectives (and had even shown real remorse after the deed had been completed). Of course, she would never admit that this was because she had never intended to kill Foster's double in the first place, and he had invented his own account: "True assassins," he had explained away, "of course feel every kill as if their hearts were being rended by your most favourite of weapons from the Compendium, the Five-Fingered Metal Skillet that shears, tears, rips, grips, and sautés anything moving slower than a hummingbird's heartbeat. It is the best assassins, however, who use that feeling to fuel other means, be it escape, a bluff, intimidation, or even suicide. True power comes not from blocking emotions or even hiding them, but by allowing them to wash over you, spurring on things that would otherwise be called impossible." Marietta didn't have the heart to tell him that after Geoffrey, her heart was as carefree as a Stumbler sow that had somehow stumbled into a catatonic ward. She reasoned that a good assassin need only care for one thing: money.

A large, swarthy man whose face dripped more wine than sweat, with a bald, shiny forehead and an elaborate moustache that curled three times before reaching the folds of his nose, was escorted by three light-filled doppelgangers: one green, one darker green, and the third a midnight blue. The Pilgrim girl wearing the purple armband in the matron gown, with made-up wrinkles and powder in her hair to make it look like she was going grey, had a sunny-coloured sister, another one of mustard, and a third that was somewhere between chartreuse and pistachio. The more intense the colour, the more intense the emotion; the darker, the more desperately it was hidden. Green meant interest and blue was complete infatuation. Yellow was disgust and red was passion. In a strange bit of counterintuition, black was complete happiness and white was murderous hatred, but grey was moral ambiguity that could be swayed by as little as a lingering smell of burning feathers. Chartreuse was just plain madness, but given that the Pilgrims' niche was to be as motherly as possible to their clients, to see it in Polly was understandable.

Every one of the clients and most of the girls were on what Marietta referred to as the Oblivion Spectrum—absorbed in the things immediately in front of them. They wouldn't notice the new girl with the blue armband slithering through the gathered crowds, biting her lip and looking for a landmark, a street sign, anything to tell her where that dive called The Slaughtered Celery Stick could be found. Any colours like orange, coral, and even salmon were a warning that someone was, in three seconds, going to start becoming contemplative. It was at persimmon that she would be in danger of being discovered.

Mottled blues, spotted greens and diaphanous yellows sparked everywhere as she wandered. Either the maps from her prostitute informants had been wrong or the bar had been moved. Normally she would think the former, as prostitutes were technically in the ward of Ladybird, Foster's older brother, and thereby would do everything in their power to avert her mission. But Ladybird's wards were on the other side of town and still too young to walk the streets. Probably the girls had just gotten their directions mixed up.

She finally found a landmark—a fountain of a young boy running from a cluster of iron Star-Crossers to mark the day when they first attacked from the forests—and knew that The Slaughtered Celery Stick was close by.

The peeling, overcooked asparagus-green walls showed half-rotten oversteamed broccoli-grey wood beneath the paint that flaked off if brushed with even a delicate fold of clothing. Marietta made a beeline for the bartender. Cleavage and coquettishness weren't going to work with him, so she pulled a small silver coin from her corset and set it on the counter, keeping one finger on the edge so he couldn't take it without making eye contact with her first.

"Diana says hello," she said, wagging her eyebrows and pushing the coin towards the large man with the even bigger hands. He snatched it up, bit down on the edge, licked his lips, and then put it away someplace she couldn't see.

After a few seconds of him wiping down the bar and rubbing

out a few water spots on an otherwise filthy glass that needed more attention than just a soapy sink, she cleared her throat and proffered Diana's salutations once again.

"Listen, I can tell you're new," he said, looking her up and down and then sideways. "So first of all, it's the Queen on the money and her name is Victoria. And you can't just say that she says hello, you got to say how she says hello. Like with the shilling you just gave me, you would say, 'Vicki the Judas says, 'top o' the morning,' which the top part would mean this is the furthest you'll go to bribe me and the morning bit means that you want whatever it is done by—"

"The morning, I get that."

"No, it means you want it done by midnight. So shut up and listen, because there's a lot you need to—"

Marietta took out a small dagger she had hidden in a sheath between her breasts and slammed it down between his fore and middle finger, just a hair's breadth from the soft, webbed flesh there.

"Diana from Darjeeling's Denim Dauphins, you twat, not the Queen. I've been sent here by Diana. She said you'd get everything ready."

"You must mean Maurice. Didn't make it in today. Came down with a Hungolian Hangover."

"So everything's not ready?"

He squinted, spat on the table and wiped it into the grains of wood, then gave her a surly look. "Define ready."

She sighed and pulled the dagger out of the dark wood. The real bartender was an ex-consort of Ladybird—as was Diana—and therefore more than willing to help her get her man. Without him, though, she was banking on the fact that the place was empty and that, even if he wasn't going to help her, Maurice also wouldn't be quick to help Byron.

She settled down at the table furthest from the bar, allowing the shadows from the glowing green candles stuck on human skulls in the middle of every table to hide her face.

The target, she had been told, was a regular at this fine establishment. Often after he was drunk, he would find a girl and take her away where she wouldn't be seen for weeks; even then, sometimes she would be missing things like fingernails, teeth, and eyelashes. Once, as she had been told by Carlotta, a Copper Concubine—one of the few bands of unaffiliated prostitutes—a girl had even lost her right big toe, along with her sense of alliteration. But he had paid them all ridiculously well, so a few missing bits wasn't enough to call in any authorities. And they all talked about how dashing and charming he was, regardless of the strange habit of wearing—

"A lady's glove on his left arm," Marietta whispered to herself, watching with watering eyes as the target moved through the tavern doors as if he were the owner's son. He sat down in the middle of the room and waited without saying a word, trusting that the staff already knew what he wanted and would get it to him ahead of those who had been waiting longer. Within seconds, a busty wench had poured him a shot of whiskey and left the bottle. The assassin watched as he looked over his shoulder at a Pinkerton girl licking the ear of some aristocrat, patted down his pockets, and finally found a snuff box. He pinched the powder and added it to the shot before leaning his head back, slamming the glass into his mouth—Marietta could hear it clink against his front teeth—and pounding it back down onto the table, causing the three couples around him to stop their conversation for a second. The near-future selves of everyone around him turned a blazing coquelicot before simmering down back into the Oblivion Spectrum.

She studied his face, nodding to herself that he was indeed an attractive man, with his dark hair and olive complexion, strong jaw, and bright green eyes. But where he should have looked robust, he looked sallow. His gums were greying, as was the hair at his temples; his cheeks were sunken in and his lips were the same shade of sickly yellow as the corners of his eyeballs. But even his seeming illness lent a certain beauty to his features, as if stopping just short of perfection made one realise how close he was to it. The only thing that seemed out of place was the black glove on his left arm, tucked into his shirtsleeve so that not a bit of his flesh could be seen. His right hand, however, was large, and poured another drink of whiskey and pulled a bit more snuff and scattered it into the amber liquid, leaving a slimy residue on the side of the shot glass.

After every shot, his intentions would turn a dark brown before lightening back to a murky feldgrau. Like everyone else in the place, he was drinking to forget something, causing his intentions to become more and more muddled as he worked his way through half the bottle. Marietta decided to approach him when his inhibitions were low, but he was not quite so roaringly inebriated as to either cause a ruckus and be kicked out or whimper into the arms of alcoholic oblivion in the corner.

She sipped from a drink that a wench had given her with a wink and contemplated, making a face at the bitterness of the first few pulls. When she looked up, the bartender who was not Maurice was talking to her server, and he raised his glass to toast Marietta. She smiled, ingratiating herself so her target's imminent grisly death would be less ungracious, and took a long swig. She knew it was poisoned—part of her training had been to build up an immunity to the thirteen most common forms of poison—but it was still her second inkling that something wasn't right. The first was the failed attempt to bribe the bartender. It would take one more thing for her to abandon the mission; until such time, however, she would just have to be as cautious as a pressure valve inspector.

With empty cup in hand, she stood up, straightening herself to make it look as if she had too much to drink and keeping one eye on the bartender to see his reaction, and sauntered over to the target's table. She balanced on the ledge so that he was face-level with her bosom and leaned over to talk to him, glassing over her eyes and peering through the goggles. His aura inflamed with a passing spark of red, then simmered down to its normal state with a burst of eggshell towards his feet.

"Most guys come here to find someone to share their pain, and though I don't discount the solace found in—" She picked up the bottle and read the label: "Captain Stormseeker: Don't Let Your Mouth be as Dry as a Star-Crosser's—" She blushed as she almost read the next word out loud. "While whiskey can make you forget, it can't make you remember. Believe my next sentence with whatever convictions you may have left: you will remember me until your deathbed. Even then," she said, leaning over with elbows on the table, so that her face was inches away from his, "your last words might be my name."

He looked at her over a small pair of round spectacles darkened to be as black as pitch. His aura was beginning to flare into a vibrant aureolin. "First, your breath doesn't stink of alcohol and your words are far too measured to match your feigned drunkenness. Second, your armband is far too obviously nothing but a silly joke to yourself. Third, you are far too prudish to be a prostitute if you can't say—" A girl broke a mug at that moment, drowning out his next word, but Marietta blushed all the same. "And yes, I've been watching you in that eerie green light with your Mismatched Temporal Animus Lenses. Though it is flattering to be followed so," he said, putting a finger across her lips for silence, "any other girl would know the rumours by now and have demanded from me, upfront, an outrageous price to allow me a round of drinks, a night of passion, and a keepsake, be it a lock of hair, eyelashes, or something more." It was his turn to lean in closer, almost touching noses with her. But the sentiment behind the gesture was more feral and hungry than playful and coy.

His aura flared a blinding white and Marietta backed up, realising that most of the other couples had left for the night. There were only the serving wenches and the bartender—none of whom were too friendly with Marietta, and all of whom clearly knew the man across from her. Had Maurice actually been held up his end of the bargain, she would have been accompanied by at least one person in her employ and thus have a chance to escape. A cold tendril of fear lanced her stomach.

The man grabbed her wrist and she struggled, reaching for the small dagger in her corset. But his intentions calmed down and he slumped back into his chair to take another pinch-filled shot. Part of her wondered whether she should back off and try a different approach. But the sting of another failure pricked more than just her pride, so she sat down in the chair next to him and pulled it close so that they could talk without anyone hearing. In the back of her mind, she cringed at the thought of remaining near this man any longer. Her intuition told her his very existence was somehow wrong, somehow off, and that instead of being close to perfection, he was probably as far away as one could get. But the well-trained part of her shrugged it off; whatever violence he would threaten her with, she knew at least ten dozen rebuttals, and she had handled far more threatening targets before.

"Besides," he continued, a small hiccup in his voice; his eyes remained unfocused, staring at the floorboards, the green light deepening the already-dark shadows under his eyes. "How am I to remember your name if you haven't told me yet? Unless I am to make one up for you? With those ridiculous goggles on, I can barely fathom if you're a woman or not, even with the corset. Corsets, I'll have you know, have been the undoing of more than one woman, and I'm not just speaking literally. If you've ever heard the story of Zylphia, of the Zaffre Zygomatics?"

"Zygomatic isn't slang for a prostitute," Marietta interrupted, wondering at the strangeness of this man who spoke to her as if they had grown up together. While she had made a lasting impact on his childhood, she doubted that he was aware of it. "It's an anatomical term."

"My dear," he replied, signalling for another glass and pouring her a shot, refusing to tell the rest of the story until she drank it, "if it exists, there is someone out there who finds it even remotely erotic. And if it is even remotely erotic, there is a prostitute who specialises in it. Of course, for one as delicate as you, I wouldn't delve into the deviancy of the common gentleman. But behind the perfectly charming mask of our neighbours," he said, pulling his face into a wide, bewitching smile that allowed Marietta to further understand his allure, "there lurks a beast, hungry for whatever life it can pull with its shambling hands into its open mouth." The corners fell and his dapper demeanour instantly changed into a rictus grin.

"So men are like Crossers?"

"My dear—I shall call you the Princess of Wails, for the goggles you wear that so adamantly protect your identity—all human beings are like Star-Crossers. They are nothing if not true reflections of ourselves, our base instincts and carnal needs unfettered by higher thinking or existential quandary. Strip a man of everything that makes him respectable, presentable. Strip a man," he said, gesturing to the skull on the table as he idly stirred another shot, turning it the colour and consistency of dark ash, "into nothing more than a green shadow, cast against a wall by a poorer fool whose face has been repurposed as a base instrument of illuminational derivation. Take away all this." He began to count his fingers. "His name, his title, his money, his rightful position on this sad, meek little planet, and you have nothing that a Star-Crosser doesn't already possess: the need for satiation."

"Do you always make horrible puns when you're drunk, or is this a phenomena of your sobriety as well?"

"All that, and all she gets out of it is humour more fit for Shakespeare than a man pouring his soul out for a stranger whilst poor Yorick sadly looks upon." He picked up the skull on the table and admired it with a sense of sympathetic apathy. "Well, he would if he had any eyeballs. No, my more entertaining aspects stick to my person...much like a sense of illegitimacy sticks to you."

"And my name is Marietta, though you may call me Rabbit."

"A rabbit! Fortuitous that we should be talking thusly. My name, what I have left of it, is Byron." He gave her a sticky hand that she reluctantly shook. "And a rabbit is precisely what led me to this wonderful junction in the series of circumstances known formerly as my life. But, to continue the previous sentiment, I'll bite and ask how you received such a nickname. I'll venture that it was because of your demure ways—before becoming a lady of the night, I'm sure."

"A jar containing a preserved Star-Crosser rabbit fell upon my head as a child."

"That," he yelled, his aura turning black for the first time during that night, "deserves a drink!" He poured another whiskey for her, not realising that he had drunkenly switched glasses, so that hers now carried the blackish soot and he had the clean one. He took his shot and Marietta recognised the taste in hers as common dirt, but its purpose was still a mystery. "My tale is not as jocular, I'm afraid. It all started with an origami bunny, Sanskritian

Death Worms, and a ravenous wolf, the heroes being, of course, myself and my best friend, whose life was almost lost—"

"Perhaps," she replied, placing a hand on his leg, "you'd like to continue this story in private?" She swooned a bit, this time not in dissembling, but because of some strange reaction between the dirt in Byron's shot and the poison in the drink from before. (It was not uncommon for her immunities to have erstwhile effects, like turning her eyes yellow or numbing her tongue so it slipped down her throat or even growing the hair on her toes so long she could braid it and wrap it around her ankle.) This type of drowsiness was concerning enough that, pride be damned, she knew she had to leave. But if she could get Byron to come with her, there was still some hope of redeeming herself.

They staggered out together, Byron too tipsy to tell which of their four feet were his and Marietta vainly struggling against the aborted poison. As she lifted one of Byron's heavy arms—how could such a lanky man weigh so much?—she saw the bartender and the wench who'd served her wave.

"Ladybird says hello," the bartender chirruped.

By the time they arrived at a small inn—The Spotted Raven, the sickly bird on its sign suffering from what Marietta assumed was some sort of avian venereal disease—the three-second Byrons flashed sangria, vermillion, and amaranth, respectively, until Marietta felt that she was seeing in triplicate and her head began to pound. She rubbed the goggles around her eyes and then smiled, pulling Byron into the room after her. She didn't know this inn from any other, but the pain at her temples had precluded the possibility of going further and her training told her to seek shelter, regardless of the fact that she would be walking blind into a potentially threatening situation.

The innkeeper barely glanced their way. With a smattering of coins dropped into his greasy palm, they blundered into a room and into a graceful clump on the noisy, springy bed.

"You were saying about your best friend?" she prompted as she began slowly undressing him. He was obviously a man who liked to talk about himself, which could only work to her advantage.

"Hmm?" He had poured the rest of the whiskey into a flask from which he now drank, swishing the contents with his left hand. "Best lad I'd ever known. Stuck with me through think and twig. Or, rather, twin and wink. Regardless," he slurred, sitting down on the bed to watch with fascination as Marietta pulled off his mud-encrusted boots and peeled away the grimy socks underneath. He laughed when she wrinkled her nose. "What was I saying?"

"Your best friend," she began again, now standing up so she could unbutton his shirt. A few pounds against the back of her eyeballs and she felt as if she, too, could wake up with a Hungolian Hangover.

"Ah, yes! Unselfish type, always risking his neck to save mine, until he no longer had a neck, that is. Really good at finding stuff, too. I once buried his favourite toy in the backyard and the champ found it faster than a whore asks for money." He looked her up and down. "Begging the vulgarity of such a statement, Miss Rabbit. He liked rabbits, too, now that I begin to think about it."

Marietta began to open his shirt, kissing him along the neck and down to his chest. The taste of him was salt and something else, something bitter. It reminded her of the dirt encrusting the edge of the shot glass.

"And your best friend, does he know why you like your so-called keepsakes? What do you do with them?" she asked between kisses, hoping to keep his mind occupied so she could peck at the truth.

"All of the other girls will take off their masks once they've realised that their partners are neither common shills nor Guardsmen with appetites bigger than the Star-Crossers against whom they supposedly guard us. Why do you keep yours on? Oh, I forget," he murmured, clearly not forgetting at all from the way he winked at her, "you're not an actual prostitute, though you certainly do know all the tricks." He screwed his face up and then broke into another smile. "I just made another pun! Perhaps you are correct in that the ratio of calembours to libations are inexorably intertwined." The white of his aura was lessening and she relaxed as the pain in her head faded slightly.

His hands were in her hair, pulling out the pins and letting her curls tumble down her shoulders and over his arms. She straddled his legs to work at the buttons on his trousers. He found the strap to her goggles at the same time she started to peel back the glove on his left hand. They both stiffened, her hands going up to keep the goggles on and his to grab her wrist.

His intentions flared the brightest white she had ever seen come off of a human being. She quickly shut her eyes to avoid being blinded; mere mortals weren't even capable of registering such a colour. Her head pounded worse than ever and she lost her balance. Collapsing onto the bed, she looked up to see Byron, completely sober and sharp-eyed, his tongue stuck out between his teeth in concentration. He was now on top of her, scratching at the goggles, which he pulled off along with a large clump of her hair.

"You'd like to know about the keepsakes? Shall I tell you about those, or do you want to know why your head is pounding? Well, I expect it's pounding now because of the large wad of your hair that I now possess, but the reason it was pounding before?"

She tried to struggle, but the weight of him was too much and both of her arms were now pinned. "They poisoned me at the bar. Or maybe I should just blame your incredibly cheap taste in whiskey? Even two shots of that, and I feel like I was tackled by a hare-lipped bear."

"Why should a bear care if it has a hare-lip or not? No bear has any sense of self-consciousness and thus would not be any more angry than a bear without a hare-lip."

"Fine. Tackled by a hare-lipped bear in the middle of salmon spawning, angry because fish keep slipping out of his mouth."

"Acceptable. But, unfortunately, still wrong, regardless of the motivations of the ursine creature in our similitude." He took her hair and, keeping his knees on her arms, patted down his pockets until he found the right one and placed the clump in a small blue glass phial. "Your head is pounding, my little cunicular critter, because of the whiskey, but not because of its paltriness. It's meant to keep death away—but if you've never been touched by the icy pale rider, then it has quite the opposite effect."

He spat into the ampul then. Marietta watched in horror as his phlegm ate away at the hair until it was nothing more than a brownish bubbling concoction. He added the sludge to the flask with the whiskey and dirt and took a long, gulping quaff. He smacked his lips and his skeletal smile crept through. Marietta felt the tips of her fingers and toes go numb simply from such a stare.

"Acidic slaver?" she squealed. "How many times have you dreamt that you're a puddle run over by a carriage? I've heard they're rather horrific. Is that your supposed brush with death? Melodrama and puns must occupy the space in your personality where clarity was meant to go. I've known men who have chewed burnt Star-Crosser tongues for thirty years, and none of them have ever described it as a harrowing experience."

"Not so horrific when the carriages are replaced with steamcars. Wonderful things, really. My Uncle had a whole fleet built for him and would drive a different one each day, depending on the pattern of his pocket square. The process to heat them up in the mornings took an entire fleet of servants as well, with their own pocket-square patterns to worry about, so that it became quite the conundrum to solve without an overseer. But when you're the creator of clockwork limbs, you have enough money to spare on such trivialities. Did you know that he actually coined the term car? Short for carnage, apparently. And I'm glad to see that you're keeping a sense of blitheness appropriate to the situation."

"The situation being my impending death? You wouldn't be telling me all this otherwise."

"As the colloquialism goes, and I apologise for the plebeian-ness of it: yahtzee! And your spoken question, as to what I do with all of the souvenirs I take from the girls I frequent, shall be answered by your unspoken question about what lies beneath my glove. For I have never tasted a burnt Star-Crosser tongue...aside from my own." He took another swig of the flask, grimaced, then loosened the fingers of his glove with his right hand, pulling them longer so it looked like he was popping his fingers out of joint, much like a snake unhinging its jaw to cause its mousy prey to recoil in preternatural terror. The edge of the glove began to scale away from his skin, revealing a neat line between live, pink flesh and grey-green decay, with scabs and pustules and open wounds like a pitted battlefield. "I can survive on odds and ends discarded by people that were once alive—hair, fingernails, flakes of skin and the occasional hallux—but I had resigned myself never to take a life to sustain my own. Seeing, however, as you're the cause of all of my problems, since the day you broke into my house those many years ago and tried to kill me by infecting Quincy with Sanskritian Death Worms, I'll make an exception."

Marietta's eyes grew as large as the orbits in her skull. "So let me go and I'll give you all of the halluxes you'll ever need. I won't be dead, you'll not have gone back on your promise, and we both win."

"Halluces, my dear. Third declension: a noun ending in u and then a consonant, such as x, will inevitably decline with a C-E-S ending," he droned, his eyes wandering until they snapped back to attention and burned through hers. "I find it odd that you don't even deny trying to kill me. As you let it slip, however, that you're a frequent cohabiteur with those who chew Star-Crosser tongues—a habit peculiar to the Wasp's Little Stringers—I'll say that you've been an assassin since a very young age and have finally come back to finish the job. Did you think I didn't recognise you? That your clever disguise of hiding the bridge betwixt your eyes and the tops of your cheeks could fool me when your dusty face has scarred my dreams for the last fourteen years? However," he said, and he spat on her cheek so that the soft flesh began to blister, "if you're good and give me the name of the man who wants me dead, I'll eat you head-first, instead of the other way around. As I have yet to lie to you—lying is a personal anathema of mine that I try to avoid at all costs—I'll tell you that I am very adept at keeping people alive, even when they're missing sixty percent of their internal organs."

"We don't know who hires us. Clients come into a confessional with money and give Wasp a name; he then calls one of us into that same shriving-pew and we do our duties. I couldn't even tell you what he looked like."

He leaned in closer to her face. "Then how do you even know it's a 'he'?"

He spat again and she screamed as it rolled down her cheek.

"Because...!" she started. He propped himself up on his elbows, face inches from hers. "Because...!"

"Yes? Do you need something to drink to make your throat less dry? I've heard that caustic spittle is a close second to water."

"Because!" she screamed as she finally worked her hands free. She thrust out her elbows to unbalance him and whipped her head forwards to knock him unconscious. The hope was to be able to withstand the pain it would cause, but as she saw his body falling towards hers, she realised that she had miscalculated. She had just grasped the hilt of a knife hidden in her garter when he crashed into her and she felt an excruciating pain in her neck. It was only when the blood was gushing out, dribbling down her shirt and colouring her entire world incarnadine, did she realise that he had bitten her.

She felt cold and knew it was because of the blood loss. The pain was subsiding only because her brain was losing oxygen, and with the ragged hole in her windpipe, the fuzzy feeling of disconnectedness continued to grow. She knew she was dying; to experience, finally, the other side of the journey, to be the victim instead of the perpetrator, gave her an odd sense of peace. Her vision narrowed until all she saw was the top of Byron's black hair as he bent over her, tearing at the muscles and cartilage of her throat. The tip of his nose was bloody as he stopped to breathe and she would have laughed at the absurdity, had she still had a larynx with which to laugh.

Over Byron's face, as if in a double exposure of film, she saw the Doctor's leer, the coils of ruffles and rubies and rumours, and she wondered at the intelligence of tea leaves and how they had been able to predict that her death would come because of the inventor. She had always thought that the worst way to die would be by a Star-Crosser's dead hands, feeling their rotting teeth digging into flesh. Now that it was happening, she felt silly for her previous pusillanimity, and even imagined that, with the last fading buzzes of pain travelling through her perishing nerves like fireflies bowing to the greatness of the sun, she was sitting up as Byron rolled off of her and phantom hands tried to piece her throat back together. Were they hers? It didn't even matter.

It wasn't until after the fourth stubborn attempt to reattach part of her windpipe—they were hers! in her gauzy state, this fact pleased her—by simply looping it under ruined tissue and disjointed bloody fibre that she realised that Byron was laughing. She hadn't recognised the sound because it seemed like her ears were filled with water. It pulsated through her brain, like a warped record playing through a gramophone stuffed with old socks. It was the bleakest laugh she had ever heard, hawkish and blank as a statue's eyes.

He turned around and held his once-gloved hand up to her to show that it was pristine, a perfect replica of his right one. The sallowness had left his cheeks, a shine had returned to his hair, and his eyes were once again bright with health, no longer corrupted with atrophy. It was a shock, then, as she looked down to see that she had taken that part of him, the disease, the dying into herself; she had made it back up the rabbit hole, but not entirely in one piece. She had become a Star-Crosser.

In Which We Finally Meet the Nefarious Ferret, Or: The Lord of the Unforgettable Yawn

"Asunderers," Byron said as they walked through the cloaked and hooded crowds of the Mephistopheles Market, glancing at wares and trying to push their way towards the head of the congregation. "Amuckers."

"Amaretto?" Marietta responded, stopping by a booth that was selling painted Crosser fingernails.

"I'm sorry?" Byron said, pawing through a bargain bin of half-broken nails and cuticles and mumbling to himself when he couldn't find an acceptable one.

"I thought we were saying random words that started with the letter A."

"Breachers. Cleavers—no, that's a type of cutlery used for chopping the heads off animals to put into stews. My father's old cook would carry one around in his belt with blood still dripping from it and tell the maid that one of us had been murdered by a dwarf-sized serial killer with bad teeth. The bad-teeth phobia was just a leftover from a doctor who once told her about the dangers of desultory oral hygiene. But the dwarf-sized bit came from her father, who was a side-show freak and would oftentimes scare the girls who paid halfpence to see him by drinking pigs' blood diluted with, strangely enough, amaretto."

Marietta gave up on having her question answered and started looking at the wares herself. The nails were used to cause intense itchiness if they broke the skin and drew blood. Which colour they were painted with advertised the duration and intensity of the itch. It varied between a minor inconvenience that would merely cause one to scratch until blood blisters appeared and an itchiness so horrible that one would be driven to cut off the offending appendage, then go on scratching at the bloody stump. In the worst cases recorded, the victim would even go on to maul the lingering phantom limb, scratching at the air like a madman signaling unseen zeppelins.

"I am trying to think of a new name for Star-Crossers. I mean, has anyone ever stopped to think why they're called that, other than the obvious connection to the Homunculus Star? Preposterous, I believe. And the best way to go about finding a new name is alphabetically. There is nothing that cannot be solved with practical logic and a stable system of trial and error."

Marietta hadn't been listening.

"Your scarlet 'Everything-Looks-Like-a-Hammer,'" she started saying to the vendor, reading a plaque above a row of cracked, peeling fingernails, some of which were still attached to tissue (and one that was even still trying to move on its own), "is clearly just a yellowed and expired nail that you've repainted." The vendor gave her a sharp look as another customer scoffed and walked away, pulling up his hood so that no one could see any distinguishing features. "It's not going to make anyone or anything itchy, save for a wallet that wishes it could have been emptied for a better purchase."

"Sorry," Byron said to the one-eyed vendor, pulling her away from the counter and flipping him a silver-speckled coin that Marietta knew to be a worthless piece of hammered metal. "You," he said, pulling at her arm and walking them into the waves of people flocking to and from various booths, "should remember that the only reason I made you look this human, at quite the cost to me, is so that you wouldn't attract attention." He wriggled his left hand to show off the glove that covered it. The entire arm was decayed and barely worked, save for gesturing and the occasional wave.

"The more you play with it," she warned him, "the more likely it'll be to fall off. Don't worry, though, we're close to the hands and we can get you a new one." He glared at her as they passed a booth selling Star-Crossed hands as thief's aids; each one would act as a third hand when placed anywhere on the body. "What should we name it? Amuck? Cleaver? It certainly makes the ladies split." She knew that taunting him at the Mephistopheles Market in the midst of the humming crowds left him powerless to retaliate—but she hoped that by the time they were back on the road, he would have forgotten, or else she was going to pay when they were alone.

"Besides," she went on, pointing to her left eye socket, where a black patch with an outline of a faded salt-encrusted skull-and-crossbones resided, "I'm still missing an eye, and could give a nasty surprise to anyone wanting to take a peek underneath, if you know what I mean."

"Dear Lord, woman, may you never speak of such vile, base—oh, you're not speaking of that underneath." He cleared his throat. "Let's just go find Ferret, shall we?" He looked around himself, straightened his pocket watch on its rusted chain, smoothed his hair, and then shook his foot to remove a stray glob of mud that had hitched a ride from a passersby.

The Market was laid out in the likeness of a human being, with each booth selling a respective part based on where they were geographically. They had entered the left hand and were making their way up through the arm, the shoulder, past the neck, and eventually up to the head—"We're like a blood clot!" Marietta had remarked to an unimpressed Byron—where Ferret, the Minister of the Star-Crossed black market, literally headed up the entire outfit. He ruled with an iron fist—the right hand of the Market currently resided over an iron ore mine—and with his vast collection of telescopes, gyroscopes, periscopes, and even kaleidoscopes, he could see every single part of the Market from anywhere within his office. It was indeed a tight ship, despite the fact that they were many miles away from the nearest body of water.

Throngs of people jostled the busy walkways over the muddy marshes upon which the Meph was built. Small causeways of wooden planks rose two feet above the muck, but there were so many people that others donned knee-high boots and waded through the quivering brown side streets in order to get to their destinations faster. In fact, one couldn't move past a major quarter of the body without hearing someone hawking a pair of cheap boots to make the way easier. Marietta knew that those boots were mismatched and probably taken from any Crosser dumb enough to get caught in the mud banks surrounding the Market. Almost everyone was wearing a hood over their face, either to avoid being recognised or because of the faint drizzle slowly dewing everything with moisture.

"Are you sure we're not in the armpit of this massive creature?" Byron said as they moved past booths selling decaying goops purported to be jellied white Star-Crosser lungs. "It's certainly humid enough that we could be walking through zombified perspiration and not even realise."

The lungs were used to dry out foodstuffs to preserve meats, cheeses and fruits, but when used in tandem with pickled adrenal glands, they boosted the human nervous system, mimicking the effects of cocaine and giving the user the lung capacity of an Alps-raised horse racing at sea-level. Marietta had once seen a man blow over an entire pig farm after having eaten such a delicacy. He had died three days later, though; when the resurrection men, who doubled as informers for the Wasp as to new and exciting ways people could die, found his autopsy at the hands of the Dean of Cadaverous Inquisitions, they reported back that his lungs had melted internally. She doubted, looking through the cloudy glasses, that these lungs could even allow someone to blow out birthday candles.

Marietta had only just started walking through the crowds of people before she realised that they were being followed. One of her many skills as an assassin was to sense any stragglers who came too close or tried too hard to blend into the background. Many an attempt on her life had been made by someone whistling a tuneless ditty or buffing already-clean nails or even looking up into the sky at nonexistent birds. If there was anyone who knew about nonexistent birds, it was her.

She put an arm on Byron and leaned in to him, as if they were a couple.

"What are you—unhand me this instant—I don't want to see what's underneath!" Byron started before she pushed him into a small alleyway and cut off his protests with an involved kiss. Her left hand pressed against the veins at his collar and paralysed his right arm while her right hand pulled a small mirror from her belt. "Number thirteen, Marietta? When we're so close to—" Byron cringed as the numbness started to work its way up his shoulder. When he couldn't talk anymore, she breathed on the glass and then kissed it, leaving an imprint of acidic saliva that began to burn through to the mirror's silver backing.

Byron, through the paralytic stupor now possessing him, began to squint and moan like a high-pitched dog as her lips burned first on the side of his cheek, then on the side of his throat, near his collarbone. She wasn't paying attention to that, though, and she closed her eyes to listen. Over Byron's muffled groans, she heard another cry of pain behind her. She quickly slid on her brass knuckles and punched the alley wall behind her.

The wall shook and released a small avalanche of grey stone, pinning her attacker to the ground. She straddled him, fist raised high, ready to make his brain coagulate and drip out his nostrils if need be. But curiosity got the best of her and she threw back his hood, splattering droplets of dew.

"Spittle?" she asked, surprise galloping through her.

"Scab, actually," he replied.

She blew on the compact again and he writhed at the pain in his cheek.

"Scab has a port-wine stain under his right nipple. And I know there aren't any clusters of moles on your backside...so we meet again, Spittle."

"Swiss worm cheese, they told me you was dancing with the squirmies and drinking with the lord of the unforgettable yawn. To see you here, though, flesh-peddling and boot-stomping for waggon bits, makes a Spittle use his hard-boiled noggin." She noticed as he talked that his teeth were blacker and his eyes were a little bit wilder since last she saw the apprentice assassin. She tried not to think about the time before, when he had accompanied her from her last assignment, before she died in Byron's grasp to be reborn. Too many bad memories would start to rise from the soiled dredges of her past.

"I believe he has mistaken you for a lady, with all his prattle about dancing and lords. And cheese. I miss cheese. Not the curdled proteins you uncivilised barbarians eat, but Gouda, Waterloo, Cheshire, fine fettle Yorkshire, Wiltshire loaf, and anything else ending in -shire. The first thing I shall do when I've won back my inheritance is buy a wheel of cheese bigger than my head," Byron remarked, rubbing the marks on his neck and collarbone where the stinging had been. He cleared his throat and re-creased his collar.

"He thought I was dead," she said in an exaggerated tone,

looking at Byron so he would catch her meaning, "which is obviously a blatant lie."

"Like you being a lady. Yes, I can understand how this game works."

"And you, Spittle—" She turned to face the boy, "—last I saw, were just an apprentice, drinking milk with the rest of the babies in the outside courtyard."

Byron grunted behind her and began to get up, shaking off the effects of her nerve pinching. As he limped towards her, he pulled out a small dagger and began picking at his nails; it was a favourite pastime of his when he was trying to preserve some dignity. He smoothed his hair, straightened his shirt, checked his shoes in between scrapes, then glared at her. She barely glanced at him, though, figuring that if he was angry at her, it wouldn't be the first time he showed his displeasure with pain.

"Friend of yours?" he asked as the sound of metal against keratin echoed in the small alleyway. He blocked the narrow and darkened entrance so that all anyone outside would see would be the sweat-stained back of his dirtied shirt. "And what was that?" He rubbed his cheek.

"Remember when we met The Patch-Skinned Cloaker? Barley-Toothed Hounder? And, let us not forget, the Blacketeer?"

"Is this what being you feels like when I talk?" he replied as she glared at him. "No wonder you've tried to take out my tongue, if I'm constantly spraying out non sequiturs like a gap-toothed, lisping auctioneer selling Spanish Hissing Tusks. My mother, may the Great Lighthouse take pity on her poor, ravaged soul, whenever she saw a tallow candle, would go off on stories about the advantages and disadvantages of the different types of fat and their relative smokiness and clarity. Poor old woman was losing her head even before she became a Star-Crosser."

"Yes, that is exactly how I feel after more than ten seconds with you. Instead of taking out your tongue, however, I feel the need to puncture my eardrums. And all of the things those men have in common is that I've kissed them, like I've kissed you—I'm still trying to get my lips clean—and like I've kissed Spittle here. I try to kiss everyone I meet, so if I'm ever followed..." She pulled out the small mirror and made to kiss it before Byron snatched it out of her hand. "I can find out if it's someone I know or not."

"Dear Lord, woman," Byron said, looking with horror at the compact mirror, "may the saints preserve me that I never allowed you to kiss me anywhere else. I knew a man in Nantucket who—"

"Lived to the ripe old age of eighty without anything remarkable happening to him, which is something that neither of us will be able to say. Now," she continued, turning back to Spittle and easing her legs off his chest so that he could breathe, "what are you doing here?"

"Looking for a new set of eyeballs, I suppose, for whomever has the unpleasant burden of having to look upon him," Byron quipped, continuing to play with his dagger. Marietta hissed at him and waved him away. He held up two hands like he was surrendering and waved back in a courtly manner. "Ask him if he's been sent after me because you failed." She spat and missed as he jumped back. "Twice." He held two gloved fingers in the air. She didn't miss the second time.

"You?" Spittle spat. Bloody, acidic foam hissed in the corner of the alleyway. "I couldn't tell your ticking clock from any other of these watch parts scampering around here. No, I was sent after the top hat of this entire organ in the organisation."

"Ask him where he learned to speak, because I can't understand a bloody word," Byron said. "Ooh. Maybe he's here for a new set of vocal cords."

"He said he wasn't after you," Marietta translated. "He's here for Ferret."

"I'm rather wounded," Byron mused, staring at the drizzling sky and pretending to wipe his cheeks. "Surely my head is worth more than that poor bastard's."

"Bastards fit in flea wine casks and in dog ones too, but all end up a dark stain on the lips of the yawning lord. It just pays more to send some to his parties than others, and looking at your grandfather clock, you're worth half a straw stick," Spittle related.

"He said that—"

"I can understand the gist of it," Byron interrupted. He had tightened his grip on the dagger. Marietta knew that his legitimacy was a prickly subject; it was the rumour that he was a bastard and not the true heir to the Llewellyn-Cave fortune that had gotten him disowned and disavowed by the upper echelons of society.

"Well, this grandfather," Byron started, "has business with the estimable Ferret. And if you do anything to obscure my dalliances, all of the body parts in the entirety of this damnable Market will not rectify the crooked lusus naturae you will become after my cessation with you."

Marietta wanted nothing more than to see the two of them fight, but knew that she would pay for it one way or the other. "Calm down, Byron. He didn't mean anything." She turned back to the boy and softened her voice. "This is your first assignment," Marietta said, patting Spittle down and relieving him of several crusted, dull weapons before helping him back up with a proffered hand.

"No," he shot back, rubbing at his chest and dusting himself off. "Spittle's as dog-eared as any unflappable novel. Look at my pages and you'll see written, 'here Spittle's yanked out this Saint

Job on the sidewalk' and 'there Spittle's cranked out this Holy Ghost in the back of a carriage.'"

"I meant without your brothers. Where are they, by the way?"

"Oh," Spittle said. He looked down at the ground and then back up at her, biting his lip. "They crossed the wrong red Rubicon a few months back."

"They got turned," Marietta translated to Byron, who had gone back to picking at his fingernails.

Spittle nodded and continued: "We got flanked by an empty-stomached playground of Seekers, fast in the night like the curtains drinking arterial lifesblood. They snatched up Spider and Scab, took 'em from the ashy pit by their sauntering joints, and all I heard were their froggy croaks rubbering off the splayed woodsy fingers."

"Seekers grabbed his brothers while they were sleeping."

"I saw 'em, a castlenight back, slinking in the barkies, tangling with the undergrabbers, their eyes steaming with stomach-gurgling might. 'Fore I could nock a penny for their peepers, they smoked into the ink."

"He saw them, but couldn't kill them before they—"

"Yes, the poor orphan boy is now bereft of what little family he has and he assuages his conscience by killing others, hoping to ease his own pain by bringing solace to those miscreants unfortunate enough to be put upon his death list. Murder, intrigue, plot twist, climax, denouement. It sounds like a plot from the penny dreadfuls the Lady de Leon would read late at night, in hopes of bonding with me over the sordid details of greasy spies chewing gristle and loose ladies chewing other things inappropriate for the ears of a youngster. May we please get on with our own quest here? I'd like to reach Ferret before I have to buy a new razor to shave off the beard I've grown in the time we could have talked to him, negotiated for more information, and already started on our way towards my Uncle. And the chances of me finding a razor here not infected with Hippocratic Fever are higher than whatever price you may have put upon Ferret's head."

"Nuh-uh," Spittle said, pulling out a handgun in some sleight of hand with which Marietta was unfamiliar. She had been gone long enough from the Assassin's Guild that she was behind on the newest techniques. He pointed it right at Byron's head and gestured him away from the entrance, back into the alleyway and next to Marietta. The gun was a small thing, no bigger than the palm of Spittle's hand and holding only three bullets, but Marietta tried to put as much distance as possible between herself and Byron. "I have a clockwork contrivance revolver and no bottlenecked wrench the likes of you is going to foul it up."

"So you're going to stop us with your pea-shooter, is that it? Peasant, I've seen bigger guns carried by the fleas in a hunch-backed grandfather's beard."

"Byron," Marietta whispered, "that's a Soliloquy-Inducing Close Burst Revolver. If it hits you, you'll be wracked with agonising pain until you can recite a 24-line soliloquy in dactylic hexameter. If you don't do it correctly, the pain only grows until you can complete your closing remarks. I once saw a man hit with it take two weeks to die because he couldn't find a rhyme for disembowelment."

She held her hands out, trembling as the sights turned from Byron to her, aimed squarely between her eyes. Byron yelped and dashed behind her. He was hiding, but that was hard, given he stood many handspans taller and wider than Marietta.

"It's what they would have wanted," Spittle said. "Me, pupating into a flying botfly."

"Why don't we just calm down and take a few seconds to realise that we all want the same thing?"

"We most certainly don't!" Byron yelled from behind Marietta. He had crouched down to make himself as small a target as possible and was covering his neck.

"Spittle, listen to me. We need to see Ferret, and so do you, if you want any hope of getting close enough to kill him. He's rather guarded—understandably so—but he knows us and will let us in to see him. We'll take you to him if you promise not to kill him until after we've gotten the information we need."

"And if you don't kill us first," Byron squeaked.

"A Spittle has been gestating a bit o'er how to bump in some noses with the grey slush."

"He said that—"

"I understand most of the slang about bumping things within a fifty-mile radius and in six different languages, so I can understand what he said, thank you," Byron interrupted. "But why anyone would want to do such a thing with the grossly pocked Ferret is beyond me." He suddenly jumped up from behind Marietta and started checking his pockets for the bottomless one to find the Star-Crosser parts they needed for bribing Ferret. He finally found it in the pocket sewn into his right sock and he clapped his hands together. "Now that we're one big happy, shall we be on our way? Ladies first," he said, smiling and gesturing to Marietta to walk back onto the path leading up to the brain of the market-sized human.

Marietta bared her teeth more than smiled and walked out into the drizzling cold. Being dead, the cold didn't really bother her, and neither did the heat; in fact, she didn't feel much of anything, save for the times when Byron stitched together her parts and made her look more human. The depressing, slow-moving, humid drivel pouring from the sky was more like oozing pus than actual precipitation, however. It unnerved her, as if it were sinking into her bones and eating them away, faster than any decomposition she had seen in her body for the past year. It was the closest feeling to pain as she could get now, and she found herself wondering at why she missed its sharp bitterness.

She didn't bother to look back, walking as quickly as she could in a skirt weighed down with weapons; they clattered against her hips and the backs of her knees. There were the even, dainty steps of Byron in his highly-polished, expensive-looking-yet-eaten-through boots, followed by the soft, papery stumblings of Spittle as he dragged his feet, remembered he was supposed to be quiet, then forgot and started the cycle all over. As soon as they hit the main vein up to the head, however, the bustle of other people drowned out her companions. The booths leading to the head of the Market were usually the most crowded, selling Star-Crossed neck muscles for house insulation and jaw bones for enchanted boomerangs that would bite their victims and return with a chunk of flesh if instructed by a series of hollow tongue clicks. As she expected, the crowds got rougher and more of the people around them began to resemble the pictures of Star-Crosser victims that Marietta had studied in her youth, due to her terrified obsession. There were parts missing: eyes, arms, legs, and even more hidden beneath clothing. Some had been replaced with hissing clockwork parts, but most had not, so that a motley, rag-tag group of fractional humans trudged through the Mephistopheles Market, looking for pieces to replace parts of themselves. She wondered if any of them would ever find what they really wanted.

Reluctantly, Marietta went out into the street slick with dew and people. She felt her clothes sticking to her back, but also the sticky stare of one—or both—of the boys trailing behind her. Byron made small noises of disapproval to let her know that his shiny boots were not taking kindly to the ever-growing swampiness of the mud. Spittle just grunted as he went out of his way to plop through all of the puddles. Marietta continued to walk with resolution, not caring if the boys were following her or not.

They had just passed a booth selling epiglottises and the horrible stench accompanied by them when Marietta began to feel a twitch in her right femur. As she turned halfway back to catch Byron's eye and see if he felt it too, a wailing cry echoed through the dimmed ceiling of the sky. Every hair on the back of her neck stood straight up. Spittle tensed like a man hit with a nerve-crunching round of paralytic ammunition (used specifically to make the ensuing corpse strain and pop, moving its lifeless limbs as rigidly as a marching soldier's, thus ensuring not only death but desecration when it was inevitably mistaken for a Star-Crosser).

"Byron, I don't feel so well," Marietta said, clutching her right leg.

"There's no way they should have been able to sneak up on us. Unless—"

"My ear itches," Spittle observed just as hundreds of Stumblers started limping towards the edges of the Mephistopheles Market.

There were a few surprised screams from the people closest to the churning mud-trenches before the first Scouts scrambled into the moats and simply disappeared up to their shoulders. They tried to continue walking, not realising that they weren't ever going to get any closer to their prey. The screams turned to dry chuckles as the Meph's patrons pulled out axes and shotguns and enchanted jawbones and started killing the Stumblers as they writhed, helpless in the protective ravines.

Marietta sidled up to Byron and spoke in a hushed whisper so Spittle didn't overhear. "Why didn't we sense them coming? I haven't felt the presence of any other Star-Crossers for weeks now, especially not this many. And why is my blasted thigh hurting? If this is another one of your stupid tricks—"

Byron interrupted her with clipped words and an outstretched hand. "Would that I could cause you to feel pain simply by using some intangible extra-sensory brouhaha, but I fear that these Amuckers are under the control of someone else—or rather, something."

"I wouldn't necessarily call your inane ramblings an extra sense, though they are intangible and rather painful, so—ow!" She put both hands around her leg and tried to massage the pain out. "Do you see any Seekers around? Usually I feel them more than Stumblers, but not like this. Never like this."

"Nothing like a squint's worth of melodrama to coax out the duelling knuckle punches, eh?" Spittle remarked as he passed them, not even deigning to look at the Stumblers as they tried with outstretched hands to grab any passersby and chomp on their foreheads.

They had made it to the top of the head, past the sugar-coated eyeballs and the sun-dried stapedes. Two beefy guards, their arms barely crossed because of the sheer girth of their biceps, stood on either side of a large door covered with extravagant red velvet, leading to a large, grandiose tent with so many colours and points that it looked like a confused sea urchin. The guards were equipped with long-tipped spears that whistled like drowning dogs when thrown. The sound was thought to mimic the squeaking noise that half-decayed teeth made when biting into a fresh brain, therefore distracting the Star-Crossers.

When Byron sauntered up to them, one arched an eyebrow before looking back to an objectless spot in front of him. Byron cleared his throat, produced a small index card out of his bottomless pocket, and coughed a bit into his hand before singing a few lines of a dirty ditty revolving around the exploits of a bosomy blonde with a clockwork brain. He stopped upon realising that he was reading the wrong thing and flipped the card over.

"The comet," he started, reciting from the card in a loud, extravagant voice accompanied by grandiose hand gestures, "passes the sturgeon." He stopped again, squinted at the card and brought it closer to his face, then lifted his eyebrows in comprehension. "Dungeon, I'm sorry—passes the dungeon at midnight."

The guards grunted, uncrossed their spears, and allowed the three of them through. They found themselves outside a lush red curtain that belonged more to a high-class theatre than a black market for undead human parts.

"What were you saying about melodrama before, lad?" Byron asked, rubbing his gloved left hand absentmindedly, his voice far away and distracted. "I'd expect chorus girls of at least mediocre quality to pop out from behind such a curtain if we were in an entirely different atmosphere."

"A less-than-brilliant deduction about something," Marietta remarked dryly, pulling back one of the curtains so that the others could duck beneath into the darkened room, lit only by a solitary, flickering candle. "You must be distracted, indeed."

Byron grabbed her arm and spoke into her ear: "Those Star-Crossers...there's something else out there. Something other than me controlling them."

"We're not going to go off into Charred Thicket tracks for Star-Crossing Queens again, are we?"

"Are you using 'Star-Crossing' as an actual modifier pertaining to the status of the Queen or as a derogatory epithet pertaining to my mental acuity? It's hard to tell with you sometimes. Either way, I don't think I like your tone of voice."

"Buzzing like a set of in-love crickets, rubbing each other's legs to make whisker soup, you two are," Spittle breathed out of the corner of his mouth, clearly exasperated.

"Yes, it is surprising that they think we can't hear them, even though they're whispering. The novice mistake of thinking that theatrical asides are possible in real life." Both Byron and Marietta jerked their heads up. "Your alienating erudition is showing, Byron," said a man behind a beaded veil that showed only his silhouette. "And it's unsightly."

Wafting incense climbed through the gossamer curtain, curling at the ceiling until it pooled there in choking clumps that stuck to Marietta's hair and caused her to scratch her scalp out of habit. The actual feeling of itching was almost foreign to her by now. The man stood up from the table at which he perched; his shadow seemed to stretch further than humanly possible, as if he were not a man but rather the leg of a massive spider. Marietta always wondered how he didn't ever seem to topple forwards due to the sheer height and lack of any balancing appendages. As he drew closer to the curtain to open it, his shadow loomed, his chest seemingly a mere paintbrush thick, his legs even more galline. Three pudgy fingers on each hand pulled at the webbing and the large man stepped through into the room.

"And here a Spittle's gestating that Ferrets should look like their namesakes. You're a flamingo matchstick if I ever had a bottle o' crackerwater." Spittle said, puffing out his cheeks in a way Marietta knew was meant to tell his brothers that Ferret would be a pushover. When she caught his eye, he began staring at his feet in order to avoid her pity.

"You didn't tell him about Ferret's insecurity vis-a-vis his appearance?" Byron whispered into Marietta's ear.

"When was I supposed to do that? Between him trying to kill us and the Star-Crosser attack?" she hissed back. "I never really understood, either...why he would call himself Ferret if he was so uptight about how he looks?"

"I can still hear you," Ferret replied, smoothing down the three strands of hair crossed over the top of his shiny forehead and trying to straighten his robe over the two feet of bare shin, ankle, and foot. He began walking out into the flickering lamplight of the Oriental paper lanterns shaped into different organs that hung from awkward spots in the ceiling, so that one always felt he would walk into them at any moment and start a fire. Marietta figured there was enough incense scattered about to make the place go up like a powder keg. "And you, young man," he spat, starting towards Spittle, who cowered as the ma ssive man sprigged his way and began poking him in the ribs with his six lanky fingers. She had always wondered how Ferret had lost both of his pinkies, but had never had the gumption to ask. "You should know that I've chopped people up and sold their parts for less."

"'Splains the missing pokers. Now a Spittle can chirp why the namesake rattles thusly." Ferret had stepped into the light underneath a paper lantern shaped like a pair of pulsating kidneys, revealing an ear-to-ear port-wine stain that covered his eyes from the middle of his forehead to the bottom of his nose, making him look remarkably like the spry, hirsute mammal in face, if not necessarily in body. "Spread your fishgums so's we can see if the munchers line up."

"Your own teeth better be made out of gold, if I'm to sell you bit by bit and not have you still be alive when the bits start becoming important."

The port-wine stain seemed to grow, as if his whole head had been dunked into a vat of purple dye, when the sound of screaming filtered up through the stairway. Ferret walked over to the window to pull aside the dark, thick curtain; the bright sunlight that shone briefly in a respite from the clouds made all of them flinch. The sun then ducked behind the clouds once again and the light deepened into grey. Anger radiated off of Ferret still as he tried to assess the situation outside.

"Ferret, Ferret, Ferret!" Byron said, trying to place a charming hand on the back of the cantankerous chief. He wasn't quite sure where, however, not knowing precisely where body parts joined they were so elongated, so his hand hovered around Ferret's left shoulder. Finally Byron grimaced, as if taking a shot of low-quality whiskey in a disreputable bar, and settled on a relatively safe area he thought to be just under the shoulder blade. "The boy's young—a bit addled, between you and me, rather a charity case that we picked up because of Marietta's indiscretions. But I digress. The real reason we're here is because I've picked up some rather rare specimens of the greatest quality and I wanted to make a trade." He pulled out his various jars of Star-Crosser parts in dark liquid and rattled the collected teeth together, keeping them just out of Ferret's reach. Well, as best as he could, given the wingspan of such a man. "This exquisite product—for information about my bastard Uncle. Bastard in the sense of his questionable morality, not in the sense at all that he is illegitimate. In fact, quite the opposite, as everyone involved in my family is completely, resolutely, irrevocably legitimate, and I have papers to prove that—"

"Your tongue better be made out of gold, too. But I digress," Ferret said, his brow furrowed underneath his stretched skin, so that he looked either exceptionally angry or rather unsettled in terms of digestion. (Even then, his face was so far up that it was hard to tell exactly what it was doing, rather like trying to see the expression of a cloud-covered Zeus upon the throne at Olympus.) "For I know it's nothing more than pyrite: pretty to look at, but awful to taste." He picked up a large speaker to what looked to be his gramophone and yelled into it. "Why am I seeing Star-Crossers that are not being chopped up for their bits? Why are there whole Stumblers stumbling through my Market? What is happening?"

"I'll see to it, sir," the voice of one of the guards barked back, distorted through the series of copper pipes back up to Ferret's office.

"There were Stumblers at the edges of the moats," Marietta chipped in, standing on her toes so that Ferret could see her over Byron, then realising that the man had a birds-eye view on everything. "There seemed to be quite a lot of them. Maybe they concentrated their efforts and filled up the moats with the Scouts first, allowing the rest of the army to walk over them and into the Market."

"These are undead, rambling sacks of tissue that run amok without a genuine thought in their heads about anything other than grey matter. I doubt they've studied the military tactics befitting Waterloo necessary to such a well-executed plan," Byron said, sighing.

"Why are we talking about cheese again?" Marietta asked, cocking her head sideways like a type of bird.

"It's like you two are eating the same Star-Crossed brain and sharing each other's thoughts," Ferret interrupted, "because I can't make sense of your coupling. Lieutenant, report!" This last was shouted into the gramophone. The pipes rattled as if the words became stones and unbalanced the conduits. One of them popped and steam started streaming out with a shrill whistle.

"Brains! Exactly! I found this," Byron said, putting aside all of the other parts and opening the jar of jellied brains. "This has got to be worth all of your information about my Uncle." He tried to pull Ferret close so that each man's eyes were all the other could see, but getting the large man to stoop down took a little bit of convincing. "It proves that there is such a thing as a Star-Crosser Queen, and you—" He pushed his finger into Ferret's chest and had a hard time getting it back, "—could be the one to help pave the way for discovery of such a being." He snatched the jar back. "If you tell me where my Uncle is, how many men he has with him, and whether or not he's finally gotten rid of that horrible ascot of his. You know the one I'm speaking about...the one with the polka dots and smudges that are meant to be painted sparrows."

Ferret, with a strange harrumphing sound that poured out of his nostrils, took the jar (with a yelp from Byron) and held it up to the light, a begrudging expression crowding out the port-wine stain on his face. His brow creased and he was about to throw the jar across the room when he stopped, arm cocked.

"What's this?" he cried. He pulled back another curtain to show a bubbling, boiling chemical lab with strangely shaped glass tubes and beakers connected through conduits that shook with the force of the liquids rushing through them. Still others were clamped in strange metallic hands that whirred and whizzed and delivered the perditious contents to other ends of the lab. Intricate metal instruments, pointed and starred, chiselled and honed, littered every single flat surface so that each countertop could examine, dissect, and even toast. There were microscopes and series of lenses layered over one another, some coloured, others opaque, and still others translucent but frosted so that the world, seen through them, became disjointed or upside down or, best for Marietta, mapped out such that the pressure points on any given person or object were visible. (She had once killed a target by severing the connection between his brain and his eyebrows, so that his dog— which took commands via eyebrow gesturing—ripped out its own master's throat. She had yet to try the technique on an inanimate object, but she doubted it would lose any efficacy.) The largest thing in the room, however, was a telescope that looked into a chunk of sky carved out of the perfumed and veiled ceiling.

Ferret clambered over the delicate glassware and instrumentation, infinitely more nimble than Marietta could have possibly thought, and stuck a finger into the jar so as to rub some of the purplish goo off onto a glass slide and inject it into the opening of the microscope. He fiddled with knobs, making noises of discovery and disappointment, adjusting until he finally cried out and stood as straight as his frame would allow, his index finger raised in the air like that same terrific Zeus about ready to hurtle a lightning bolt.

"This makes no sense! Where did you say you found this?"

"Within the Charred Thickets," Byron said, sidling up to the microscope and trying to get a peek of what had so enraptured Ferret. "I believe it belongs to a Star-Crosser Queen, a being so magnificent, with powers beyond our mere comprehension as living beasts, able to control other, lesser Star-Crossed through psychic vibrations that she sends through—"

"Do you ever shut up?" Ferret yelled back, prompting a tingling from one of the copper speaking pipes.

"Is everything okay up there?" a tinny voice echoed throughout the lab.

"Yes, yes, have you figured out what is causing this surge in Stumblers? I haven't seen a deluge this bad since before the Guard was instituted." Ferret leaned back from the speaking gramophone and steepled his fingers, face slackening and eyes growing glassy. "I've been thinking," he continued, "that there's no reason why Star-Crossers should still exist. Seekers, quick-witted and fast, turn into Stumblers after the zenith of the Homunculus Star; Stumblers, trudging prey with sludge for legs and brains, are quite easily picked off by the Guard. There's got to be another reason for their continued existence—and I believe it to be the Homunculus Star itself!"

He poured himself through the small tables and squeezed into a chair so that he could look up through the telescope and into the drizzled sky. His knees seemed to come up to Marietta's shoulder.

"Blast!"

"The Star-Crossers have firepower?" Marietta wondered, crouching and looking up to the ceiling as if waiting for an explosion.

"Heavens, my dear rusty monocle," Byron said.

At the same time Ferret said, "No, you dolt! The sky is too clouded to observe the Homunculus Star! I can't corroborate my findings if I can't see the Star!"

"Wait, I'm confused," Marietta interjected, leaning into the space between Byron and Ferret.

Byron made a small protestation, as he had been leaning over the telescope and Ferret's face, vainly searching the sky for whatever Ferret was looking at.

"I'm sure it's because not even Ferret could see your brain from underneath his microscope, as small and whittled-down from disuse as it is."

"You are what you eat," she retorted, looking back to Ferret. "You can't see the Star. It's not in the sky right now. Believe me, we'd all know if it was." She gave Byron a significant look filled with undead wisdom.

"Exasperating, I know," Byron responded, shaking his head.

"Marietta," Ferret said slowly, nodding as if he were speaking to a small child, "the Star orbits the Earth unlike any other celestial body I've observed. What we call its zenith is when its trajectory is closest to the Earth, but it moves too quickly at times and too slowly at others. The Star is not able to be seen by the naked eye—"

"Who's starky now, eh?" Spittle popped his head between Marietta and Byron so that all three of Ferret's guests were crammed into the small space, trying to wedge themselves into a better vantage point.

"Exasperating, I know," Byron repeated.

"—but can be seen with such instrumentation as mine before it reaches climax," he finished.

"Now I know this is one of 'em bee-dultrous teeth chompers what not fit for mine waxy hearing," Spittle observed, making a face as he slowly edged his way out of his position.

"Because of its unusual nature, I've been theorising that it is not just a celestial body, like a comet or a star or any such thing, but rather visitors from outer space—"

"Here we go," Marietta said, stepping backwards as well and putting her hands up. "Byron, you know how he gets when he hasn't had anyone to talk to about his theories for a while."

"What it is is neither here nor there," Byron said, able to get as close to Ferret as he dared now that the other two were poking at glass tubes and swirling liquids in bottles and other very breakable things. "Will this help to prove that Queens exist?"

"Byron, has anyone ever told you that you have the finer qualities of a dog on the run, unwilling to let go of its grisly bone, despite the fact that it will eventually get its head caught in a stair and be unable to extract itself due to its sheer stupidity and greed?" Ferret sighed, returning to the telescope, but this time swinging it downward so as to see the rest of the Market.

"And they call me indecipherable," Spittle whispered to himself.

At the same time Marietta said, "That was a rather long-winded metaphor." She was examining a beaker of bubbling blue liquids as they coalesced into a green, putrescent snot. Her eyes became twice the size of her face as she looked through the curved glass.

"A quality," Ferret continued, "that I do believe your wife found exasperating as well—"

Byron stopped cold, then swung around to face Ferret toe-to-toe—or rather, face-to-stomach—and sized the large man up. Marietta had never seen Byron as inhuman, even when he was touched by the Homunculus Star, since the night he had killed her. To show that kind of emotion—to let his mask dip so deeply—she knew that Ferret must have touched, no, gouged some sort of nerve. Byron was looking for a weakness, and when he couldn't figure the placement of any major organ, he took a chance and swung his entire arm around Ferret. At the last second Marietta, trying to deflect the blow so as not to alienate their last buyer of Star-Crossed parts or anger Spittle (who still held the Revolver), realised that what she had mistaken for his shoulder was actually his neck. Byron ended up hitting the giant man in the windpipe, knocking out a good portion of the air in his lungs.

"I am sorry!" Byron said as sarcastically as his nasal voice would allow.

The scientist let out a large cough, but couldn't seem to inhale afterwards.

"Lieutenant!" Ferret yelled in a raspy voice.

"Now, is that really necessary? It was an accident!" Byron yelled, trying to stop Ferret from heaving himself up from the chair. "I was trying to give you a manly embrace for your exploits!"

"Lieutenant!" Ferret cried again, this time louder, having ignored Byron completely like a great oak ignores the lovelorn initials of carve-happy couples. He threw open the door and started waddling down the stairway, looking like that same tree trying to learn how to walk. "Lieutenant!" he kept on shouting down the hallway until he reached the foyer out into the Market proper, five minutes later. Marietta and the rest had simply taken each stair one at a time, waiting for the tower of a man to catch his breath and continue. Byron had stopped trying to calm him three steps into the descent.

Once they were at the bottom, Ferret opened the door, but hadn't even gotten half of his height out of the impossibly small-looking frame before three Seekers descended upon him with ravenous mouths and grappling fingers. All Byron and Marietta saw was Ferret's top half, lying sideways as his six fingers tried to get a grip on the frame so that he wouldn't be dragged off.

"Marietta!" Byron yelled. She already had two axes in her hands and was running down the stairs. As she passed Byron, she saw him pull out his small flintlock welded to a dagger and rolled her eyes, but kept her commentary to herself. For whatever reason, Byron knew how to kill a person six ways to the Seven Circles, but became squeamish about killing Star-Crossers with anything heavier than a damp napkin. (Which, of course, in the right hands—namely, hers—could be a lethal weapon.) She burst over the threshold with a strangled war cry and axes teetering in her hands, itching to be thrown. What she saw made her drop the one in her left hand, and almost her jaw as well.

The entirety of the Market had been overrun by Star-Crossers, most of them agile Seekers. Everywhere she looked, bodies were strewn about, the booths now filled with human body parts and feasting zombies. The three Seekers had bitten Ferret, leaving him unable to get up as their poison spread through his system to turn him into a fellow Star-Crosser, but then left him in search of other prey. She didn't have time to stop and think about it, however; she picked up her axe and her years of training and unleashed another cry that made her teeth vibrate.

She began to run into the ruckus, but before she could get any further, Ferret caught one of her ankles. She landed on her chin and felt something shatter. He motioned for her to come closer. She looked around to see how close the Star-Crossers were, just in time to see Byron bemoaning that his recently shined shoes—which had been muddy anyhow—were now covered in the exploded heart gloop of a rather undecayed Seeker.

"Met—" Ferret choked out, followed by a gush of airy blood.

"Metric system?" she asked, and he shook his head. "Metaphysics?"

He shook his head again.

"Metamorphosis? Meticulous?"

For a third time he shook his head.

"I give up—amaretto?"

He continued to shake his head even more vigorously with each passing word until he slapped her, put his six-fingered hands around her neck, and drew her close.

"Meteorites." He coughed and some blood splattered her cheek. "From the Homunculus Star. They can—"

A slimy Seeker tackled her, pushing her into the dirt a few handspans away from Ferret. Getting up, she threw her left axe and struck the Seeker right in the neck, cleaving the spinal cord. She saw that his sliminess came from trails of intestines hanging out of his mouth. She pulled the axe back out and he fell down, truly dead. She slicked her right axe with her own blood, then tucked it into the crook of her arm and began running, so that the outward-facing blade sliced at the Seekers as she passed. Once her blood mingled with theirs, they would follow her and clear the path for Byron to do whatever it was he intended to do with the dying Ferret. She gave the fat man a once-over, understanding the pain of becoming one of the undead, before leading the Seekers away like some miscreant Pied Piper, going over Ferret's last words in her head and finding little sense to them.

Once they were at a safe distance, she saw Byron kneel over Ferret and apply pressure to his bleeding wounds. She barely ducked in time when a Seeker threw his arms around her, as if to embrace her with one hale limb and the other half-decayed to the point where a nub of femur scraped against her cheek. She missed, however, the Seeker whose bottom half had been cut off reaching for her ankles. She fell down, face hitting the dirt, and she rolled over to see the one who had tripped her gnawing on her calf with three rotten teeth and slimy green gums. Another two quickly tried to swarm her. Before they could reach, however, there was a small popping noise and one fell down mere handspans away, its brain leaking out of a dainty hole in its forehead. The other she garroted with a sharp line of wire that had been wrapped around her wrist.

The one chewing at her heel had found the tendon and torn into it before she could grasp her brass knuckles and hit him between the eyes. A reverberation started in the middle of his forehead, the skin rippling and starting to peel off, as the magnitude grew and grew until the brass knuckles were ringing and the Seeker was being torn to shreds by the percussive violence. She stopped the vibrations by dampening the knuckles in a puddle of mud before standing up, limping on the leg whose tendon had been snapped.

The dagger-pistol was still smoking as Byron lowered his raised arm without even looking at her. He never took his eyes off Ferret—who was slowly succumbing to the bite, his skin greying, his words slurring, and his fingers beginning to curl—as he fired another three shots in various directions, with three more fallen Seekers to show for it. The last bullet he fired straight up into the air, not hitting anything that Marietta could see.

"Does it look like I'm wearing your skirts, Marietta?" he yelled. "Last I checked, I believed that me being the brains of this operation would be a little less literal. Now get up and clear the area!" He pulled up Ferret's head—the only part of the man he could lift—and slapped it as Marietta limped towards a post to balance against. As she pulled a very large blunderbuss out of the back of her belt, Byron shouted, "These are your dying words, Ferret. Use your last breath to tell me where my Uncle is. You have nothing to lose, man!" He smacked him again, trying to ignite the dying nerves into coherent thought.

Marietta aimed the blunderbuss at an approaching Seeker who was missing an eyeball and pulled the trigger. Gears interlocked with other gears, ticking and scratching their way up the side of the engraved gun until grapeshot exploded out of the wide mouth, smattering the Star-Crosser with large green smears that ran down his shirt but barely slowed him down.

"Byron! You filled the blunderbuss with actual grapes? They're afraid of vegetables, not fruit!"

"If a filthy tomato is a fruit, then a green grape can be a vegetable!" He went back to browbeating Ferret. "The poison will soon reach your mind and raise you again as a Star-Crosser. I doubt your size will allow you to survive even that meagre afterlife for too long. Don't go into the Great Ocean without easing your conscience!"

"Never—after what you did—you can go to hell—"

Ferret choked up some blood that splattered against Byron's face.

Marietta reloaded the blunderbuss with a cartridge of rolled lettuce leaves, soaked in wax to form a stony slug that would explode upon impact, showering the offender in leafy green shrapnel and taking out large chunks of flesh. She fired again, allowing the mechanism to click and clatter its way to ignition, taking out the four Seekers closest to her and hitting another three that looked at the green mess with horror. Or quite possibly disdain; it was hard to tell from their disfigured faces, especially the one whose eyebrows had been blown off with a stray lettuce shot.

"Spittle!" Marietta yelled, frantically reloading as more and more Seekers began running towards the blunderbuss's ruckus. "Spittle, get out here and help! I'll tell Foster that you ran and he'll break your legs and leave you for the Stumblers outside of the Lighthouse!"

"At least tell me anything you know about a Queen, someone who can control the Star-Crossers!" Byron said, frantically trying to keep Ferret conscious. "Do they exist? Ferret? Ferret!"

"How—do you think—" He coughed, splashing another smattering of blood across Byron's now-sodden shirt, "—they did all this? Psychic control of the Star-Crossers does not start and end with you, Byron." Byron sucked in his breath and looked around, seeing only the chaos of the tattered marketplace. "You thought I didn't know? There are worse things out there than you can imagine—even being one of them yourself."

"Is that a yes?" Byron asked, almost breathless.

Marietta dodged another swarming attack and yelled again for Spittle to help. She was working her way back towards Byron, trying to find a safe spot amidst the overrun Market.

"Star-Crosser Queens—ask the Queen! Marguerite had a met—!" Ferret yelled.

"Metric system?" Byron asked, desperately grasping at the

folds of skin at Ferret's neck and trying to massage an answer out of them.

Ferret shook his head and said again: "Met—!" With one final gurgle, he died.

"No!" Byron screamed and threw the body down.

"If you," Marietta grunted, pulling a small twisted dagger from a Seeker's neck that was supposed to finely knit arteries and veins together so it not only cut, but confused the circulatory system as well, "want to keep him as a pet instead of me once he rises, I won't take offence. I can't say he'll be as talkative, but I know how sometimes you like the quiet ones—Spittle!" Her head twisted around, looking every direction for the boy, wondering at her newfound compassion for him. She could count the number of people she didn't want to come across half-eaten on one hand, and Spittle had surprisingly found his way to the top, along with her parents, Grandmother Oculus, Foster, and strangely enough, her first boyfriend, whose name had been Ambrose Dinklehoffer and who had been a hell of a kisser until a mysterious football injury had ended his kissing career.

"No, I refuse," Byron started, standing up and wiping the blood off his face. "He'll come back, and when he does, I'll get the truth out of him. He'll have to do what I say. I'll make him point the way or draw a map in his own blood or slobber in Morse code, I won't care, just as long as he tells me."

"That's great. One big happy. Now, if you could…?" Marietta grunted as she continued to garrote more Star-Crossers. She was quickly running out of ammunition and she could only stand on one leg for so long before her bad circulation caused her other knee to weaken and eventually collapse. Even she couldn't survive being torn limb from limb by a horde of angry Seekers.

Byron pulled out his hip flask, took a large sip, chewed on

several worms that accompanied the whiskey and graveyard dirt, then began to pour the rest of the bottle into Ferret's open mouth. It came back out in a torrent; Byron began to massage the dead throat when suddenly Ferret sat straight up, his eyes feral and bloodshot. He immediately grabbed for Byron and tried to take a large bite out of his chest, catching only a mouthful of his cotton shirt. The undead Ferret spit it out and lunged for another bite when Byron closed his eyes and mumbled a few nonsensical words. Marietta felt a shock like someone punching her in the stomach.

She turned around to find that the top half of a Seeker (merely axed in the throat before being chopped in two) had indeed punched her in the kidney. But then she felt someone thread a needle through the organ and pull ever so slightly in Byron's direction. She doubted that the Seeker was an undead tailor, unliving his last moments of embroidery in some scrabbled sense of fulfilment as a Star-Crosser; Byron had contacted the power in him to control Swarms, shaping their thoughts like shepherding sheep.

Ferret stopped, too. The moaning in his throat became a high-pitched keen as Byron broadcast a signal that made Marietta, Ferret, and all of the Seekers within thirty yards stop and want to spill their innermost secrets. Since most of their vocal cords were rotten, the magic's effect emerged as a cacophony of mumbles, with only a few words jumping out like gold teeth in a prostitute's mouth.

"…garrrgggle…"

"…wife's sister…"

"…mrrrph…"

"…fluffy layers of petticoats under my knickers…"

"I got a bloody nose while baking zucchini bread and then I served it without telling anyone," Marietta found herself saying before she clamped her hands over her mouth.

"Your Uncle is in another mansion...!" Ferret screamed before all of the Star-Crossers, Marietta included, slumped as another power washed over them, stronger and more cohesive than Byron's slippery grasp.

"What? What is this?" Byron gasped, clutching his left arm as its decay spread until putrefaction peeked from below the glove and began moving to his elbow. Before Marietta could tell if she was becoming even more human, she felt the alien presence of another mind within hers. And it sounded familiar as it told her to gank the greasy-lipped horsefly.

"Spittle?" Marietta asked, looking around to see, finally, the boy walking down the stairs, two slumping shapes still hidden in shadow behind him. They moved tangentially to him, as if he held the middle of a long string that tied them together. He was clutching his left leg, rubbing at the tendons as if it were giving him great pain. "Spittle?" This time, her voice held neither relief nor anger, but trepidation. The two shadowed creatures seethed behind him, one hissing and spitting, the other smacking its teeth together with a horrible gnashing sound. "But how...the Homunculus Star has passed since your brothers turned. How can they still be Seekers? They should be Stumblers, right? Tell me I'm right. Anybody?"

Everybody else—including the Star-Crossers—was waiting silently, drifting sideways as if their balance were incomplete, staring at the young boy and his two undead brothers. A niggling sense of mastery emanated from him and Marietta felt herself slipping in his direction.

"I chirurgeon them up, real neat and stitchering. I say kernel up and they do more'n lather than other Ruby-Crossers."

"I am speechless for the second time in the day," Byron interjected, "and I must say, I find it frustrating and irritating...

rather as if I were of mediocre intelligence instead of my true genius. How exactly have you turned yourself into a Star-Crosser Queen, my dear lad?" Byron started polishing his dirt-caked nails with a near-ruined handkerchief. Marietta recognised his affected nonchalance as an attempt to hide the burning curiosity sifting through him.

"Crowney-cronie? Spittle's no tongue-lapper for anybody. They are mine. My family," Spittle responded as his brothers Spider and Scab rubbed their faces against his calf. Marietta almost gagged as Spider took a small nip from the ankle and she saw that more than half of Spittle's left leg was rotting away, gangrenous and pustering. It was a Stumbler bite; his brothers had been bitten by Seekers, turning them almost instantly into Star-Crossers, leaving Spittle to lose only his leg to the bite.

"You need to get rid of that leg, Spittle, or you'll die. The rot will spread and you'll go insane before it kills you in the most painful way possible," Marietta said, trying to edge away from Spittle and towards Byron, wondering why she would feel safer with the man who had repeatedly tried to kill her.

"I believe he has already arrived at that particular depot, my darling rust-pot," Byron muttered, folding his handkerchief and placing it delicately back into his ruined shirt.

"No! I can ear them and they mail back. What's a Spittle without his blood tree?"

"You can still talk with them? Spittle, Foster can't know about this. He would never condone it," Marietta said.

"I learned more about amucking and splintering from 'em than ever I did with the Great Lightbeam. Great Firebug is more like. I'll quash him like a polenta. Spittle's the shiny-best little stinger since you met with the Yawny Lord."

"I am not—" Marietta began, but was cut off.

"No? Then why is your postage in my branium?" He tapped against his head. "Fate worse'n the yawny apocalypse. Fivever here, forever not there. You want I should dictate you, post-haste?"

"If dictation has anything to do with dying, I'll keep this meagre afterlife of mine. I'm not so sure there's something beyond. So, thank you, but we're done. Ferret's dead—let's just shake hands, or bite legs, or whatever is appropriate for a show of respect, and be on our merry?" Marietta began tugging on Byron's shirtsleeve, not caring when he bristled at her touch. She whispered into his ear, "Who knows how many more he has out there? We should just go. We can't fight them all and I've run out of rubber-mallet bullets."

"He reneged on our deal. I consider that one of the greatest sins known to mankind, amongst lying, thievery, and wearing white after Belabouring Day," he whispered back.

"Crickets! Makes a pound in my orbits that travels to my stump," Spittle said, gritting his teeth hard enough that Marietta could hear it yards away. "The ess-lets are much sprier with their vocabubrary books." The Seekers that had stopped seethed again and inched closer to the two of them. She could see the struggle on their slack-jawed faces between listening to Spittle and his brothers and simply lunging upon them to tear them apart.

Byron slipped a hand to her belt and pulled out one of the axes she carried by her hips. It was such an easy movement and so quick—as blinding fast as Byron ever could be—that Marietta expected an attack just as quickly. Byron, however, threw the axe in the air and caught it with a deft hand, spitting on the edge and wiping it clean with the tail of his uncharacteristically unbuttoned shirt.

"You, sir, are neither a gentleman, nor a scholar, nor even fully a human being—not that that is a prerequisite for morality and judgement of character, for who of us here is completely human? But I abhor those who renege on their words. You will cease and desist or suffer the wrath."

"Of what, your shiny axe?" Marietta quipped. "Or rather, my shiny axe? Or, if we're going to split heads, Liza's axes?"

"Who you holy roman empiring?" Spittle spat back. "Cliff-hangers for all if'n your teeth keep chomping."

At that moment Marietta closed her eyes, grabbed hold of Byron—who seemed, for once, not to mind her grip upon his upper arm—and waited for the Seekers to tear them limb from limb. She wasn't even quite worried that she would die because of it; rather, she was terrified that she would live through the experience. It wasn't until she felt the warm sensation of the sun against her cheeks, followed by the sluggish feeling that high noon always produced in her, that she realised what had happened.

"Your last bullet..." She yawned and stretched, looking for a place in the shade to lie down along with the rest of the retiring Star-Crossers. "It was…a…" She yawned again. "Sunshine Shellacking Slug?"

"Of the fourth order. I always put one in the last chamber of my gun for emergencies such as this. Learned that trick from the dead—well, recently undead, but even more recently truly dead, as in: his body is floating headless somewhere within the murky confines of the Thames—Comte de Bassoon, whose musical explorations were matched only by his penchant for torturing Star-Crossers. Wanted to find out what musical instrument made them cringe the most. Surprisingly enough, it was neither the oboe nor the bagpipes, nor indeed any of the double-reeded family that succeeded in making them cover their ears in an almost human gesture, but rather, the bongos," Byron responded, squinting in the sunlight and putting his rotting left hand up to shade his face, but remaining otherwise unaffected. All of the Seekers were slowing down, piled on top of each other or their half-eaten last meals, like groggy dragons protecting their treasure. Only Spittle and Byron remained standing, as even Spider and Scab began to curl up and go to sleep at the boy's feet. Byron stepped over the slumping bodies towards his foe.

"Stratosphere stamping won't work longer'n a few clicks of the potters," Spittle began, backing up slowly and pointing the Soliloquoy Revolver at Byron's heart. "Prepare to table under with the Great Sputtering Firefly."

"Death, like anything, my dear boy, is a final foray into something incomprehensibly new. And while I intend to visit the place, it shall be neither by your hand nor because of your malicious intent. If either one of us is going to meet your Yawny Lord, it will be you, and my name will be listed as your deliverer into his cabal."

"Byron…no," Marietta said weakly, holding up her hand for a few seconds before it wavered and she collapsed back onto the ground. Visions of everyone she held dear, including Ambrose Dinklehoffer, charged her folding eyelids.

He stopped within a few feet of Spittle, concluding, "But such a halcyon rest is not for those as you and me." Then he dashed forwards. Before Spittle could react, Byron had swung the axe high and brought it down upon the assassin's leg, severing it mid-way down the thigh. "We deserve screaming pain and the knowledge that we are alone to keep us shivering in the night."

"My selves!" Spittle cried out and fell backwards, clutching the stump of his leg as brackish blood seeped out of the wound, turning red as the contamination bled out. Scab and Spider barely stirred in their slumber, but Spittle crawled to their bodies and began cradling them. "It's an iron void, clumping up the greying pipes like drifting soot souls. They're gone and even the Yawny Lord can't spyglass them without shuffling stars to swamp the way."

There was a dull popping sound, like someone firing a muffled gun, and darkness spread over the area once again. Marietta rubbed at her eyes and slowly started standing up, but Byron tugged on her arm hard enough to pop something out of place and started pushing her towards an exit close to the neck of the Mephistopheles Market.

"Good morning, my lovely bedpan, how did you sleep? Can I turn down your sheets? Or shall I get you some eggs and bacon before the rest of the Seekers decide that we, as tainted as our flesh is, are a good way to break their own fast?"

"But…Sp…Spi…"

"Splitters? My dear, that is an excellent nickname for the Star-Crossers. But I'm afraid that now, when we are surrounded by the hungry undead, is not a good place for this conversation."

"Spittle. We can't leave him." She pulled Byron's head so that he could see the still-bleeding Spittle on his back, trying to edge away from his brothers. Scab had turned to devour his amputated leg; Spider, however, had gotten scent of the fresh blood and was struggling towards his brother, trying to shrug off the effects of the sunlight.

"As grandiloquent and bombastic as I may be, I don't actually believe he should suffer. 'Twas simply a narrative technique I picked up from a foul-mouthed wandering bard who specialised in spoonerisms and liked to tell stories about Robin Hood and Friar Tuck. I do, however, believe that he should die, and getting ripped to pieces by those he once controlled is as fitting as if I had written it myself. So, verbiage and symbolism aside, if we don't want to be caught into his destined comeuppance, we should leave."

"It's not his fault he's the way he is, Byron." She pulled her arm away and started retracing her steps, bashing a few awakening Seekers on the head and pulling out a large flail.

"The rustic candour of your psychological machinations continue to amaze me. Here, I'll help: Yes, you are similar to him. No, you don't have to save him on the logic that, by doing so, you are helping yourself. May I now continue to save the both of us? I won't let you die until you tell me the name of the person who hired you to kill me, and I'd be loath to go after you once you enter that gelatinous quagmire. I just shined my shoes." She looked at his mud-spattered feet. "Metaphorically speaking, of course."

"What? I guess we can save him, too, but I just wanted my hand-sharpened flaying dagger back. I noticed he stole it off me right before we went into Ferret's office—he's been a little thief since the first time I met him—and I'm not leaving that behind."

"Oh. Well, in that case…" He took her hand and leaped into the Seekers, which started to get up and claw half-heartedly at the two of them as they massacred their way towards Spittle. Marietta eventually reached the boy and hauled him over her shoulder so that he was facing the ground, still struggling to connect to his dead brothers. But the loss of blood overpowered him and by the time they reached the safety of the surrounding forest, he was close to fainting. Marietta began dressing his wound, finding her dagger in his satchel and taking it as Byron tried to slap the boy back into consciousness.

"You have your dagger, so let's leave him for his brothers and get back to finding my Uncle. I have an idea where he could be from what Ferret told us," Byron said, sighing and leaning back to rub his strained slapping arm. "My father—may the Great Lighthouse alphabetise all of his voluminous tomes—and I had a secret code that my Uncle—may the Great Lighthouse strike him languageless—adopted as a way to rub salt in the proverbial bastardisation wound. By saying that Archibald is in another mansion, he means that he has taken a new identity and as such, and if I know my Uncle at all, is to be found right back where all of this began."

Marietta thought for a second.

"The brothel?"

"Despite that being the only place fit for a mind such as yours, no. But come, let us be hence."

"Wait." She took out a worn and faded paper, ripped off a piece, and scribbled something with the stub of a pencil before placing it on Spittle's slowly rising and falling chest. "Okay. Let's go. Though how you got anything out of his incomprehensible chatter is beyond me."

"What was that?" Byron asked as they walked along the path, inclining his head behind them.

"My father's the ink-maker for the Undersecretary to the Department of Ancillary Extremities and Supernumerary Quanta. Spittle is eventually going to need a new leg, and for every referral, my dad gets a couple extra quid. That should pay back for almost killing us."

"Your conscience may be assuaged by monetary recompense. But I have to live with the image of his brothers eating his leg for the rest of my life."

"Not the worst thing you've ever seen."

"Not even close."

In Which the Mysterious Personage of the Heretic Appears, Or: The Electric Slide

"…we believed the old abandoned mansion to be haunted by the ghost of the personage we called the Bumbling Baron of Borscht. There were several beetroots planted about the property and whenever we—my servants and I, of course, as I had no friends growing up as a child, save for my best one, who almost fell through the rotted spiral staircase on our second foray into the spiderweb-bedecked halls and, had it not been for my brash heroism, would have certainly fallen to his death—ventured upon its hallowed ground, we would find the plants crushed by boots. We would follow the seemingly bloody footprints into various rooms and they never quite led to the same place each time we were there. My friend assumed that the walls moved between our excursions, but I knew it was just our youthful lack of spatial recognition that did not allow us to remember the darkened halls every time we went back, making it seem a different architectural layout each time."

Marietta snorted awake and half of her nose came off, leaving a rather gaping hole in the middle of her face that showed the bones of her nasal passages. Her eye was still missing, covered by a patch, and she wondered what she could do now to make her face look less horrifying. Then she realised that with her left arm ending at the elbow, trailing a bundle of dangling nerves, and her ribs showing through the ragged slits of her dirty and yellowed shirt, there was nothing left for her to do. The Homunculus Star was quickly approaching its zenith and there was nothing Byron could do for her either—save for allowing her the blissful hours of sleep induced by the droning nasality of his voice.

The covered steamcar they rode in hit a bump and Marietta

braced herself for impact. A clump of hair sloughed off the back of her head with a wet slop as she hit the flimsy top of the compartment. Byron smacked his head against the window and, when he shifted his weight to see if he was injured, stuck his hand right into the rotting mass of what was once Marietta's scalp.

"I say!" Byron said, leaning his head out of the carriage by opening the curtains and slapping on the wooden door. "I do say! Driver! Driver! This road is entirely too bumpy for my delicate derriere. Can't we take a different road? One that's less prone to making this infernal contraption vacillate as if we were in the stomach of some large giant doing cartwheels?"

"You wanna get there when you told me you wanted t' get there or do you wanna get there when the Star is in orbit? I take a different road, pal, and we're lookin' at getting' Swarmed before you 'n the dilapidated missus can say, 'We're be'n eaten aaaaahhh—my spleen, ooh—it would burn if I still had nerves left t' feel anything, aahhh—!'"

"Do you hear a lot of people getting eaten, to dramatise such an incident?" Marietta asked, now sticking her own head outside of the carriage and squinting in the half-light with her one good eye. The later afternoon hours were tiring, but not as cumbersome as high noon, and she found she could tolerate small amounts of sunlight in such a way. The wind of their movement whipped through her skull with a low-pitched whistling noise. "I must admit, it was rather convincing."

The driver looked back at her, startled badly, then shifted gears so that the bumps doubled and the trees flashed by at such a pace that she was having difficulty keeping track of individual trunks. It was then she remembered that she was supposed to be a fearsome Star-Crosser, capable of eviscerating people and eating them at the same time with just a flick of her eyelash; it was entirely because of this threat that they'd been able to hijack this steamcar and travel during the daytime towards the mysterious mansion that Byron believed held a clue to the whereabouts of his Uncle. She scowled, trying to growl low in her throat. The driver turned pale and began swallowing convulsively, as if he were going to vomit at any moment.

Both Marietta and Byron slipped back into the travelling compartment.

"I don't want to eat him if he vomits at every little thing," she began, knowing that they were probably saving the driver to eat when the Homunculus Star rose in just a few days. "Erodes the elasticity of the oesophagus and makes it crunchy. It's a strange texture, not dissimilar to jellyfish tentacles fried in chili peppers and fish sauce. Though I've found with jellyfish that they rather assume the flavor of the things around them, not really carrying a zest of their own, unlike esophagi, which are distinct enough to—"

"Life-threatening undead with preternaturally potato peeler-like excoriating powers should be seen and not heard. Everyone is afraid of your ghastly appearance, my dear. No one is afraid of your compliments, though your diction and pronunciation are enough to make even the worst professor of semiotics die in abject terror. Given that he has a weak heart, of course—otherwise he might just faint. Maybe survive with a heart murmur or something. Regardless, I intend to give him a choice about whether he wants to remain our driver until the Star's zenith...or to walk back to Shropshire without his steamcar."

"Which is a death sentence anyway, given the fact that there is absolutely nothing between here and Shropshire except for many, many Hives."

"Mr. Byron, sir?" a timid voice called from the front of their carriage. "Mr. Byron? There's somethin' up ahead that you need t' see, sir."

"My Christian name, my dear mundivagrant runt, is Byron, and you calling me thusly is horribly inappropriate. You may call me Mr. Llewellyn-Cave, and if you pronounce it incorrectly, I'll remind you of the time I was travelling with a boxcar sideshow exhibit that delighted in misshapen miscreants, including a three-armed monkey, a two-headed pig, and a rather amazing sheep that turned colours depending on which food it ate at what time of day. They were searching for the Holy Grail of carnival acts: a bearded lady. It just so happened that the third wife of my best friend, who just so happened to be riding with me, fit that description. When we found her in the jungles of untouched Laos, she had pierced her lips so many times according to the native custom that she had a horrible lisp, couldn't eat soup without dribbling down her frontside, and couldn't even begin to pronounce my name. My best friend, who was as irascible about his name as I am, bit her with glowing coals lodged in his teeth until all of her piercings were too hot to keep in and were removed, thus permitting her rise to fame as the Holy Bearded Lady, who would perform miracles of the hirsute variety—"

"How does a train get to Laos?" Marietta interrupted.

Ignoring her, Byron opened the side of the carriage, unfolded the step, and stuck more than half his body outside their compartment.

"Very well, thank you," Byron said absentmindedly. He continued speaking to the driver: "The Welsh double L is a voiceless lateral fricative, meaning that it's a guttural hissing sound most easily rendered into an 'hl,' as if one were to press one's tongue against one's teeth, grunting and pushing air through at the same time. Most people are unable to make such a noise when not actively throwing up, but I assure you, with practise it comes as easily as—"

"Mr. Byron! Up ahead! You didn't tell me we was headin' into Heretic territory!" The young boy pointed, his outstretched arm quivering in damp light of the afternoon.

"Boy, I told you that—Heretics? What in the seven shadowed halls of the Star-Crossing strumpets are you talking about?"

The carriage pulled to an abrupt stop, causing Marietta to bump her head against the forward wall and dislodge the left portion of her forehead, so that her yellowed and cracked skull showed through just above the leather string of her eyepatch. She put a hand up to feel the damage, thought better about what might happen if more skin sloughed away, and put her hand back down. Hopefully her good eye wouldn't fall out of her skull before the zenith of the Star.

"Th' Lightnin' Heretics," the boy continued. "You don't know about 'em? Crazy zealots is what they are. They fink that steam is a leftover from antiquity—their words—an' that mankind has enough intelligence t' be using new technology—their words— in order t' advance civilisation. They use this electricity—their words—t' do horrible experiments. Can't even see this stuff, 'cept for when somethin's gone wrong and lightnin' starts shootin' everywhere. Run out of the city when they burned down their last headquarters and scared all the misses with their hooded robes an' cracklin' masks. Fink this electricity stuff is magical...a god, even. Left t' their own devices, I don't fink anythin' good can come from them—my words. What kind of lunatic doesn't want t' use steampower? Good, clean steam? What's not t' like?"

"Isn't that sort of the definition of a heretic, then?" Marietta quipped, stepping out of the carriage and walking a little ways up the road to see what had everyone so spooked. The driver squealed and tried to crawl on top of the passenger compartment to get away from her.

"Please don't eat me!" he pleaded, squirming in his seat as if to make himself a smaller target.

"I was just asking—"

"Fink of my children!"

"You're maybe thirteen. How do you have children?"

"Fink of my theoretical children who will one day be borne of your graciousness in not eating me!"

"Is this the place?" she asked, pointing to a decrepit mansion overrun with dark vines, dark stains, and an even darker history. Most of the windows had been broken either by vandals or by time, and there were clearly weeds and small trees growing inside, their leaves shooting through windows and doors. The place was deserted and had been that way for quite some time. "Looks scary," she said tonelessly, wondering why the cabbie had been so afraid to go further.

The driver made small noises in the back of his throat and began stamping at the ground, clearly agitated by something that she couldn't see or sense. Then, across the night sky, in a completely cloudless atmosphere, a streak of lightning passed sideways over the mansion's roof and dissipated into the tops of the surrounding trees. She followed the path of the jutting white light and saw that down the road was a familiar sight: Byron's childhood home.

When he saw the direction in which her eye had wandered, Byron pulled her towards the crumbling mansion roughly and told the cabbie to follow in a gruff voice.

"There is no such thing as this electricity," he said, "and there isn't a cult going around worshipping it as if it were a deity. The preponderance of people roaming this earth calling themselves divine architects has risen to such a Babelic height that it makes one's neck strain; we need not inanimate objects such as this mythological 'electricity' to start boasting such hubristic claims as well."

"So that story you told me about convincing the natives of the small island of Mauritius that you were their death god because of your skeletal hand, and they worshipped you for forty days and forty nights by giving you hand-painted turtle shells carved with their teeth and made you harps out of flower stems that you played ethereally, and it was only when your best friend warned you that it was their sacred duty to mate with any and all gods that you decided you'd had enough—that was not your ego making itself out to be a divine prime mover?"

"Don't remind me," Byron said, shuddering. "If I had had to spend one night with each of those elephantine women, I would have been flatter than a badly made cappuccino—you know how I like my coffee to be well frothed and Costa Rican, just like my women. But my best friend seemed quite equipped to the task, and in fact, had rather taken to the young ladies' legs—"

"Then what do you call that mysterious lightning?" Marietta chimed in as another streak arced across the sky. Byron motioned her to stop speaking.

"Oi!" the cabbie said as Byron took him in his other arm and pushed them towards the house before him. "You keep that thing way from me. I don't like th' way it's eyein' me fingers like they're sausages."

"'It?'" Marietta yelled.

"Just don't let her kiss you and you'll be fine." Byron kept pushing.

"Why? Is that some sort o' ritual before she eats you?" The boy blanched. "After she eats you?"

"At least the pronoun is better," Marietta muttered under her breath. Now she saw that they were following a set of red-smeared footprints hidden in the dust. They were still fresh, not more than a few hours old.

"The Bumbling Baron strikes again!" Byron cackled and trod upon a few stray beet plants, taking one of the tuber-like vegetables and biting into it with a satisfied smirk as juice dripped down his chin. Marietta was about to open her mouth to say otherwise when Byron pushed her through the open door and plunged her into darkness.

"I can't see anything," she whispered. Her voice echoed off the columns inside the house, and even a few small trees that had somehow wormed their way through the floorboards to sprout inappropriately in the dining room and one of the boudoirs. The surprising bounty of nature served to make the house feel nigh-sacred, so that even the softness of her voice seemed to interrupt an important lecture on the inconstant life of man. It was quiet here—something Marietta hadn't felt in a long time.

But Byron was right behind her, and began speaking quietly into her ear: "Having one eye gives you horrible depth perception, but it doesn't do anything with your night vision. Now take the boy and look around for any sign of my Uncle." He walked away, then stopped before he reached the doorjamb to his right. "And stop whispering!" he yelled. Immediately dust from the rafters streamed down, disrupted by the avalanche of his voice. "It's not a graveyard. Though if we find my Uncle, that may change."

Marietta grabbed the boy. He screamed—dislodging more flora, so that sounds of fluttering and creaking and cacophony displaced her sense of quietude—but eventually swallowed his fear as they walked over the creaking floorboards. Linking spider webs dusted the tops of bannisters and strung themselves across hallways and doorframes. Millions of particles of decaying and dead matter shot up into the air and slowly settled back onto staircases and windowsills, but not respectively. Every little thing that moved spooked the cabbie and he clung to her side, trying to grab her rotting sleeves but receiving only shreds of dirty fabric that lined their path like breadcrumbs.

"If I'm going to be playing anything in our rendition of this fairytale, it's not the Star-Crossing piece of bread," Marietta intoned, slightly above a whisper after Byron's admonishment, but still not in her full voice. The uncomfortable feeling was still settling down into the pit of her stomach. Or maybe it was just a leftover eel that still hadn't worked its way out of her system yet.

"You want t' be Hansel, then?" the cabbie quipped. He immediately stopped and looked at Marietta with dread. "I mean— you can be whatever you want, er, miss, er, ma'am...?"

"Ma'am is my mother," Marietta growled. And it was true. If her mother wasn't called ma'am, even by her father, she would get out her bank-robbing tools and pretend the offender was a safe, poking and prodding until something opened.

"...Sir?" the cabbie meekly replied, ducking his head into the collar of his heavy jacket.

As the two intrepid explorers walked, the hallways became more and more stooped and overrun with termites and spiders and roaches, until Marietta felt the crunching of moulted skins underneath her bare feet. It seemed as if the spider webs clinging to everything did nothing whatsoever to deter insects, and rather seemed to be an invitation for all sorts to make themselves at home. Marietta swiped her arm left and right, hoping to the Great Lighthouse that she wouldn't get infested by Black-Eyed Peatles— which, like their legume counterparts, caused one to make horribly flatulent squelching noises that often led to ostracism before death—or Snubnosed Assassin Spiders, which turned any person who made a living destroying the lives of others into a foppish aristocrat who could do little more than bend a wrist and sneeze daintily into a lacy handkerchief, and since Byron currently had hers, she would have to resort to her sleeve and thereby become doubly infectious—or even the dreaded Knotted Tree Stick Bug, which made the carrier believe that everything was made out of sticks. Everything.

"Shh," Marietta replied. She put a finger to her lips, which had long since rotted away, leaving only a fine film of discoloured tissue over her teeth. What teeth she had left, anyway. "Did you hear that?"

The cabbie practically squeaked and hid himself in the folds of her skirt. With this new growth attached to her left hip, she walked awkwardly into a large dining room that had once been resplendent with light-scattering crystal chandeliers and velvety chairs and intricately patterned rugs, but now was decked with dusty grime and flecked cobwebs. The chandelier had fallen at one point, wrecking a huge hole in the floorboards and scattering broken glass everywhere Marietta stepped. She wasn't sure which was worse, the insect carcasses or the shattered glass.

A bright light flashed and flickered in the stubs of the chandelier and Marietta had to shield her eyes from the strangeness of the light before her. She took a few tentative steps towards the chandelier and ran her hand over the glowing points; they were hot, but not flame, and not gas-powered, either. They were simple glass bulbs with white-hot metal inside. Her fascination was such that she didn't feel the cabbie tugging on her arm or squealing at a pitch only dogs could hear. There was the sound of a cape fluttering in the wind and then blackness overwhelmed her.

* * *

"Uhhh…" She sat up in a darkened room, putting one hand against her head. It had been a while since she was last knocked unconscious, and though there wasn't any pain other than a slight pressure at the back of her eye, she maintained the human response of moaning and rubbing the afflicted area.

"It's up!" she heard a voice say, followed by the muffled sound of a hand hitting a bundle of clothing. There was some scuffling and rearranging of objects, like pulling a table whose legs dug into the floor. A bright light hit her face.

"Uhhh!" she cried out, shielding her sensitive eye. The knock to the head had dulled her senses a little and her movements were groggy and slowed.

"This one is really far gone," the voice from earlier said. Through her drooping eyelid, she saw two fuzzy black figures and horizontal black lines that she knew to be the bars of a cage. If her many months of imprisonment as Byron's houseguest had taught her anything, it was what being locked up felt like; there was a stuffiness to the air, even though the bars were uncovered and she could reach out up to her shoulder joint. She thought she saw a twinkle against the speaker's hip that could be a set of keys and she grabbed wildly for it, then realised that she no longer had a hand on that arm.

With her mouth squished against the bars, her "Let me out" emerged as "Lemuhhh."

Before she could pull her arm back, the other, silent man pulled out one of her own axes and chopped her already-mangled left arm off above the elbow. Black blood sprayed out, splattering on the floor, and subsided into a dribble of coagulated mess.

"Ahhh!" she cried out, stumbling backwards into the cage. There was some shuffling behind her as she fell and landed on her back. As she opened her eyes, she saw that her cage was backed up to another—from which the cabbie was staring at her with two very large, shiny eyes. He leapt backwards and made the sign of the cross with his fingers.

The two men walked up to her cage and she got a good look at them. Both were middle-aged ruffians with greasy hair and dirty faces, but that was where the casual similarity to a passerby on the street ended. Both wore black robes over their clothes; the man who had spoken kept pulling at the collar and rearranging its folds to lay better over his regular garments. There were scorch marks and healed burns on their cheeks and backs of their hands, but the most peculiar thing was that their hair was standing straight up, scalp to split end. The silent one tried to flatten it three times as they walked over, but it only sprang back up like the hairpin trigger of a Tricycle Pistol, so named for accuracy it gave while the shooter was riding one. Something to do with the ambient ratio of pedal to pavement allowed the pistol to aim so precisely, its wielder could shoot the top corner pip of a playing card fifty yards out, even without seeing the card face. Marietta had won many a drinking match with just such a feat.

"What did you do that for?" the talker asked, smacking the silent man and making the same muffled sound as earlier.

"We need eet fohr eet's bite, not eet's bark," the chopper responded. He had a rather profound French accent.

The talker smacked his own head and then that of the Frenchman for a third time, saying, "You need an idiot-matic dictionary or something, my erstwhile friend!" He started talking to the cabbie next to Marietta's cage. "Igor says stuff like, 'oh, aye do 'ope zat we can kill zeese two behrds wiz one 'am bone,' or even, 'let us stop, we ahre splitting a tomahto.'"

"Aye do not talk like zhis!" Igor cried. He picked up Marietta's leaking arm and threw it into a rubbish pile behind him. There were stacks of broken chairs, smaller versions of the chandelier that Marietta had seen earlier, and other furniture that had seen better days. It was an appropriate graveyard for the darkening churn in Marietta's stomach. "And 'oo can keep zeese expressions straight, aye ask yoo?" He was pleading to the cabbie now. The cabbie shrugged and moved closer to Marietta's cage, obviously preferring to become a quick dinner over suffering whatever the two men were going to do.

"We need it, dear Igor, for its bite indeed," the talker said. Then he spied what the boy was doing. "Hey! Do you fancy losing an arm by teeth instead of a clean knife? Turn you into one like her if you get too close, now."

"But Marcus, izn't zat ze, as yoo say, bingo?" Igor whispered conspiratorially, but still loud enough for the others to hear him.

Marcus began rubbing the bridge of his nose. "Yes, but we don't want a panic before the experiment begins." He threw a toothy grin at the cabbie and a dirty glance at Marietta. She had decided to continue the zombie act and was now drooling, leaning her head against the bars but being careful not to stick anything else out.

"Uhhh?" she asked, turning towards the cabbie and motioning with her eyeballs that there was a loose bar in his cage to the left, if only he could get to it without drawing attention. Since it was a rather complex message to deliver via eyeball, she began wagging her intact eyebrow and the eyepatch strap that substituted as her other one.

"No, but, uh, sirs," the cabbie began, swiping his dirty hat off of his head, bowing slightly, and ignoring what the assassin was trying to tell him, "Marietta promised she wouldn't hurt me. She promised on my future children and see, she wouldn't bite me. I just started to trust her, and if that trust is broken, I don't think I'll be able to handle it. Oh, Great Sailor," he said, blanching even more and finding a far-off corner. "I'm gonna lose it."

"She 'as a name, now, does she?" Igor laughed and knocked his fingers against the bars. "Ze first Seekehr zat aye 'ave evehr been acquainted wiz. And what an ugly teapot!"

"Mug, you imbecile!" Marcus yelled. "What an ugly mug! I'll be breaking all sorts of china over your head if you don't—"

"Gentlemen, gentlemen!" a voice boomed. Lights came on to reveal a masked figure. "Why so much animosity, when we have almost reached the culmination of all of our years of research?"

As he stamped elegantly into the room, the lights nearest him turned on, so that more than half the room was lit by the time he reached its centre. The sconces bore the same strange bulbs as the ruined chandelier from before. Marietta shielded her eye and went down on one knee in order to get a better look at the place. The cabbie was continuing to vomit in his corner and thus could not help her out, unless she could concoct some plan using stomach contents that included a half-eaten cob of corn.

The masked man wore a long robe that brushed the floor, similar to Igor's and Marcus's, but much more elaborate—hemmed in gold and glittering with exotic gems, sweeping up millions of dust motes into the buzzing light—and a large mask with such an elongated nose that Marietta could have skewered her chopped-off arm on it to make a grotesque kebab. The bottom half of his face was exposed, but Marietta couldn't stare for too long at the risk of alerting the men. She thought she saw, just seconds before she pulled her eye away, that the artificial light shone differently on his left cheek than his right. She groaned again to defuse any suspicion as the Frenchman looked at her like a crow before it pecks out a finger bone from a corpse.

"Are you boys sure this is a Seeker?" the masked man said, looking at Marietta through the eyeholes of his mask. She tried not to let any emotion show on her face as she rushed the side of the cage and tried to claw at him with her stump of an arm. She recognised the voice. He faltered, then made a clicking noise with his teeth and shook his head. He stared into her eyes; she tried to make them as lifeless as possible and bit at his outstretched fingers. "Yes, yes, I suppose she would be this scuffed up, even as a Seeker."

"Boss?" Marcus said, pulling the robed man away.

"From another lifetime, I knew her," he said. Both men stopped to look at him. He waved their concerns away. "It is a way she would have wanted."

Anger boiled up inside Marietta as she waggled her stump even further through the bars. This was most certainly not the way she would have wanted to go. She had always wanted to die of heavy-metal poisoning from swimming in and consuming all the gold from her assassination of the imposter prince—certainly not as a discombobulated corpse comprised of several different girls and possibly one very large pig under the power of some lunatic, necromantic rapscallion. And the masked man should have known that. If only she could will her severed arm to crawl over and strangle him...

He must have picked up on her inner thoughts, because he suddenly took a step back and said, "Yes, I see it now. Definitely a Seeker." He snapped his fingers and the two men stood at attention, drawing deep black cloaks over their shoulders and hoods over their faces. Marietta could only tell them apart by the difference in height. "Boys. Open the bars between the cages."

"What?" the cabbie squeaked, then took off his hat and dry-heaved into it. He jammed the hat back on his head and got down on his knees to plead. "Marietta, you tell them. You tell them that you're a good Star-Crosser and you're not gonna hurt me. Byron? Byron? Mr. Ll—ll—ll—" The bars raised between their two cages until there was nothing left between the two of them and all that came out of the cabbie's mouth was a barking noise.

"Ah, yes," the masked man said, "an adept of the double L of the Welsh variety. Don't worry, my boy, you'll only be dead for a second! And then we'll have you back, right as rain—"

"Aye thought eet was right as volcano ash," Igor popped in. The others threw him dirty looks. Marietta thought that the mask almost downturned its eyebrows to show disdain, but she had other things to concentrate on. A real Star-Crosser would have thrown itself on the poor boy and bitten him to pieces by now, and although she was hungry, she wasn't about to fall into whatever plot they had concocted for her. She stubbornly tried to reach at the masked man with her stump, not caring that they could now hack off her arm to the shoulder. She could always get another one.

"Hll-hggghhll—" the cabbie was saying, sounding like he was being strangled.

And where exactly was Byron, anyway? He should have heard them, unless they had moved outside of the old decrepit mansion while she had been unconscious. But she had been unconscious many, many times, and had a knack for counting seconds whilst incapacitated. And they hadn't been out for more than ten minutes, tops. Which was enough time, sure, to cause a bit of brain damage, but not enough time to move a bedraggled corpse very far. Perhaps he had finally grown tired of her and was leaving her to die at the hands of strangers, which Byron knew was the most ignoble death for one such as her. Or—and this idea merely flirted across the top of her mind—she should stop thinking about what she thought people should think of her, because now was clearly not the time.

"She's too enamoured of you," Marcus said to the masked man, making kissing noises through puckered lips. "They say that some of them keep their personalities; maybe her knowing you is throwing off the plan."

"Quite all right, my dear fellows," he replied. He took a plain glass jar from one of his large pockets and put it on a stool that he dragged over to Marietta's outstretched appendage. Black blood was still dribbling from her stump, splattering a semi-circle around the bars. He unscrewed the metal lid, then rolled up his long sleeves to reveal a strange instrument attached to his right wrist, with leather straps that looped around his arm and disappeared into the folds of his robe. He flicked his fingers and a small arc of lightning passed between the small metal box at the wrist and a similar one on his middle finger. He kept on flicking until a steady stream of captured lightning was sparking across his palm, then twisted his wrist so it faced down into the open jar.

There was a large flash that burned Marietta's good eye and then a strange popping noise, like someone was pulling on an arm and dislocating the joint over and over again. It wasn't until a few seconds later that she realised that was indeed the case. The cabbie's arm was in her mouth and she was gnawing at the exposed bone and tissue and pulling it out of the socket; the boy had fainted from pain and shock, but was still alive. She swallowed the mouthful of flesh before wiping her mouth off and backing away.

"Excellent," the masked man said, closing the jar with a squeak of glass on metal and replacing it into his robes. "The Homunculus-Star Inducer works perfectly with the addition of a little electricity. Nothing that the newest technology in electrical fields cannot solve!"

Marietta watched in horror as the boy's body began to twitch and her bite wound went septic, turning a ghastly greenish-black that spread through his veins. She had only ever blacked out like that and woken up covered in human gore after the zenith of the Homunculus Star, and that was another week away. The masked man had somehow figured out how to trigger an episode. She'd have to warn Byron before—

Before nothing. The Homunculus Star affected Byron like it did any other Star-Crosser. He became as mindless and ravenous as the rest of them were all the time. If she could somehow get that jar from the man and use it against Byron, it could be her ticket out of this pitiful existence. Dying of heavy-metal poisoning was not so far away. She could practically taste the metallic tang at the back of her throat, wafting in the air like a particularly unpleasant odour.

As the cabbie's body twitched again, she realised that the smell was just his bowels loosening as his body spasmed and eventually began to move on its own. His fingers gripped the smooth wooden floor and dragged the rest of his body towards her. His eyes still hadn't opened, but that didn't matter. Star-Crossers hunted by smell first, sight second, and there was enough humanity left in Marietta that she oftentimes became a target; it took a few tester bites before her attackers realised that she wasn't that nutritious. Byron liked to joke that it was because her mind was the only thing left to her, and it was rather like a steam-engine in and of itself, so of course it smelled and drew her brethren.

"What es zis?" asked Igor as he watched Marietta backing away from the advancing boy. His head had lolled up onto his shoulders at an odd angle and the former cabbie looked at her cockeyed. He stretched out his arms and ran the length of the cage before biting into her shoulder and again at her neck. "Aye 'ave nevehr seen zis before!"

"That's it, big boy." Marcus opened the back of the cage to put a bag over the boy's head, then picked him up around the waist like a sack of potatoes. Marietta made a move to attack, only to receive a bullet in her unbitten shoulder. She slumped back into the bars, clutching the slurping wound. "Time to zap you back to the way you were."

Marcus transferred the wrapped-up boy to Igor, who held him over one arm and used the other to whip off a sheet from a table connected to the ceiling by a series of chains. He threw the boy down—the back of the cabbie's head struck the wood with a juicy thwack—and strapped down his struggling arms and legs, splaying him out. Igor uncovered the cabbie's head and the young boy snarled, baring his teeth and snapping at any appendage within reach. His mouth was still covered in Marietta's goopy blood.

The masked man had been throwing switches and levers, flicking glass beakers of boiling multi-coloured liquids, producing steam and arcs of lightning and altogether making a kerfuffle with his arms and occasionally a leg that pounded a pedal or threw a switch. He always did like to put on a show, Marietta thought. Other robed men walked into the room and filed into a semi-circle around the masked man, partially blocking her view and forcing her to stand on tiptoe. She was too engrossed to feign mindlessness anymore, and all eyes were now on the cabbie anyway.

A low-throated chant began around the room and rolled like a wave across the tongues of the adepts as the masked man continued to throw switches. Igor and Marcus pushed a large wooden wheel counter-clockwise until the ceiling began to open up. It was a cloudless night and the moon hung full in the corner of the skylight. But from the roof, a large machine that looked like a metal stanchion with a mesh doughnut on top began to blot out the white orb. Bluish streaks of light travelled through the circular mesh like a horse race.

"Ten quid on Clockwork Kidney Stone," Marietta whispered under her breath. It had been her favourite horse to bet on back when she had been just a humble bird-watcher. One of the adepts looked back at her with terrified disbelief. She clawed at him half-heartedly. "I mean, uhhhh—" she groaned. He looked back at the spectacle and she grew miffed that she was less of a draw than whatever was about to happen.

The machinery hung halfway between the ceiling and the floor, growing brighter and brighter until the arcs were coming off the machine in calculated strips that charred the top of the walls. Marietta saw now that dozens of scorch marks, faded with time, covered the walls; she wondered how long these men had been doing this and for what purpose. Occasionally a random streak would hit someone in the face or on the arm and there would be a grotesque cry. But most of the rays missed or were deflected, and Marietta wondered at the properties of the adepts' robes.

"Guess I'll find out," she muttered to herself, and the same adept whipped his head back at her. She put her good arm in her mouth and began chewing until he turned back around.

The streaks of lightning were curving underneath the machine now, dancing around the cabbie's outstretched limbs. Every time one of them almost touched him, he flinched and snapped his teeth again, growling low in his throat. It almost matched the same pitch as the adepts' rising chant—Marietta could make out a phrase something like "Magnificent Macaque"—and she could feel her bones vibrating, including her exposed ribs. The lightning continued to flare until one, then two and finally three arcs struck down into the cabbie's heart. His back arched off the wood and the entire room was plunged into darkness, with a few small explosions and popping noises.

"Holy stroganoff," Marietta whispered, but couldn't see if the adept had looked back to her or not.

She jumped when a match strike echoed throughout the room. The warm glow of candlelight began over in the corner where the masked man had been, growing as more and more candles were lit.

"Marcus, check the fuses again! I think we blew something major this last round."

"Yeah, boss, I'll be right back," Marcus's voice said. One of the lights bobbed out of a back entrance.

Marietta fell to all fours—or rather, all threes—and crawled along the edge of the bars until she found the loose ones, near where the cabbie had been. She began to twist and pull them out of their sockets. It was difficult with only one arm and she had to work quietly and quickly before the strange lights came back on. With a grating sound, the bar pulled free and she slipped through, tearing off a bit of her dress. She heard the shuffling of the adepts around her scrambling for light. She waited for a few seconds to allow her eye to adjust, then crawled towards a large shape that turned out to be Igor's hulking legs.

"What just happened?" she heard a voice say from the direction of the table. She froze, partly in the hopes that Igor thought she was someone else and partly because there was no way she could have heard the cabbie's voice. "Last thing I remember was my arm getting' torn off by that brute of a monster, and—" Here the cabbie started screaming and Marietta had just disentangled herself from the Frenchman's legs when, with a boom and a growing hum, the lights flickered back on.

Before Igor could sound the alarm, Marietta undid a pouch at the back of her belt and pulled out a small dagger, not bigger than the width of her thumb, and quickly plunged it into seven pressure points around his neck, face, and head. Within two seconds he was dead on the floor and she had slunk into a corner with his carcass, where she hoped the deep shadows would hide her until she could wiggle her way towards the exit that Marcus had used. She took a quick bite out of his arm before she realised what she was doing; as the Star's zenith approached, she became less able to control her actions and became more like other Star-Crossers.

"Calm down, boy!" the masked man said, unstrapping the cabbie's legs and straightening his mangled arm so that he could suture it and put it in a sling. The boy's blood was once again red; there was no trace of the blackened veins that had throbbed all the way to his heart scant minutes ago. From Marietta's corner, she could see nothing left of the Star-Crosser he had once been.

Once the boy's arm was wrapped and set, he struggled to get up. But his other arm was still strapped down.

"Now hush, hush. Wait just a second. We have to make sure that we've gotten all of the horrible nastiness out of you, boy. Previous tests have proven to be...problem-ridden," the masked man said, taking the jar once again out of his coat pocket and unravelling the top with a scratching sound that echoed in the quiet. The other adepts were slowly stepping forwards, holding their hands out to touch the cabbie but drawing back at the last moment as if they had been burned. The awe on their faces was palpable. "We found that the older the Star-Crosser, the further gone from this earthly realm they were." He spread one of his arms back behind him to gesture to a small cloaked figure. She undid her cloak to reveal a scarred face, a smooth, shiny stump where her hand had once been, and a cracked smile flush with insanity. "And the less chance of returning to their former humanity. Poor Delilah here was one of our first experiments, and she came out, well..." Here he began to whisper. "A little off."

Delilah smiled again, showing loose teeth and putrid gums, and tried to curtsey like a lady before falling over and laughing, smacking the stump of her arm against the floor.

"Ate 'em up I did! All of 'em, in little bitty gobblettes that ran down my mouth!"

The masked man continued to whisper to the cabbie: "She remembers everything. Eating people, losing limbs, turning others into Star-Crossers like herself. The mental damage alone let us know that we needed a fresh victim, and voilá! You, my boy, are the first successful cure of Star-Crosserdom, and you have Tesla's Trucklers for the Advancement of the Electrical Engine to thank! I know, quite a mouthful, but first things first!"

He sparked the apparatus on his wrist and started a small electrical field around his palm again. He was about to upend it into the jar, causing Marietta to go into another frenzy and surely give away her position, when the doors were thrown open. Byron pointed the flintlock-dagger directly at the masked man's face and cocked it.

"I demand to know what you are doing in here with my cabbie. He is currently in my employ, and as such, belongs to me. I personally consider any damage to him a rebuff to myself, and I do not take kindly to those who put me in such a situation as to repeat a buff. The last man who did is now missing most of the small bones in his ear, which I surgically removed while he was sleeping. On top of the fact that he can no longer hear, he has horrible problems with gangrenous wax that occasionally tries to crawl out of his ear and take over the country of Lichtenstein. Napoleonic urges, I'm afraid, but my best friend—may the Great Sailor rest his soul—knew a man who underwent the same procedure for its supposed medical benefits and his gangrenous ear wax was always trying to sing opera, causing the man to go not only deaf, but tone-deaf as well. A more serious affront, in my humble opinion."

"Sir, as you can see, your cabbie is just suffering from a broken arm," the masked man said, gesturing to the cabbie's arm, which was not only broken, but fractured, bruised, torn apart, and scalped as only a forearm can be scalped—second to the scalp itself, of course. "He was merely helping me with an experiment, one that I need to conclude shortly." And here he upended his sparking hand into the jar.

All chaos broke loose, and fortunately—or, maybe unfortunately—Marietta was only aware of the aftermath.

This time she had gone after the masked man himself. When she regained consciousness, she realised that she had chewed off his mask, thinking it was his face, and now spat out the leather nose in her mouth. With his mask torn, Marietta could see the wasp scarred onto his left cheek and knew that her initial assumption had been correct. It was her old master, the man who had raised her, nursed her, and turned her into a terrific killing machine. She had him pinned down, and as she was about to speak to the terrified man, she heard Byron trying to talk with his mouth full.

"Ohnly wan man dat I know ofth hasth thuch a tattoo!" He had the foot of one of the adepts in his mouth and blood smeared across his face and his clean white shirt. There were at least three mutilated bodies behind him, but with so many scattered body parts, Marietta was having trouble keeping track.

"A: You're lightning fast even when under the influence of a machine-produced Homunculus Star? B: You know this man, too? And C: Yes, I can talk," she said, looking down at Foster, who was staring at her with as much horror as she had ever seen on his face—and she had heard many a story filled with dark, depraved human beings, even darker and more depraved Star-Crossers, and the darkest, most depraved orphans. "And I remember everything about you, this bloody assignment to kill Byron, and how it was you—" She poked him in the chest to punctuate every word, "—that got me killed!" Here she started punching him until Byron's arms encircled her body and pulled her off of the cringing Foster.

"To answer your questions in a rather backwards, rather Homerian order, C: Only if you warrant those garbled noises you make without a nose 'talking.' B: Of course I know this man. He taught me everything I needed to know about keeping oneself alive whilst being attacked from the inside by the insidious Star-Crosser venom, and also how to find true love, or whatever you'd like to call it. And A: I learned my agility when I visited the Guru Mordecai III, a rather reticent mountain man who lived at the top of Mt. Pele and only ate coffee beans hand-picked by monkeys in the low-lying volcanic jungle and hand-delivered every morning by a person wanting to know an answer."

"And he taught you how to move so quickly?" Marietta asked, still being held in the air while Byron talked into her ear.

"Heavens, no, the man was decrepit, hadn't moved in ages. How could I learn from him? No, my skeletal patrician, dear, that was the day the mountain erupted, spewing its hot gases and ash in a furious pyroclastic cloud that I had to outrun if I wanted to live. But more importantly, and rather first and foremost, to leave Homer in the Grecian dust where he belongs next to Achilles' shield, you have insinuated that this is the man who was hired to kill me." He dropped her and pushed her to her knees. "And I dare not believe it to be so. This man is a personal friend of mine—"

"If he's that same blasted best friend you're always harping on about, I'll have you know that this man is an assassin and also a trainer thereof. You pick your friends like you pick your—well, I wouldn't even call me anything more than a much-maligned servant who is one day going to kiss your—" Marietta received a smack that snapped a few discs in her neck out of place.

"Not quite," Byron interrupted. "But as close of a friend as my truest, in all but the hirsute sense. And Mr. Darkboat here—"

"Darkboat? He's a Lighthouse at the orphanage, and he trains the orphans to be assassins." Marietta received another smack against the head.

"You're right, the esteemed Mr. Darkboat saved me from a horrible man by the name of Ladybird—"

"That's his brother, who also runs an orphanage. In fact, he trains his orphans to be…"

This time she shut herself up as Byron gave her the coldest, most bloodcurdling look he maintained in his repertoire. She knew he practised in the mirror, but obviously not that look, or he would be going through mirrors like clean shirts. She gulped. "His name is Meriwether Foster, also known as Wasp. He's the one who gave me the assignment to kill you, but not the one giving the orders. So, as you can see, you still very much need me in the sense that not only do I save your life on a routine basis," she said, shrugging as Byron gave her a wry grin, "but you still don't know the actual name of the client yet! And that's worth my paltry life, right?"

For the second time in recent memory, Marietta found herself counting Byron's seconds of silence as he mulled over her words. It had long been an area of contention between the two of them— really, one of the main reasons he kept her alive and in working order, not just some skeleton in a closet—and Marietta knew how much he hated all of the assassins in her guild. He had even gone out of his way on numerous occasions to kill them. If he found out who hired her from Foster, there'd be no reason for her to exist anymore.

"You? You trained this despicable wretch?"

"What happened to 'patrician?'" Marietta muttered under her breath, trying to test just how tightly Byron was holding her.

"I—I—I don't know exactly how this is possible, save for a like-minded experimentation process completely independent of our own trials." Foster started to get up, dusting off the shoulders of his cloak and looking sadly at the chewed remains of his mask. "But yes, Marietta is—was—is?—the best assassin I have ever had the pleasure of meeting and training. And yes, on two separate occasions, her services were employed in order to terminate your life. But it was nothing personal!" He held his hands out in front of him as if to give Byron a hug. "I've killed many an acquaintance, few times a lover, and even an estranged uncle, but pish-posh! That's all in the past now. Now, we must concentrate on telling me how you managed to bring Marietta back—"

In a flash, Byron was strangling Foster with a leather garrote whose handles contained small spikes doused with the strongest truth serum Marietta knew how to mix up. At any point during a strangulation, one could puncture the skin of one's victim, forcing them to give true answers to any question. But since Marietta had still been only a serum-making novice before her untimely zombification, they only spoke said truth if interrogated in a high-pitched squealing voice, like one speaks to a kitten.

After a few seconds of choking the life out of the Lighthouse, Byron undid the clasp that held the spike and pricked Foster just underneath the collar bone. The effects were immediate.

"Tell me now, were you ever truly my friend?" Byron asked.

Marietta cleared her throat, made a kissing face, and mouthed, "Who's a good boy?" Byron ignored her.

"Certainly, old chap!"

"The elixir to keep the decay from a Star-Crosser bite, that was all true?" Byron held up his flask containing graveyard dirt, earthworms, and a few other things and swished it in front of Foster.

"Of course, dear friend!"

Marietta cleared her throat again, pursed what was left of her lips, and pinched her cheeks. A flap of skin came away in her hand.

Byron sighed and then started patting and rubbing Foster's head as if he were a puppy. "Now who's a good boy? Huh?" His voice was high and squeaking at the vowels. "Who's a champ? Now, tell me, why did you join these heretics?"

"I—" Foster had broken out into a sweat, clearly trying not to say what he was about to say. "I—the elixir stopped working. I heard about this strange new electricity that could save me from the bite I received fourteen years ago."

"What?" Marietta asked, getting closer to Foster and the machinery that he had used to bring the cabbie back to life. Her voice was high only from surprise, but it worked just the same.

"Yes, child, the same day that you knocked on my door asking for a cup of flour—no, wait, that was a Tuesday and the bite happened on a Saturday, so never mind."

"Who hired you to kill me, huh? Who hired you to kill me, champ?" Byron asked, pinching Foster's cheeks and making kissy faces.

Marietta began turning and pulling the various knobs and switches, not caring that she didn't know what she was doing, just hoping for a result before Byron noticed. She didn't like to think of what he would do if she tried to put herself bodily between the two of them.

"The—the first time was—was—" he said as Marietta cringed, praying as hard as she could that something would happen, "your Uncle."

"Oh," Byron said, leaning back and rubbing his hand through his hair. "Is that it? I could have told you that. Of course he was trying to kill me."

"Are you serious?" Marietta squealed from the corner and in her frustration hit a lever that threw the entire piece of machinery into overdrive.

"But the second time," Foster gasped, "the second time was someone else. The second time was—"

Lightning arced outward from the coiled machine, striking Foster square in the chest. A plume of smoke erupted, wafting a charred smell through the air; Byron had to wave his hand in front of his face to see just exactly what had happened. Foster's body was smoking badly and there was a large wound on his left shoulder, right above his heart, deep enough to see muscle. As Byron moved to close Foster's eyes, he gave Marietta another cold-blooded stare.

"…Oops?"

"Marietta, you—you—"

It was like hearing the whistle of an incoming bomb right above her head. She knew that the large explosion would render her body into as many different parts as there were versions of the story of Byron's estrangement from his Uncle. She had stopped keeping track the thirty-seventh time he charmed his way through villagers' hearts after ripping out hers with his story of woe and displacement.

"You tongue-scraping, scissor-lipped, cud-chewing, eyeball-gouging, pale-faced, candle-blowing antediluvian troglodyte! You deserve to scrape the toes of hellbound souls until your fingers fall off and you have to go on cleaning them with your tongue! How dare you compromise my ability to figure out who tried to kill me! If you thought I was a heartless bastard before, you have no idea what the lowest depths of my reptilian brain can create in order to make your life as impossible as possible."

Byron was breathing heavily, contorting his fingers in rage, towering over Marietta and ready to strike her when Marcus came rushing back into the room with an armful of fuses. One of them dropped out of the crook of his arm and the thin glass shattered the two of them into silence.

"Conductor…" Marcus intoned, looking at the charred remains of Foster still smoking on the table.

"Marietta," Byron said, clearing his throat, straightening his blood-soaked shirt, adjusting his back tooth, and slicking his tousled hair back with the cleaner of his two hands, "as a last request, would you be so kind as to tie up our friend here so that I may torture him for any information regarding the late Meriwether Foster or Mr. Darkboat or any other silly titles he may have had?" He snapped a pair of gloves onto his hands—now having two gloves over his left—as Marietta jumped into action, eager to avoid as much pain as possible.

As Byron sat down to torture Marcus, stealing the crumpled device Foster had attached to his wrist and learning quickly how to use it, Marietta knew from the gleam in his eyes that he was only just warming up for her. She gulped as a part of her throat came sliding down the front of her dress and landed in a wet glob at her feet.

Part Two

In Which the Homunculus Star is Further Explored, Or: Excuse Me, But Your Teeth Are in My Calf

Byron woke up in the ramshackle tavern with a pounding head, a pounding arm, and a pounding calf. The head he could attribute to the wild night of cheating the townspeople out of their money by pretending to kill his partner in crime, the roving Seeker who would eat all of their children and then make xylophones out of their bones. They had even stolen a xylophone from a run-down music hall, which had no need of stringless instruments because it didn't go well with their theme of silk-string acrobats, and played it disjointedly throughout the night as a sort of musical predatory call. This time, he had taken the left lower leg of his Star-Crossed companion to give as a souvenir to the local Star-Crosser hunter, who had made quite a name for himself.

The arm, of course, was due to his condition—and because the Homunculus Star was at its zenith that night, the pain would only grow until he partook of the human flesh lying to his right, his payment in the most recent form of a red-headed young lady. The calf, however, was a new mystery for him to unravel. But as he couldn't actually open his left eye, due to the sheer level of gound accumulating there, he simply stretched, limped out of bed, and groped for his shirt in order to find his bottomless pocket.

"Curse that Transylvanian huntsman who taught me the secrets of unravelling the very folds of both fabric and time!" he said aloud, rubbing at his eye and still fumbling with his shirt pockets. He moved on to his vest next, being unable to locate his trousers. "He only had one eye and carried around a dagger with an executioner-style tip. I mean, what kind of bloody idiot thinks he can behead someone with a simple dagger? I should have known then that he was a steaming pile of viscera and should have instead learned the temporal arts from his next-door neighbour, a homeless ex-military type with a six-fingered hand and an even-more jointed—" There was a loud knock at the door. "Speaking of belts and what lies below them…" He finally found his trousers, smacked himself in the left hand with the buckle, and started cursing loudly as the knocking accumulated at the doorframe. "I told you I didn't want to be disturbed! Is this any way to treat the man who single-handedly saved your pathetic little village from the wrenching teeth of—"

Standing at the door was a terrified-looking barkeep, his face so blanched that he looked two shades this side of a Seeker ready to disintegrate into a Stumbler after the Star. Acting very much like what Byron imagined him to be, the barkeep wobbled into the room and looked around, nervously clutching his fingers and opening his mouth as if to speak, but somehow forgetting to make sounds approaching the Queen's English.

"…Yes?" Byron eventually asked as the barkeep continued to waddle back and forth in the threshold. "Look, if you want me to be a godparent to your child or spit on your hand to make it lucky or some other ridiculousness, I suggest you get it over with quickly and painlessly, or you'll be the one I pick next for target practise." He patted his pockets for a weapon to twirl about his fingers into order to look more intimidating.

"I—I—"

"If this is about my payment, I thought that saving your town was enough to earn your undying gratitude, the hospitality of any warm house, and the even warmer hospitality of the young ladies who—"

"Listen," the barkeep finally said, moving aside so that Byron could see his one-legged accomplice behind the older man, "I don't know what kind of racket you're running here, but—"

At that very moment, Byron finally found his bottomless pocket. He rummaged elbow-deep in his trousers for a bit, much to the wide-eyed disbelief of a barkeep who had, admittedly, seen much that he wished he could disbelieve that morning, and found what he had been looking for: a very long piece of sausage. The girl who had accompanied Byron to bed had finally woken up; careless of the two men in their stand-off, she snatched her breakfast and began eating it with the appetite of the underfed and still sleepy-eyed.

"Marietta!" Byron yelled. The young cabbie, missing a leg and seeping black fluid from a long scratch down the side of his decaying cheek, popped up from behind the barkeep.

"Boss, I don't know how many times I have t' tell you, my name isn't Marietta, I've never been an assassin, an' I don't understand your obsession with talkin' t' yourself for long stretches o' time about things that never really happened in th' first place." He continued pushing the barkeep into the room, then closed the door so as not to arouse any suspicion from their neighbours. "'Sides, she's can't hear you from where she's at. Not tha' she could hear you anyways, not without any ears like you left her—" He stopped as he noticed the girl had stopped eating and was looking at him with confusion.

"Not only did Marietta have more tact the morning after..." He gave the cabbie a meaningful look to shut him up before he even opened his mouth, an exchange which was standard between the two of them now. "But she also still has my special man dandies!"

When he forgot to give the cabbie another glance, the young boy burst out laughing and slapped the barkeep on the back in a show of, according to the barkeep, overly familiar camaraderie.

Marietta also, Byron noted to himself, was much better at understanding what he meant. She recognised that he referred to the emergency pants that allowed him to erase the last three minutes of someone's memory if, while wearing them, he did a very specific dance meant to confuse the optical nerves and send a mind-altering impulse directly into the memory centre of the brain. Marietta would have merely quipped that he looked like a bee, showing the rest of the colony where a viable source of food was; she wouldn't delve into the physical necessities of such an endeavour.

In lieu of the cognisance-stealing dandies, he merely sufficed with punching the barkeep straight between the eyes and knocking him out stone cold. When he went down, he hit his head a second time on the edge of the table—sufficient enough, Byron hoped, to make him believe that the entire thing was merely a dream. He might pepper the barkeep's rather illustrious yet still unkempt beard with a few crumbs of jalapeños slathered with sweet cream to corroborate the story of a raucous, dream-ridden night filled with three-headed cows, dragons made of flowers, and a singing bathtub.

"There was a time," Byron started, finding a few crumbs at the very bottom of his bottomless pocket and sprinkling them with vigorous gestures, "when, after an entire night bingeing on sweet cream-slathered jalapeños, I dreamt that I was a burnt piece of Melba toast covered in raspberry jam. But all I really wanted was orange marmalade, and thus I rolled off my plate and out of the hands of the man about to eat me, until I found an Onion Johnny who kindly pointed me in the direction of an old lady who sold said marmalade, only to stab me in the back with a butter knife as soon as I tried to roll away and douse me in the foulest onion-and-liverwurst spread known to mankind. To this day I shudder when I see anything that even resembles the shape of a liver—"

"Are you going to eat that?" the girl said, pointing to his handful of crumbs with one hand and licking the fingers of the other.

"Does no one appreciate the wit it takes to tell these stories with such heart-rending pathos so as to evoke every emotion known to mankind within a mere thirty seconds?" Byron yelled, throwing the rest of the crumbs up in the air. "Pack your things, Christina," he said to the girl, hastily getting dressed while puffing up his hair with his distressed sighs. "You're leaving with us today, as soon as we're able."

"Able, Mr. Byron?" scoffed the cabbie. "You call one leg able? I couldn't even hobble up th' stairs without the help of th' barkeep, and I had t' threaten t' bite him!"

"Able?" scoffed Christina simultaneously, talking into Byron's other ear. "When's that? When I can pay for all of the gambling bills my husband's racked up? When I can buy milk for my babies? When I can feed my dogs? Unless you can promise me all that, I'm not going anywhere with you—as good a time," she said, sauntering to him, the sheets catching on the corner of the table and dropping lower and lower, "as I did have last night." She bit the air and her teeth clacked together. Byron suddenly remembered why his calf was hurting the second before Christina turned away sharply and started collecting her clothes.

He pulled his trousers up and tried to saunter over to her in the same suggestive, seductive manner, reaching to put a hand on her cheek.

"I know you may feel that last night was a fleeting moment, a wisp of breath between branches, shaking our bodies together like leaves and pulling us here and there," he said, walking his fingers along her backside until he found the wrapped-around sheet. He began to tug as his voice became nothing more than a whisper against the top of her ear. "But it is nothing compared to what could blossom between us, small and quivering like a fragile glass heart, filling and pumping life into us, flowering us into beings complete with each other, our souls touching like fronds reaching out for sunlight." He pulled her closer and began to unwind the sheet, twisting her in his arms slowly. "We could be those glistening rays of light, nourishing each other through the long, dark, cold nights." He had gotten down to the last layer of sheet before he realised that she was holding a hand-sized revolver against her naked hip, pointed straight at his crotch.

She stood on her tiptoes and kissed him on the lips while he gestured wildly with his eyebrows to the cabbie, hoping the boy would help subdue the woman-creature or at least retrieve his flintlock dagger and brass knuckles from the desk.

But the cabbie was lying on his stomach, inches away from the barkeep, salivating at the twitching fingers of the concussed man.

"Do you think these would taste all right if I rolled 'em up in flattened bread and pretended they was blood sausages? A little bangers and mash goin', y' know, just t' settle my stomach at th' thought of eatin' human flesh? I'm so hungry, but I haven't been able t' keep anythin' down save for a few scraps o' hair and toenails what we found in th' lavatories o' that one restaurant we swindled out o' a nice meal."

Byron rolled his eyes, again wishing that Marietta were there. She would be able to sedate the wild Christina and get her to go along with the both of them without any problems. The ferocious glint in Christina's eyes as she came closer to him, the revolver's muzzle pressing against the centre seam of his trousers, reminded him too much of the last triumphant look on Marietta's face as she killed Foster with that infernal machine. Before the girl could blink, Byron had grabbed the small revolver, twisted the sheets around her neck so that every turn of his wrist further cut off her air supply, and with the gun pressed her hand to the wall, feeling her bones grind against the metal muzzle.

"Now, dear..." He pressed the gun deeper into her hand until she cried out in pain. "This gun was merely a plaything, right? Like all of the other little toys we had last night. And somehow it got tangled up with the sheets and just happened to slip into your hand, right?" She kept on nodding until Byron thought that her pretty little head might fall off her shoulders. But that would be later. He shot her hand and threw her a ripped piece of sheet to wrap around the bleeding wound. "You won't need that hand for very much longer, my dear little buffet. Tonight the Homunculus Star rises and your sacrifice will be honoured so that we, your humble hosts," he gestured to himself and the cabbie, "may live. Or unlive, in his case." He scrunched his face in thought. "In my case, too."

"You shot me!" she screamed, holding her hand.

"Yes, and soon I shall tear into your flesh with my hands and teeth. So, really, when put into perspective, a little gunshot clean through the metacarpals is nothing. Besides," he said, pulling up his trouser leg to show where she had bitten him, "I shall be merely paying you back in kind."

In the end, Byron had to shoot his way through five more villagers, including the unfortunate Christina's gambling betrothed—"The only snake eyes he'll see now are the snakes actually eating through his eyes," he had quipped—brass-knuckle his way through the entirety of the orphanage, who were wailing at the fact that their favourite teacher was being carted away from the tavern over his shoulder—"Judging from the size of her derriere, these children received a well-rounded education"—and burn down the nearby Lighthouse, as its adepts vaguely reminded him of Wasp and his betrayal—"Die!"—before he got away into the nearby forest with his stolen bride and accomplice. The barkeep they merely left with a crumb-filled beard; Byron didn't like thinking that the barkeep, who knew more about them than the nosy peasants or wailing children, was the one still alive, but that's the way it had worked out. And if there was one thing Byron had learned through his rather expansive education, it was that reflecting on the past was for the paltry and the poor.

"So what did we learn about swindling towns into letting us stay in their fluffy white sheets and their down comforters?" Byron was saying, walking with the cabbie to his left and the agonised Christina still thrown over his shoulder.

"T' be more subtle in the way tha' I mimic other Star-Crossers so as not t' give away th' fact that I'm not going t' eat their children and make their bones into xylophones and—hey, do you fink that if I twirl her hair up in a fork, it'll taste like spaghetti? I used t' love spaghetti so much..."

Byron downed a few bitter swallows from the flask in his hip pocket. After he adjusted his tooth, he began chewing on one of the longer worms he had found on a particularly rainy afternoon while hunting down information on the Archduke Velo and his wife, the Heelduchess Judith. They were the two names he had gotten out of that fool Marcus while he pushed the shavings of a rubber eraser further and further up one nostril while prodding with a charcoal stick up the other, in order to simultaneously retrieve and erase any information. By the end, Marcus didn't even remember the name of his mother (and had one hell of nosebleed), but had divulged that Foster had been rather cushy with the Archduke, who was also a known associate of his Uncle's. Since the same torture technique had yielded only the barest of results on Marietta—whose nasal passages had unfortunately decayed into nothingness, and there just wasn't the same level of passion if it was so easy to see the targets of her sinuses right there on her face—he could only hope that one man who wanted to kill him would know of the second. And there was the bothersome and unresolved issue of his inheritance as well. As soon as he heard that the Archduke was nearby and a friend of Foster's, a plan started to cook in his mind.

"…covered in some marinara sauce, o' course it would taste like spaghetti, or maybe even some fettuccine, if I wanted t' make a nice cream sauce with some fresh basil on top t' garnish it," the cabbie had been saying.

"You shot my fiancé!" Christina yelled, "and my father and those poor children—"

"I merely grazed their curly-headed mops with my brass knuckles—"

"That cause horrible explosions, so that even if some of them did survive, they're probably scarred by what they saw happen to the others."

"Remember how you won't be needing your hand? Well, you also won't need a fiancé or even a father where you're going."

"And where exactly is that?" she said as he set her down. Byron guessed that her feet had lost their feeling during her voyage on such a strange mode of transport; she wobbled before falling down on her backside.

"A wonderful ball where the women are exquisitely dressed like statues carved in glistening marble and the men are immaculate in their blacks and whites, so that they look like exotic fauna glittering in the night. The wine is as deliciously dark as the topics of conversation. It is a most wonderful, floating source of intoxication—also like the topics of conversation—preparing one for the even more ecstatic dessert, a taste unlike anything conceived by man because they have so much money that they are able to hire witches to brew their culinary concoctions."

Christina looked up at him in wonder, a smile breaking across her face.

"Really?"

"Of course, my wailing pallbearer—or should I say whaling, given the size of your backside? I never lie." He pulled off his hat and wiped the sweat from his brow. "You'll be dead as a doornail, I'm afraid, animated by the strange dark prestidigitation that lulls all Star-Crossers back into their blistering afterlives, but you'll be at that party nevertheless."

How he loved to see the crumbling hope as her face fell and the harsh lines of reality once again crept across her brow. Dismissing her with a hand, he began to pace.

"And there quicker than I intended, too—there being, of course, across the threshold of death and not the party, which is, of course, a fixed point of time and therefore cannot arrive earlier than the time for which it is arranged—for I fully believed we would be at the next town over by the time the Star rose. But alas, even the best laid plans…"

"…get roasted and fried like a chicken on a spit," the cabbie finished, coming into the fading light so that Christina could see both men edging towards her, salivating and growing gaunt around their cheeks, skulls shining underneath their thinning skin. "Oh, can we, please?"

Just over the tops of the trees burned a small bright light that trailed its tail of shimmering ash over the sky. It lit up the gloaming so that even Byron could feel its warmth against his back as he and the cabbie moved closer to the girl. Her heart was beating, her flesh was churning with life, and he wanted nothing more than to dip his hands—rotting and sloughing skin, pussing and puking, for his true nature shone through just like the Homunculus Star—into her and he didn't care if they charred, he wanted that life for himself. The Star seemed to cut through the trees, endowing them with twisting shadows, blanketing the entire earth in a greenish glow that animated any zombie under its preternatural light to find, consume, and ransack everything within reach. Under the Homunculus Star, the Star-Crossers would be driven into frenzies, turning into buzzing Swarms that sought to establish and cultivate new Hives. Before its deadly reach had started to affect him, after his marriage to his wife, Byron had seen towns cut down in seconds by the roaming beasts under its influence. Houses were consumed by pitch-black figures, like amassing ants charging through rivers, using their own bodies as bridges.

He was distantly aware of himself as his hands dug into her intestines and started scooping them into his mouth, just as he was furtively aware of their taste between his gums and tongue. But there wasn't a damn thing he could do to stop himself, or even to do more than observe as events unfolded. Not that he cared overly much for Christina's life or for the cabbie that he had taken because he needed an assistant with Marietta's unique skills—the intelligent Star-Crosser ones, not the assassination ones, though he was beginning to realise that those were awfully useful as well. He felt helpless in this state, nothing more than hunger and want; though that was his waking life, too, at least he had the fine British capacity to take it with a stiff upper lip, keeping calm and carrying on and drinking tea. He could never drink tea in a state like this and it was that rebellious freedom that thrilled him.

Footsteps crunched towards him. His instinctual feasting body looked up with a bloody mouth and gore-splattered hands and jumped up into the safety of a tree just as a shining sword sang through the air and decapitated the oft-maligned cabbie. His head spun through the air three times before hitting the ground and rolling to a stop at the bottom of the nearby ravine. Byron heard himself hiss, launched himself out of the tree towards his attacker, felt himself receive a slash to the stomach in return. He hissed again, knowing he was defeated, and grabbed a leg of his prized carcass to start dragging her through the forest, looking for an escape. As it just so happened, he met another group of rambling Star-Crossers, mostly defunct Stumblers missing the necessary parts to propel themselves further than a few feet at a time, and led his pursuer straight into the depths of arms and legs and crawling stomachs that tried to bring him to ankle-level so they could bite him into unconsciousness—or, in the case of the stomach, spill a little stomach acid on him in the hopes of toppling him over for easier digestion.

Byron spent the rest of the zenith eating the internal organs of the girl, then recuperating as the Star passed back over the curve of the earth and disappeared into the treeline once again. His faculties slowly returned; he drew in his breath as he concentrated on healing the gash in his gut and the lingering decay of his transformation. The time after the Star collapsed back into space, where it wouldn't be seen for another three months, was always when he felt his best: a full stomach, a full head, and a full body. Even his left hand would be a fleshy pink for a few days before it returned to its normal greyish green and he would have to cover it up with a glove again. And now that he didn't have to worry about making the cabbie—he realised he never even knew his name— look human, and Marietta was as far away from human as she could possibly ever get, he could reap all of the benefits himself.

The entire spectacle lasted maybe an hour.

And when he heard the rustling of footsteps against the soggy ground again, he didn't hiss, he didn't move a single eyelash, but just slunk back into the cover of the tree branches and waited, slitting his eyes so that their glassy whiteness wouldn't attract attention. The glint off his hunter's drawn sword was enough to allow Byron to track him through the darkness. It was a sword he recognised, from its Spanish tip to its intricate hilt and razor edge; it belonged to the famous Star-Crosser hunter to whom he had delivered the cabbie's leg back in the village. This close, he could even see the delicate carving on the side of the scabbard: a round, mottled shape that could either be a pear or a—

"Hehctor Aguacate—achoo achoo achoo!—knows no defeat, choo foul beast!" the man said with a slight Spanish accent and a quick swish of his sword. "I demand dat choo comb back here and face me like a man!" He sneezed and sneezed again. Just when Byron thought that the man was done and he had pulled out a lace handkerchief with which to wipe his nose, he sneezed three more times in quick succession. He rubbed his dripping appendage with his right hand: a shiny black hook that seemed to eat instead of reflect light.

"You know, dear old chap..." Byron stepped out of the brush after making sure he had wiped off all of Christina's blood and buttoned his jacket over his dirtied shirt, hoping that the darkness would swallow any bloodstains on his trousers, "I have a friend who has an intimate connection with the Department that makes clockwork limbs for accidents such as yours." He nodded towards Aguacate's right hand. "And they actually work fairly well. I should know, as my father was the one who invented them. Superb technology, really—"

"Show yourself, choo coward!" Aguacate yelled and pointed his sword straight at Byron's heart.

"I don't know how else I am supposed to show myself, since I am, quite literally, in front of you. Unless you're talking about a different kind of show altogether, and in that case, I've heard that the Lovely Lollipop Ladies of Lancaster can show you as many different contortions of their—"

"Ah, choo, Meester Llewellyn-Cave!" Aguacate yelled again, sneezing in place of the hyphen and butchering his last name so badly that Byron smiled crookedly, took his outstretched hand, and shook it gently, hoping not to catch whatever horrific cold Aguacate had picked up that made him sneeze every three seconds and around any proper noun. He would dread having such a cold; one of his favourite things to do was see how many times and in how many different ways he could say his entire name. The record was at thirty-two, with the thirty-second being an expression of bamboozled ennui. (His favourite, of course, was the seventeenth: near-catatonic rakishness.)

"Please, call me Byron," he said, if only never to hear again his last name butchered in the snot-filled nostrils of such an uncouth personage. When he got his hand back he wiped it on the back of his trousers, preferring to have viscera on his hand over Aguacate's sickness. "All of my friends do." He neglected to mention that all of his friends were dead, which is what he was hoping would quickly happen to the unlucky hunter. He reached behind him for the small hand-held electric mechanism that he had stolen from the masked Foster and never kept far from his person.

He had just snapped his fingers, activating the small humming electrical current, when the bushes behind him began to rustle. Aguacate pushed him out of the way and started stabbing his sword in every direction in the dark, punctuating his exploratory parries and thrusts with sneezes.

"I warn choo wit caution, Meester Llewell—I mean Byron, sir. I was chay-sing some foul Seeker, faster and queecker than any I, Hehctor Aguacate—achoo achoo achoo!—have known."

"Are those three rapid sneezes part of your name? Like a Junior or an Esquire or something?"

"Hehctor Aguacate—achoo achoo achoo!—knows no fear!"

"We've heard this part before," Byron muttered, hoping that it was, indeed, a large group of roving Seekers who were about to mash Aguacate into guacamole, when he remembered his ill-tempered meal. Since there was no way that he would be going back to the town he had decimated, he needed Christina's body in order to deceive the Archduke. "Mr. Aguacate, your deft-handedness, may I suggest that we head back to your encampment? I too have seen many a thrilling Seeker tonight and fear that it may be too much for—"

"Hehctor Aguacate—achoo achoo achoo!—knows no fear!"

"Yes, I'm aware, but I know fear. So very well, in fact, that we play bridge together every other Tuesday. Fear is a terrible cheater, I'm afraid, and always tries to hide cards under the table in his sock bands and then pretends to have an itchy ankle due to some horrible career-ending injury he received from an errant arrow decades earlier. Which is quite the contrast to my best friend, however, who was so fiendishly clever—at cheating, not at bridge—that we were kicked out of every gambling house this side of the Thames." Aguacate was looking at him with a slack jaw. "What I'm trying to say, my honourable hook, is that we very much need to leave. Now."

Just then, Christina jumped out of the forest and lunged towards Byron. Thinking quickly, he threw himself in front of her with a shout, as if he were out of his mind with terror and his haphazard flight just so happened to block Aguacate's sword. At any other time, he would have very much enjoyed saving damsels from other men's swords, but given the context and the lack of the Lovely Lollipop Ladies of Lancaster, he was becoming rather exasperated.

"Hout of de way, so I may keel de foul beast!" Aguacate yelled and then sneezed as Christina pounced on Byron, kissing him with large, voracious smacking sounds. It was dark enough and Aguacate was sneezing hard enough that Byron decided he could still save the situation.

"Mr. Aguacate, please stop. This is my…" He paused, wondering if having an incestuous sister or a disembowelled wife was worse. "My fiancé." He thanked the Great Lighthouse—out of habit, not any religious compulsion—that he and the cabbie had only taken large chunks out of her easily hidden midsection and avoided her limbs. If kept in low light, the fact that most of her internal organs were now sitting in Byron's digestion tract was almost inconspicuous.

He grimaced as she started kissing him again. Her breath was as foul as the smell under his Uncle's powdered wig—which is where his Uncle kept most of his money, being untrusting of the banking establishments in general. However, the tonics that he used upon his bald pate mixed with the human skin oils captured on the paper, causing the money to become hairy and his head to acquire the unfortunate smell of currency. This led to horrible confusion whenever he did go to an inferior banking establishment—those staffed by somewhat trained and impossibly well-dressed automatons made out of recycled clockwork limbs. Which, in turn, only served to reinforce his hatred when the tellers tried to deposit his few ghastly strands of hair.

"Choo did not tell me dat choo were engaged whan choo 'anded me de foul leg of de foul beast which choo had slayed!" Aguacate said, finally managing to say a whole sentence without sneezing once. Byron believed it to be because of the surprising situation—the unfortunate meeting place, not that someone would actually want to marry him, as he had once been very happily married before the troubles had started.

"It doesn't usually manage to come up whilst handling disembodied parts of devastating creatures, I admit," he replied. At once a large pat landed on his back and a lit cigar appeared between his lips, billowing acrid smoke. He coughed at the same time that Aguacate sneezed and Christina tried to kiss his ear with a voracious amount of her tongue somehow involved. Her amorous advance missed its mark and landed straight on Aguacate's nose, which protruded from his face like the sideways sails of a slowly sinking ship (and seemed to discharge as much mucus as rigging did oil).

Aguacate jumped back, flushed, then started twittering about how his own wife had been killed by the same Star-Crosser who had taken his hand and now he was on the search for the foul beast. Why the promise of romance would cause a man to remember a horrific incident involving dismemberment and murder, Byron couldn't understand—until he began thinking about his own marriage, which had involved both and quite a bit more.

"So although I am flattered by your ohffer ohf a pre-nuptial lambada, I must, unforchoonately, decline hout ohf respect for my dearly departed and de fact dat I am on de trail ohf de one who took my hand. Choo wouldn't, by any chance, Byron—ooh, how delighted I am dat choo have indeed allowed me to call hyu by your Chreestian name!—like to join me? Two rapscallions such as us on de hunt after—"

"Fowlest of fowl beasts who fowlishly took your hand—didn't happen to look like a chicken, did he? Now I am the one to offer my regret, as I must decline. You see, Christina—" He pointed at the girl, who had wandered off to gnaw the branch of a tree to see if it tasted anything like brains, which was a common occurrence in newly awakened Star-Crossers, "— is devilishly afraid of any light brighter than a small torch. It's quite the reverse of the usual situation, but the poor dear cries out like a small kitten when exposed to a roaring fire and, goodness me, the screams she makes when the sun comes out and shines through gauzier-than-usual curtains. Don't even get me started on a gas lamp behind a slightly damp napkin. I was just taking her to the next town over before the sun rose and she had yet another epileptic episode when we were attacked by the creature that you must be searching for. Dreadful, really, her eyeballs go every which way—not literally, man," Byron said, guffawing rather obnoxiously and not at all organically, "for that would be ludicrous, and her arms will spasm—in a completely human way and not anything like a Star-Crosser, no! So I am unable to help you, though I do wish you luck on your endeavour, and may the Great Lighthouse shine your way into getting your handsome revenge."

He tried to lead Christina away by the hand, their backs turned to Aguacate so as to avoid any unnecessary discoveries, when she began to moan and grope for Byron. Some part of her brain still remembered who she was, though it was uncertain whether she was driven by the memories of her night with Byron or the knowledge that he was her murderer. She took a friendly bite from Byron's cufflink, spat it out, and chewed on the fabric before bounding off into the middle of the forest without a trace. The part of her throat that still functioned made a cackling noise that refracted wildly off the trees.

Byron counted to twenty in order to allow his anger to subside as Aguacate cried out and began untying his horse, which he had hitched to a nearby oak with a twisted trunk.

"Ay Dios mío, man, choor fiancé! We must rescue her before she falls prey to de unsavoury elements about!"

"I'm sure they'll be perfectly savoury to her," Byron muttered under his breath, wondering if he should just shoot Aguacate right between the eyes, abandon all prospects he had with Christina, and find a replacement redhead. Of course, he did need a new accomplice with which to trick towns out of their wits, and if Aguacate was already missing one hand, it was just one less body part to replace once he was a subservient Star-Crosser. A bite now, when Byron was in his right mind, would make Aguacate like himself and the cabbie—that is, very much unlike the clumsy Christina, who had been bitten by the Crossed cabbie and thus deteriorated into a weak-minded Seeker almost immediately. A new plan started to hatch in Byron's mind. He slowly pulled the flintlock dagger out of his belt and pointed it at the one-handed Spaniard.

"Men!" Aguacate yelled. Three large dogs with three large men attached melted out of the forest, as if the colours of the trees had simply created them out of thin air. Byron blinked a few times and sighed, uncocking the gun and placing it back into his belt. He wondered if Marietta had left her candle and twine so he would be able to follow Christina, then realised that, with the passing of the Homunculus Star, he should be powerful enough to locate and control some part of the errant Seeker with his mind.

"Yes, men!" Byron interrupted, walking into the small circle they had formed while Aguacate debriefed them on the situation. "The able-bodied kind who are able to split up and find my fiancé before anything happens to her! But remember, she hates light, so the darker we can be about our search, the better!"

"Perfect!" sneezed Aguacate. "You t'ree go dat way and light up a flare if you find her. Byron and I will go en de last direction we saw her and do de same if we find anything. Certainly two such capable hunters as ourselves can deal wich hany mischief before choor Christina finds further harm."

"No, really, Mr. Aguacate, I think that it'll be much better if I look for her by myself. You know, so she doesn't get frightened into impaling herself on a tree branch or whatnot. I've seen it happen. There were three neighbour children who lived next to me, in what is now the ex-haunted headquarters of the ridiculous, electricity-worshipping Heretics, who went running through the forest one day without their shoes on, very much against the advice of my best friend and myself. When we searched the forest three days later, we found that each and every one had somehow slid down a muddy bank into the operating nest of the Star-Crossed Long-Eared Legion, who proceeded to eat everything but their skins, which they left flapping in the wind like tiny bed sheets—"

"Dhis way! I bet I'm not de only thing attracted to her in dhis blasted forest, and Hehctor Aguacate's nose knows when dere's a Star-Crosser! Achoo achoo achoo!" He mounted his horse and galloped away, leaving Byron to run through thickets that tore at the seams of his trousers and jacket. His tailor was a very rich man after all of his gallivanting into the forest after clues to regain his inheritance. In fact, more of his inheritance than he would have liked was already earmarked to said tailor; Byron began to contemplate the benefits of having a mending-woman as an accomplice instead of a Spanish swordsman.

"That is my fiancé you are talking about, my—" Byron stopped before he defended the honour of an undead prostitute. He instead decided to whine about how no one listened to the ends of his stories anymore, which were undeniably the best part. Like a petulant child, he poked and prodded his way through the forest, all the while complaining to himself about how excellent of a foil Marietta was to him, until he remembered just exactly how that foil had foiled his plans. But the cabbie hadn't tasted nearly half as good, and didn't soak up even half of his death like Marietta had...

No, he couldn't possibly like Marietta. That was just his

memory getting mixed up because of the Star; he was never quite himself for hours afterwards. It was only because of the similarity of their names—his long lost love's and Marietta's—and nothing more. No, nothing more at all.

By the time he caught up with the Spanish swordsman, he was out of breath and in sore need of a tailor. All of the Christina he had eaten earlier was not settling in his stomach after all the bouncing and churning of his midnight romp. Whenever he was this out of breath and it was this dark outside, it was almost always because of a woman.

"My sneezes—achoo!—'ave intensified—achoo! The beast must be close!" Aguacate said as he came to a small clearing before a man-high thicket of thorny branches and black roses intertwining, as if someone had planted a privacy hedge in the middle of the forest. Aguacate was just about to pull back some of the vines when Byron stopped him.

"These are Skeltering Hell Blossoms," Byron said, pulling Aguacate's hand away very slowly so as not to disturb any of the petals. "Grown only where vast volumes of Crosser blood have mingled with the local flora to produce an incredibly savage yet beautiful flower with a fragrance not unlike the last breath of a dying man—stale and finite, the last dissonant note of a violin as it is smashed by a music-loathing mongrel. The pollen itself is a powerful narcotic, sold in places like the Mephistopheles Market as a drug for exorbitant patricians. But one touch of those silken petals..." Here Byron pushed Aguacate hard. The thorns drew blood as he stumbled into the thicket and the petals of the roses brushed up against his exposed flesh. "Like a mere mortal toyed with by the King of Fairies and his mercurial Puck, you instantly fall in love with the first thing you see—don't look at me, you one-handed, tickle-nosed fop! Unlike in the play, however, it's a passion so intense that you begin to hate your very beloved, but are unable to break away, forever miserable and forever infatuated in your star-crossed love." Being careful of the blossoms himself, Byron parted the bushes. Christina was in the field with several other Star-Crossers, all digging avariciously at a fresh deer carcass with their clawed hands and bloody mouths. "Huh. Normally my puns are better thought out and less abstruse."

Aguacate stood up and, as he tried to brush the thorns out of his wounds, caught sight of Christina. By now, he knew that she was, indeed, a Star-Crosser, but did not care—but then again, cared too much, in such a way that then made him care less, but only in such a way as to allow him to care more. He went up to her and embraced her, getting deer brains all over his fine shirt and fine sword, and kissed her on the mouth just as she returned the favour. He sneezed in her face, spraying deer brains and saliva all over her, and she simply licked it up.

The other Seekers, however, still riled up from the Homunculus Star and just itching to Swarm, wanted to take a bite out of Aguacate in quite a less romantic manner. The wheels in Byron's head were churning as quickly as the movement of the Homunculus Star (shooting past the dark side of Venus by now) as he calculated how easily he could get rid of the bodies and escape the three large dogs and the three large men.

His best bet, he realised, was to save Hector, thereby winning the gratitude of the Hunter and counteracting the rumours about him somehow naturally being of the Crossed persuasion. He didn't care if people thought he was a Star-Crosser—indeed, he almost liked the comparison—but the idea that he had never been human maddened him to the point of pulling out his own fingernails. As if he wasn't good enough to be human or Star-Crosser, but was, like he had been for his entire life, something other. He wanted more than ever to reclaim his inheritance so he could ban the use of the word "disinherited" entirely by hiring goons to kick anyone who dared in the shins. Indeed, his inheritance would be enough to do that and much more.

He closed his eyes and reached inside himself to find that ravenousness touched by the passing of the Homunculus Star. That unfeeling part knew no pain or satisfaction or even the basic sense of touch—only hunger and the barren, gaping maw of death.

And then he skipped over his conscience and found the part of himself that was a Star-Crosser, and had been from the very day he was born.

It was as if he had planted his feet in the ground and started growing roots that searched through the earth like blind moles. As his psychic roots spread out and started blossoming under the Star-Crossers, those underling things stretching their undead limbs and mouths towards Aguacate, he began to see out of five different pairs of eyes, then seven, eight, fifteen, twenty-two. Forty-four arms came out of his twenty-two chests. He had become the goddess Kali that he had once seen in a gorgeous tapestry when he had been combing the Orient for his Uncle. As he tentatively took twenty-two single steps away from Aguacate, he looked at the heavens and thanked the Lighthouse that his puppets were relatively calm and had not yet smelled blood in the air. Once that happened, he would lose all control of them, and Aguacate would be torn to shreds. Admittedly, there was a chance that he could be included in this meat-grinding possibility; unlike him, however, Aguacate couldn't come back.

He ignored the pain shooting up his left arm as it decayed into slime-stained bone held together by a few rotting tendons and slips of gristle. But the pain shooting up his leg was new, and not entirely unlike the pain he woke up with this morning. As soon as he made them shamble off to a safe distance and stopped controlling them, his flesh would grow back almost like new—but this new, crippling aggression in his calf was troubling. He didn't have time to lean over and roll up his trouser leg, however, before he shooed the rest of the Star-Crossers away from Aguacate.

As Byron beamed with hubristic self-importance, he saw that Christina was holding two arms. She had taken them off a nearby wrecked Stumbler and was using them to defend Aguacate from the now-retreating hordes. Instead of congratulating him, his true saviour, Aguacate's eyes were shining with violent love at his blighted sweetheart and swimming with sickening appreciation.

When all the Star-Crossers had left, Byron collapsed in a heap on the ground, clutching at his ankle and wondering what exactly was happening. Aguacate gave Christina another large kiss on the mouth, this time taking a few teeth with him and spitting them out like white watermelon seeds. He kissed her hand, smacked her, then kissed her cheek. She demurely tried to pull his arms out of their sockets.

"Byron! In my country eet ees proper for someone to tell choo whan dey mean to apprehend choor fiancé and steal her for heemself. I must inform choo dat you have de right to challenge me to a duel if choo want to regain your precious betrothed, but I warn choo—"

"Yes!" Byron cried out in exasperated pain. "You are the best swordsman, having practised slicing off Star-Crosser heads since the time you were three and your first words were 'en garde!' I understand—but you can have her, my good man. She is yours and I shall not be reclaiming her anytime in the future…because she is dead. She is a Star-Crosser! The very thing you hate!"

"I know," Aguacate replied, looking back at Christina. "Isn't eet wonderful?" His triple sneeze blew away several chunks of her hair.

As the two of them galloped off into whatever sort of future they were going to have as a couple, Byron slowly peeled up his trouser leg to find that his right ankle was now swollen, gangrenously pulsating with what looked like embryonic bot-fly embedded underneath his skin.

He leaned back onto a nearby tree. His infection was spreading. Even with Marietta having absorbed the entirety of his decay, he was still falling apart.

In Which We Are Reunited with a Ginger Character (Or Three), Or: Byron's Got the Biggest Balls of Them All

"They were quite rapaciously snogging each other after I had dispatched thirteen or more unlucky Star-Crossers—"

"Back to Star-Crossers, are we? What about Rippers or Jack-Knifers? Or, considering your sudden unaccountable fascination with that horrible electricity, Shockers?"

"—with my blazing swiftness of foot, not unlike a winged Hermes, if, indeed, he were to cut down the undead with his caduceus instead of merely, um, holding it?"

"Holding caduceuses? Is that what they're calling it these days? How long was I gone exactly?"

"But holding it in a godlike way, as gods are wont to do— and it's caducei, by the way, my barking hyena. And the way that Christina and Aguacate were insatiably mashing at each other's lips, I was surprised that there were still lips to be had—on her end, not his, for why would his lips be falling off? Unless he were stricken with some sort of horrendous disease, like syphilis, only it strips your lips instead of your nose, like I saw in the Australian penal colony as it was ravaging those who had arrived by boat with their feet tied to large metal balls—"

"So the slang is not holding caducei—and how do you know the pluralisation of all of these obscure words, anyway?—but rather stripping noses or tying feet to metal balls? I was gone for a very long time, indeed. If I ever make it back to the girls at the Catscratcher District, they'll laugh me out of the wharfs."

"Exactly! They were snogging precisely like how you and I were snogging the second time we met," Byron said, drifting closer to Marietta as they followed the crowd of masked guests. The path leading to the large, gas-lit castle where the ball would be held was lined with thousands of delicately folded paper flowers. "How fortuitous that you should think now of the exact comparison I did then. Oh…" He paused to dig into the bottomless breast pocket of his tail-coat, where his pocket square would have resided had it not kept slipping into the void. "I remembered that you needed a new one of these." He pulled out a small ear and pushed back Marietta's hair to reattach it to her right side. "It may be a little small," he said, inspecting it from afar with his tongue poked out, moving his head side-to-side in order to examine the proportions and even sticking out his thumb to ensure levelness.

"You shouldn't have." Marietta's tone was flat. "I'll name my right ear Christina." She stopped and faced Byron until he forced her to look ahead again so he could continue checking. "That is who it came from, right?"

"We'll say yes because I don't remember the cabbie's name, and what fun would it be if we knew the names to all of your parts except for your ear? Though I suppose we could just call it Eustace," Byron said. Marietta narrowed her eyes and he stood back, aghast, a hand on his chest. "Dear singing uvulas, woman! Beyond the tympanic membrane is the Eustachian tube. Did they teach you nothing at assassination school? Though I suppose knowing who was doing the teaching and seeing him fried to a crisp makes your gaps of common knowledge understandable."

Marietta was about to respond when Byron cut her off with a slashing motion across his neck. (For once his left hand bore a man's glove, not a full-length lady's opera glove as he was accustomed to.) A masked couple in elaborate dress was passing. His wicked smile, full of teeth but devoid of any warmth, quickly unnerved the strangers and the man put a hand on his lady's back to hurry ahead. Once they were gone, the smile slipped and Byron knocked his top hat forwards, enshrouding what little of his face wasn't covered by Foster's long-nosed and hastily repaired mask. Marietta, on the other hand, was wearing a very decorous black-and-white dress replete with ruffles and whalebone and long, fingerless gloves.

Indeed, everyone else filtering into the paper-flower garden was wearing only those two colours. The men were resplendent in their coattails and shining top hats and the women were—well, dressed like Star-Crossers, some to exaggerated, comedic effect and others with shocking anatomical correctness. One particular lady wore a white gown that had been absolutely coated with a fine, slippery layer of red ink that was supposed to be blood, but was too red and too runny to be even halfway realistic. Another had attempted a decayed cheek, only for the make-up to smear until it looked as if her mask were Crossed and not her.

"Hacks, all of them," Byron muttered as they passed a couple where the man was wearing an equine mask and his companion was a dead jockey with a riding crop sticking through her chest. "And they do this in honour, not in jest. Could have fooled me."

Only the butlers were clad in pure white, with masks covered in vines that curled around their temples to hide the telltale straps. Every other butler lining the path held a tray full of snuff adulterated with powdered Star-Crosser teeth, so that with one inhale, the imbiber felt as if the entirety of his respiratory system was being chewed at and cleansed. Those who repeated the procedure—for it was a rather addictive rush—sometimes complained of their various body parts making chomping noises. Which, in a sense, was accurate; small Star-Crosser teeth formed in plaque-riddled passageways and ravenously tried to consume everything, but, being only a few teeth without gums or jaws, were rather ineffective. Byron took a pinch and inhaled with a sinus-rattling snort.

He never could get through a ball without some sort of drug to either keep him awake so as to enjoy the festivities or sedate him so as to better enjoy the festivities. His childhood had been filled with many such drab affairs, and he couldn't keep his bow tie straight enough or his coattails behind him enough in order to stop the twitching memories from seeping into his delicate plan. The last one he remembered had been held for his seventh birthday; one could imagine how hard it had been to procure biscuits laced with opium that still tasted like honey.

"These damned black and white masquerade balls! How horribly confusing it is for those who suffer from black-and-white blindness that doesn't allow them to see those two colours—"

"Shades," Marietta interjected.

"—and thus are confined to seeing black as a strange wobbly sort of chartreuse and white as a static-filled hot pink. My father, may the Great Sailor rest his poor, ravaged soul, was such a victim and therefore could never go to any sort of funeral where the company was wearing all black, because he would burst out that they all looked like sun-beaten tomatoes bleached by an inexperienced washerwoman. He was kicked out of my grandfather's—the illustrious Maximilian Norish Llewellyn-Cave, thank you for asking—wake because of his unseemly outbursts."

"That explains so much," Marietta remarked as she trundled along, occasionally misstepping or almost tripping over her own feet. "I think this is the first time I've ever heard you talk about your father, lie or not."

"You impugn my honour with your idle tongue! My father was the best of us all, killed horribly when he forgot that his wife had been turned into a Star-Crosser and went in to kiss her one morning, encountering her hungry maw in place of petal-soft lips. After that, my Uncle had the two of them burned at the stake, forcing me to watch so I would never have the same lapse of memory as my father. Though what damage could have been done by such an innocent mistake in temporal cohesiveness, now that the bodies of my very biological parents were charred away into nothing more than ash?"

"I can't even tell if that's a lie or the truth, it's so disturbing."

"My honour!" he snapped back.

"Is so neglected that it's beginning to wilt. Nothing I say or do is going to make a damn difference. Does it look like I have a watering can?"

"Hidden beneath the folds of your skirt, I've no doubt you have at least twenty different weapons. And I assume that in assassination school they did teach you how to kill someone with a watering can, given the opportunity."

"Yes, the class was called Tenderising the Garden—"

"Invitation?" the last of the white-clad, forest-themed butlers asked, holding out his gloved hand and looking above their heads at the amassing crowd. Byron gave Marietta a squinting glare out of the corner of his eye and started patting down all of his pockets. However, his hand never strayed to the pocket sewn into his left sock for the direst of emergencies—for what sort of gentleman reaches into his sock at such an elegant ball, and further, what sort of gentleman allows his hand to drift further down than his elbow into such a well-hidden pocket? Byron prided himself on knowing all the etiquette befitting his station and always took the opportunity to show others his enlightenment. He saw himself as a Calvinist of propriety.

"Dear me," Byron cried out in faux alarm. "I seem to have misplaced the thing. But never mind that, I am a close, personal family friend of the Velos and—"

"Without an invitation, you'll have to step out of line and go back home," the butler responded, yawning as if he had seen it all before.

"My florid-faced manservant, do you not recognise me?"

The butler gave Byron the look of a saint's statue frowning at the orgy going on in front of him. Between his very large, shiny black top hat, the long-nosed mask that hid the better part of his face, the crude tattoo that had been hastily drawn on with a mixture of ash and spit (and had smeared in their rush towards the party), and the stubble he had tried to grow in so as to further resemble Foster, the butler would have had no chance of recognising him had he been the Queen of England.

"I," Byron replied, puffing himself up and bumping his chest into the torso of the butler, "am none other than the Heretic."

He heard Marietta slap herself in the forehead behind him. He kicked her in the shin to remind her that she was not to speak nor make any human gestures if they were going to pull off their con artisanship later that night.

"Nice costume," the butler said to the rag-tag Marietta. Other than her fancy dress, she was a mere skeleton held together by loose tendons and lackluster tissue. Byron was saddened by the fact that her immensely green pallor ruined the black-and-white effect, but she did look positively ghastly when all of the other women merely looked somewhat spooky. Egged on by the butler's comment, he took a step into the part and was stopped by a large arm.

Byron smiled again as the butler motioned to two very large men holding two large blunderbusses with shining brass muzzles. He may not have known as much about weaponry as his companion, but he knew the Guard when he saw them, even when they, too, were masked like the butlers and dressed all in black.

Marietta began coughing behind him—something that a Star-Crosser had been known to do on occasion. As she hacked, she hung onto his arm to get closer to his ear.

"Hggggffff—bwaaaakkk—kwoffff—Tesla—" He smacked her on the back until he realised what she was saying while trying to reattach her finger without anyone noticing.

"Ah, yes!" Byron said, whipping off of his top hat to show his hair, which they had dusted with flour to grey it. A misty cascade followed the arc of his head as he bowed. "Silly me! Of course no one else calls me the Heretic to my face! That was just a joke betwixt friends. And what need do friends have of twixes?" When the butler continued to stare with righteous indignation, Byron dropped the smile and stepped very close. "I am the Conductor of Tesla's Trucklers for the Advancement of the Electric Engine, and if you, sir, presume to stop me from entering the party into which I have been invited by the Archduke Velo himself, you will not only be the first person whom I reanimate with my electrical arc…uh…thingy," he said, springing out his wire-covered right hand and deftly playing a small lightning bolt between his fingers, "even though you are not dead yet, but also one of the first to smell yourself cooking and be able to describe it to your friends at a later date—and possibly, if enough time passes, with amusement instead of abject horror!" Byron cocked the top hat forwards again and cleared his throat. "Rather reminds me of a time when my best friend tried to sneak onto a pirated trolleybus when the only change he had was the remnants of a dog biscuit, and he bluffooned his way onto the decks by promising to show him his trick where he would roll over and do an immaculate imitation of a dying cockroach—"

"Haaaaaaaaaack!" Marietta coughed again, pushing him inside as the butler wiped a fine sheen of sweat off his brow and let the last few stragglers of the evening into the ballroom.

"Did you just call me a hack?" Byron had a chance to say before they were both awed by the spectacular scenery.

The entire hall was decorated in thousands of crisply folded paper cranes that had been strung from the ceiling with invisible wire, so as to look as if they were floating. Curtains of cranes hung from the dark wooden rafters forty feet above their heads all the way to the floor, separating the dancing hall, the cards tables, the dining area, and the entertainment. Beyond the paper wonders, painted into the ceilings and curling halfway down the walls, were sky-blue murals populated with every cloud formation seen by human eyes.

"Let us do hope they don't employ any fire-jugglers at this particular party, or if they do, the cranes are non-combustible," Byron whispered, still under the spell of the enchanting décor.

All of the guests were in their finest jewellery and dresses. The women wore feathers and tight-fitted corsets and layers and layers of petticoats—underneath the Crosser make-up—so that they resembled the paper cranes come to unlife (albeit drained of colour). The men were handsome in their cornered suits and boots that rode up to their knees and flickered with the curved reflections of the low gaslights. High laughter and shrill screams echoed through the hallways, dampened by a soft crinkling as the papers shuffled against each other.

Byron scanned the room for the Archduke as he came to yet another butler, who demanded to know his name so he could announce him to the rest of the guests. As he and Marietta walked down a series of spiral staircases and into the ballroom proper, he heard from the rafters:

"The Glorious Conductor of Tesla's Trucklers, not to be confused with the Inglorious Mangler of Tesla's Treacles, which is a different thing entirely," the announcer said. Byron had been mouthing the words and nodding with as much fatherly pride as he could with Marietta attached to his side. "And guest: the lovely Miss Greta Blanche von Eustace."

He felt a small punch to the back of his arm. He very deftly popped off another one of Marietta's fingers to let her know that he did not appreciate her touching him, his familiarity with her earlier had been a mistake, and he would just as easily put her back into that rancid closet as a skeleton for another three months if she did not cooperate to her fullest extent. As a waiter passed by, he picked up a flute of champagne and quickly deposited Marietta's finger into an empty glass. The waiter continued on as if nothing out of the ordinary had happened.

"A very elaborate prop, my good sir," Byron explained, patting the waiter rambunctiously hard on the back.

Byron took a few spins around the dance floor by himself, waiting. It wasn't until a few seconds later that they heard the screams and Byron smiled, stuck out his elbow in a jovial stance, and invited his red-headed companion to scour the crowd while they spun. He downed the champagne and threw the glass to the floor. A few of the guests glanced over at its shattering pop; he sneered at them and grabbed at Marietta's arm to tug her through the amassing crowd.

"Come, Miss von Eustace! This party is entirely too prosaic for us! Let us see if we can find some culture in the other, better rooms," Byron said in a haughty tone—one he had perfected when he and his best friend had indulged in a contest about who could be haughtier, though he had had to bow out as his best friend had misunderstood and started to build a bonfire around his feet. Once they were in the hallway, he pulled his companion close and began whispering in her ear: "I know it's rude to speak ill of the dead, but do the same rules apply if I am speaking as the dead? Out of everyone here, we are probably the only ones close enough to actually do it. Now, on top of ruining Foster's reputation, we must find the Archduke and make an even bigger scene." The girl leaned over and tried to bite at the outreached arm of another patron, who was looking for another snuff of crushed Star-Crosser teeth. He smacked her on the back of the hand. "I know I told you to act like a Stumbler, but dear, not until we've found the Archduke." He then squinted at her masked face. "Didn't you just have one violet and one blue eye a second ago?"

She growled at him and gave his shoulder a small, sopping kiss; when she pulled back, a thin line of spittle drifted between the two of them. Byron patted her on the head and pushed her away, still keeping a hand on her so as to restrain her from attacking the other guests. As it happened, the latest dance craze was to keep a stiff arm around the upper part of your partner's arm, so his tight grip didn't seem extraordinary to any other guests. Indeed, Byron even overheard someone comment upon his skillful style when he heard a familiar sneeze.

Hector Aguacate was coming towards him. The Spaniard carried a flute of champagne as well and was darting through the droves of condensed people to make his way to the couple. He was a fencing master, after all, so his deftness was unparalleled as he wafted through the ladies and gentlemen. Unfortunately, his hooked hand kept snagging on their gossamer fabrics and he had to continually stop to excuse himself, sneezing all the while, as he made his interminable way towards the impatient Byron.

"Choo dere! I say, choo dere good sir!" he cried out, tripping over the train of a lady's dress and flinging himself into Byron's arms. "Are choo de eenfamous Heretic—I mean," the man replied, blushing at his social faux pas, "Glorious Conductor of Tesla's Trucklers? Chor experiments into dat positively apostate method of energy h'are dazzling. Achoo! Excuse me, I seem to be allergic to something. Has my fiancé been asking choo about chor incredeeblay discoveries has well?"

"Fiancé?" Byron responded, looking around the room for Christina, wondering if her affections for him had worn off. Which was ridiculous, of course; no woman could resist him, alive or dead, with or without his necromantic skills. Even said skills were a draw to the ladies, though some were squeamish about such things—which was, the more he thought about it, understandable, as necromancers were not usually known to be very good people. Then his indignation at Aguacate having stolen his previous fictional fiancé flared again. "My dear Aguacate, you may have snatched my lover once before, but I shall be a twice-blasted cuckold if you—" Something bumped into his shoulder and another slobber-filled kiss left his sleeve sopping. He remembered that he was no longer Byron, but Foster the Heretic. "I apologise, sir, for my outburst. I was hit by a stray arc of lightning a while back and it has since caused me to adopt the personalities of those I have recently met. As I have recently met that gorgeous man Mr. Byron Ulysses Llewellyn-Cave, I cannot help but channel his essence in moments of extreme emotion. You should have seen me after I met the second cousin to the Earl of Rochester; I was twittering like a pregnant horse, hee-hawing my way through the uncouth and decrepit hallways of my vastly unclean estate. Between you and me," Byron said, leaning in close to Aguacate, who began to sneeze almost uncontrollably, "I believe it to be infected by disease-ridden Teacup-Filching Rats." He patted the long nose of his mask meaningfully.

"Uh, yes," Aguacate replied, trying to inch closer to Byron's companion. "I do apologise for my sneezing. Usually I'm only like dhis when I'm around Star-Crossers—achoo! Do choo think cho'll be able to give us a demonstration of your power later dhis evening? I know the Archduke would be delighted to see chor work and anything eet may accomplish een the realm of fighting de monstrosities dat are growing so bold as to overrun our civilisation wit dheir flesh-eating treachery."

Aguacate slipped his arm around his own companion's waist as Byron wondered if that was some strange Spanish way of greeting the female gender. He decided to play it humble to get a better reaction.

"Oh, I don't know if the Archduke would be interested in such trifling upheavals of everything we hold sacred and true. Given the context, it might feel almost like a cheap party trick."

"Oh, no! Never!" Aguacate protested. "I am a very good friend of de Archduke and he ees very interested een what choo and chor comrades have been researching h'out een de forests. Besides, eet will take his mind ohff ohf more concerning matters."

"Yes," Byron proclaimed, continuing to push people out of the way and leading the other two over to the buffet table. He began nibbling at various exotic fruits crushed between sprightly biscuits and roasted meats with nose-drenching spices, only to put them back on the table marred with teeth marks and slobber for others to discover. "I have heard of the unfortunate disappearance of his wife, the Heelduchess Judith. Have there been any further inquiries as to what exactly may have happened?"

"Unforchoonately, no. I haf been commissioned for de upcoming search party, but de outlook ees rather grim, as she has been missing for more dhan four weeks now. The good news ees, none of de local Guard have seen a Star-Crosser matching her description; if she ees dead, at least dere ees nothing left ohf her to come back. Which is why we held dhis ball in her honour and why everyone ees dressing up like de Star-Crossed. Eet ees to make her feel at home if she has been turned."

"Well, when we see the Archduke, I will tell him that I, too, am willing to enlist all of my services and men in order to help in her search as well," Byron responded, licking his fingers and then going through a small pile of grapes until he found the one he wanted at the very bottom of the bowl.

"Oh, no, no, no. I will have to introduce choo, ohf course. De Archduke never just casually accepts people into his circle."

"Even if I control the very essence of god-like lightning itself?" Byron skewered a pig ear and began chewing the cartilage with loud pops. He then stuck a hand in his mouth and adjusted his loose tooth with a squelch.

"Amazing. De shock choo took even makes choo mimic Byron's gestures? I saw heem do de exact same thing when I stole his fiancé!"

"Is it normal in your culture to widely proclaim one's cuckoldry?" Byron whispered conspiratorially. "We Brits tend to be a little bit more subtle and stiff-upper-lipped about the whole process."

"Ah ha!" Aguacate honked and slapped Byron on the back, making him spit out a full half of the pig ear. It landed on the plate of a large-busted woman sporting a beehive hairdo, filled with actual bees in a delicate framework of close-knit chicken wire. "I will introduce choo! Hector Aguacate—achoo achoo achoo!— knows no fear ohf awkward social situations! Allow me to find de Archduke and I will present him to choo!"

"You mean, me to him? I, of course, already know the man. It is quite the opposite that needs to happen," Byron intoned, pulling Aguacate close. The Spaniard nodded, causing his hook to clink against his sword scabbard, then clicked his heels together and spirited himself away in search of the Archduke.

"Excellent," Byron whispered into his plate of food, then threw it onto the ground again and looked up for Marietta. He saw the back of Aguacate weaving through the crowd with another red-headed lady that he assumed was Christina. He sidled over to Marietta to reconnoitre.

"Can you believe our luck? Of course, the Fates themselves are on our side, given that I am fighting for the restoration of my good name and my inheritance, which was so rudely and inappropriately taken away from me at such a young age, when I had no means to defend myself. And Aguacate was a bit handsy, too, don't you believe?"

Marietta looked at Byron with a cocked eyebrow and a questioning glance.

"Weren't your eyes brown just a second ago?" Byron asked as they wallowed through the crowd. "I know we've been through several sets, but honestly, I can't for the life of me remember what colour they naturally were."

Marietta continued to glance at him with a dry expression and a lined mouth. Finally she shrugged her shoulders and grabbed at a passing waiter for another flute of champagne. Byron stopped suddenly in his weaving and his companion ran into him, dislodging his top hat and making him cringe as he bent over to pick it up. He clutched his right calf and then forcibly straightened his features and body, not letting anyone know the extent of his pain—least of all the person standing right across from him.

Byron could scarcely believe the sound he made: a low growl, rising from his chest. He cleared his throat and realised that the sound was not coming from him. He blinked around to see his red-headed companion snarling at their adversary, the unexpected Spittle. He put an arm on her to keep her from doing anything rash before they met the Archduke.

"Marietta, my dear, you are a much better actor after being locked away for three months," he whispered. "Although I suppose if I couldn't speak or move or do anything but think during that whole time, I, too, might become more adept at monologuing—but just because you can doesn't mean you should. A great part of acting is timing, my dear thaumaturgic thespian. Don't strut and fret before your time is ready. And green eyes now? Didn't you just have heterochromia a second ago, followed by brown eyes?" He leaned in closer as she began to grab at the air in front of their foe. "And besides, you saved this wretched creature, so now you have to face the consequences. Horrifying, isn't it? Which is why I never leave anything dangling: plot lines, enemies, modifiers—"

"Who you calling a grammatical error?" their enemy yelled, spitting in their general direction.

"What devilish sphincter did you crawl out of, poor boy?" Byron spat back. His hand was still on his companion's shoulder, holding her back as she growled and snapped. Their interlocutor snarled back. Byron thought that the harshest insult known to man was to call someone poor; without the power of wealth, one was nothing more than a dust mote in the trash bin of history, liable to be swept up by a newfangled automatic steam-powered street sweeper known to take off dirty limbs if the walker hadn't bathed within three and a half days.

"Poor'n'Shoeless? What wanker dares to call a Spittle shoeless? Do you not eyeball these fine stitched tree limbs? I mean..." Spittle cleared his throat, pulling off his brass pince-nez and buffing the lenses on his jewel-encrusted vest. "My dear sir, you do impugn my honour with your hurtful words. May I ask the name of you, sir, so I may redress you in public?" The young boy was cleaned up, his hair slicked down without even a trace of fish bones or chicken skin. His mouth was clear of acidic slaver and a set of veneers had been attached to his teeth to hide the damage from all of his tongue chewing. In effect, the boy was an entirely new man, except for the fact that he wasn't a man just yet. He started to take off one spotless white glove; he would have to jump in order to slap Byron's stubbled chin, but it was a faux pas he was willing to commit.

Byron had once again forgotten that he was acting as Foster, the Heretic of Tesla's Trucklers, and allowed his hatred of his foe to overwhelm his logic. It was his turn to clear his throat and begin to pull off his own glove, only to realise that the only glove he had on was the one covering his left hand. Although it was only a minor affliction at the moment, there was still a tinge of gangrene hanging about the beds of his fingernails and a flap of loose skin that revealed the muscles of his metacarpals. He went to pull off his companion's glove instead and came back with her full hand, which he was about to throw when Spittle stepped forwards and peered up at Byron's face under the bottom of his mask.

"I just saw Mr. Aguacate running off towards the Archduke, blathering about some electrical experiments to be conducted by the Conductor himself. What a surprise it will be for all if I tell him that his Conductor is nothing but an insulated fool known as Byron Ulysses Llewellyn-Cave, the disappointment of ages. You know, they still tell stories about you and your disgrace. In my previous circle, we would call you a carriage-licking comb-over. The worst of all possible insults."

Byron wondered at how well Spittle had cleaned up. Or at least, he would have, had the mention of his ignominy at the hands of his blasphemously unfair Uncle not enraged him. It took a few seconds to restrain himself from taking a bite out of Spittle's good leg; the other was a puffing, steaming, state-of-the-art clockwork limb. Such a fine display of technology could have only come from his Uncle.

"Posh, you ragged, day-old pastry! I don't know what you're doing here and I don't see how a little crumbly, hard-around-the-edges, inappropriate starch like you thinks he has any rapport with the Archduke anyhow! He'll flick you off like a spot of jam stuck in his beard and you'll land in a newspaper that can soak up your sob story about how poor disinherited Byron was mean to you. Maybe you'll even learn a better vocabulary from the harrowing experience, too!"

"I'd forgotten how convoluted your metaphors can be," Spittle responded, picking at his nails as he walked closer. His clothes were immaculate, his hair was oiled in the latest coiffure, complete with waxed, and shaped sideburns, and his mask sported enough jewels to feed a small country. Provided, of course, that the country's inhabitants could digest rubies and sapphires and emeralds; everyone knew that diamonds were unpalatable and tasteless, even to the most cast-iron of stomachs. "I, I'll have you know, am the adopted son of the Archduke Velo and heir to his entire fortune, fame, and name." He lowered his voice so that no one else could hear. "When the batty trophy finally meets the Yawny Lord and sleeps with the wormies, I'll be the one picking up the royal pieces and piecing 'em into a newspaper cake."

"Adopted?" Byron felt sweat start underneath his armpits and down the middle of his back. The Archduke was a very influential person, and if Spittle had any sort of influence over him, it placed Byron's inheritance that much further out of his grasp. His fingers couldn't get any longer without breaking some bones—and they would not be his own.

"You are looking," Spittle said, glancing around and puffing his chest out, "at the world's best son. Even got me a mug that says so."

"I'll give your mug something else to say in a second," Byron responded, arcing the electricity across his hand and balling it. "With my fist!" He felt a touch and looked back to see that his companion was holding his arm, shaking her head. He lowered his arm; the guests around them were staring and whispering. "You're right. The whole 'with my fist' was a little too overdone. It was inherent in what I was going to do, considering the intensity of my actions, and I made the fatal mistake of narration in a crucial action scene. I apologise." He bowed to Spittle a bit and made a reassuring face. "With my other fist! Didn't see that coming!" His decayed left hand struck the living flesh of Spittle's cheek with a wet smack, sending the small boy flying. The adopted heir landed in a crouch and brought his hand up to wipe the blood away from the corner of his mouth. What looked to be a palm-sized rock flew out of his pocket and landed between them with a clatter. "No teeth?" Byron said, disappointed when Spittle stood up and only spat out a small spot of blood. "I always do enjoy hearing teeth rattling around things that aren't mouths."

Behind him, his companion let out a vicious snarl.

Everyone in the room had frozen. Champagne glasses were raised halfway to mouths, appetisers were sliding off small crackers and hitting the floor with wet, slobbery plops, arms were raised in salute or in dance at awkward angles, and all eyes were on Byron. They all swung around, however, to watch a red-headed blur race after the small boy, who picked up his rock and fled from the room.

Byron cleared his throat, letting the electricity fade from his palm, and clasped both hands behind his back. He rocked on the balls of his feet in a preponderance of exasperated thought about how each of his three companions in the past three months had abandoned him—running away to their deaths, falling in love with Spanish swordsmen, chasing off after young boys. A lesser man might have thought himself deficient in some way. Byron, however, merely shrugged, drained another flute of champagne, threw the empty glass on the floor, and stormed into the next room, where

Aguacate had prepared the Archduke and a few other important personages for him.

Byron entered the room with a dramatic sweep of his arms, startling a few older ladies with salt-and-pepper hair into spilling dabs of their tea on their fancy dresses. He was about to close the doors when a flustered Marietta rushed through and curtseyed for her lateness. He made eye contact with her and cleared his throat.

"Did you finish giving Spittle his dental check-up?"

Marietta looked confused.

"You know, knock out any teeth? Check for any fist-related cavities?"

She furrowed her eyebrows.

"What was it that he dropped out of his pocket, anyway? Looked like some kind of rock."

Her eyes grew big.

"Weren't your eyes green just a few seconds…" He trailed off as he remembered that everyone else could hear them. One of the tea-stained ladies huffed in his direction as if he had insulted her mother viciously and personally. Three men squinted at him through their cigar smoke. Two other red-headed ladies in corsets and dangling flesh looked back through black feathered masks.

His mind snapped together like Star-Crossed cogs bursting through the back of a grandfather clock in search of clock faces to eat. (He had once overheard about such a thing through a crack in the wall of a dining room where they served foods that began with the letter R only to people who could prove that they were rather famous criminals in their past lives. The restaurant boasted that they had served the likes of Brutus, Genghis Khan, and Ivan the Terrible. Their house specialty was Roasted Rabbit with Ravioli in Red Sauce, which happened to be his favourite dish.

He had claimed to be the tenth reincarnation of Philip Herbert, the Seventh Earl of Pembroke, but was quickly kicked out when it was discovered that his mathematics had been severely off and he spent the rest of the night combing through the trashcan before thusly hearing said conversation through the copper pipes of the building.)

Byron narrowed his eyes at his own red-headed companion. She took her ordained spot in the corner of the room and waited, staring ever so slightly at the other two women, who didn't look like her at all save for the red hair. Not even their dresses matched. He had been talking to all three that very night, thinking them to be Marietta. One—the brown-eyed broad—was clearly Christina, but the other's identity continued to elude him. It was the violet-eyed one, the one who couldn't possibly be here, that buzzed around his brain like a half-remembered song.

"Señor Foster!" Aguacate nervously patted down his trousers as he stood up and pulled Christina along with him. She made a vague notion towards his neck before kissing it and losing a tooth in the process. A flap of skin from her cheek peeled away to show two rows of greenish teeth, blackened gums, and a wart-riddled tongue that lolled around and spattered brown-specked drool. "Aye didn't think that choo were going to show up so quickly. Please allow me to introduce choo to—"

The largest man in the room stood up, his lacy geyser of ruffles almost taking the front of the table with him. He sniffled, walrus moustache twitching, so that it looked less like its namesake and more like a beached whale struggling to breathe. The distinct sound of a hissing, gear-turning crunch told Byron that this man had a clockwork leg almost equal to Spittle's in calibre and ostentatiousness. He narrowed his eyes behind his mask and tipped his hat forwards even more.

"Never mind that!" The large man pushed out his chair with his voluminous backside and waddled towards Byron. "I have heard so much about you, I've practically been dying to meet you. I've been starved for a good conversation with someone who has a differing opinion on just exactly how this entire Star-Crossing infestation began in the first place! I'm curious, Doctor: How exactly did you word your conjectures again on the disintegration of higher functions between the 'Seeker' and 'Stumbler' stages? The conclusions you draw between the related intensification of tissue rot, especially in the post-primordial conditions, are so eloquent— I'd rather my guests hear it from your mouth than mine."

"To answer your question: very monkishly. But that is not the reason I am here, Archduke Velo. I have heard about the unfortunate circumstances of your wife's disappearance and I am here to offer you a trade."

The Archduke's face grew even more florid. Byron could not help but liken it to a teapot, then wondered when the ladies' cups were going to be refilled with the snot boiling over into Velo's moustache.

"If you, sir, have any information regarding the disappearance of my wife, you had best give it to me before I—"

"Not only do I have information, my dear bicycle, I have your actual wife!" Byron spread his arms wide again and Marietta stood up in the corner, whipped her mask off, and made a beeline to the Archduke, holding her arms at odd angles and gurgling noises that might have been, "I love you"—or, more discernibly, "I love food."

The entire room gasped. One of the salt-and-pepper ladies fainted into her teacup, causing a small storm of brown bubbles to erupt from her nose. The cigar-smoking men choked on their own smoke and frantically fanned at the air. The only two not to react were Christina and the mysterious red-headed lady. Christina was gnawing at the edge of a table, perhaps mistaking the wood grain for a nice, brown, wrinkled brain. The other woman was staring intently at the crouched figure of Spittle, so that Byron could see only her throat and the bottom of her chin; a discoloured purplish-green, like a two-day-old bruise, was beginning to snake its way up her throat.

"You—you—you—!" The Archduke was curling his fingers as if Byron's neck was in their grasp instead of across the room. Or perhaps, Byron thought, he was trying to massage the air itself into corporeality so that it would do his bidding—which was, at that precise moment, to pull out every strand of hair on Byron's body with blunt tweezers dipped in the juice of the world-renowned Toledan Spectre Chili, one of the hottest peppers known to mankind's collective tongue.

"I did nothing of the sort. I simply found her; she was already in this state. And if you have been paying attention to my recent claims of undoing the damage of Star-Crossing with my electrical studies, you would stop wriggling your fingers about—you're confusing your wife into thinking that they're worms, look, she's practically salivating—and listen to what I have to say."

The Archduke slapped his arms down to his sides, defeated. Byron inspected his nails, chewed off a particularly bothersome hangnail, and started buffing them against his shirt. It wasn't until he had gotten halfway through shining his right hand that the Archduke burst out into a stream of such vulgar oaths that even Marietta blushed. (Which, as everyone knows, is actually not exceptionally difficult, and can be attributed to the lack of pigment in her undead cheeks rather than a true blush.)

"Well, what the devil are you waiting for? Speak up!" the Archduke said, after finishing the sticky strings of profanity that left his mouth dry.

"No, I think you need to wait a few minutes more."

It took another ten minutes to calm the Archduke down so that he could listen without the threat of apoplexy.

"In exchange for giving your wife her life back—literally—I ask only one simple favour. Rumour has reached my ears," Byron said, having pulled up a very large smoking chair with three layers of plush seating, and hanging one leg off one of the arms and his other around one of the chair's own legs, "that you are in contact with the elusive Archibald Llewellyn-Cave. I'd like information as to his whereabouts for, uh, personal matters. For a simple scrap of paper with his location, I will imbue your wife with the life that was so wrongfully taken from her by the teeth of a ferocious Star-Crosser."

"Doctor," the Archduke responded.

"Yes?"

"Not you—Dr. Archibald Llewellyn-Cave. You will give the man proper respect when addressing him."

Byron narrowed his eyes; the sting of epiphanous rumination hit him for the second time in as many quarter-hours.

"To the parlour!" Byron cried. He pointed one finger up in the air and started marching in the direction of what he perceived to be the correct hallway. He had been walking for three minutes, with only a slightly stumbling Marietta lagging behind, before he realised that no one else had followed him. He popped his head back into the room where everyone else was still reclining—or, in the case of one of the salt-and-pepper ladies, still treading tea in their teacups—and demanded again that they follow him.

"But, sir," one of the mustachioed smokers squeaked in between inhalations, "we are in the parlour!"

"Really?" Byron looked around at the ceiling and in the

corners, even scratching the wallpaper with one of his fingernails. "This just seems more like a foyer or a salon or, at best, a den. I was once in the parlour of the Queen of Falkland for an entire afternoon and found that each individual crystal in its seventeen chandeliers boasted the initials of the Queen's many lovers, painstakingly engraved with the vibrations created from said nocturnal friction, and here I see nary a chandelier with even a string of crystal! And besides that, a parlour would need more…paisley."

Narrowing his own eyes, the Archduke responded, "Why, in all that is holy, alive, and Uncrossed do you need to be in a parlour? Can't you please just turn my wife back to normal, and I'll tell you where the good Doctor is and we can all continue on with our lives as if we had never met?"

"Elementary, my dear watt—by the way, did you know that is what electricity is measured in? Everyone here is not who they say they are, which, colloquially speaking, means that there is something very much afoot—" He cut himself off.

A small rabbit had hopped into the centre of the room. It twitched its little bunny face and looked directly into his eyes. After a few seconds, there was a small popping noise and all that remained of the rabbit was its foot, a quivering glob of speckled phlegm, and quickly dissipating fog. Byron mumbled to himself: "Who would have ever thought that my magic would last that long?" Then much louder, to everyone: "Grab the nearest piece of furniture and follow me!"

He picked up a small gas-lamp stand and started walking out of the room, towards what he assumed was an exit leading to the field behind the expansive, isolated mansion, but still close enough to the railroad to facilitate his escape. (Byron never went anywhere without first researching how far away he was from the nearest fast-moving vehicle, whether it be a train, a steamcar, or even a gouty, three-legged ex-racehorse with one eye.)

This time when no one followed him, he popped his head back to see that the salt-and-pepper lady who had collapsed into the teapot was being eaten from the left foot up by the rest of the Star-Crossed Long-Eared Legion. There was barely even that much left of some of the other guests. Only teeth and diamonds remained where dukes, earls, viscounts, and even chimney sweeps had stood; all were reduced to their molars and a few bloody scraps of clothing. The few guests still alive were screaming and running around the room until Byron halted them with a loud whistle.

"If you want to live, you will grab the nearest piece of furniture and follow me. There is a train departing from a station not far from here, and it is our only chance of survival."

Marietta picked up a small footrest covered with blue velvet and golden tassels and marched towards Byron with an eager look on her half-decayed face. The others merely continued to stare in horror or tried to climb up the walls, since Byron and Marietta were blocking the only exit that wasn't covered with swarming killer bunnies. One of the smokers tried to put his cigarette out in the back hind leg of the nearest Star-Crossed rabbit, only for the creature to dodge his blows and chomp with its little buck teeth at the man's left foot.

"Why do we need the furniture?" one of the other smokers asked, getting up as quickly as possible after seeing what was happening to his compatriot. By now the old woman who had fallen into her tea was nothing more than a leering skeleton, and even that was being picked apart and scattered amongst the twitchy-nosed killers.

"Because I've always wanted to have a parlour scene and I can't have one without the parlour! And since we must evacuate and I cannot bring along the physical parlour, I need the furniture at the very least!"

No one picked anything up.

"Because it'll save you. I have wiped down all of the furniture here with the elusive Dead Man's Tongue Oil, vine-ripened and aged with an assortment of wilted lettuce, foetid carrots, and eau de lupe, a specialty of mine specifically chosen for its ability to repel the Long-Eared Legion! If you keep it within a hare-span of your body, the Legion will not attack you—but only if the pieces are in the air! The cologne won't disperse unless you lift it up!"

Within seconds everyone had snatched up the furniture around them, some even going so far as to fight over a small table, cracking it in two so that each ended up with a broken leg. The guests started following Byron out the back entrance of the mansion. Down the hallways they could hear the tortured screams of those being eaten, and more than once their path was blocked by several corpses that looked hale from the waist up, but whose lower halves were nothing more than gnawed bones barely held together by cartilage and tendon. As they trundled along, a body was propelled through the servants' quarters, hit the wall, and exploded into a shower of splintered bone. Marietta stopped to suck on some marrow before Byron picked her up by the arm and shoved her in front of the furniture parade with the small pull-out drawer attached to his stand. He then used it to clobber a few rabbits out of the way.

It wasn't until they got outside into the brisk night air that Byron took the lead. He used his end table to push forwards through the high grass and dry reeds, allowing the others to follow in a straight line after him.

They had almost made it to the raised train tracks behind the mansion when Byron set down his end table, wiped his brow—

digging underneath the mask to dab at the ring of sweat that had formed there—and scraped a small hole into the hillside in an attempt to stabilise the piece of furniture so he could sit down. Again he splayed his limbs every which way and laid his posterior upon the table so that it began to believe it was, in fact, an end table in the most literal sense. The others behind him kept on glancing over their shoulders, afraid and incensed at the delay, certain that every flutter and rustle of the reeds was the Long-Eared Legion come to eat them in this darkest hour.

"I can still hear them!" one of the smokers said. Reluctant to give up his cigar, he had put it in the band around his top hat, so that he carried a smouldering light and the stench of burning fabric.

"No one has ever escaped from the Long-Eared Legion! Why are we stopping?" one of the ladies cried out, clinging to the elbow of the Archduke and nestling herself in the crook of his armpit.

"I beg to differ, my illustrious pit viper! The wondrous and melodious Byron Ulysses Llewellyn-Cave once escaped from the death that stares from those beady red eyes, from the very clutches of the Legion's alpha male—"

"Rabbits don't have alpha males," the mysterious ginger with the bruise on her neck said. It was the first time Byron had heard her speak that night. He paused only slightly to tell her with his eyes that of course rabbits had alpha males, and if she wanted to discuss the pack structures of the lesser Sciuridae, there was a private room—actually, just a spot behind the curtains that a smallish man with a bright, shiny bald head was holding about him like an elaborate paisley toga—where he could spend all night discussing biological matters with her. She shot him a return look that said rabbits were in the Leporidae family, a fact he should well know.

"Regardless," he continued, looking away from the

mysterious lady and sweeping his top hat off again, releasing another culinary reaction of a cloud of flour into the air, "that wonderful boy escaped, and just a few short months ago, told me the secret of how he survived. I found it so brilliant, I almost never wanted to hear another story in my lifetime, as I knew it would never live up to his. And that's including my best friend's story of the time he washed up on a desert island and had to use coconut water as a blood transfusion after getting into a row with a coconut crab, in which he defended his honour using only a rusty fork with two missing prongs—it was a relish fork, mind you—and a pair of shoelaces."

A loud whistle sounded to the east. The dark outline of a train began to encroach on the horizon.

"I do believe our ride is here!" Byron replaced the top hat with a pat that sent flour gushing out the sides of his ears, as if there were a small train inside his head letting off its own steam.

"It's not going to stop for us out in the middle of nowhere! And there's no way we can get to a station before those beasts catch up with us!" the smoking man said, still unaware that his hat was smouldering. The ginger woman knocked it off his head and began stamping it out, to much guffawing and pishposhing from the old man. "My hat!"

"Ladies and gentlemen! Archduke!" Byron replied. Thinking that he had already swept off his hat, he flourished his hands and sent another cascade of flour into the air with a resounding, hollow thunk. "I have taken care of everything!"

The rumbling of the train grew louder. All of the guests began to feel its vibrations crawl up their feet and into their calves as the dark, sleek object grew on the horizon. Byron stepped sideways to reveal three small babies tied to the tracks. They wriggled in the moonlight; the harsh locomotive's headlamp cast long shadows against the shifting basket in which they were encased. There were several horrified gasps from the crowd.

"All will be well! Sooner or later—preferably sooner—the train shall see these precious obstructions and slow down, thus allowing us to board as if it were the most natural thing in the world." The smile that accompanied this statement could have chilled a frostbitten nose.

"You horrible villain!" one of the women shouted. Spittle, who up until this point had stayed out of Byron's view, tried to run up to save the children. But Byron merely picked him up and held him squirming in the air, his clockwork leg puffing and steaming to no avail.

"My dear madam!" he said, putting his other hand to his chest in shock as each one of the guests weighed the lives of the three babies against their own survival and came up steadily in their own favour. "And I do mean madam in the sense of a brothel owner, what with that hair"—an updo that left her bangs dangling in her face—"and your shoes"—high, shiny button-up boots that clacked even in the dirt—"and the pitiable choice of furniture"—she was carrying an unfortunately shaped gas lamp—"everyone knows that a villain is a moustache-twirling silk-snatcher with a bass voice and hairy toes! I don't even have a beard!" He showed off his chin by jutting it forwards, forgetting the stubble that he had grown for the occasion, and walked over to the hirsute Archduke. "Now this is a moustache for the deft-fingered rogue!" He twisted his fingers around the hair sprouting from Velo's upper lip. His face mimicked his audience's in anticipatory surprise when the moustache popped off in his fingers just as the train ran over the baby-filled basket. "And as for hairy toes, I once had a travelling companion who assured me that she was the last of her family and that her horrible ilk were going extinct."

Throwing the moustache over the top of the brake-squealing train, Byron clapped his hands together as the sky began to rain white powder.

"Not to worry! Not to worry!" he assured them as their horror gave way to confusion. "A couple of left-over flour sacks from my disgui—I mean, from my cooking class earlier this morning, which I magicked into the illusion of squalling children! That and a few tricks of stage make-up, and voilà!"

Sparks flew from the metal wheels as the train finally slowed to a stop with an ear-wrecking final lurch. Byron shooed his companions into an empty boxcar and slammed the door. He then undid his mask, threw away his top hat, took his normal brown bowler out of his bottomless pocket, shook out his hair so that it returned to its normal black, and brushed off his shoulders. They had only a few minutes before the conductor would come out to find what he had hit, and the stage had to be set.

Banging on the side of the car, he yelled, "You better be rearranging the furniture in such a way as to allow all of you to view my upcoming feats of extraordinary wonder."

"You're going to save my wife?" the Archduke's hopeful voice said through the wood amidst the scraping of table and chair legs.

"Just watch," he replied to himself. He stretched his arms and pulled off his glove, finger by finger, revealing the decayed mess of his hand, which was little more than bones held together by green gristle and black, mould-riddled skin. He flexed the joints painfully and slapped the side of the car. Slimy remnants of skin remained in a handprint-shaped smudge. There was a shudder as every Crossed creature within forty yards flexed to his projected will; each of the three red-headed ladies inside the neighbouring boxcar raised their heads towards him as if he were a rising sun.

As he slid open the door, everyone turned to him with a shout of "Imposter!" Only Spittle remained silent, crossing his arms and glaring as Marietta, Christina, and the mysterious lady all bared their teeth at the other guests and began snapping.

"They are all real!" one of the beehive ladies squealed. "They're not in costume at all!"

"Choo are talking about my wife!" Hector brandished his sword, flicking its point into the air to establish a defensive perimeter around Christina. She gurgled and tried to bite, only to lose a few teeth on the metal.

"Of course Christina is Crossed," the man holding the broken leg of the end table said, ducking his head to avoid Aguacate's long reach, "but we mean the other two ladies."

"So I'm not the only one who confused the three of them!" Byron said, pointing a finger into the air. He cleared his throat and let out a carnivorous smile. "You are now my captive audience." He hopped up into the boxcar and closed the door behind him. As if on cue, the dog-eared man who held a dog-shaped lamp struck a match and illuminated the room with a faint gas glow. Byron found the large smoking chair, sat down, and willed the women a few steps closer to anyone who dared to display their outrage. "It has come to my attention that we are all imposters here—"

"I should have known you were that irascible fool Byron!" Velo screamed, trying to clutch Marietta closer to him, only to barely escape her sharp teeth. His saving grace was the feathers coming off her mask, which became stuck in her mouth and forced her to chew through them first. Black feathers hung from her lips and the continual tickling of what was left of her nasal passages started a horrible rhythm of snap, sneeze, snort, snap.

"As I was saying, I'd like to rectify that situation. Yes, I am an imposter, but not nearly as much as the Archduke here!" There were gasps as Byron flung his arm to point at the de-mustachioed

Velo. Marietta finally spat out the feathers and chomped at his mask, tearing it off his face. "Or should I call you Archibald 'Rhinoceros Slayer' Llewellyn-Cave? My nefarious Uncle, who stole my inheritance and killed my father?"

"That's Dr. Rhinoceros Slayer to you! And I haven't heard that name in years. Not since Africa, when you killed my wife! And I was right to disinherit you, you bastard!"

Byron stopped cold. The anger that overtook him was quiet, rolling like a pot ready to boil over. His entire body quivered with the unstoppable force of the rage coursing up his calf and into his zombified arm. The three gingers started wailing as they encircled his Uncle, becoming more and more agitated, snapping at the air in front of him.

"This is exactly why I gave myself a new identity!" Dr. Llewellyn-Cave cried, backing up until he stubbed his toe on the leg of an antique wardrobe with curled feet and intricate brass handles that poked him in the ribs. "You have ruined everything I have ever loved, including my brother!"

Byron's roar started in his chest and came out of each of the ladies' throats—ruined or not. Finding no further room to back up, Dr. Llewellyn-Cave tried to squeeze himself into the wardrobe until his rotund body could fit no more. With a squeal and a hiss of his clockwork leg, he closed his eyes and braced himself for death.

As one, the three ladies each took a bite out of him. He fell to the floor, writhing in pain and clutching the wounds on his neck and side; his right leg was left to squirt blood across the room, painting the ceiling and everything in between.

"Do you know, my dear masticated Uncle, that there are seven chakra points on the body? And that, if some of them are bitten in a specific order at a specific nerve bundle, it can make your death interminable? On average, it takes three hours for a Star-Crosser bite to become septic and either turn the victim into a zombie himself, if bitten by a Seeker, or rot until amputation is inevitable, if bitten by a Stumbler. For you, however, the pain will double every fifteen minutes...and you shall not be released from it until three days from now. Which should be enough time," he pondered, holding a finger to his temple, "for me to unmask everyone in this room and make you all finally understand that I am not the villain in this story, but merely the poor victim who only wants what is rightfully his."

"Three days?" one of the ladies squawked. Dr. Llewellyn-Cave screamed in agony, frightening her back into silence.

"We should just squeak by with that allotment." Byron took off his coat, carefully readjusted his suit and tie, dusted off his shoes, reset the pocket watch with too many hands that had belonged to his father, and crookedly applied his hat, so that he looked rakish enough to begin his tale.

244

In Which There is a Scene in a Parlour of Sorts, Or: Bony Prince Byron

"Like any mortal man, I was borne of a careful set of precipitous circumstances lending to the profundity of my existence—"

"Why're we chomping for your cocooning, eh? Brain me a story-sized carp, will ya?" Spittle said from the corner. Dr. Llewellyn-Cave had enough presence of mind to give his ward a stern look before crying out as another spurt of blood frothed from the teeth marks in his neck. "I mean," Spittle corrected, coughing into his sleeve and wiping at the pince-nez that dangled upon his chest, "it is unnecessary for us to hear your entire life story, Byron. May you speed it up?"

Byron flexed his will and Marietta trudged closer to Spittle, snapping and clawing at him from an arm's length even as her expression filled with regret. Spittle quickly backed up and gestured at putting his mouth into a treasure chest, digging a hole, and burying it where only pirates could find it. It was a rather complicated gesture.

"I trust there will be no further interruptions. Not unless you'll be wanting chunks—of your flesh, not of narrative. I prefer either, really, as I've always had a strong stomach. Which was first discovered when I was three and decided to swallow an entire hive of bees living underneath the sycamore tree that my great-grandfather Preston Camus Llewellyn-Cave—may the Great Lighthouse preserve his soul like jam, but not necessarily in a jar, because I'm not quite sure how much fresh air a soul needs—had transplanted—quite literally, from Trans-Siberia as he passed through—"

There was a whine from Archibald that could have been either "you're a bastard" or "my waistband is elastic."

Byron glanced at the bleeding man's trousers and scoffed: "Indeed, it is quite elastic. But hush, or I shall give your tongue to your supposed wife in the hopes that it'll help with her dreadful pronunciation of the word coupon. Where was I? Oh, yes…having swallowed an entire hive of bees, I experienced only a rather stinging indigestion and a swollen mouth, such that I had to survive for a week on the three litres of honey and waxy comb I had consumed, as no food could pass my puffy lips. But I digress!

"My precipitous circumstances rest on a single, seemingly innocuous mammal: a beady-eyed, twitchy-nosed, hoppy little rabbit."

There was a scream as one of the ladies thought that one of the Long-Eared Legion, which they had left far behind, had somehow gotten into the hair of her companion. She started swatting every curl she could see until one of the curls bit back and she found two of her fingers being swallowed by Marietta. She only screamed louder until the mysterious redhead wrenched the grey lady's mouth open, tore out her tongue, and devoured it with a choking sob, clearly not wanting to do such a horrible thing but unable to control herself.

"Now, if there are no more interruptions?" Byron said each word slowly and carefully, as if his own tongue were having sympathy spasms. The rest of the guests sat still in their chairs and on their ottomans and on the floor with rapt attention—all except the grievously wounded. "Yes, a rabbit decided the course of my life and brought us all here, to this very moment, in this lovely parlour—minus the parlour, of course—in order to hear my tale of woe. Because, like the lowly rabbit with its glistening whiskers, wet nose, and somewhat predatory instinct to eat its own young if it senses the need, all of us here are not what we appear to be!"

"That doesn't make any—" the redhead said before Byron quieted her with a snap of his fingers and a push of his will.

"Stop speaking in tongues," he replied as the other tongue slipped out of her mouth. "You most of all, you slipshod, slipless, and simply slippery imposter!" The girl looked down at her dress, wondering how Byron knew she wasn't wearing a slip. "But," he said, pinching her cheeks, "you are my climax—metaphorically speaking, though we did have our moments, didn't we?—and I haven't even gotten to the rising action yet." With each word he gave her a pat on the cheek: "Wait your turn." Abruptly he pushed her away; her decayed frame wobbled and fell.

"No!" he yelled, pointing at the writhing former Archduke, "we start with you! It was that moment when I was five, when you found me eating the rabbit's brains, too young to understand— it was then that you decided you hated me! That you vowed to disown me if ever the chance should arise—say, if my father were to die under circumstances that did not implicate you, thereby giving you control over the family fortune!

"I've gleaned together every infinitesimal fact of what exactly happened to my mother—may the Great Lighthouse shield her soul from all that is wicked, including you, the rampaging Star-Crossers, the tattooed men who cannot get knuckle tattoos because they cannot think of four-letter words that they like enough, and the highest tenors in barbershop quartets. Actually, my best friend once auditioned for such a position—despite my discouragement, but he wanted a hobby that didn't involve me in order to differentiate ourselves as we matured—but was turned down for quote-unquote 'howling' too much.

"Regardless: my mother began as a simple flower girl, who

occasionally sold the honey she collected from her beekeeper brother's farm. Then she attracted the eye of my father—may the Great Lighthouse keep his pants clean—and was raised to the status of second-richest trophy wife in all of England and its colonies—discounting the Falklands, of course, which are known for their vast assortment of bronzed, brassed, and framed trophy wives. A year after giving birth to me, something went horribly wrong and she was taken in the night by what seemed at the time to be a band of marauders. I discovered from my older sister Dorcas, who had witnessed our mother's abduction when she was three and retained only vague, traumatic moments from that night, that one of them had been a previous beau of hers—another beekeeper who was upset at her spinning the Rota Fortunae and coming out on top, rather than on top of him. For he had received the bottom of the wheel, quite literally; it was his job to clean the bottoms of the bee chambers, presumably a most disgusting endeavour. That last bit I found out after torturing—or rather, having my assistant torture—the beau's brother, who incidentally was a skilled archer." He looked to Marietta, who was busy eating the tongue-less woman whose bleeding face had posed too much of a temptation in her decayed state, then realised that she was supposed to be the Archduke's wife and looked away again. "She also learned that the band of marauders was somehow working with Star-Crossers. By the time the Guard had found my mother— may the Great Lighthouse always fill her nostrils with the scent of freshly baked biscuits—she had already been turned into one of those soulless creatures. Both my father—may the Great Lighthouse ensure that his shoes are always broken in—and Uncle would spend their lives concocting clockwork limbs for the victims of such terrible fiends. The irony, ladies and gentlemen, was not lost upon them. But lo! What clockwork piece could ever hope to replace my dear, sweet mother—may the Great Lighthouse grant her eternally spearmint-flavored breath? Thus my father, unable to let her go, kept her as a sort of pet even as her humanity slowly eroded before his eyes, giving his children entirely unfit and confusing thoughts about the separation of the realms of life and death! Forever altering their healthy perceptions of what is and isn't acceptable within mixed company of the alive and reanimated! And leading you, my dear Uncle, to make your attempts on my life!"

Byron looked around, his arm still poised in the air, accusatory and righteous. But the guests stared blankly, without a single reaction appropriate for a parlour-esque exposé. When his eyes met Marietta's, she lifted her eyebrows and stopped eating long enough to gasp.

"It's your Uncle! The man who hired me—rather, an assassin—to kill you! But how did he become the Archduke?" Marietta said. Byron beamed, radiating the proudness he felt for Marietta for knowing him well enough to figure out when to play along. The other two redheads glared at Marietta jealously; they had been unable to communicate for the duration of Byron's spell. The assassin merely shrugged and wiped her mouth.

The mysterious ginger, master of unspoken communication, gnawed on ear cartilage in a way that declared: "I refuse to let these kinds of situations change me in any manner whatsoever, even if it is for the best."

"...de Leon," the Archduke, or rather, Archibald, grunted in pain—or possibly "stinking peon." Byron, hearing the latter, pushed out his cheeks in anger and took several breaths to calm down. His agitation spread; the Star-Crossers in the room began to squirm and claw at the air.

"Yes, my dear partially digested Uncle—" Byron began.

"Doctor!" Archibald gurgled. Or: "Mock her."

"Yes, my dear tidbit Uncle, I do. Mercilessly and perpetually do I mock your choice of wives, even into death. But! How he became the Archduke has much in common with my own tale of woe, so we shall continue. Yes, you decided to kill me so you could marry a horrid woman whose face was too long, too orange, and too whiskery; indeed, she looked like her namesake. How well am I mocking her now, Uncle? You took pains to make yourself as suitable a suitor as possible by getting rid of everyone who would stand in your way. For you needed time to change the will so that you would inherit after my death, instead of the family fortunes going to some obscure, estranged, and hirsute cousin. You!" He pointed above the Archduke, forgot that the man was lying on the floor, and lowered his arm. "You conspired to kill my father, my sister, and eventually me!"

Byron waited, still pointing at the injured man—who merely groaned—for some reaction. He sighed, slapped his arm to his side, and rubbed the bridge of his nose.

"Have none of you ever been to a melodrama? A simple theatrical production with a clear hero and an even clearer, morally offensive antagonist? A bloody Punch and Judy show?" he screamed.

"I've never seen a Punch and Judy that had actual gore," squeaked the dog-eared man who had been trying to hide behind his slowly burning lamp. "But after the Star-Crossers, I suppose it's possible that they had to change from blunt-force trauma to something more visceral to appease their audience's new tastes…" When Byron turned his gaze upon the speaker, the man squeaked again and put the lampshade over his head. A brilliant beam of light fell upon Byron's brow and illuminated his stark green eyes.

"Let me make this as clear as possible," Byron started. "I am the narrator and therefore the hero—"

"Of moral offensiveness?" Spittle chirped.

"I prefer morally suspect! Even heroes can be that! As I was saying, you cheer for me. The villain, the one who plots to kill the hero's family so he can marry a feline—the closest human relative of a large cat that I could ever find, and everyone knows how much my Uncle loves the smell of ammonia—receives hisses befitting of his wife's clawed state. When I expose a villain, you, as an audience, are expected to cheer for me and boo for the culprit. Should I have our beehive lady explain it better? Oh, wait, she can't!"

"No," Marietta chimed in, "she can. She has her tongue." She pointed to the mystery woman.

Byron sighed. "Thank you for unveiling my veiled threat. It has become so much more evocative now. Truly, I thank you."

He turned back to his Uncle and once again pointed.

"I became so intrigued with glamours and poisons and the like because of you. Unbeknownst to you or your betrothed—who was always looking at my father's backside and then mine once I had grown a little older, but still not old enough for it to be even remotely appropriate—I would sneak into your room at night. When you were gone, my boyish curiosity got the best of me, given that I was bed-ridden at such a young age—"

"You always were sick!" the Doctor guffawed. Or: "Suck my..."

A woman screamed her frustration at being led on this crazy chicken chase—her words, as she was from the United States and had a loose grasp on the English language—and demanded to be released so she could warn the nearby town in which her family lived that the Long-Eared Legion was on its way.

"Audience...?" Byron asked, holding his hands out palm-up and staring very calmly at the apoplectic woman.

"Boo?" someone said quietly, testing the waters.

"Hiss!" another joined in.

Soon the entire boxcar—save for Spittle and the mystery redhead—began booing and hissing. Someone even threw a tomato he had been holding onto from the buffet in case he got hungry during their escape. Marietta picked up half a nose and threw that too for effect. The woman wiped off the rotten food and sat down in the corner, desperately trying to stop herself from sobbing too loudly so as to avoid any more unnecessary attention. Byron finally could feel his grip over his audience tightening and it thrilled him to the bone.

"As I was saying: The fact that I was a sickly child, always green-faced, pale, skeletal, more dead than alive, meant that I had an insatiable curiosity for all around me—from the hidden books on magic and glamour to the rabbits that sniffled in the garden. I read every single one of your books, dear masticated Uncle, and so when I saw the telltale signs of the four transparent fingerprints laid against poor Dorcas's arm, I alone knew that you had snuck into her room at night to clutch her arm in the moonlight, your fingers painted with a mix of Star-Crosser bile and the blood of drowned porcupines. You ensorcelled her to look, act, and feel like a Seeker until the next new moon—and by then, it would be too late. I watched in horror through the slats of the staircase as Quincy took the axe we used for firewood and chopped poor, immobile Dorcas into pyre-wood. Only I knew she was still alive. Before, of course, her head separated from the rest of her body.

"Our eyes met and she blinked as her head rolled down into the dying ashes of the fireplace, some part of her still alive in the fading glow of her wide orbs. Their intelligence only departed when her veins pumped the last of her blood onto our expensive rug, hand-woven by tear-streaked orphans from the hair of Chinese white tigers, inbred so as to be fine and delicate instead of rough and coarse.

"My father's arms around me were the first sensation I remembered after the brutal massacre. And to make matters worse, because of an injury he had sustained while fighting against Seekers—who had, in life, been a band of travelling Renaissance jousters who put on shows for sport, and still retained their nigh-impenetrable armour that only came off when their limbs popped out of their sockets from advanced decay—he dropped me onto the blood-covered rug. I have hated tigers and tomatoes ever since." Byron fell silent.

"Byron," Marietta said, putting a hand on her heart. A small, joyous thump went through Byron's own chest at the gesture. It wasn't her own hand, but the old woman's that she had been munching on. (And technically, it wasn't even her own heart, but that of a twenty-year-old seamstress by the name of Lenora.) "I never knew that about you...wait. Why tomatoes?"

"The pattern on the rug was tomato-themed."

"I'm so sorry," she replied.

"That never happened!" the Doctor groaned. Or: "You're so dapper!"

"Yes, I believe I am, but I refuse to be persuaded by compliments. That changes neither my perception of you nor how I will portray you in these reminisces. For after the trauma of losing my sister, when I saw you dosing my father's tea with ground-up, sweetened whale fat mixed with the root of the Lethe moss, I knew you meant to murder us all to retain the rights to the clockwork limb designs and finance your debauchery far into the afterlife. I tried to stop the fatal consequences by throwing all of Father's tea into the river by our house when he was feeding Mother her daily allotment of rabbits. The poor man thought I was re-staging the events of the Boston Tea Party and patted me on the head, affectionately calling me a damned Yank. But he had one tin stashed away—as you well knew—and he took his tea as normal at 2:15 on the dot, sealing his fate with a cup of Darjeeling served with a splash of heated milk. However, he usually took it black, and the milk reacted badly with the Lethe root; instead of making him forget, he remembered everything he ever did in his life, with the exception of those times when anyone had said the word parrot.

"Thinking of his wife in all of the aspects he had ever known her, even the ones before they had met, he went into her room. She became a subtly shifting series of images, as if seen through a collapsing telescope with a cracked lens whilst the sun sets, throwing off strange colours, muddy purples, burning oranges and shadowy greys, phasing from a young, dirty flower girl to a duchess to a Seeker to a Stumbler and back again. Then her pet parrot—who only ever said his own name, which happened to be Popuguy, the Russian word for parrot—spoke aloud at his presence, causing every single thought to bleed out of his brain and my dear father—may the Great Lighthouse keep his fingers forever free of newsprint smudges as he eats his breakfast—went to unlock Popuguy's cage and release him. But the bird had been bitten by my mother—may the Great Lighthouse prevent her crumpets from breaking apart in her tea—and when I went to ask my Father—may the Great Lighthouse safeguard him from indigestion even after the largest meal—if I could have another piece of caviar on rye bread for a snack, I found only his henpecked body, with the bloody Popuguy squawking over him. I've hated parrots and tomatoes ever since."

"But you told me your father—" Marietta interjected.

"Rotten tomatoes were Popuguy's favourite food. And even though your plan backfired, he still ended up dead. I knew then that I was next."

"That's a complete lie!" Or: "Demand and supply!"

"Which," Byron continued, ignoring the outburst, though wondering about the economics of his Uncle's situation, "leads me to my next unmasking. For it was you who tried to kill me!" He pointed at Marietta.

This time, half of the audience gasped, having caught on to Byron's nigh-insensible demands. Among them was the Archduke, who moaned about his wife's honour and how she would never hurt a fly—or perhaps something about being a spotter for unsavoury types. Regardless, Byron, chuckling and still trying to get the flour out of his hair, pulled off Marietta's mask and flung it into the corner of the boxcar. There were a few more gasps from the more intelligent members of the captive audience.

"Yes! You didn't think I never knew? You snivelling, sorcerous, cream-faced loon! May the devil damn you as black as chewed Star-Crosser lungs dipped in preservative tar, because no part of your soul shall be saved for any reckoning that will ever happen for the blackest of black fiends."

"Byron?" Marietta added sheepishly, "are you talking to me? Because of course I know that you know that I was hired to kill you, so..."

"No, sorry," Byron replied. "I just thought that, since you were the focus of the next mystery-esque exposé, you should be, well, my focus."

"That's...that's not my wife?" the Doctor said. "What did you do with her?"

"Of course it's not your second wife!" Byron responded. "Because you're sterile, and you have been since you were thirteen and kicking down anthills to watch them scatter, their homes wrecked before their beady little compound eyes. Even then you knew how to squash what you saw to be insignificant...not realising that the anthills had been built over the rotting corpses of fifteen rabid raccoons, which had been ostracised from their respective families and found support with each other in their delirious, hydrophobic states, and that the soil was freshly turned from that morning's Star-Crosser hunt. The ground gave way, plunging your right leg into the undead, unrabid raccoons' lair. They gnawed off your right leg, and along with it, half of your manhood. You were always a quarter of the man you had been after that.

"But I digress. I knew all of your tricks by this point—the plants and the glamours and the powdered poisons and the sleights of hand. You couldn't poison what wouldn't eat and you couldn't glamour what was too strong-willed for simple magicks, so you hired an assassin from the Lighthouse. The cheapest one you could find, so as to keep your barely gripped coffers full. They sent Marietta after me—"

"I am not cheap!" Marietta looked down at herself and thought about what she had done. "At least, not in that manner."

"I remember that day as the one that changed every single moment after it.

"I had gone into the garden earlier to catch rabbits for my diseased mother and father, who had joined her in the locked terrace—may the Great Lighthouse always pop all of the kernels in their popcorn, so they will never bite down on a hard seed unsuspectingly. It had been raining. The fog was rolling through the grounds like scores of small orphan hands wriggling their stubby fingers and caressing my ankles underneath my trousers. I loved the small creatures—the rabbits, not the imaginary orphan hands—both for their innocent curiosity as to what and who I was—much like I had been before you killed my entire family— and because they kept my mother—may the Great Lighthouse keep her nail-beds free of those strange white marks—strong and, if not necessarily alive, then at least less noisy. Have you ever heard the sounds of a hungry Stumbler? Like a mewling kitten being both drowned and eaten by fire ants at the same time. But that day, among the several live rabbits I caught and delivered for my mother's repast—may the Great Lighthouse allow her to eat celery without getting those strings stuck between her teeth—there was something of such beauty as to make even my increasingly jaded eyes tear up with wonder. It was a perfectly crafted rabbit in the delicate Eastern tradition of origami.

"I don't think description really does any sort of justice to the beauty it inspired in my young mind. It was as if all the stars had rearranged themselves into constellations just for me, constellations that my father—may the Great Lighthouse never give him a hangover that is not worth the partying from the previous night—used to tell me about from the books he had read as a child. Unlike those I created myself, they had been filled with heroes and villains and faithful friends who went on grand adventures to save humankind, triumphing over great evil that was always destined to fail but just needed a general nudging in the right direction. Or it was as if the mountains would move for me if I stepped down upon a path specifically made for my small, orphaned feet, and then those mountains would become my companions, singing their songs through the bitter Arctic winds—"

"Get on with it!" the Doctor yelled at the same time Spittle yelled: "Stubble's about to erupt out my tongue; it's had too long to mushroom out!"

Byron glared at the two of them and snarled.

"Regardless! My adolescent mind was filled with such joy that someone would have known me so well, would have observed me and left me such a perfect present without ever revealing themselves—that I was loved and never knew it. My heart was suffused with such warmth that I was barely able to sleep that night. And well I did not, for it was no present, no proof of the intricate rumblings of a gracious universe, but a trap set by my Uncle via his agent, Marietta Margot Pierre-Lapin! An assassin, trained since birth by an orphanage-master also known as The Conductor, the man I've been impersonating tonight. For the irony, mostly, in knowing that the arbiter of my downfall shall be channeled through me in order to orchestrate the downfall of everyone else in the room.

"That fateful night, I heard the most terrible sound known to my small, orphan ears. I woke up from my excited half-sleep, still infused with the light of hope invested in my fellow human beings, only for that hope to become horror. The paper rabbit had jumped off my nightstand and fallen between it and the wall. There was a great rumbling that I didn't understand at first, thinking it was some new magical element to my mysterious gift. It wasn't until I saw the flashing teeth that I realised the paper had been soaked in the brine of thirteen slaughtered whales stolen from the depths of their watery homes, whose oil had then been burned while thirteen blind bumblebees looked on. Anything this concoction could be absorbed into would be filled with their salty hatred if given a sufficient amount of light followed by utter darkness. As a child, unlike most, I believed that monsters lived in shadows, not simple darkness; if there were no lights, then there could be no shadows, and I was safe in the nebulosity of my lightless prison. But as I stared into that gaping maw of paper teeth, sharp enough to shear through human flesh, I realised how naïve I had been.

"The creature reared up and knocked over my desk, thus allowing me to escape into the hallway. I ran into our faithful servant, Quincy, and babbled of the horrors appearing in my darkened bedroom. Like my father—may the Great Lighthouse preserve his hair from split ends—the butler knew me to be an over-imaginative child and thus thought that I was simply reenacting another scene from the American Insurgency—the trials of Concord and Lexington and the psychological impact of that monstrosity, interpreted as a large, ravenous paper rabbit. He hushed me, trying to calm my adolescent nightmares, and escorted me back to my room.

"When he opened the door, the paper monster sprung. Mistaking the butler's arm for my scrawny orphan neck, it chomped down and tossed Quincy around like a ragdoll until releasing him into the wall, where the force of the impact cracked the plaster—and poor Quincy's head.

"I was left alone with the encroaching creature.

"Surely I would have died if not for the bravery of my best friend, who happened to have slept upstairs instead of by the burning embers of the fireplace in the servants' quarters. He charged the foul beast using his every available weapon and finally bit down on the rabbit's foreleg, holding himself there until the beast collapsed. As a stream of wood pulp and whale blood poured out of its fatal wounds, my friend killed it with one swipe to the jugular. Thinking we were safe, we celebrated...never aware of the danger lurking in the guise of my faithful butler.

"The bite, you see, had slowly been changing him into a paper monstrosity. His arm became a two-dimensional crinkling limb. His face became a drawing made of graphite and eraser marks. The lingering rabidity of the slaughtered whales, pining for their precious deep, however, was too much for him; as the paper protozoa took over, the rage of being two-dimensional in our depth-filled world was too much for his flattening brain. He lashed out, picking up my best friend and saviour and throwing him at me with such force that I bit into his backside, accidentally taking a chunk out of the fleshy spot next to his spine. He fell to the floor, whining and pawing at the air as the light faded from his eyes, looking at me with a fear of the unknown and an undying loyalty that grieved to leave me by myself. As I held his dying body, I didn't care that the butler was crawling towards me on rapidly transforming legs, eager to kill me for existing in three planes. I didn't even care that he had brushed up against the candle he'd set down when he came in and was now drenched in flame, his screams like scrunching, tearing paper. No, I only cared that my best friend had died, and by my own teeth.

"That's not how it happened at all—" Marietta started to say, then realised something else. "Your best friend, who saved you from Quincy that night, was a dog. Your best friend is a dog? This entire time, all of those stories...they were about a dog?"

"Not just a dog! His name was Sir Cardigan, and he was the most loyal, handsome, and fearless creature on this planet."

"But most of your stories about him happened after I tried to assassinate you. Were all of those lies?"

"No, my dear bait-and-switch! For this is the moment that changed my entire existence and preconceived notions about the thin line separating humans from Star-Crossers! The next day, my Uncle buried Quincy and I, my faithful friend. That night, though, I rolled over in my sleep, and in some blissful part of my brain that had not yet processed his horrible death, I imagined that he was lying next to me, curled up in my lap and peaceful in the knowledge that I was safe. As I petted him I relaxed, enjoying my carefree dream until my hand slipped from smooth fur into rotting, squishy intestines. It was then I realised that this was no dream; he had somehow come back to me. And what I saw as a joyous event—reunion with my best friend—my Uncle, sole guardian and arbiter of my fate, saw as ghastly.

"'The dog's been turned!' he yelled when I woke him to display the midnight miracle. 'He's a Star-Crosser!'

"'But no!' I responded. 'Look! He still barks, he still understands me, and he has no intention of eating my flesh or my brains. Not even my bones! I tempted him with a phalange and not even one bite. Though he may look like a Star-Crosser, he is, in spirit, the same faithful companion he ever was in life. Even more so—he braved death to come back to me!'

"That was when you, my dear acidic, ulcer-causing Uncle, stepped back with a look of soul-curdling terror and abject, as the German would say, getiavayfrommingmegeisheit, and said word-for-word: 'Abomination unto all that is pure and un-Crossed, I knew that the far-flung consequences of your birth would haunt my very marrow. You bastard child, you take your cursed dog and never come back, or I will kill you myself. Only the memory of your dear mother prevents me from fulfiling that promise here and now.' You shuddered then, as if you were touching the innards of a seasick whale. 'And my terror prevents me from treading any closer. May the Great Lighthouse forgive me for what I am about to unleash upon the unsuspecting world.'

"That was the day I discovered my necromantic abilities. That was the day you kicked me out of the house and began your twelve years of legal tomfoolery to cut me out of my father's otherwise ironclad will. And that was the day I swore vengeance upon you and yours—and your slanderous tongue. After I dispatched the Lady de Leon, you found another wife—the Heelduchess—who desperately wanted children, so you said you would adopt, and adopt you did. Under a new persona, you collected children in need like old dirty pence—" here Byron frothed angrily towards Spittle who spat into the corner "—from the gutters next to brothels. And then you made change!" Byron screwed up his eyes and gesticulated wildly with his hands. "You know, with their souls!"

Byron stepped closer to his dying relative and gripped the man's cheeks with both hands.

"Having an affinity for controlling the undead does not make me a bastard, at least in the sense of illegitimacy. And saying that to a boy of barely twelve is a horrible stain upon his delicate psyche. Boys who have been loved by their father figures rarely grow up to be friends with Star-Crossed assassins, alleyway murderers, those skilled in the arts of mountainous seduction, and general all-around cads with no regard for the consequences of their far-flung actions.

"For where else do you think a cold, starving, and devastatingly handsome—even for such a youngster—orphan is supposed to go? Where do all unwanted and homeless children go? I fell in with a buck-toothed, rabbity-looking itinerant with a bald patch on his left cheek—not that one, dear," he said, wriggling his dusty eyebrows at Marietta, "—that, if he looked at the mid-morning light while Mercury was in retrograde and the Homunculus Star was two weeks to its zenith, could prognosticate the manner in which people's pets would die. He made a living off warning the parents of small children about their beloved family beasts, thusly forestalling any existential observations about death at a too young an age. When such happenstance and circuitous circumstances evolved between us, and with the rather timely but not permanent death of Sir Cardigan, the toothy man could only see the brutal manner in which the faithful corgi had met his maker and then—excuse the vernacularity—promptly punched his maker. Thereafter he was unable to see any other deaths and thus make any more money. He sold me to a rather hirsute individual whose gender I could not ever discover, even to this day, who—"

"You were grinding on, draining 'bout double-backing?" Spittle interrupted.

Byron looked to Marietta to translate.

"You were talking about seduction?" she answered with a shrug.

"Ah, yes! We eventually ended up where the endless drain of all homeless youth ends: the orphanage. And not just any orphanage, but one belonging to a man known on the streets as… Ladybird!" He pointed to no one in particular, but almost everyone, now having fully understood the rules of their confinement, gasped at the non sequitur—Spittle in earnest.

"You fell in with that spotted leaf-munching amalgam?" Spittle said, connecting the thoughts that had gotten scrambled in the drawn-out storytelling. "You didn't tongue 'bout the snake-charm. Out of all Foster's milk ribboners, Ladybird was the covetous one, always munching on the priestless and sliming their visages for kingdom done. If you caverned with his organ-grinding, no wonder you're fanged up like a man-working viper."

"He better have said how well Ladybird's instruction allowed my natural and voluptuous charm to work through the rough edges of my childhood. Like polishing a stone by throwing it into a river, only the river is a brutal and hierarchical world of brothel ownership and prostitution."

"Uh," Marietta looked between Byron and Spittle, trying to decide what else to say. "Yes. Kind of. It's just that we all have a prejudice against Ladybird. You see, Foster—Wasp—had two older brothers. All three of them inherited an orphanage when their own parents died from the initial Star-Crosser attacks, before the establishment of the Guard and the fail-safes. In their excessive sibling rivalry, the boys made a bet about how much money each of them could make off of their orphanages. The oldest, Tarantula, turned his orphans into thieves. The middle, Ladybird, turned his into prostitutes. And our master, Wasp, made us into assassins. Their competition was bitter; we were all brought up to hate the orphans from Foster's clansmen. The rumours of what the other two did—Ladybird especially—made Wasp's methods seem tame in comparison."

"Au contraire!" Byron burst out. "He was the only one who ever showed me what it really meant to be a man. And that was to pleasure a woman, to elicit such a feeling from—"

His Uncle coughed loudly, dark blood frothing from his lips.

"Best andalay this up, top-hat," Spittle said. "Else Uncle Doctor Bad-Ass will fade into that tymphanic skin and won't boom back like any boomerang in this cold night. And where will your passing down be?"

"All in good time! I've killed enough people to know how long it'll take for them to die. Never rush the ending to anything, my dear lad—also advice I picked up from the much-maligned Ladybird. You must allow these things to breathe organically... unless, of course, they don't.

"It was there that the second most important event of my life happened—"

"You lost your Mary lamb?" Spittle asked. Marietta turned bright red and was unable to translate.

"If you don't quiet down, I will make you bleat so hard that even a most seasoned shepherd would mistake you for one of his flock," Byron said, becoming impatient at the many interruptions. "So can it. And I mean that quite literally. I've studied my Uncle's inferior clockwork limbs enough to know how to sabotage them from afar. Unless you want to be doing the can-can every time you mean to walk, you should respect that some of us have found true love and, for even those brief moments, known exactly what it means to live wholly and inexplicably for and through another." Byron paused a moment, overcome with the emotion that he had tried for so many years to stanch.

"When you start out as a junior partner in Ladybird's service, you are first primped and coiffed, then taught to bring out the same beauty in others, even the most slovenly of hapless creatures. I was apprenticed to a girl named Pepper. While highly sought after, she was a piggish girl whose beauty was marred by her jealousy. For, like in a fairy tale, there was one yet fairer than her: Marguerite, a goddess of red hair and glowing green eyes. Pepper instructed me to use my knowledge of the arcane arts to poison Marguerite's favourite lemon-poppy scones with clotted cream, so that her hair would turn the ghastly orange of a particular type of mould that only grows in the nasal passages of Cyclops Horses, found in the mutagenic volcanic wastelands of the North. Oh, and they were supposed to make her teeth turn a particular shade of brown—"

"A hairless baboon's backside! Get on with it!" someone yelled and then, to avoid retaliation, ducked out of sight behind a bar that had been lopsidedly carried by two men and now seeped a steady fount of amber alcohol.

"I couldn't go through with it, watching Marguerite daintily eat her scones and cheerily sip her tea with her pink-coloured pinkies up. Here was this celestial being, brought down to earth to be one of its best creatures, and I felt that even breathing on and fogging a window through which her beauty could be seen was an atrocity. Just the thought of destroying such perfection was enough to make a man contemplate a particularly painful suicide. So I switched their teas and watched as Pepper's beauty faded and the men stopped asking for her. Eventually I was no longer her servant. And I had gotten my heretofore unknown wish: I was now in the employ of Marguerite. I washed her hair, cared for her clothes, readied her make-up, and even solved complex math equations, all like a guardian angle. I watched over her and made sure she was ready to face anything.

"I debated with myself sixteen times a day about if and how

I should explain the depths of my love. But how ridiculous! Me, a mere boy proposing my slobbering adolescent affections to such a magnificent, clandestine creature. No, I would have to prove my merit first. I began wandering the streets when I was supposed to be sleeping in order to find a worthy quest. That's when I stumbled into an old man by the name of Darkboat, a grizzled old thing with a bluish tattoo scarred upon his cheek, weathered hands, and an even more weathered story. He was sitting in the gutter, sighing and cradling his head in his arms. Being the caring boy I was—your uncouth bashing had yet to make me completely morally numb at this point in the tale—I asked him what was wrong, even though I was running out of time to get back before Ladybird noticed I was gone.

"'Nothing a young lad like yourself could understand,' he sighed.

"I noticed a glass eyeball in his left hand and a glass tooth in the other. They were covered with a luminescent oil that was pooling and absorbing into the lines on his palms, scintillating briefly before disappearing into his skin. It was a strange magic, but almost familiar: a bastardisation of the cultured glamours I knew, mixed with savagry and desperation. All the signs I did recognise, however, dripped of lost love, of seeking redemption and of proving manhood. All the things I wanted.

"'Who was she?' I asked. I must have surprised Darkboat, or so I thought then—I know the much darker truth now. He asked how I knew that he had been seeking his love. When I told him of my Uncle's work and all that had happened to me, his eyes lit up and he asked me the same question: Who was the woman I pined for?

"'Sounds like we have the same problem,' he said, and clasped my shoulder so that I sat down with him and watched the dirty water from the alley slosh over my ratty, holey shoes. 'It's much too late for my dear Mybelle. She was unable to overcome the allure of a perfectly chiselled chest.'

"'Another man?'

"'Another statue. She has miniscule seizures in her eyeballs that make her perceive all statues as live, moving people. I was unable to win back her love from a memorial devoted to the first fighters against the Star-Crosser plague. That's why I made this,' he said, indicating the glass parts. 'They're supposed to allow you to see what it is your true love wants most in the world, and then to—'

"'Eat it?'

"'Consume it. Or rather, just grab it.'

"'Then why not make a hand?'

"'It's not as symbolic!'

"'But it's more realistic—'

"'Not the point! I will help you, young boy, for though love has passed me by, you will have a chance. Here,' he said. Before I could interject, the glass eyeball's slime filled in the love line on my palm and bright light suffused the air. In a few seconds, the tooth and eye became accustomed to my physiognomy; the light-filled love line snaked along my wrist and arm until it settled somewhere around my heart. Then the line lifted off my palm and shot out, far to the north and into the wildernesses that the Star-Crossers had claimed as their own. My eyes began to water from the pain. An outline of the object most desired by my love flashed in my vision: a small, ovoid thing lit by mysterious grey light, which so severely bleached its colours that I could hardly tell what it was. All too soon the light faded, shooting stars behind my eyes.

"I had lost it before even discerning its identity. I began to sob—and I am not ashamed to admit this, for I am comfortable in my masculinity—as if someone had told me that I would live out the rest of my days inside a sock, forever in darkness, squished between smelly toes and jostled by sheep-sized, bleating athlete's-foot bacteria.

"'My boy!' Darkboat cried. 'What is wrong? I know sometimes the path to a woman's heart may seem treacherous and their wants absurd and fantastic, but that doesn't mean you can't do it! My love, My—I call her My for short, as an inside joke—before she fell in love with the statue, wanted a tooth from a Megalodonian Pie! A razor-toothed archaic pie baked by stone men who thought that simple foods that didn't bite back were not worth the trouble of eating. Tell me, what did she want?'

"'That's just it!' I yelled. 'I don't know what she wanted at all!' I began to describe it and the direction the eye had shown me.

"'My boy!' he cried again. "It's a Franciscan Cork Egg! Laid by the Franciscan Flying Caged Bird—they carry their own cages around their heads made out of their spindly feathers, dirt, and saliva, which they fashion into mating helmets so that the females cannot escape. The bright blue-green shells of their eggs can be fashioned into the finest eyeshadow known to Man—or should I say, Woman. Any lady who wears that shell-colour around her eyes becomes so desirable that every four-legged creature for miles will stamp in rhythm to her heartbeat, allowing all to know how excitable she becomes. If you give such an egg to your lady, she will no doubt love you to the ends of the earth. Just don't let her wear the shadow, or you'll be fighting off lions and tigers and bears—oh, My!" Darkboat yelled. A woman, presumably Mybelle, had started running down the street after a young urchin whose job it was to dust and polish the statues. When she didn't even recognise him, Darkboat sighed and slumped again.

"'Where do I find this egg?'

"'Surely the eye showed you the way?'

"I pointed and the old man's face fell even further.

"'That way lies the deadly Thickets, covered with ash and twisted trees. Only Star-Crossers rule out there, and even deeper, darker things. Rumours reach my ears of a controller of the Crossed, a manipulator of the mangled, a royal reckoner of the reamed! It will be a fight for you, boy—but what lady's heart isn't worth a little blood and guts?'

"'I've already got those!' I happily held up my left hand, which, after an accident involving a rogue ice cream cone, a feral alley cat, and a drunkard, bore an unhealed hangnail that had started to peel back. The nail's bed was discoloured and every day Ladybird said that he would kick me out if I didn't improve my hygiene.

"'My boy!'

"By this time I was irritated.

"'I am not your boy. I am my deceased father's boy, and he would be very cross indeed to hear you calling me such. My name is Byron Ulysses Llewellyn-Cave, and the only reason I haven't trod upon you in disgust the way one of my stature should is because I have been disinherited and cast into the street, like a chewed-upon rib not even fit for table scraps! Please do not injure my pride any further by reminding me of my orphaned state!'

"'Disinherited because you've been bitten? My boy—' I glared. 'My Star-Crosser, is that better?

"'Explain yourself, sir,' I replied tartly.

"As the man rolled up his trouser leg I shuddered, looking away in disgust, then realised that he was merely showing me his underdeveloped calf. Clearly the man had never been a ballerina, nor had he ever done the intensive cardio necessary to prepare one for a roll in the hay—if you catch my drift—as I had. But far more interesting was the gangrenous, decayed bite. His wound looked old, but under the skin, faint blobs of black lines wriggled like worms—similar to those on my own hand—all up and down the normally blue-tinged veins in his leg. It was healed, but strangely still putrefying just under the surface of his skin.

"'I share your affliction. Got bit a few years back. I've been fending off the infection with a strange concoction.'

"'I still misunderstand you, sir. I have never been bitten by anything in my life, save for my Star-Crossed companion.' Here I showed him Sir Cardigan and his eyes grew wide, as most people's did. 'But that was quite a few years before he acquired his current state.'

"'Still makes sense. Sometimes animals can hide their bites better'n anyone. He could have transferred the Star-Crossing affliction long before either of you noticed. Your bite'll soon get worse, though, and you'll need some help.'

"I immediately grew suspicious. Even as a child, I was acutely aware of the perils of being beholden to anyone.

"'Why would you help me?'

"Darkboat smiled and looked off towards his love as she scrambled back to her statue and tried to kiss it, even though it was three feet taller than herself.

"'Love, my boy. Love pure and simple. If you catch it, you'll never understand, but if you lose it, you'll never want to see that loss in anyone else ever again. Promise me you'll love that girl, and I'll tell you all about how to stave off the effects of the bite.'

"So I trained and became strong, lifting weights and preparing myself for my eventual foray into Star-Crossing territory. I counted the years, not wanting to be the least bit unqualified for whatever the journey may have thrown at me. Finally, when I was sixteen and about to be plucked away from my duties as Marguerite's assistant, I snuck away in the middle of the night. By that time, my hangnail had spread up that finger to the knuckle, giving me the perpetual look of a boy who constantly skinned his fists in brawls and an accompanying, unearned reputation of hard-assery.

"Before leaving, I broke my own vow of silence, and whispered into Marguerite's ear as she slept of all my hopes and desires. How I wished we could grow old together and, in our advanced and wrinkled state, reminisce about our lives—and those reminisces would be better than our actual lives, until we would get to the end and thus have to start the cycle over again, each time becoming greater and happier and more joyful until we simply burst from it all. I left her in the middle of the night with these thoughts permeating her dreams, never to return without the object her heart most desired.

"So I travelled. By beast, by locomotive, by any means possible, with the exception of my own two feet because that's how peasants walk and I'll be damned if I'll ever be a peasant—"

"But we walk everywhere all of the time," Marietta said.

"I said my own two feet. What makes you think these are mine?"

As everyone pondered that, Byron continued: "It was only after all of these events that I found the old man to also be an imposter! You see, he was the brother of Ladybird. He didn't want to save love, as he had told the gullible young orphan me, and he never had a wife named Mybelle who fell in love with a statue. He wanted me to be a pawn in his game. For the old man was...Wasp!"

He pulled out the mask he had been wearing earlier and accused it in his own hand.

"He wanted to get rid of Ladybird's top prostitute and thus sent me away on a quest! I was nothing more than a means to an end—and, unfortunately for poor Marguerite, it would be her end.

"But I have strayed too far ahead of my story. For years I travelled north into the Charred Thickets. Sir Cardigan, always my faithful shadow, hopped beside me—or hobbled, rather, as his decay had only advanced. At last I reached the base of the volcano and glimpsed the tree with its precious ova, my eyes filling with the same mysterious light held in the glass eyeball. The stubby legs of a corgi didn't allow for tree-climbing, decayed and missing or not, so Sir Cardigan took a nap in a nearby bush as I attempted the ascent.

"Little did I know, even with all of my research and intuitive knowledge about Star-Crossers, that the sound that most attracts Star-Crossers is the sound of corduroy trouser legs rubbing against bark; it mimics the sound of brain waves echoing throughout the cranium. As unfortunately dressed as I was, Seekers instantly surrounded me—and from my perch, I could see Stumblers drifting in behind them, waiting to feast upon whatever remained of me after the quick Seekers had their way.

"I was as prepared as I could have been for such an eventuality. But even my measly supply of repellant leafy greens and gelatinous globules painted to resemble brains was not enough to stop the encroaching horde. I needed to act quickly. I licked a few lettuce leaves, applied them to the bark, and struck the tree with my brass knuckles—which I had picked up from a one-lunged wooden-plank salesman, forged to protect him from his clientele of scurvy-ridden pirates, whose gold teeth he could make reverberate in their mouths and shoot up into their brains. As the reverberations scattered the green vegetables onto the Star-Crossers and they began wailing about how many more bites they had to eat before they could get to dessert—that is, myself—I spotted the nest of the elusive bird I sought. Balanced on the precarious branch,

I stretched my arm out, wishing I had traded for a wooden plank instead of the brass knuckles, when I realised my fatal mistake.

"There is a particular bird known to ornithologists—"

"Which is exactly what I am, if my parents ever ask," Marietta interjected.

Spittle shot her a look. "Instead of what, a member of the legion of the undead?"

"—as the Lazy Filching Flying Fiend—"

Marietta, shooting back the same look but missing the desired effect because half her face was falling off her skull, finished Byron's sentence for him: "That, even though it lives in the same volcanic environment, has mutated only to become lazier than its non-volcanic brethren. Their modus operandi—Latin, see? Means I'm a real ornithologist—is to steal the—"

"Don't spoil it!" Byron said, putting his hands out to stop Marietta's words. "Their modus vivendi, rather, can be likened to the fable of the grasshoppers and the poor ants which they enslaved, forcing them to eat their own children until their gene pool was so small that they had no choice but to inbreed. The grasshoppers then put the resulting grotesqueries into tiny sideshow acts so as to amuse themselves, demonstrating their own laziness in their inability to entertain themselves without the tears of orphans.

"Likewise, the Lazy Filching Flying Fiends push other birds' eggs out of their own nests and replace them with their own vile and vicious offspring. When the chicks hatch, the horrible stench of their leftover egg yolk causes their surrogate parent to hallucinate that it is a rock and thus belongs on the ground instead of in the sky. Its subsequent death-leap provides the newly hatched Flying Fiends with their first meal.

"Ladies and gentlemen, Star-Crossers and evil uncles alike:

"There I was, teetering over the hungry hands of the heinous hellions, and—ladies, this is not for the faint of heart—I moved the branch out of my way, expecting to find the bright blue-green shell so sought after by ladies of all persuasions, only to find the vomit-coloured, blood red-speckled egg of the Lazy Filching Flying Fiend. If my heart had been beating the fastest tattoo it knew, it now dropped into my shoes, burning a hole all the way down so that I felt as if my feet and brain had switched places.

"That's when I heard the fateful bark of Sir Cardigan, my best friend. The bush he had chosen for a nap shook and his decayed nose and dangling eyeball pushed the branches aside—only to reveal the egg I so desperately desired, unharmed by its fall. It must have landed in the soft grass, so delicately fertilised by all of the roving Star-Crossers, and rolled into the very same bush that Sir Cardigan had chosen as a delightful nap spot. I blew my kisses of thanks towards the Great Lighthouse for my incredible luck.

"But one of the Seekers had finally persevered enough to climb the trunk of the tree. He had been watching my feet dangle long enough to get the rhythm of my swing, and on its backwards arc, my ankle landed precisely between the last two teeth in his mouth. A sharp crunch sounded and I realised I had been bitten. My entire measly life flashed before my eyes—catching rabbits, cups of tea, gruesome deaths, cups of tea, Sir Cardigan's death, Marguerite's sweet face, another cup of tea. Everything started to go dark and I felt another force taking me over. I thought I had already turned, that I was now a Seeker, before I understood that I had crushed the Filching Fiend's egg and it was just the neurotoxin that made me believe that I was a rock.

"Using all of my willpower, I made myself believe wholeheartedly that I was a hot-air balloon—the type they launch in the wee hours of the morning, so that the bottoms of their baskets reflect the rising sun and cast spots of light on the awakening town of my youth. The upward lift of my thoughts and the downward thrust—please keep your vulgar thoughts to yourself or I shall never finish—of the toxin's persuasion evened out and I was able to make myself understand that I was neither a chunk of mineralised earth nor an aerial mode of transport, but merely myself: Byron Ulysses Llewellyn-Cave.

"The Seekers, however, not being so able-minded, started dropping to the ground like nuts and burying themselves in their irresistible urge to once again to become part of the earth. I carried the egg with me as I climbed down, dribbling bits of yolk over any rambunctious Seekers who had yet to become faithful rocks, until I found Sir Cardigan and my precious heart's desire.

"I held the Franciscan Cork Egg in the waning light of the sun and finally breathed a sigh of relief after six years of searching and fretting. I began my journey home, the egg secure in the bottomless pocket I had procured by stealing the sacred rocks crafted by a travelling band of kite-riding gypsies who only ate primary-coloured foods. One such food was a yellow bass that lived in the deepest lake known to mankind, high on a cliff that could only be reached by those with control over the winds. These fish ate the rocks found at the bottom of the so-called Devil's Throat, and when the gypsies ate the fish, they would imbue these stones with the properties of the deep lake by carving them in their very digestive tracts with certain traditions known only to the kite-riders. From then on, the rocks would be as cold as the frigid lake, release a darkness so black it felt like swimming through ink, or—in the case of my pocket—create a depth without boundary.

"My step was jovial as I walked—"

"But you never walk!"

"—on the backs of two Star-Crossers that, coming out of their hallucinatory stupor only slowly, believed themselves to be small salamanders carrying food back to their dens in Ladybird's orphanage.

"I was resplendent in my triumph, glorious in my prodigality, and shining in my prize. I opened up the doors to Marguerite's private chambers; finding her with a client, I picked him up by the collar and left him on the stoop, trouserless and loveless. Then I got down on one knee and proposed to my love, holding the egg in my hand as if it were her actual heart that I cupped.

"She seemed puzzled, unable to place my face after my long absence and all of the changes wrought by my exposure to the elements. Indeed, I had met an alchemist with a horrible lisp who, in trying to turn all of his copper teeth into enamel, had only succeeded in turning them into wood, so that all of his friends and family believed him to be re-enacting George Washington's crossing of the Delaware. As fellow victims of mistaken historical posturing, we became friends. He taught me exactly how to part my hair so as to minimise the exposure of scalp and avoid an infection of Star-Crossed lice, who not only eat your hair follicles, leading to horrible dandruff that craves to eat every dust-bunny within a two-centimetre radius, but eventually burrow deeper into the skull and clog brain function—fatally, in cases where no viable ducts can be scoured. But without the classic part that I had worn throughout my years as a denizen of Ladybird's orphanage, Marguerite was unable to figure out who I was until she saw the tell-tale rot of my ring finger —which had by then spread down to my first knuckle—and she assumed that I was still getting into fights and continuing my hard life of unmerited fisticuffs. The years of my absence, combined with my grown stature and my newly parted hair, made her realise that she had been pining for me all along.

"'Well,' I said, my arm growing tired from holding the rather heavy egg for thirteen minutes while she figured all of this out, 'are you going to take my gesture of love?'

"'What…is it?' she said, daintily pecking at the shell with a fingernail.

"'It's what you've always wanted! The very thing your heart has always wished for, but was out of your reach because it was surrounded by volcanic ash and Star-Crossers and Filching Fiends!' I said as I began to panic.

"'The thing I've always wanted is my mother's opal locket. She was buried with it and I didn't even know she was dead until three years after the fact. She's right over there, in the Cornerstone Cemetery.' She pointed in the direction I had just come from. Not thirty yards away was a cemetery; I could just make out a gravestone with a weeping angel and her surname on it. 'That egg is about the same shape and size, though.'

"The last entire six years of my life had been wasted on something she neither wanted nor needed. I had risked everything to prove nothing. She must have seen my face fall, for she threw her arms around me, letting me know that she didn't care about quests and baubles; she loved me for me, for my honesty and integrity. She kissed me until there was a cough—then a loud throat-clearing when she didn't acknowledge the former. Ladybird stood in the doorway, looking back and forth between the two of us.

"'Unless you're paying her, boy, you need to leave. And speaking of leaving: I have half a mind to lock you up for the rest of your adolescent days, you delinquent! Do you know how hard it is to get a stipend for an orphan if I can't prove that he has room and board here? After all I did for you, after all the training that went into making something out of you, you have the nerve to run away and then try to steal my top girl? You got me in trouble, but it'll be nothing compared to what I'm going to do to you and your girlfriend for the next twenty days before she turns eighteen.'

"'It's not his fault, Ladybird.' Marguerite turned to me. "Byron, I can't be with you. You understand. You…you have to pay.' It was the first time that my name had ever passed her lips and the first time I had ever seen her embarrassed by her station.

"I wanted to stay, to fight for my love, but I was not then the man that I am now. I was innocent, filled with the conviction that life was precious, no matter the squirming form it may have taken. It wasn't until later that I realised that life is no more precious than death. We spend all our time fighting the inevitable, but I learned to join the winning side on the greatest battlefield. I became its lieutenant, its commander, and its flag. Death is our end; why shouldn't it, at least for some of us, be our beginnings and our middles, too?

"But, at that moment, I was a mere green boy in the struggle for my future love. I would have surely lost Marguerite, cowed into submission by one I thought to be worthier of her, when I saw Ladybird's eyes dart to the egg. That look I had seen many times before on many different people, but on Ladybird, it was reserved for whenever a prominent official, a peer of the realm, or an important member of the Guard visited his establishment. It was the same look a Seeker gets when it finds itself at the tar pits next to the gangster dens after what they call 'spring cleaning.'

"He knew the worth of the egg, but so did I. I jumped up from my proposing knee and hid the egg into the bottomless pocket, which had taken up residence in the hidden compartment of my hat-band.

"'The girl for the egg,' I responded, puffing out my chest and pushing my hat forwards. It was then that I realised that I was a man, mostly grown, muscles developed from my trek, mind sharp from surviving a hungry horde, and machismo bolstered from Marguerite's reciprocation of my love. 'It'll more than cover what she could make for you before she comes of age.'

"'She's my top girl. It'd take a lot more than just some coloured shell for me to give her up,' came his scathing response.

"'More than that,' I replied. 'Sure, you sell the shell, and you get more than enough to cover her cost for the next twenty days. You use it, however,' I said, rolling my hat around in my hands and watching his eyes somersault, watering as if they were his mouth salivating over a large meal, 'and all of your girls will be as marketable and desirable as Marguerite. Men will come from miles away to use your services. And not just paltry men, but everyone from the highest-ranked generals to the Queen's consorts themselves! You,' I said, coming closer to him and lowering my voice to a whisper, so that he had to strain to hear me, 'will blast your brothers out of their comfortable, wealthy lives. Let's face it, you've been behind their rather insurmountable assets for a few years now...but it's not your fault! Think of the cost you have to put into your orphans!' I put a hand behind his back and started to lead him over to a couch to sit down. 'What does it take to dress a thief? Nothing but rags. An assassin? The price for black dye has gone down threefold in the last few years. But for your boys and girls? I doubt the Queen even looks as nice in her fineries—'

"'You watch what you say about the Queen,' Ladybird warned. But I could tell that I had gone fishing in the right lake; if there was one thing Ladybird's patronage had done for me, it was to make me an excellent fisherman.

"'Now, you take this shell and you turn your lowliest girls into queens of the Nile! Beauties that could conquer Rome itself! Greek goddesses, wrathful but willing to change their minds if given the right incentives! Horse-riding princesses! Diamonds in the rough like eyeballs in a beggar's empty head! Think of the looks on your brothers' faces when your establishment has queues going around the block. They will positively piss themselves—excuse the vulgarity of the idiomatic expression—at your success.'

"Ladybird thought it over, weighing the options in his mind while Marguerite trembled, waiting to hear her fate from his thin, greasy lips. I kept silent as his mind ran through the imaginary numbers of made-up girls and the profits their shell-shellacked eyes would bring. My palms sweated more that day than any other I can remember, including the time my best friend accidentally gave me a sweating tonic instead of my usual graveyard-dirt fare. Have you ever felt the peculiar sensation of your eyelashes sweating? I'm not sure even my prodigious skills of descriptive prose are up to the challenge.

"I'm not sure what I would have done if he had refused. I would have paused, I think, unsure of my path, knowing I could have once had love, could have known the peace it may have brought me—but I would have walked away. As it was, Ladybird's announcement changed the outcome of my life. I lifted Marguerite up, twirling what was left of her dress after her nightly forays in the cool damp air of the brothel, and could have sworn I was in paradise, surrounded by the smells of passion, the sounds of those trying to work up their passion, and the sights of those trying to recapture passions lost long ago.

"In my ecstasy, I visited Darkboat to thank him for his advice and to return his tooth and eye so that some other lover could bring his aloof dreams and inaccessible wants to fruition. The old man was in a sorry state indeed when I found him. He had left a business card with me at our first meeting and I dutifully found the address. The building in which he lived was old, falling apart but still majestic, with an annoying number of children about.

"I introduced him, bedridden wretch that he was, to my soon-to-be bride. Beautiful girl that she was, she blushed, as demure as the innocent flower she certainly was not—"

Here the mysterious ginger grunted and crossed her arms. Byron, angry at the interruption so close to the emotional crux of his troubled past, sent out a brief psychic hum. A small hole appeared on her left cheek that left her teeth visible, even with her mouth closed. She clasped a hand to her jaw and the anger that burned through her eyes came from more than just this small slight; this was an echo of a past fury, a past transgression.

"—when I told her of our saviour. Darkboat coughed, a small stream of dribble catching on his chin, and told how his life had fared in the past ten years. Alas, his own love had committed suicide. Mybelle and the statue had been engaged for three months before one too many pigeons had (how to put this delicately?) defecated on her, and when she attempted to kill the filthy flying rats that had so ignobly treated them, she had been admonished for publicly brandishing a gun without intent to kill the undead. After a horrible argument with her fiancé about how he needed to stand up for himself and assert his dominance over the pigeons, she eventually drowned herself in the river.

"I nodded towards Darkboat's bad leg and asked, while Marguerite was busy looking through the treasures that he had acquired while searching for a cure for his love, if the cause of his sudden illness was due to his affliction. He shook his head, saying that he was heartbroken over Mybelle's death and having financial trouble after spending the last of his money bailing her out. His leg, he said, was just fine, and he was glad for the chance to speak to me before my wedding about the concoction that would prevent my own affliction from growing.

"'You need to start with a good strong whiskey,' he began.

"'Is that for disinfection?' I responded, giving my fiancé a small wave and a smile. She was picking through a series of preserved animals that Darkboat kept next to a picture of what I could only assume to be his family when he was much younger. He had two brothers and a rather austere father, standing beside a wispy waif of a mother. How stupid I was not to realise that he was Wasp, the brother of my own saviour, surrounded by orphans as we were! They kept on running in and all over the place, but the strength of my love made me oblivious.

"'Certainly not, my boy!' he guffawed. 'It's for the horrible taste!'

"He went on: 'Graveyard dirt will do from anywhere. The only difference is in the taste. A cemetery full of sinners, cheaters, backbiters, and gamblers will give it a gamey flavor, but saints and nuns and priests lend a citrus taste...which sometimes can backfire if the worms are too fresh, because then the mix will curdle. The worms themselves should be of the same quality as those you would use for fishing—'

"'Something I know a lot about!' I winked at Marguerite as she studied a cracked jar that held a small Star-Crossed rabbit. It twitched something horrible when she shook it. I then asked for a cup of tea and she left to procure one.

"'Indeed,' Darkboat muttered darkly."

Byron lifted his eyebrows a few times, trying to see if anyone had understood the wordplay, but all he received were a few bored stares.

"He seemed to be thinking about something else, before he described the rest of the life-saving recipe. 'And remember: You will be tempted to eat human flesh, especially in moments of passion,' he said, waggling his eyebrows as Marguerite toyed with one of his dolls, 'but you must not give in. Such behaviour will only serve to expedite the decay and turn your mind away from what is left of your humanity. Perhaps the lady will be able to help you with whatever you may need?'

"'Never!' I cried in alarm. I had to quickly smile and gesture for another spot of tea so as not to rouse Marguerite's curiosity any more. 'She must never know the truth about what I am.'

"'You're Byron, the man I love and the strongest, most honourable beekeeper I know,' she replied, hanging her hands around my neck. (I had told her that when I wasn't working for Ladybird or off on quests for young ladies, I toiled honestly making honey that could never be as sweet or as golden as she.) She handed me a small, steaming china cup filled to the brim with black tea and two sugars.

"In that moment, I didn't care about my inheritance. Even though I knew that we could have all the money we wanted if I pursued my Uncle, to make whatever life we could with all of the gold and jewels known to mankind...I could have been a poor working man, so long as I was with her.

"But," Byron continued, slicking back a stray piece of hair and straightening his tie, "it wouldn't have hurt to be as rich as morally bankrupt assassins."

"Which," Marietta interjected, "is really, really, really rich."

"Our wedding was a small ceremony in the graveyard nearby Marguerite's only known, yet tragically buried, family, since all of mine had either died or disowned me. Her dress was beautiful, as grey as the cobwebs that littered the grounds, her red hair as vibrant as Mars high in the night sky and just as auspicious. But it was her beautiful green eyes, as jewelled as the dying flowers left by those who still remembered their dead as corpses and not as flesh-eating monsters, that made the night special. Darkboat was my only guest, and he left as soon as he saw Ladybird marching over the hill with a few of Marguerite's friends in tow like tarty ducklings.

"Afterwards, in order to escape the poor memories we had of London and of England in general, we moved to the Black Forest. The Star-Crossers had not been as much of a problem on the Continent as on our own island; their spread through Europe had been stymied by the wild Cossack divisions who made it their mission to eradicate the impure beings. Alas, most of the valiant men of the Cossack divisions were hydrophobic and thus never made it to our hallowed shores, leaving us adrift with our dead.

"My wife and I believed ourselves to be safe in our little clearing, surrounded by the deep, mysterious forest that we both loved for its silence and its temperance. We had no need to fear the night as we had in our own hometown; soon, the thought of a Star-Crosser attack became as distant as Marguerite's former clients.

"It was peaceful there. We built our own house, raised our own food, planted, sweated, and carried on for three years that way, only going into the nearby town if there was something we could not produce ourselves or if we wished to hear news of our motherland.

"At first she seemed put off by Sir Cardigan, who had, naturally, crossed the Channel with us. Once she realised that the two of us were inseparable, however, and that Sir Cardigan was actually the best friend that Man could ask for, she began to see through his gruesome exterior to the kind dog that had faithfully served me almost my entire life. She never questioned how he obeyed me or why, if he was Star-Crossed, he didn't try to devour our eyeballs at night on the way to our brains; he merely kept the household clean by living off of insects and other vermin.

"As for my affliction, Darkboat's concoction kept me mostly symptom-free, and the decay slowly receded back into my fingernail alone. I had to hide my ruined hand less and less, and her questions about why my fighting wounds weren't healing eventually disappeared altogether. There were many days when I considered telling her about bringing Sir Cardigan back as a Star-Crosser and my strange ability to control not only him, but—as I had found out during my quest—other undead creatures as well. But I always stopped syllables short of the truth. On the days surrounding the zeniths of the Homunculus Star when I hungered for her flesh or felt myself slipping into a catatonic stupor, I did my best to hide from her by foraging or going into town for supplies.

"Like Darkboat had mentioned, the times when we were intimate were the hardest to control such thoughts. But we wanted children so badly, and she was so beautiful when she asked if we could try just one more time...I quickly learned how to control myself and soon discovered that I was more concerned with procreation than with mastication.

"We never became pregnant, however. The doctors were baffled; we were both in such good health and she had birthed many children during her former occupation. Clearly the problem lay with me, and there was a small part of me that knew my affliction was at fault. Something written in the stars didn't want me to pass along my cursed heritage—or maybe the universe was trying to protect such a delicate flower from giving birth to a monstrosity like me.

"I decided to track down Darkboat to see if he had any remedy to my latest predicament, but I was unable to locate him. His home was empty and the statue that Mybelle had fallen in love with had been destroyed at the last zenith by a bunch of confused Star-Crossers, likely thinking that bronzed brains would taste just as scrumptious as their fleshy counterparts. I assumed that he had left, since there was nothing to keep him there any longer. Ladybird, when I asked, didn't know about whom I was talking, but he asked me to give him a good description. No sooner had he received the egg from me than it was stolen by one of Tarantula's thieves, and the following day, it hatched into the wrong bird—and not even a Flying Filching Fiend, either, but a Disgruntled Dragonbat that had shot fire out of every newborn orifice, burning down half of Tarantula's orphanage and half of his orphans with it.

"Ladybird guessed that only a clever assassin could have planted such an idea. It wasn't until a few weeks ago that I understood the full implications of Darkboat's—or rather, Wasp's—actions. He had manipulated me into marrying Ladybird's top prostitute and into retrieving an egg that he knew Tarantula would steal because of its value, crippling both his brothers' enterprises at once. We were all merely pieces in his puzzle—but Marietta and I had the last laugh when last we saw him. Well, me more so than her; she didn't have much of a mouth or a tongue or even lungs at that moment. My only regret is not getting Wasp to admit who had hired Marietta for my second assassination attempt before he was burned to a crisp by his own invention." Byron sparked the small instrument on his hand, showing all of the witnesses in the room what power he possessed. "No matter, however; I have since figured it out and will get to that shortly. There is still the matter of my downfall to discuss, the impetus of my own hard-driven thirst for revenge and retribution.

"Dejected by the news of Darkboat's disappearance and slightly less dejected to hear that Tarantula and Ladybird were both suffering, I went back home to my wife without a cure for our reproductive woes, hoping to resume our blissful but quiet life.

"On our way through the forest around our cottage, Sir Cardigan and I passed a strange structure. Like an obtuse boy in a fairytale, I paid no heed to his warning barks, but merely noted that the large cocoon dripping greyish goo was something at which to marvel rather than worry.

"The moment we arrived home was the last moment I was ever happy. Marguerite was knitting by the fire, absent-mindedly staring at the sparking flames and their quivering shadows. She had yet to see or hear me, so I marvelled for longer than I should have. The rise and fall of her tiny chest made the fabric of her floral dress crinkle, so that it looked like a wind-swept field of poppies in the gloaming. Her hair had fallen in front of her eyes, the light refracting through its silky redness, and the lines of the individual hairs on her brow made her seem a figure captured on textured canvas—for how else could such a beauty exist in real life? She scratched her head and the clean smell of her disrupted scalp wafted over the smokiness of the fire. And when she looked up, startled and overjoyed all at once to see me, oh!" Byron gasped, his hair disheveled, his coat askew and hitched up on one shoulder, his eyes welling up with complexion-smearing tears as he looked up towards the ceiling. For once, everyone was silent for all of the right reasons. Byron knew he had them hanging on to every word. His heartbreak was their catharsis. His woe their every thought. "How ecstatic life was in its quietude, in the solemnity of our happiness! Every day was the same, but we never tired of its perfection." He then coughed, remembering who and what he was, and put himself back together. The only difference from a few seconds before was the fading red in his eyes. "Then Sir Cardigan ran into the room and jumped onto her lap, yipping—or rather, gargling pridefully— at having brought her back a present when I was so empty-handed. The one and only time, ladies and gentlemen, evil Uncle, I have ever been jealous of a dog.

"'What have you got there?' she said, attempting to wrench the large femur bone from his mouth until his entire lower jaw came with it. Marguerite panicked, tried to put the entire thing back into his mouth, and only succeeded in making him edgy—when there was a loud thump at the door. All three of us froze. When it happened again, only Sir Cardigan moved, jawless and tired as he was. With a growl, he jumped off my wife's lap and pawed at the door, whining and looking back at me for some recognition of the danger he perceived. I had barely started to figure out what he was trying to tell me when the windows burst and the door buckled, splintering against a flood of Star-Crossers.

"Marguerite screamed—a sound I never again wanted to hear in my life but would, sooner than I had ever thought—and I pulled her behind me. Arms, too many to count, pushed in from every opening to the outside. Everywhere I looked were hands battling their way in, reaching for her—I already knew that my infected flesh held little appeal for their appetites. She picked up a poker from the fire and began slapping at them.

"'They are not errant schoolboys!' I yelled, grabbing the end of a flaming log and pushing them back with the whirling fire.

"'What else can we do?' she screamed back. I could only agree as another crash sounded and the door finally gave in. We had mere seconds before they would be upon us, merciless in their attack. I was still in my infancy when it came to my powers and could not yet control creatures of such irredeemable malice. I knew, however, that they would tear her apart first—that much I could glean from their primitive brains. But as I briefly contemplated killing her with my own hands to spare her the horror of being eaten alive, my best friend saved my life for the very last time.

"Sir Cardigan, more aware of the situation than either the poker-wielding Marguerite or my flaming log-wielding self, picked up the femur with his broken mouth, nudging it with his broken nose, and dragged it between the legs of an approaching fiend. Miraculously, the half-decayed man looked down; I could feel his need to return that femur somewhere with that part of myself hidden deep within my left ring finger. (That urge was, of course, only slightly ahead of his hunger for my wife's brains, but that goes without saying.) He bent over to follow my courageous friend as he disappeared into the darkness amidst the sounds of hundreds of Seekers and Stumblers alike, all converging on our small domicile.

"'My leg!' I heard a female voice cackle from the inkiness. Between my panic to protect my home and the rising smoke from the extremely flammable bodies, I could barely make out a one-legged Star-Crosser, austerely regal, with a crown of finger bones around her head and a scepter of a small leg in her hand. She was reaching to retrieve what I could only assume was her own thigh bone from Sir Cardigan's broken mouth.

"She then picked him up and tore him to pieces, flinging them to her minions, who started to retreat—mostly from the flames, but also because their mission was complete. Their master had gotten her prize. It was then that the idea of Star-Crosser Queens congealed with all of the rumours I had heard and I learned just how much of an abomination I truly was.

"I fell to my knees, both out of grief for my only friend's sudden and horrendous death and the intense pain wracking my decayed left hand. Every aspect of my infected nature that I had believed under control rushed to the surface—and Marguerite was their unfortunate victim. The need for her brains, to take them back to the enigmatic vision in the forest who had just destroyed my best friend and only remaining symbol of my childhood happiness, overpowered my love, my cognisance, and my own will.

"My wife watched in horror as my left hand began to decay all the way to the wrist and my eyes went blank. I moaned like they do; we all know the paralysing sound, the loss of humanity and the incongruity of such a noise coming from a civilised mouth. She screamed again just as my teeth sank into the sweet-smelling scalp

I had so admired minutes before. That horrible sound brought me back to myself—but too late. The damage was done.

"She ran up the smouldering stairs to escape the horror that her husband had become, not daring to go outside lest the invading beasts be encountered once again. I caught her wrist at the top step, furiously trying to explain what had happened, how I had successfully kept my infection under control until Sir Cardigan's undeath was somehow pushed back into me. But she was hysterical, and in my passion to get her to leave the now-burning house, I am sorry to say that I struck her. She returned the favour and knocked one of my molars loose. In the ensuing struggle, she tripped and fell backwards down the stairs, breaking every important bone in her body with a series of sharp cracks and ending with her neck at the bottom."

"How do we know that you didn't push her?" the redhead said. Spittle nodded in agreement.

"History is written by the victors, my dears, and the victors are most certainly those still breathing. As she no longer breathes, I am left to tell her story. Know that I loved her more than I love myself—a great feat, I must emphasise—and have no cause to lie, as I still blame myself for her unfortunate death. Perhaps this is not enough to convince you, but I hear her scream every night before I close my eyes and every morning before they open. If I had pushed her, I do not doubt that I would hear that scream every second of my life.

"I bent over to kiss her fragile, rose-petal lips once last time, but in doing so, my back tooth loosened entirely and slid down into her throat. With her last breath she choked, succumbing to asphyxiation instead of the harshness of her wounds."

"You were frenching with a corpse?" Spittle pondered.

"A corpse that was my wife mere seconds before, my poor sir. I see nothing grotesque about it.

"I lifted her shattered frame in my arms, the sun having risen and scattered the Star-Crossers and their rather mythological leader to the four corners of the covered forest. I found a burial spot for her in the clearing, next to the flowers that she had loved to pick and that still decorated the burned ruins of our house. I spent all day digging her grave in the hard ground and all night fashioning a marker out of a dead branch, despite the advanced decay of my hand. The concoction helped, but I could not bear to take any dirt from my deceased love's grave to make more. It would be the first of many downward steps into a grief that would subsume not only my best friend and my wife, but my humanity as well. More salt stung the earth that day than all of my days before or since. I resolved to shed no more tears so as not to cheapen the emotion—"

"You just cried two days ago because of a rock in your shoe," Marietta interrupted. Spittle snorted. This time it was the ginger who shushed them, receiving a wink and a smile from Byron before he continued.

"I curled up in bed mere hours before the next sunrise and dreamed that my love was somehow still alive, sleeping next to me with my fingers entwined in her downy red curls. It was only when my hand squished into the rotted skin of her left cheek, releasing a small torrent of pus-contaminated saliva, that I knew I wasn't dreaming.

"I bounded out of bed and embraced my Marguerite returned to me. As a Star-Crosser, yes—but like Sir Cardigan before her and Marietta after her, she retained her memories, her faculties, and her essence because of my bite. With my arms wrapped around her, I imagined continuing our life together, infected but perfected in our abnormality; we were now equal, with no secrets and no limits to what we could achieve in a deathtime together. She pushed me away at the height of my imagination, however, and demanded that I change her back.

"'But,' I explained, 'there is no way to do such a thing! Even with my strange powers, a mere mortal cannot simply turn back Death's clock. But think—Sir Cardigan far outlived any normal dog! You and I...our love could last forever.'

"'He was a decayed mass that could barely bark! The only reason I put up with him was because I loved you. And even our marriage was a sham! You never told me anything about your past, your life, anything from before you came to the orphanage or the years you disappeared hence. And I never questioned you; I told myself that you would tell me when you were able. How could you do that to me? How could you keep such a big part of yourself locked away and pretend like it never existed? When I vowed to love you, I meant the entirety of you—not disjointed, piecemeal bits flashed from behind a thick curtain. What else haven't you told me? Did you ever even want children, or was that another lie? Are you truly unable to cure me, or do you just want to keep me like this for your own selfish reasons?'

"'I don't know! I've never tried!'

"'Well, now would be a good time to find out.'

"I closed my eyes and concentrated, afraid that I would undo too much of whatever had brought her back and reduce her to a corpse again; I couldn't lose the happiness that had been so lately returned to me. And then, there, niggling at the corner of my consciousness, was a small strand that bound us together. If I had thought that we were connected before, how poor of a man in love I had been to have mistaken one thing for another! I threaded her through me, a proverbial needle trying to push her soul close to a heaven made for the two of us, and stitched her up.

"Her ruined cheek knit itself together. Her ribcage, which had been hanging open like the door of a safe to show off the squishy, putrid spots of decay on her internal organs, swung back with a snap. There was barely even a mark against her ruined clothes to show where she had once been imperfect. If before she had looked like she had dragged herself through hell to get to me, now it seemed that she had merely gotten a little overexcited with the trowel while gardening.

"'There!' I replied, so overjoyed with my success that I didn't realise the pain in my left hand had worsened. The foul stench in the air was no longer coming from my wife, but my own corrupt flesh. My skin was the horrible green found only in bodies that had lain in germ-infested waters for weeks, bloated and crawling with swimming rats. The flesh had peeled back from my knuckles so that four white, shiny spots reflected in the fading moonlight; the muscles twitched with brackish grease that seeped into the cuff of my shirt.

"Then came my horrible realisation: she was not saved, not cured, but merely changed at the expense of my hand. I would have gladly taken it off if she had wanted, but she railed against our fate and, just like on the stairs, refused to listen to my pleas about adapting to the circumstances life had thrown at us.

"She ran off into the night just as the blazing comet of the Homunculus Star crested in the sky. She felt it first, I know, because she buckled, clutching her stomach. Then it crashed into me and emptied all thoughts out of my skull. My previous attacks of inhumanity seemed tame by comparison; if that was what a Star-Crosser feels all the time, I can see why they are so vehement in their quest to eat us.

"The last thought I had, before blanking out completely under the swarming effects of the Star, was how large that bright object hurtling towards us seemed to be getting. Pain shot up my left hand, curling my fingers into a misshapen claw that tried to tear the sky in two.

"When I awoke hours later in the sunlight, I felt exhausted and lethargic. I was covered in blood, with bits of intestine and brain matter smeared on my lips and tongue. I panicked, hoping it wasn't the flesh of my Marguerite, until I saw the rabbit lying in pieces a few yards away. I sighed and looked for my wife. She was on the shore of a lake, the water dragging her arm back and forth with its small crests. There was a smouldering rock sticking out of where the left side of her face should have been, and she was unresponsive to my pleas or my touch or even my tearless weeping.

"The same thing that had happened with Sir Cardigan's death had happened again with hers. The rot had spread up my arm up to the elbow; my hand was little more than a skeletal remain of what it had been. It was nothing, however, compared to losing Marguerite yet again.

"I buried her body, along with the fatal meteorite that had fused with her face, in the sand where I had found her, lacking the strength in the sunlight to drag her back to her previous grave and unable to go near our ruined house again. There were no memories left there for me, and this death was so permanent, so present in the decayed mess of my arm that I could barely stand the thought of staying on that soil for one more harrowing second. I was, however, able-bodied enough to fetch the grave marker I had made. I stuck it at the top of her sandy grave and said one last word for her eulogy: Never.

"I would never love again, never laugh, never feel, never do anything that I had done with her. I moved back to England, bent on finding my inheritance; only money could make me forget, or rather, pay others to make me forget. I went to every brothel I could, trying to find that same spark, still denying the half of me that had awakened when Sir Cardigan died, making do with fingernail clippings and mats of hair instead of the true flesh I craved. Then, the very same night that I could stand the cravings no longer, that I decided I didn't care if I became a Star-Crosser and consumed what had been taboo from the very beginning...I found that the girl I had hired was none other than the assassin sent after me as a child. She was what had started all of this nonsense. What did her life matter, I thought, after all those she had taken?

"And so I ate of her flesh and she became a Star-Crosser like Marguerite and Sir Cardigan. The sickness that had been overwhelming my body disappeared, though; instead of becoming more monstrous, like Darkboat had predicted, I became strong and healthy again. Thus, every zenith ever since that night two years ago, I have killed and eaten people to maintain myself on my quest to regain what is rightfully mine.

"The question that remained, however, was who had hired the lovely Marietta a second time. That mystery had plagued me ever since Wasp let it slip on his deathbed—until this very night. Someone in this room is responsible, and I intend to unmask them as the villain that he or she," he said, glancing over the ginger, "truly is."

He sighed, his gaze coming back to rest on the emerald eyes of the mystery lady, and pointed a finger at her that wobbled with exhaustion in the light of the dim boxcar.

"Why, Marguerite? After all this time, after everything we went through, my thinking that you were dead, why did you hire an assassin to kill me under my Uncle's name? More importantly, how did you survive the impact of a comet to the head? And why did I feel your death in my soul like I had with Sir Cardigan? Death is no boundary for the likes of us, but there are some cliffs that even we cannot come back from."

"You presume too much, Byron," Marguerite said, tearing off her own mask and revealing the soft, delicate curls of her red hair against the decayed ruin of her left cheek. Only Byron noticed that it was the exact same pattern of rot that she had come back from the grave with, no more and no less. The years of their separation had been incredibly kind to her; she had not progressed into a mumbling Stumbler like Sir Cardigan had, and like Marietta would have if they had not been replacing her parts along the way. While a normal Star-Crosser would be frozen in death, however, she appeared to have aged into her late twenties. "I fell in love again, years after surviving the horrible meteor impact. It was I who convinced your Uncle to murder you, for turning me into a despicable creature and for lying about our love! I didn't tell him, of course, what had happened to me; I was able to hide the decay quite effectively using what I had learned from Darkboat and the eavesdropping I had done while we were together. But your Uncle, as infatuated with me as I was with him, decided he was done with you, not wanting to ruin our relationship with any foul thoughts of the past. So I dressed up as the Doctor, went to Darkboat—Wasp— and ordered that he rectify the ruined opportunity from so many years past. It was I who hired Marietta the second time, and I stand by my decision!"

This time, only one person gasped, and that was the three-quarters dead Archibald Llewellyn-Cave. It was three-quarters the moan of a Star-Crosser, with just a hint of cognisance behind it to let everyone know that he had not yet turned.

"It seems there is more unmasking yet to be done this night!" Byron said, taking his hat off to rub his dusty temples.

"Archie, I'm so sorry I never told you about my life before you married me—" Marguerite started.

"The same thing you accused me of!" Byron interrupted. "I see hypocrisy is a learned trait."

"I didn't want your hatred of your nephew to taint our relationship!"

"The bastard is not my nephew," Archibald gurgled.

"Relationship?" Byron squeaked, unprepared for the torrent of images that ran through his head. It wasn't until his former wife had said the word out loud—and in regards to another man—that the actuality of it struck him.

"I could never hate you, my wife," Archibald said. He raised a hand and Marguerite pressed it against her left cheek. "No, the other one," he grunted in disgust. She held it to her beautiful right cheek until his arm went slack and hit the floor with an echoing bump.

"Archie!" Marguerite burst into tears.

Byron, flabbergasted at the display of familial love that his Uncle had never showed to him, debated whether he should make her eat the remains of her dead husband out of spite. Then he remembered that he had studied every line and space of his Uncle's will, looking for loopholes in the otherwise ironclad text. A small smile appeared on his lips.

"We were never legally separated," he whispered, mostly to himself. Only Marietta heard his feeble words.

The train's brakes squealed horribly and all of the furniture and passengers inside lurched forwards. Only Byron kept his footing as the rest scrambled to keep the parlour looking spic-and-span enough for their captor. Byron pulled out his pocket watch with too many faces and hands, checked it, frowned, closed it, and looked to the front of the train.

"Just in time," he said, loud enough that everyone could hear. "More or less. Ladies and gentlemen! Star-Crossed and human alike! May I permit you to step out into my domicile? I find it only fitting that, since you have entertained me in this parlour for the past three hours, I invite you into my own house and do the same for you." He waited until the train fully stopped, then opened the boxcar door into an abandoned train yard. Rusted boxcars spilled their dilapidated innards over miles and miles of ruined track and dusty, unused switches. People were reluctant to leave until he made the three Star-Crossed ladies snap at them, herding them into another empty boxcar and into cages, where Byron forced them to await their fates.

In the heated kerfuffle of the moving masses, Spittle slipped from between the man who was still desperately clinging to his lampshade and the American woman who was still sobbing, wiping with the sleeve of her neighbour at the massive expanse of make-up that had started to migrate south with her tears. The controlled Star-Crossers were too slow to react and the slippery thief started running, his clockwork leg echoing a metallic clunk every other step.

"I'll get him!" Marietta said, running off after the young assassin until the two of them crested a hill and disappeared from Byron's sight.

The floors of the cages were littered with bone fragments, like the den of some predatory cat that liked to sleep on the remains of its previous meals. A few guests realised right away what would happen to them in a few weeks when the Homunculus Star rose once again. Still others were trying to push such thoughts away, thinking that, as strange a man as Byron was, he would not save them from the Long-Eared Legion just to kill them off later.

Once the passengers were secure in their cages and watching Byron and the three ladies—Marguerite trying to look away as her lover's corpse began to turn into a Seeker—with sad eyes that begged for freedom, Byron cleared his throat to end his tale of woe:

"Fear not, my friends, for this story shall have a happy ending after all. You see, now that my Uncle has been killed by a few rampant Seekers who accompanied the Long-Eared Legion, all of his money goes to his wife. And now that his wife is dead," he said, taking out a sword from one of the compartments on the other side of the abandoned boxcar and swiping off Marguerite's head, "all of his money goes to her first and rightful husband: me."

In Which Byron Cheers Himself Up, Or: Come Two, Come All

"What do you mean all of his money doesn't go to me?" Byron demanded, sticking his hand through the bars at the young clerk who was desperately trying to escape his neck-wringing reach. Byron and a somewhat human-looking—though not entirely blemishless—Marietta stood at the front of a line of a barrister's office after trying to claim his inheritance through his connection to his Uncle's deceased wife.

"You've been living with one," the clerk said, squinting at a piece of paper filled with finely written script and adjusting his pince-nez, "Marietta Margot-Pierre Lapin for two years, yes?"

"I wouldn't necessarily say 'living,' but yes, we've been together. But not that kind of together, if you understand. She's more of a servant, but not that kind of a servant, if you know what I mean, and we just rather have a complicated relationship—and I know the impact of the word relationship, having just recently been bombarded by images I would rather never have envisaged. But what of it?"

"According to your Uncle's will and the agents that he sent to make sure you weren't getting into trouble," the clerk continued, looking Byron up and down and scoffing at his rather disheveled tailcoat—ruined by his Uncle's blood, the Star-Crossers' various body fluids, and the fluff of some rather mangy Long-Eared Legion compatriots—"he made sure that if, after your marriage to one Marguerite Annabelle Lee Gretchenson, you lived with another woman for more than two years, she would become your common-law wife, thus invalidating your marriage to Ms. Gretchenson and forfeiting any claims she held—including your Uncle's fortunes, now that Marguerite Annabelle Lee Gretchenson is well known to be Heelduchess Judith, the Archduke's third wife."

"My fortunes!" Byron yelled. Everyone else waiting in line behind them glared at him and his common-law wife.

"I am sorry, sir, there is nothing you can do. And now that Marguerite is dead, all of your Uncle's fortunes go to his adopted son, one Jebediah Hiram Blackmore."

"Who?" Byron and Marietta asked together, causing everyone in line to look at them again. "And, I repeat, my fortunes," Byron added.

"Also known as...Spittle?" finished the clerk, squinting at legalese. Byron wanted to push his hands all the way through the bars and wring the fine print's neck. If such a thing were possible. Even if it weren't, he would find a way to do it.

"When I get my hands on him—" Byron started yelling. He caught himself when he noticed a policeman among the other customers, twirling his nightstick and clearly itching to clobber someone in the gut with it. "I will pat him on the head in congratulations."

"Let me try." Marietta sauntered in front of Byron and set her elbows on the clerk's desk, squeezing her chest up and out to give him a lovely view of her cleavage. "Surely there must be something you can do?" she cooed, twirling her hair with one hand while passing a crumpled bill into the clerk's window with the other. She was human-looking, but just barely. "A few teensy scratches of the pen to turn that two years we've been living together into a one—"

"But not together together," Byron interjected.

"—will make all of this just go away." She lifted her hand like a leaf being tossed in the wind and let the clerk's eyes follow the curve of her side.

The clerk unravelled the dirty piece of paper and said flatly, "This is the label from a can of soup." He slammed the small wooden door shut so quickly that Marietta had to pull her fingers back.

"Hey! Hey!" Byron yelled, knocking on the window. "I demand the right to appeal!"

"This office isn't a court of law," the clerk's voice came through the thin wood.

"Then I demand the right to fight the articles of my Uncle's will! There was never any such clause when I studied it! I demand that an inquisition be formed to research the legality of such an amendment!"

"And this document isn't a constitution!" the clerk replied.

Byron continued yelling every swear and curse he knew, flinging insults like mud, until both him and Marietta were flung out onto the street by the many hands of the people waiting in line behind them. Once ejected, Byron sat down in the gutter, resting his head on his knees and covering it with both arms. He had never felt this miserable before. Well, there was that one time, when his best friend had challenged him to a pickle-juice drinking contest, but that had been a different situation entirely.

"What am I to do now?" he asked no one in particular, seemingly unaware that Marietta was sitting in the gutter with him, partially shielding him from the splash of horses' hooves as they carried steamcars past. He began to push around the filth with the toe of his boot. "This is the second time I have found myself in such a guttery situation—"

"Just two weeks ago, we were covered in the guts of some unfortunate militiamen who were trying to keep their properties free of the cottonwood-tree fluff, thinking that the tree was the first of many spies sent by French avant-garde invaders who only wear clothes made of cotton candy," Marietta interjected.

"Guttery as in gutters, not as in guts. Or let me phrase it this way: guttery as in guttersnipe, a particular brand of lowlife with which you are intimately familiar. Since my wretched youth I have spent the entirety of my life—"

"Unlife?"

"—trying to get my inheritance back. I finally had it in my clutches, only for it to be ripped away by unfortunate legal circumstance. I have been plunged into an unearthly depression from which I am afraid I shall never escape."

"But," Marietta said, her face in ponderous thought, "you didn't know that Marguerite was alive yesterday, let alone that she was your Uncle's legal beneficiary. So you must have had some backup plan when we found your Uncle at that party. What were you going to do before the Long-Eared Legion attacked?"

"I was going to corner him, turn him into a sentient Star-Crosser like you, and then command him to leave me everything in exchange for some flim-flam that I could turn him back. But I let my emotions get the best of me, and they spilled over into you and the others; when you attacked and bit my Uncle, there was no chance for me to turn him. So that avenue has long since passed. Actually," he said, lifting his head and staring at Marietta, "it's your fault for—"

"What do you usually do to cheer yourself up?" Marietta changed the subject quickly.

Byron put his head back down and mumbled something from between his arms.

"What was that?" she repeated.

"Go to the circus. My father used to take me there on his days off. We would skip the tiger tamers and the elephant trainers and go straight to the sideshow. The freaks always cheered me up with their strange mixture of the absurd and the macabre. I liked seeing others with stranger lives than I and knowing that they earned a living in spite of their differences, much like how I assumed I would live when I received my father's money. But that was all dashed to hell—"

"Come on, get up," she said, pulling him to his feet as if he were a child. "Let's go to the circus, then."

"What, what, what?" Byron spat. "How absurd for a grown man and his common-law wife to go the circus together without any children."

"We could steal some and then it wouldn't be so strange."

"No, no, that would never work. The thing would be complaining the whole time for his real parents—"

"Not if we stole a young enough one that he didn't even know we weren't his real parents."

"And what would we feed it? I don't even have enough money for me to enjoy Frenchman-free cotton candy. If we didn't get any for it—"

"We steal that, too," Marietta replied, shrugging. "Look, there's a kid." She pointed at a small child in a carriage whose mother was staring into the window of a jewellery shop. "And there's the circus." She pointed to the other side of the street at a travelling circus that had just come into town. "Strange the barrister's office let it set up so close. It's practically begging us to come in."

"Inanimate objects cannot beg, so clearly it is you who are projecting your own begging upon the place itself. It wouldn't be the first time that you've begged for me to come inside your big top."

"You do know how to show a girl a good time," Marietta retorted. Keeping an eye on the mother, she deftly stole the baby carriage, pressed Byron's hands onto the handlebar, and pushed him forwards. The three of them strolled across the street to the box office. Some legerdemain on Marietta's part easily convinced the ticket-seller that they had purchased their fares already, and he let them in with a cheery smile and a promise that they would have the time of their lives. Byron made a mental note to ask her to show him that trick for future reference. Circuses were an expensive habit to have.

They walked along the mulched floor, kicking up sawdust and peanut shells, smelling the over-buttered roasted corn and turkey legs dripping fat. Lions roared, elephants trumpeted, whips cracked, and the people who had gone to see the Bearded Lady tittered nervously. Signs for the various sideshow performers hung everywhere, their rough wooden displays more weathered than most of the guests who read them. Peeling paint, cracked and knotted knobs, and a few bullet holes told the story of a circus that had seen its fair share of travel—not all of it safe. Though Byron couldn't fathom how the circus had acquired its few disturbing salt-water rings.

Marietta tugged the carriage towards the lion pits, where a tamer was attempting to stick his head inside one of their open mouths. But Byron ignored her and continued to push the baby towards the small tents near the back.

"It's all fake," he muttered when she protested.

"How so?"

Byron stopped and looked at his companion with incredulity.

"You have seen me conjure a rabbit out of paper and men fried to a crisp by machinery that controls Zeus's lightning itself. How is it not fake for a pompous, pomaded, moustachioed top hat to stick his entire head inside the maw of such a beast? Besides, when have you ever caught me lyin' to you?"

"…Was that a pun on the word lion?"

"Heavens, no!" Put off by the mere suggestion, Byron pressed his hand to his heart to show how she had wounded him. "You'll make Cardigan Junior cry if you continue to talk like that."

"You named the kid after your dog?" She tried to drag Byron over to the elephant enclosures; the sign promised an elephant ride if she waited in line long enough and could bear the horrible smell of the gargantuan beasts for more than a few minutes. Byron, who had seen the world from the top of many things, rolled his eyes again and pish-poshed her wish.

"Irrelephant," he responded, waving his hands in the air. Marietta squinted at him. "And I didn't name our kid after just any dog. I told my best friend on his deathbed that I would name my firstborn in honour of him. He was dying of what is only known as the Red Recondite Consumption—"

"What's that?" Marietta nabbed a batch of cotton candy. She allowed Cardigan Junior to suck on her sugary fingers and passed a clump on to Byron, who continued his story with his mouth full of the sticky fluff, already a smile blossoming where before had been abject depression.

"Exactly, my dear. And stop monkeying around!" he yelled as they passed the enclosure of squawking, hooting primates, throwing tufts of fur and other substances to get them to come closer. One monkey danced outside the cage as a man in deep red velvet with gold piping cranked a dying organ in desperate need of a transplant. "The only thing known about the horrible disease is that one gets it when one talks about oneself, in a classic example of illeism, despite being not of royal blood. His face was covered in horrible red marks that oozed pus whenever someone blinked. His vocal cords had been beaten so raw by the ravaging recondite pustules that you could hardly hear what he was saying. He promised that, if I returned his bones to his homeland—"

"The pound?" Marietta suggested.

"—his ghost would look after me like a guardian angel instead of haunting me. That's another effect of the Consumption, to haunt the last person you see while living."

"Now I know you're lying. Sir Cardigan was ripped to shreds by what you believed to be a Star-Crosser Queen."

"You, my dear common wife—"

"Common-law," she corrected.

"I said what I meant—are walking on a tightrope here," Byron responded as a pair of funambulists flipped and turned in the air above them. The slapping of their slippers against the hard, narrow rope echoed through the big top. Byron watched as Marietta squinted to see what was happening above her, loath to be dragged away before she got a proper look at the jovial excitement happening all around them. He wondered at his patience with her; more than ten minutes of anyone else's company would be enough to start him wondering how their flesh tasted. "You saw the cocoon same as me in the Charred Thickets, so you know that there must be something more to the Star-Crossers than what we know. Think of my own ability to control them. What makes you think there aren't others like me?"

"Oh, Great Sailor," Marietta stopped in the middle of the circus. Several clowns bumped into her and squeaked and cursed as they went by. "You mean there might be more of you?"

"Quit clowning around and see what Cardigan Junior wants,

will you? He seems to be leaking." Byron pushed the carriage towards her. She picked the baby up, sniffed, turned him upside down, and declared that he was just fine. She put him back into the carriage and the two of them finally found the sideshow at the back of the circus.

"Ah!" Byron exclaimed, clapping his hands and rubbing them together. "Where should we go first? The Bearded Lady? The Tattooed Man? The Torturer's Apprentice? The Insane Doctor? The...Beekeeper? What do you think of all the—"

"You say 'buzz' and I'll leave you here with Cardigan Junior. Who, by the way, is a girl, so I think we should name her Tallulah, after my favourite gun."

"Is he? I have the darndest time figuring out the sex of those things. And I was going to say, what do you think the other circus acts feel about being next to a beekeeper? Let's see him last. How trite, to display such a normal profession next to the wondrous marvels of those too irregular to be part of normal society! Ostracised to the fringes, they must create their own societies, where abnormal is normal and anyone lacking an extra appendage or a horrible lisp or deformity or, at the very least, a tattoo of a mermaid doing unspeakable things with a sailor, is the outcast. You would fit in perfectly as the Girl Of Many Parts, but that, of course, makes it sound as if you have multiple—"

One of the elephants trumpeted loudly so that Byron couldn't even hear himself talk. But he started thinking about everything they had been through in the past few days as they went into the Torturer's Apprentice tent to look at old Inquisitional paraphernalia. A black-cowled man with piercings all over his face and stretched earlobes, nostrils, and lips explained how the various contraptions worked.

"When the bottom was heated, the rats trapped inside would be forced to burrow through your stomach as you wailed…"

"So, the birds and the bees, eh?" Marietta said, elbowing Byron in the ribs. Ever since she hadn't tried to kill him after he'd locked her in a closet for killing Wasp, he didn't mind her touch as much. He had even remembered missing her presence—or rather, having her face to talk at as he came up with his brilliant plans.

"Dear Lord, woman! Don't you think Cardigan Junior is a bit young to have that conversation? He is, after all, only a mere babe."

"She is only a mere babe, and I was talking about you and me," Marietta whispered. They passed an iron maiden, complete with a sedated Stumbler inside that squealed every time it closed, so that the patrons could fully experience the tortured screams of those who had wronged the Grand Inquisitors.

"Puncturing spears placed at precisely the same height as many vital organs, including…"

"It's a little late for both of us. Especially you, I think," he responded.

"I meant the literal birds and bees! Don't you find it strange that my parents think I'm an ornithologist and your dead wife believed you to be an apiarist?"

They passed a rack on which a Stumbler was tied and slowly being stretched as their guide mumbled on. The Stumbler's arms and legs were far longer than they were supposed to be; Byron thought they must maintain some sort of flexibility not found in the living.

"I only said that I was an apiarist because it was the first thing that popped into my mind. My mother came from a family of bee-related professionals, either beekeeping or flowers, like her. It only seemed natural that I pass along the tradition."

"In which the fingers and toes would oftentimes be crushed very slowly…"

"And your false profession was also that of the men who stole your mother away before she gave birth to you," Marietta said, blinking in the sunlight as they came out of the tent of the Torturer's Apprentice and headed into the Bearded Lady's section. Rows of people watched as a very large lady indeed screwed up her eyeballs, growling through clenched teeth, and jutted her chin forwards so everyone could see the length of her impressive beard.

"Just what exactly are you insinuating?"

"Have you ever stopped to think that maybe your Uncle is right about you being a bastard? That the men who kidnapped your mother raped her? I mean, I've seen your Uncle, and you look nothing like him, so I can only assume that you must resemble—"

Byron's ringing ears cut off all other noises in the room. Whatever she saw upon his face, Marietta cut herself off at precisely the right moment before he would have desiccated her flesh right then and there. His blood rose to his skin so that all of him, not just the feverish left hand and cancerous right foot, felt as if he were standing next to an open oven. His hands twitched, wishing for a fine string of legalese to wring. Or, Marietta's exposed neck.

"Think of the children!" Marietta cried, shielding herself with the baby carriage from his explosion of vitriol.

Byron stopped—not because he was thinking of children, but because everyone in the room was looking at them instead of the Bearded Lady. While he would have been able to control the situation if there were a few more Star-Crossers in the vicinity, it no longer seemed worth it to continue to struggle against Fate's endless roadblocks. His inheritance had been within a finger's reach, only for it to be taken away because of the woman next to him. And as much as he wanted to decay her into nothingness, into something so decrepit that not even bones remained, he found he couldn't do that, either. It wasn't a matter of going soft, nor a lessening of his want for revenge, but the part of himself he thought long dead—the part he thought he had buried with Marguerite—seemed to be stirring. What had risen in him wasn't love, exactly; he merely didn't hate Marietta. Which was more than he could say for anyone else.

Except Marguerite. He could never hate her, even after everything she had done to him. But she was neither here nor there. Well, in fact, she was there, but Byron had yet to tell anyone else that.

And Sir Cardigan. But that was it, really.

Calmly straightening his tie, Byron took Marietta by the hand and led her and Cardigan Junior into the next tent: The Insane Doctor.

"…marvelous mysteries unfolded to yours truly about the magical wonder of the phenomenon known as Siamese Twins!" the not-too-insane-looking Doctor announced, winking as Byron, Marietta, and Cardigan Junior took a seat in the back amidst the coughing and general shuffling of the bored-looking audience. The Doctor, wisely deciding to cut his patter short, bent down into a cabinet on the stage and pulled out a large jar containing a two-headed, two-chested, two-legged baby preserved in yellowish fluid. Its slight drifting movements through the warbled glass made it look even more monstrous than it really was. "Ladies and gentlemen! This is just one of the specimens I have collected throughout my travels of this strange phenomenon, in which two children share the same womb to devastating effect."

He rummaged around the cabinet for more creatures and continued to stack them on the counter, inviting people to come up and look at them firsthand. When Marietta and Byron went on stage, the Doctor—a septuagenarian with kind eyes and crinkled hands and a disposition far from insane, who had introduced himself as Dr. Milton—gasped and whispered to Byron to stay after the show so that he could talk to him and his "lovely wife." Marietta gave Byron a knowing look and sat back down demurely, folding her skirts over her knees in a very ladylike manner, and started rocking the carriage.

The audience listened with much more attention now that Dr. Milton had displayed the creatures in his repertoire, all various cases of chimaeras, conjoined twins, infants with extra appendages on both their exteriors and interiors, and other newborn lusus naturae.

"I came across one of my strangest cases back when I still practised. There was a woman who had been in love with a man who had recently turned into a Star-Crosser, sweet thing that she was—" Byron sat straight up and cocked his head sideways "—and when I first examined her a few months afterwards, there seemed to be two heartbeats in her womb. When she gave birth, I delivered one shining boy and waited for the other, only to find nothing left. Not even a stillborn. Which led me to assume that, sometime during gestation, the stronger of the two somehow absorbed his twin, thus leading to the birth of a single entity."

"Okay," Marietta whispered into Byron's ear, "now I know why they call him the Insane Doctor. Let's get out of here and go check out the Beekeeper. It's got to be more plausible than this, whatever his shtick is."

Byron shushed her and kept his rapt attention on the Doctor. People left, dropping their coins into his outstretched hat or trying to duck out early so as not to seem cheap. Byron's knee twitched nervously up and down, bouncing Sir Cardigan Junior, who cooed with delight as his kidnapper watched the remaining stragglers with urgent eyes. If he could trade in all of his substantive powers—well, minus the big one of controlling the dead, of course—for the power to make people leave, he would do so at once. Once everyone had left, Byron stood up and approached Milton as the doctor started putting away the examples of deformed twins.

"Ah! I had hoped it was you after all this time!" Milton said, pulling Byron into an embrace. He tried to fight as politely as possible by twisting, gesturing, and making awkward noises. "I pride myself on being able to recognise all of the babies I've ever delivered, and you are by no means an exception! Byron Ulysses Llewellyn-Cave—how are you, my lad?" Milton's genuinely joyful interest threw Byron off; he was as unaccustomed to kindness as he was to people pronouncing his name correctly. But that only strengthened his hunch that this man was going to help him now that he had hit rock bottom. And he had complimented Marietta, which meant he had unknowingly complimented Byron's work at making her look human.

"So you knew my parents, then?" Byron asked.

Milton gestured for all of them to sit down in one of the long rows so recently vacated by curious spectators.

"Knew them? I'd treated your mother since she was a little girl! One of the most beautiful ladies I have ever had the luck to be friends with. A horrible thing when she died, really—and the tragic circumstances of your birth!"

"I'm sorry?" Byron asked hesitantly.

Marietta put a hand on his shoulder and he found it to be calming, despite the rising tide of his blood.

"That story I ended the show with! The mysterious case of the vanishing twin—why, that was you!"

"Oh Great Sailor," Marietta whispered. "You mean there could have been more of him?"

"And may I comment on how lovely your wife is?" Milton bowed a little in his seat and tipped his hat to her.

"She's a—handful." Byron gripped his left arm, which was throbbing with tension as he maintained Marietta's human appearance.

"And what a beautiful baby girl!" Milton gasped, lifting up the infant and rocking her gently in his arms.

"Cardigan Junior. Apple of my eye. Seems like we just got him, it's been so blissful raising him," Byron responded, anxious to get back to talking about his own childhood. "But what about this vanishing twin?"

"Not much is known, other than what I've been able to piece together from old wives' tales and medicine on the fringe. It's made me the laughingstock of the entire medical community, I'm afraid, and it was your case in particular that pushed me over the edge into unexplored, maddening territory. See, I postulated that not only did you absorb your twin, but that your twin was actually a Star-Crosser. That was why you were born with the grim, ghastly appearance of a stillbirth, but yet still breathed. I wanted to keep track of you for the sake of my theory, to see if there were any other adverse effects...but after your mother died and your father started keeping her as a pet, your rather overbearing Uncle barred me from seeing your family in the medical sense. I've heard about his death, by the way; let me offer you my sincerest condolences. Being eaten by the Long-Eared Legion is a fate reserved for the most wicked of men, and even then, still a bad way to go."

"But how could my twin be a Star-Crosser? That makes no sense. Even if it had died in the womb, unless it was infected..." Byron trailed off, unable to finish his sentence.

"Did no one tell you?" Milton asked. "You were probably told that your mother was attacked by a roving gang of Seekers and suffered a fatal bite mere inches from her doorway, thus turning her into the Crosser you so well remember. Well, that was a story to save face, you see! Everyone thought it strange that she should be found uneaten and whole after the attack, until your Uncle realised that the Star-Crossers she had tangled with were once the very same squad of sailors to which belonged your mother's long-lost beau! They were rather smitten with one another in their youth before he was taken by the mysteries of the sea and she chose the fortunes of a clockwork-limb scion over a poor sailor's meagre, salty savings. When his ship returned, your mother, in a fit of youthful passion, slipped away at night to see them into port, only to realise too late that they had been infected during their voyage. Each one had surrendered to the rampant disease in the course of their three-month journey, so that by the time the doom ship docked, sick men, Seekers, and Stumblers alike disgorged into the terrified crowd.

"Your mother's beau was one of the relatively fortunate; he was merely infected by the time he staggered off the ship, and was able to save your mother from a rather vigorous Seeker by throwing a knife into the back of its skull just as its teeth were about to clamp down upon her serene face.

"Passions high with her rescue, hearts hammering from the encounter all surmounted, there occurred a—ahem—how to put this delicately, and in front of your lovely wife and child, no less?—a night of abandon betwixt the two. He must have turned soon afterwards, perhaps when they were gently drifting off to sleep, still embracing each other in their sinful sensuousness, but the damage had already been done. His seed spread to create a child at the exact same time that your father's did, creating half-brothers within the same womb, though one less, well, alive than the other. Figuring out how the timing alone worked could have been the basis of a grand thesis leading to yet another doctorate, but I digress.

"It was eventually this event that led to her death, for the Crossing disease, I postulate, comes not only from a bite. But!" Milton said, brightening up, "we learned another possible transmission route of the infection!" Then he tried to look sober again. "Which is not a consolation at all, and I am very sorry indeed to be the one telling you this. I would have thought your father or Uncle would have confided it long ago."

"I am a bastard after all?" Byron whimpered, his shoulders falling and his back bowing. He seemed to be collapsing into himself, as if all the air had been forced out of him.

"As to that, I cannot be sure with one hundred percent accuracy. But one of the possible explanations of your birth is that both your father's spermatozoon and this soon-to-be-Seeker's each fertilised an egg and then the two of you fought for dominance in the womb. Had one of you not absorbed the other, you would have been half-brothers; same mother with a different father. Stranger things have happened, if my research across the country has led me to believe anything at all," Milton explained. Byron's face started to light up. "However, the more plausible scenario is that, because this man had yet to succumb to the infection, his sperm was still human and you are, indeed, a bastard. The green of your eyes is rather unusual, given your parents' heritage." Byron's face fell again. "And, of course, in the case of the former theory, you would have shown many more inexplicable symptoms, like decay starting at an extremity that eventually consumes an entire limb, or strange psychic phenomenon that allows you to interact with and understand Star-Crossers in ways the rest of us can only dream about. You seem to be a perfectly strapping young man with a normal family and a normal life—although your taste for ladies' gloves is rather strange."

"Well!" Marietta interrupted; Byron felt her arm on his, trying to cool his rising frustration, which seemed to be affecting Cardigan Junior as well. "We should be off. Tallulah's getting fussy."

"No, no, no! Of course, I understand!" Milton started showing them out. "I need to get ready for my last show. Before you leave, however, please go to the Beekeeper's tent! He's been out of sorts lately because nobody seems to want to see him, but his show really is worth it! Please, for just a few moments!"

"All right," Byron responded, still dejected, kicking the dirt as he made his way halfheartedly to the neighbouring tent, where the Beekeeper was just about to start his show.

Millions of thoughts spread through Byron's foggy, depressed mind. How could no one have told him about what had happened to his mother? If he was indeed the bastard of this Seeker, how was he even born at all? But as Milton's predictions echoed throughout his head, it all made sense. He had never believed Darkboat's or Foster's or Wasp's—or whatever you wanted to call him—theory that Sir Cardigan had infected him before showing any sign himself of being Crossed. It was only after he bit Sir Cardigan that the dog had turned—and the same went for Marguerite and Marietta after her. All of these things were inexplicable unless he was half Star-Crosser. The mere thought made his half-dead blood run cold in his half-dead veins.

"…going to tell you a few facts about the common honeybee that are very interesting and not widely known," the Beekeeper had been saying. He was a small man with very thick glasses that magnified his beady black eyes to three times their normal size and he had a habit of rubbing the top of his balding head, scratching at the few remaining strands of dirty, shaggy blonde hair while forming his next sentence. Underneath his glasses, he wore a chicken-wire device that kept his face free from the cluster of bees he had released into the small tent. Most buzzed around him, but a few strayed into the audience, where they started pestering the only person other than Byron, Marietta, and Cardigan Junior waiting to hear the Beekeeper's story: an old woman with three teeth, grey hair that fluoresced a strange shade of purple in the light, and a dress so ragged that she must not have changed it in fifteen years. A strange odour and a faint snoring sound wafted from her. She didn't even cringe when a bee landed on her nose and started crawling around the contours of her face.

"Can we go?" Byron hissed like a small child. He wanted, no, needed to find some way to make the world pay for the unfortunate circumstances of his birth. He thought he would start with finding Spittle and enacting the plan that had so failed with his Uncle, or trying out some techniques received from the Torturer's Apprentice. Alternatively, he could turn the Apprentice into a Crosser and see if a Seeker could fathom new ways to torture someone using undeath as a weapon.

Marietta merely shushed him, pushing the carriage back and forth to calm the fussy Cardigan Junior.

"…send out a scout in order to find profitable flowers, which will then tell the rest of the colony where the source of food is by dancing…"

"I believe that woman over there died of boredom years ago, and they merely left her body where it fell to make this place look more populated," Byron hissed back. He felt more unbearably surly with every moment stuck in that tent, unable to do anything to make his life right again. The bee had stung the old woman's nose, finally, but she had yet to react.

"…worker bees are known to sting once before they lose their internal organs with their stingers…"

"Are you sure this man even knows what he's talking about?" Byron said, trying to remember what little he had learned from his mother's family.

"The man is clearly very knowledgeable about bees. Yes, his demeanour could use some work for the context in which he's chosen to give his lectures, but that does not make his intelligence any less valid. It would be as if I were giving a lecture on all the ways to kill someone with a Blundering Barnacled Back-Hoe. Since I am not a sideshow freak," Marietta said, receiving a look from Byron, "at the current moment, it would not be the best venue for me to expound upon my favourite way, number seventeen, in which the operator of the Back-Hoe upchucks the target into a spinning vortex created by—"

"Oh, Great Sailor, please make it stop." Byron got up, unwrinkled his trousers, and made for the exit at the back of the tent.

"Wait, sir!" the Beekeeper said, setting a sputtering candle out on the table and wafting the smoke towards another clump of bees that he pulled out of their hive at the bottom of the stage. He handled something in his palms, cradling it as if it were the last picture of his mother. "Don't you want to hear about how queen bees are made?"

"I, sir," Byron responded, grabbing Marietta by the wrist and pulling her upright, "would rather have my eyeballs forcibly extracted from my face, rolled around in rough bark strips, and then placed back into their appropriate sockets." He turned to leave.

"But it's the most interesting part! You merely feed a larva on an exclusive diet of royal jelly until it grows up. Depending on what it is given to eat, any bee could become a queen. "

Byron stopped, afraid that Foster's contraption on his right wrist had malfunctioned; he felt as if he had just been struck by a bolt of lightning. He ran back towards the Beekeeper and kissed him on the mouth. Then he found his ruined top hat from his bottomless pocket and put it on the other man's balding head, smacking the top and kissing him again.

"I apologise for my previous behaviour; I've lately been under a great deal of stress. You, sir, are a genius and a miracle-worker. When I get my inheritance back, yours shall be the first debt I repay. Tell me, what is the thing you want most in life?"

"I want for someone to listen to my entire act," he said in a quiet voice.

"Done!" Byron replied, sitting in the front pew with rapt attention.

322

In Which Byron Gets His Inheritance Back, Or: The Queen is Dead, Long Live the Queen

"Thank you for your interest in solving the Star-Crosser Plague," the guard said, blowing the feather on his hat out of his face with his breath, so that he wouldn't have to take his hands off his sword or the incredibly large blunderbuss that he held like a staff. "Your information will be processed and an investigator will be with you in three to four weeks. Next!" The guard craned his head to see around Byron, Marietta, and the large cart she was pulling in order to greet the next person waiting in line.

"Did you not hear me through that extravagant plumage drifting in front of your face like a dispirited peacock, lamenting that no one wants to mate with it? I have valuable information concerning the Plague with me now!" Byron gestured to the cart, which squeaked every time Marietta shifted the weight from one shoulder to the other. There was a small popping noise as weak tendons gave way and one of her shoulders dislocated to hang limply at her side. Byron smiled and tried to hide the bad arm behind him. "I demand to see not only the Queen, but all of her court. What I have with me will change the course of our struggle with the damned creatures—it cannot wait three hours, let alone three weeks. And I expect to be compensated for my efforts immediately after my presentation."

There was a loud sigh behind Byron from the next person in line. Marietta pushed the cart backwards and ran over the man's foot. Byron heard the grunting squeal and smirked inwardly at the assassin's innocent look of horror.

Buckingham Palace was in disrepair. After a rather prodigious attack of Seekers five years ago, in which the roving undead had thought its walls were flesh instead of stone and crisscrossed them with corrosive tongue-tracks, Queen Victoria had decided she wanted something that could defend against the walking dead. As a result, the Palace was always embroiled in construction as she changed her mind this way or that, always trying to make its defences impenetrable to the Crossed. At that moment, dozens of men were bustling around, laying brick, sculpting defence towers, sticking out their thumbs to get a lay of the land, and much more. It was all so very distracting; Byron wanted to put in his own two cents about the proper way to defend a castle, given that he had once done exactly that against the Battle Hordes of the Shrieking Choir, who, like banshees, could dissolve stone with a mere shriek.

"If this is such big news, why don't you just show it to me?" the guard replied, eyeing the cart with suspicion. His grip on the blunderbuss tightened.

"Because it's not quite ready yet—but trust me, in an hour, you will wonder how we fought the Star-Crossers at all without such a vital piece of information in our hands." He looked back, put a hand against the cart, and closed his eyes. "Well, maybe an hour and a half."

"Buddy..." The guard leaned on his blunderbuss and sighed, looking for all the world like he wanted to just drop both weapons and rub his temples. "I've seen it all and heard it all. Believe me, there is nothing under that tarp I haven't seen before. And if I've seen it, then so's the Queen, and if the Queen's seen it, then she doesn't want to see it again. Trust me on that. So take your cart somewhere else, and we'll process your request and get back to you in three to four weeks."

"Yeah, move it!" the man behind them yelled, nursing his broken toes and glaring at Marietta.

Byron came close and lowered his voice to a whisper: "I very much doubt that you've seen what I have." He pulled a corner of the tarp back to reveal a large, dark purple pulsating thing that dripped steaming goo onto the guard's shoe with a loud hiss. The guard backed up, crossing himself several times, and waved them forwards without another word. The creaking of the tumblers in the gate doors lifted the hopes of everyone else in line, and they watched with hungry eyes as Byron and Marietta rolled into Buckingham Palace.

A bubble of excitement grew within Byron at the thought that finally, after so many years and so many setbacks, he was finally going to get his inheritance back. Then he realised that the trembling feeling came from the child in the cart undergoing a growth spurt. It was almost ready. There were only a few more things to do before it would be complete.

All around them, people scrambled to open up a hall so that they could have an audience. Men in white livery were scuttling back and forth, yelling at others to get everything prepared for their meeting.

"Ah, yes, this is how it should be! People leaping to meet my every whim!" Byron sighed, stretching his arms out wide.

"How is that any different than what I do?" Marietta asked, grunting with the weight of the cart.

"I said people, my dear workhorse."

"I am not a horse. Especially not a working one."

"A working girl, then. But if you think about it, you are dead, and I have beaten you several times. If it neighs like a horse…"

At last only two large clockwork doors barred their path. The last of the liveried men had disappeared and the sound of trumpets filled the air. It sounded like they were inside a grandfather clock as the doors opened and the brightness from the outside filtered into the dimly gas-lit room. Once inside, the doors closed behind them, and Byron ordered Marietta to roll the cart into the middle of the room. Half of the walls had been painted and hung with ancient tapestries and dark wood furniture, but the other half was a dumping ground for various weapons that hadn't found homes in the defensive lines of the Palace, so that it looked as if a very old and very bloodthirsty, pipe-smoking, axe-wielding grandfather lived there. They both waited for their eyes to adjust to the creeping darkness.

"Stand behind me, Marietta," Byron said, pushing the assassin behind him and preening himself like a cockatoo. "I want my face to be the very first thing the Queen sees when she enters the room."

Three, four, then five minutes passed and Byron still stood there, back straight and palms sweating with nerves. (That reminded him to recheck his bottomless pocket for the nerves he had gathered from a few errant Seekers and make sure that he could still sell them when another Mephistopheles Market opened up.) He cleared his throat and finally looked away from the throne, hoping to catch someone's eye and remind them of why they were there. He was just about to hiss at one of the liveried men when a large door at the back of the room opened. A darkened figure strode into the middle of the room and sat down on an immense throne, throwing a cloak over its carved back.

"I am here to hear what evidence you have brought that will help our glorious crusade against the ill-mannered Star-Crossers," a nasal, masculine voice said. He was very short, with an aquiline nose that could have sunk a boat and shaky hands with bigger veins than some people had wrists. His skin was pale and lay tight over his bones, lending him an aura of constant sea-sickness. Every time he opened his mouth, Byron wondered if he was going to throw up.

Byron took a few steps forwards and cleared his throat. "Excuse me, I am waiting for the Queen. You are…?"

"None of your business, boy. All you need to know is that I am the one you're going to report to. Now who are you?" he whined, puffing out his cheeks and tipping his immense nose forwards in his anger. His teeth smacked against his cheeks so that he made a horrible squelching noise with every word.

"No, this is not how this is supposed to work. I am supposed to talk to the Queen and she is supposed to give me a boon for my hard work and diligence. If I'm not talking to the Queen, I can't receive my boon, and if I can't get my boon, what am I doing here?"

"A fine question," the stranger whined, exhaling a long wheeze. "What are you doing here? Certainly you have yet to produce anything worthy of my attention. Do you know the penalty for wasting my time? For every minute of mine that I believe you have wasted, I will have that many hot pokers pressed into your extremities…and then into your centre. Thus far," he said, looking at his jewel-encrusted pocket watch, "it has been three minutes. How much do you value your kneecaps? If you don't care for them, I have an entire trophy room full. I appreciate them very much. Especially the ones with intricate scorch marks in interesting patterns."

Byron stood still for a few seconds, thinking about his options. He eyed the door behind him, but it had shut tight, the gears enmeshing in criss-crossing patterns that were indecipherable to him. They were locked in. He had not thought to have an escape plan, despite his general rule of having at least three; he had always assumed that he would need to break in to Buckingham Palace, not break out. The man in the throne started tapping his fingers against the golden armrest and sighing. Finally, Byron saw no other way.

He went up to the cart and unwrapped it with a flourish that sent the tarp swirling in spirals until it settled into a neat clump on the floor. Underneath was the large, dripping cocoon that Byron and Marietta had found in the Charred Thickets almost a year before. It was no longer open, however; the sides had knit over. A dark shadow the size of a person was pulsating inside, pushing at the edges, the imprints of hands and feet showing through the dark purple membrane like a heavily pregnant woman's belly. The entire thing had taken on the shape of a giant brain, its surface packed with wrinkled ridges. There was a central groove where the membrane was thinner and one could see the chunks of brain matter floating in spinal fluid that the figure inside would eat at its leisure; Byron and Marietta had been scavenging for it over the last few months.

At Byron's mental urging, the figure convulsed, pushing at its boundaries, almost breaking them before tiring and sinking back to the cocoon's centre to feast on more collected brains. While feeding, it reminded Byron of the rabbits he used to get for his mother. The bond he felt with this creature was more intense, more intimate; he loved this thing with not only the protective pride of a father, but the ardent desire of a lover. This was his daughter, his wife, his everything, rolled into one neat little creature that was finally going to make life all right.

"What…is it?" the man said, pinching his nose even though the smell was musty at worst. He pulled his feet into the chair so as to get as far away from the cocoon as possible. "I've never even thought of a punishment for every minute that someone disgusts me; it has never happened to this extent before. Get it away before I throw up my lark-wrapped escargot." He made frantic shooing motions.

"This is living proof of the pinnacle of Star-Crosser evolution. This," Byron said, hands framing the cocoon without touching it, "is a gestating Star-Crosser Queen. She emits low levels of psychic signals that can control any Star-Crosser within several hundred yards, possesses a level of self-awareness not found in other Star-Crossers, and can, according to my own theory, help us track down and kill the other Queens. Without Queens, there would be no Swarms, and the rate of new infections will decrease until the Crossers can no longer maintain their own populations. The guidance of the Queens is why all our efforts to exterminate the Star-Crossers have failed; root out the Queens, and they will simply wither away."

"Eeew! Get it away! Get it away!" the man shrieked as the cocoon began to thump, almost dislodging itself from the cart. A small fissure appeared in one of the wrinkles on the side, oozing sticky grey matter. A small puddle formed and, because of the unevenness of the floor, began to creep towards the throne. "I will not sit here and take this any longer! Get out! Get out!"

The liveried men pulled knives from their coats and started marching on Byron and Marietta.

"Marietta! The cart!" Byron yelled. His eyes were wide with urgency.

She picked up the rope just as one of the men slashed at her. She unhooked both of the axes from her belt and prepared to fight until one of the liveried men picked Byron up and carried him to the door. She threw an axe and hit the servant in the arm holding Byron, so that he fell with a wince. But by that time, too many servants had come into the throne room. They were surrounded.

"Well, the last time I was surrounded, there were considerably less tights about, but the level of hirsuteness seems to be on par. And no, I'm not talking about the lovely ladies of The Cheeky Scullion—they were much more hospitable than the court of my very own Queen and country!"

"So you're saying I have a magicked guardsman's foot that

you're going to spit on, and it's going to make all of them run away so we can escape?" Marietta squeaked, throwing her other axe and searching her belt for more melee weapons.

"Alas, Hurricane Harvey has no mixture of spittle, feminine hormones, or the promise of a deep, dark inkwell in which to dip their pens—if you will excuse such language in the most hallowed halls of governance and upper-crustdom, though the latter is rather more crusty than it is upper—but I have something better than all of that."

"Really? Because it's all you ever seem to talk about!"

Byron pulled the flintlock dagger out of his bottomless pocket, aimed it at the closest of the liveried men (smushing the back of his arm into the side of Marietta's face), and pulled the trigger. Nothing happened. Marietta opened her cringed eye to see as the liveried man laugh and continue to rush them. Byron lunged forwards and stabbed three men in an eye, a throat, and a pectoral, respectively, then turned the bloody blade around and pistol-whipped the fourth. Then he realised that the butt of the pistol was too small for such an endeavour; the man merely rubbed the small red spot between his eyes and charged again.

Blood-stopping screams rent from the stabbed victims, giving pause to the other liveried men and even the dandy on the throne. The sloppy-mouthed youth stood on his tiptoes to watch the proceedings as those who had been stabbed started to liquefy and melt into their own shadows, bleeding flesh-coloured and white drippings as their actual bodies filled with inky blackness. At last the flattened men beat at their two-dimensional prisons within the floor while the inky shadow-men stood dazed in the real world, confused and blinded by their new, unimaginable, terrifying freedom.

"Get them away! Get them away!" The crowned man jumped

up on his throne again, shifting back and forth on the balls of his feet as if the shadows were rats. The few remaining footmen, who had been joined by guards rushing into the room, backed away in silent horror from the outstretched hands of the dark men, who were trying to glean as much information as possible about the new dimension of depth they had been so suddenly introduced to.

"I didn't know that was a Shadowglass Dagger," Marietta intoned in awe of the shining blade, reaching towards it as everyone else cringed, only for Byron to start dragging her out of the throne room.

"Got it at a garage sale," he replied.

Marietta stopped in their egress to look at him questioningly.

"That's it?"

"No, it most certainly is not it! We've left the most important discovery of the past twenty-five years back in the throne room, I have gone through the largest emotional blunderbuss-shot known to mankind, and I will not simply allow it to end with a 'that's it' and a hasty escape from a poorly planned situation." He unceremoniously guided her out of the tangle of rooms, one hand gripping her arm and the other on her waist, until they reached the front doors and slipped out into the foggy sunlight through a couple of holes scheduled for repair.

"No, I mean, you didn't get your Shadowglass Dagger from a poxy-faced blacksmith who has made a metal mask corresponding to each emotion and constantly switches them out in the hopes of curbing his Hephaestean tendencies—"

"Good mythological allusion," Byron piped in.

"—or a snaggle-toothed hobo who whistles each different part of a symphony at the same time each day against the walls of a canyon until one day the entire musical piece comes to life in the coalescing echoes, or some ridiculousness such as that."

"That, my dear marmalade, sounds nothing at all like any character I've ever met in all my years of traversing the globe and consorting with the fringes of society." He opened his arm to invite her to hitch a ride onto a cart driven by a gouty, three-legged racehorse with one eye and a crusty Jolly Roger eyepatch over the other.

"Now who's talking about hasty, poorly planned escapes?" Marietta sighed and fluffed her skirts around her legs. The car carried them off to reconvene at The Cheeky Scullion.

Byron put down an extremely large mug of foamy beer and flicked the moustache off his face, barely missing Marietta. She took a swig of her own drink and waited for the story to finish. He was talking to the serving wench; by this time, she had learned to avoid the table at which they sat, but couldn't help passing by.

"...kicked me out, do you believe the nerve of it? I can't imagine what could have possibly made them think that my offer was worth less than all the other swill anyone else has brought to them in the last ten years. There haven't been any advances in fighting on the Star-Crosser front—the Guard's weapons were discovered too long ago to be effective! It's almost as if they don't want any more information, and merely wait for people to find them knowledge that would advance the cause so they can quash it! Not that it's my cause; I could care less whether Star-Crossers were wiped out or took over the world, so long as I had my inheritance back. And now my Queen is gone, and I'll never even see what she looked like!"

He felt Marietta's hand on his back and his first thought was comfort, not the imminent fear of death. There had to be a first time for everything, including falling in love with a dead girl. (Well, a second time for everything.)

"I'm sure she would have been…" Marietta searched for a word.

"Glorious? Magnificent? The most incredible sight in the entire history of eyes? I agree," he muttered into the bottom of his mug. "Wait," he suddenly said, pulling his head up, "what did I just say?"

"'The most incredible sight—'"

Byron cut her off. "Before that."

"'Magnificent?'"

"Before that!"

"'As long as I have my inheritance back?'"

Byron eyed her. "You know the exact thing I am thinking of, so why not just tell me?"

"If you know that I know it, why don't you just say it?"

"Just—!"

"The part about how the Queen is intentionally suppressing all knowledge about Star-Crossers and that's why we were kicked out?"

"Yes! You're brilliant!" Byron kissed Marietta's head in a moment of passion before realising what he had done. He cleared his throat and threw a few coins onto the table, pulling Marietta's arm to get out of the tavern as quickly as possible. As he passed by the tavern wench who had been serving them, he winked and blew a kiss. "The next time you see me, darling, I will be a king, and you know that kings treat their subjects like they do their mistresses."

"Keep them in the dark?" Marietta suggested.

"And you would be both!" he yelled on their way out the door, ignoring Marietta's interruption.

They disappeared into the shadowy street. The sun had set while they had been drinking their problems away and Byron used the darkness to sneak around to the outside wall of the Palace. He began knocking at the bricks as if he were waiting to hear a mouse scuttle through the walls of his house. He concentrated, moving his ear along some complex pattern that only he could discern, until his eyes went wide and he nodded to himself.

He pulled a monocle out of his coat pocket and placed it over his left eye, squinting and readjusting to find the perfect angle. The glass was tempered so that he when he fogged it up and cleaned it off, it would show the architectural blueprints of any given building that he had been inside of for more than sixteen seconds. The trick, however, was the material used to clean the lens off. Wool would reveal the plumbing, silk the steamlines, cotton the landscaping, and chainmail any secret passages. The problem with chainmail, however, was that, if done improperly, it would leave scratches in the glass and ruin the monocle forever. A new lens could be ground only by blind monks trapped in caves originally dug out by primitive Man thousands of years ago for the sole purpose of drawing crude pictures that appeared to move by flickering firelight, thus recreating dreams that the blind monks could neither appreciate nor disapprove of.

"Give me some of your chainmail," Byron whispered to his companion.

"I don't have any chainmail," she whispered back.

"Don't lie. I've heard you clinking, and since I can't see it, I can only assume that you wear it as undergarments to protect what you consider to be your most valuable bits."

"Fine," she sighed. "But don't look."

Byron closed his eyes as he heard the sound of ruffling fabric and a few grunts, then finally he felt the warm chainmail in his hand. He pulled the monocle off, carefully fogged it up with a blast of breath, and used the chainmail to clean it off. There were small squeaking noises as the metal scrubbed the tempered glass. Then, putting the monocle to his eye again and taking small steps, he worked his way down the wall until he let out a small gasp of discovery.

"Here," he said, putting a hand to a small brick and pushing on it until a man-sized door swung into the labyrinth of Buckingham Palace's inner chambers.

"Lead the way, O fearless leader," Marietta breathed.

The tunnel twisted and turned, through passages so small that they had to squeeze sideways and galleries that could have fit five guards and their horses. At one point they heard faint male groans through the wall; Byron cocked his eyebrow and made a rather obscene gesture.

"You would know, given that you were raised in a brothel," Marietta responded. He gave her a brief glare before moving forwards.

After more than thirty minutes of wandering around, Byron put the monocle back onto his left eye and sought a way into the throne room, from where he hoped they hadn't moved the cocoon. He was just about to ask for Marietta's other piece of chainmail when he felt a small crackling inside his head, as if something were chipping away at his brain.

"Do you feel that?" Byron asked, tapping out the rhythm against a piece of brick with one finger.

"Feel what?" Then Marietta's face went slack.

"She's waking up," he breathed. He hurried on, no

longer needing the monocle or any other instrument save for his connection to the Queen breaking out of her shell. It was reminiscent of the connection he'd first realised he had with Marguerite after he turned her; the thought made him break out into a crooked smile.

He slipped out into a darkened corridor and looked up and down the hallway for any of the guards or servants that had kicked them out earlier. There were only two guards standing vigil in front of the room that he knew housed his Queen, and they were both falling asleep on their feet, their spears dropping slightly every so often as they nodded and snapped alert again. Byron stuck out a hand and Marietta slipped one of her axes into it. Using his blinding speed, he cut both of their throats and opened the door into the throne room before their bodies hit the floor.

"Marietta, bite those two men."

"Excuse me?"

"Please. That's not even the strangest thing I've asked you to do this day. We're going to need them."

"You bite them. I'm not hungry."

"I didn't say 'eat them,' I said 'bite them.'" He scrunched his face up and pursed his lips, trying to imitate the expression that African Spray-Nosed Feral-Bottomed Baboons made before vying for dominance through a show of seeing who could sit on the other the longest. He was about to start their traditional wail when she sighed and knelt down to carry out his command. "And then put these bowler hats on them." He reached into his bottomless pocket and pulled out several hats that matched the very one he was wearing. "I shall return forthwith."

He sped down the hallways, finding and killing as many guards as he could and returning with their bodies. As soon as Marietta had bitten each one, he pushed a bowler as far down onto its head as possible, so that they wouldn't shrug them off in their newly awakened search for brains and flesh. In fairly short order, a clump of ravenous Crossers were bumping into each other in the hall, looking at lot like Byron if one squinted one's eyes, cocked one's head to the left at a thirty-five-degree angle, and then blew one's nose fairly loudly.

"My plan is to confuse the rest of the Buckingham guards by having multiples of myself stashed around, bumping into each other and causing a general ruckus while we carry out the rest of the plan," Byron whispered into Marietta's ear. He motioned for her to spread them around the hallways with a vigorous pumping of his arms.

Marietta rolled her eyes and began to herd the Crossers out into the hallway, making the international sign for 'brains are over there,' and left them to their undead devices. As she returned, Byron began following the Queen's pounding in his own head; he led Marietta into the promised room.

There, pushed into the corner, was the cocoon—and struggling to break through the thick, gooey membrane was his Queen. One hand shot up out of the membrane and he ran to grasp it and help pull her out of her confines. A loud sucking noise suddenly released as she spilled out onto the floor in a small wave of brain matter, strange purple goo, and the bits of his decayed arm and leg that he had put in there to spice things up.

She took her first few wobbly steps and looked up into Byron's eyes to see who her creator was.

"You," she whispered and tried to pull away.

"You may call me your King," he responded, his eyes glistening with love and admiration. "It worked! I can't believe it worked. Feeding an untouched Star-Crosser exclusively brains and allowing her to gestate for months actually creates a Queen!"

"What have you done to me?" She looked in horror at her green hands and arms, the dripping brains sloughing off of her, the crown of bones that had started growing out of her own skull. She looked like a gangrenous goddess. Her black lips were full, her eyes clear and a bright, glowing agate, and her nails were strong and dark. She stood up and wobbled a bit, catching onto Byron's arm before he drew her close.

"Chosen you to be the greatest manifestation of my love," he said back, kissing the top of her head and licking its goo from his lips.

"You're sick," she responded.

"I've been telling him that for years." Marietta popped in between them to wave to the other woman and help wipe off her forehead. "We have had oh so many discussions about appropriate and inappropriate responses to things. Appropriate would have been: 'I pretended to kill you and then carted you off'—actually, he had me cart you while you were unconscious—'to the Charred Thickets, where we put your body into a cocoon we found a while ago and fed you only brains for nine months'—a supply which mostly I was responsible for securing. Or 'I made you into something the world has never seen before, or at least has not been exposed to that much.' I even would have accepted 'you're dead after that horrible incident with the roof and the five liters of Tongue-Stomping Rum and this is the afterlife' as a cruel joke. What he said is just downright creepy. By the way, Marguerite, how do you feel?"

"The last thing I remember is you cutting off that poor Christina's head." She stretched her limbs and wiggled her fingers. Byron thought every movement to be a physical symphony of perfection. He thought his smile would break his jaw.

"I had to make everyone believe you were dead so I could

inherit my personal fortune via your connection to both my Uncle and me. But alas, because of legal trickery and loopholes invented to destroy rather than protect those who find themselves under the shadow of our governing system, so that..." He trailed off as he noticed that neither Marietta nor Marguerite were looking at him anymore, but rather, something over his left shoulder.

He turned to find a veiled, white figure, covered in lace and fastidiously demure, sauntering by the open doors to the room. She was not much taller than Marguerite and about as waifish. Her nightgown was still rumpled, as if she had just woken up, and her movements were jerky and sluggish. In her hand she held a glass of opaque, slightly green viscous liquid. She shuffled in her rabbit-fur slippers so that the only noise any of them heard was her shushing gait.

Byron wasn't quite sure if the eerie glow of the liquid was giving her a greenish tinge, or if there really was a sallowness to her skin underneath her fluffy layers of nightgown and cross-stitched veil. But when she cleared her throat, Byron—who always had a problem distinguishing between a clearing throat and a whining dog—began to feel the earth for remnants of the workers who had given their lives to build the palace and were now buried deep beneath the foundation. The old and the new, the renovations of and the additions to Buckingham had disturbed their slumber, making them easier to call upon and rile up. Nothing was more rile-able than a worker killed in a horrendous construction accident and left to become part of the décor. He began to concentrate, spreading his arms palm-down, so that he could start the call if his presumptions were correct.

Marguerite, to Byron's right, stepped onto the black square of tile next to his white one and was struck with a strange turmoil. Her bony crown began to grow, the hair on her arms rose, and a low growl started in her throat. Marietta, to his left, pulled out her one remaining axe and began twirling it in her fingers, feeling the same agitation—though to a lesser extent than Marguerite, who was practically buzzing with aggression.

The veiled figure stepped into the throne room with that same, sleepy shuffling gait and set the glass down next to the throne. Byron could now see that it was full of curdled milk and maggots, crawling up the glass sides only to slip back into the gooey swamp. She placed her bony bottom upon the throne and settled her arms at the sides of the chair in a completely erect posture.

"Loyal subjects—" she began before Byron cut her off.

"I am most certainly not a subject, but rather an object, due to the inferred inferiority of sub-anything, and I will demonstrate such by objecting to my subjectification with abject apathy. I have seen through your lies, trod through the unwieldy mess left by your servants and henchmen alike, and found all of them to be lacking in the faculties necessary to run an eel farm, let alone an empire. Even the loyalty which you so wish to attribute to me will do nothing but clearly excoriate what little dyed-in-the-wool mentality remains in the dregs of my psyche. If anything, I am a wolf under that dyed wool, and soon you will discover that it is dyed with blood. And I will let you guess in that domestic-stock-sized brain of yours whose it is."

"Um, excuse me," Marietta said, curtseying and dipping her head to the stately yet partially somnambulistic woman, then rushing to Byron to whisper in his ear. "Byron, that's Queen Victoria."

"I am quite aware of who—and what—she is, my dear, and despite her name and title, she is going to leave this room as neither the victor nor the Queen." He took out his flintlock dagger and started polishing the blade and checking the chamber. He had done some testing while Marguerite had still been pupating and prepared three bullets made of sunbaked graveyard dirt, the peels of rotten carrots and cucumbers, and a special ingredient, just in case Marguerite couldn't be controlled. Now he was going to have the opportunity to use the bullets on someone else.

"Wait, I'm sorry. Hold on." Marietta held up a finger and sighed. "How are you going to get your inheritance back without a Queen to grant you a boon? Isn't that the whole reason we came here?"

"Because, my dear pawn, I am going to be queening." He blew into the chamber of the gun and began to polish the outside.

"Is that where you dress up in women's clothes and look at yourself in the mirror and tell yourself how desirable you are to the opposite gender? Because I think you'll need to tone your calves up some more if you want to be wearing high heels."

"It's a common term in the gentlemen's thinking game of chess for promoting a pawn to another piece, most often a queen. Thus, players say 'queening' instead of 'promoting'—who wants a silly knight or a rickety castle when one can have a majestic, formidable, and loyalty-inspiring queen?"

"You...you're going to make me a queen?" Marietta rested one hand on her chest and batted her eyelids.

"Silly girl," Byron scoffed, pulling back the hammer of his flintlock dagger and aiming directly for Queen Victoria's heart, "I already have a queen. You can be a pawn, as I already mentioned. And considering your previous occupations before finding me, I'm relegating you—" He pointed to a white checker-square to the far left and one row ahead of he and Marguerite. "—to where you can be the gambler pawn."

"This is regicide! I demand you put down your weapon at once and think about the consequences of your actions!" the indignant Queen shouted, waving her hands around and sloshing some of her milk onto the floor. "Guards!"

"I'm sorry," Byron responded, his extended arm not even wavering as he spoke, "they're dead and shambling around. By now they're being sought out and destroyed, much to the bitter disappointment of their fellows, who thought they had finally caught a rascal like me but received a poor, Crossed imitation instead. That doesn't mean much, because we're dead, too—and this may come as a shock to my compatriots, but you're dead as well. Death is the great equaliser, as I've always avowed; this time, however, I shall make an exception, for some of us are about to become deader than others."

"Ooh!" Marietta shrieked. "I finally get to correct your grammar!" She pondered for a moment and then shook her head as another thought grazed by. "She's dead? In the sense that the monarchy lives on through its respective ruling heads, and she's just another in a long chain of the mantra 'long live the queen, the queen is dead?' Or—"

"She's dead," Byron responded just as Victoria unveiled. Her skin was the same sallow green as Marguerite's; she bore the same black lips and fingernails and the same bony crown, only fully formed and ornate with intricate carvings, looking more like a stag's rack than the princessly tiara of Byron's lost wife. "That's why there's been no advancement against the Star-Crossing Plagues, the Long-Eared Legion, or any of the other horrors to come from the passing of the Homunculus Star, and no mention within the last twenty years of anyone receiving a boon. You've been advertising for information in order to find and kill those who learn the truth. And if the truth will set you free, is naked, and comes from the mouths of babes, then we are your free, naked babes."

"Clean," Marietta clarified. "The truth is always squeaky clean, so we're clean, free, naked babes."

"And should be taken with a grain of salt," Byron added, "so we're clean, free, naked, salty babes."

"No, the saying is just 'take it with a grain of salt.' It isn't necessarily truth that should be taken that way. Though the truth does hurt, and if one were to theoretically take it with a grain of salt, that would make it sting more. So we'd be masochistic, free, naked—"

"Enough!" Victoria yelled, pounding her glass of curdled milk down. It shot to the ceiling and landed on the floor with a spongy splash. "I've had enough of your games."

"I doubt that very much, my literally mortified monarch. How fond are you of chess?"

"Is that what you think this is? A game of wits? Hardly. This is a game of numbers." Victoria laughed, throwing her head back to the ceiling. "And yes, my Guards are dead, but they are hardly a fair match to your paltry army. One queen, one poor excuse for a king, and one pawn? I have a stacked board." She closed her eyes and Byron could see the dead Guards in the hallway walking jerkily, as if they were attached to strings at the ends of Victoria's fingers. He hadn't expected her control to be so swift or complete. The distant sound of marching boots munched up the hallways and echoed into the throne room. Within minutes there were eight foot soldiers—including the two from the doorway, their necks smiling like open mouths—two bishops, two knights, and two very large albino ravens. All were Star-Crossed and in various stages of decay, so that when they entered the room, moulded feathers scattered and detached limbs crawled of their own volition behind them, leaving slimy trails and wet splotches of boneless tissue.

"Stacks and racks," Byron mumbled, still pointing his gun.

"For being such an austere paragon of propriety and repression, you certainly do use transparent terminology. And rooks instead of castles? My grandmother can do better, and she's—"

"Dead? Yes, I understand the concept," Victoria sighed in exasperation. "It was the best I could do given the shortness of the demand."

"No, quite alive and well, thank you, and a master architect at that." Byron scratched the side of his head with the barrel of the revolver before aiming it again.

"I'm glad to hear that," she said, standing up and placing herself opposite Marguerite on their large chessboard, an empty space beside her where a king would be, "Now attack—"

Byron held up a finger on his other hand for patience. He closed his eyes and felt for the bones he had discovered earlier from those who had died to build the palace. With his right hand, he grasped Marguerite's shoulder and forced her broken will to power his own for the upcoming endeavour.

The floor began to shake, the neat-edged tiles cracking apart and coming up at the seams, so that the rolling breaks made a disjointed and broken chessboard. Out of the exposed patches of dirt and foundation rose a bony hand like a botfly issuing from the bloated leg of a drowned corpse. A veritable hodgepodge of bones shook out of the ground, revealing themselves in the exposed earth under the palace and rearranging themselves into their proper places, until there was a lumbering, mismatched skeleton army more fitting a stew than a force to match the Queen's. Some were missing arms, most were missing ribs, and a group of about six gathered around a coveted thigh bone and began wordlessly arguing over who would get it.

Byron felt a familiar pain in his left arm and right ankle, this time accompanied by a stinging sensation at the top of his head. He pulled off the glove from his ruined hand and felt with its skeletal digits the beginnings of his own bony crown. Seven bony black protrusions peeked out from his hair. He cackled gleefully as the ragtag soldiers began to orient themselves forwards, disregarding the proper etiquette of turns or how each piece was supposed to move. The raven to Byron's left took flight and the one on his right floundered until it lost a wing with a squelch and started trudging forwards with the rest of the Queen's army, far slower but far more robust than Byron's own.

He let out his own war cry and his rickety troops stumbled ahead with a great clacking and shuffling. Byron released Marguerite and a similar scream issued from her own throat as she charged, jumping over skeletons and through rotted flesh in order to reach Victoria. Having learned much from the Beekeeper, Byron knew that the instinctual surge of a Virgin Crossed Queen to seek out and destroy one who was so unfit to rule blocked out any doubts she may have had about working for the man she hated and had tried to kill several times in the past few years.

"A Virgin Queen—one who has never eaten flesh outside of her cocoon, that is, for Marguerite is as far from pure as muddy Lucifer himself—who senses that the previous Queen is unfit for command will, more often than not, kill her predecessor and take over her Hive. The drive is pure instinct," Byron yelled to Marietta, who was hacking at the throat of a rust-armoured dead knight. Once she had sawed through the metal, dulling her blade, his head came rolling off. He soon fell apart, his pieces clanking and crawling over the board, trying to trip any passing skeleton in a last gesture of malice.

"Fascinating!" She threw the ruined axe away and pulled out her brass knuckles, only to be surrounded by five pawns shabbily dressed in the garb of their former occupations. Each and every one of them had been bitten by Queen Victoria herself, lending them the power to remain animated even after being chopped up, burned, or anything short of totally destroyed.

Marguerite, on the other hand, commanded a phalanx of skeleton soldiers, who had elected a president for the advance formation and discharged committees for weapons retrieval, scouting, and attack. They democratically marched through the clanging masses towards the still-seated Queen, who watched over the battlefield with an almost glazed expression. Her bishops had crossed her throne with long, metal crucifixes with which they thwacked anyone who ventured too close. Since Marguerite's skeletons had no gristle to hold them together, only magic, they easily fell apart into mere bits of bone, which still others used to parry and thrust against Victoria's zombies.

At first, the committees worked well. Some picked up the still-crawling bits of the Queen's Star-Crossers and were gathering arms, legs, ribs, and even a jaw to use as wriggling weapons against the enemy. Still others had perched on the flagpoles on which hung all of the heralds of Victoria's various titles, cupped skeletal hands over their eyeless sockets to gain any weaknesses in the enemy line, and communicated what they saw through dancing gestures; they looked either like bees telling the rest of their hive where a source of food was, or like very angry carriage drivers who had gotten into an accident and were trying to convince the befuddled police that blame lay with the other party.

"Byron!" Marietta yelled, being rapidly buried underneath a mountain of pawny unflesh. "The device!" She gripped her right hand in the air—the only visible part of her—and mimicked the gesture he used to activate Wasp's electric arc. Byron took it off his hand and threw it. The device maintained a perfect arc as it sailed through the air, only to land six feet away from her grasp. She sighed loudly and disappeared under her enemies.

Marguerite's phalanx, bolstered by her own power, had stayed together quite well, until the president that they had elected suddenly stopped three yards away from the Queen and started wordlessly gesturing to his comrades about the unfairness of the entire situation. Marguerite, master of body language and unspoken communication, watched in horror as the skeletons decided—democratically, of course—that they had neither instigated nor even voted for the war in which they now found themselves. One of them shouted—with his arms and fleshless face—to give him either liberty or death. The others quickly took up the cry, and within seconds, all had decided that death was indeed the better option given their current situation. They fell into rickety pieces right on the chessboard, raising such a cloud of dust that no one could see what had happened for a few seconds.

When it had settled, the other knight was holding Marguerite in the air by her throat and trying to toss her around like a rag doll. Marietta was being pecked at by the flying raven and four more pawns. And Byron—who had stayed behind the fracas like his counterpart sitting on her throne—was desperately trying to dodge horseshoes being thrown by a former blacksmith whose gritty face, despite its advanced decay, looked almost normal due to the sheer amount of soot disguising it.

"No!" he yelled, punctuating each phrase with a dodge of his neck and a lazy shift. "I…refuse…to…give…up!" He stopped manoeuvering around the thrown pieces of horseshoe and stamped the ground, rolling the floor and shaking the remaining bones. The less sturdy pieces lost their footing and fell to the ground. He closed his eyes, muttering under his breath with hissing S's and writhing vowels. Every skeleton still fighting for him, every Star-Crosser under his command--including Marietta and Marguerite— curled up, feeling the impact of his words as if they had been hit with every letter. Any wounds they had sustained during the course of the battle were healed. Peeling flesh glued itself back to their tendons and muscles so that both looked as if they had never even been dead in the first place.

Byron, however, grabbed his left arm in agony as the rot crept up to his shoulder. He swayed and shifted all of his weight to his left leg; the right had become little more than squishy flesh that could barely even bend at the knee. He poured himself into the ladies, urging them to fight, to toil forwards for the ultimate prize of both the throne and their continued existence. Marietta threw off the three pawns surrounding her, punching one so hard with the brass knuckles that he exploded into a putrefying mass of tissue too small even to wiggle. She then reached into a pocket that Byron had never seen opened before and pulled out a long whip lined with small blades. She snapped it in the air and a painting that was hanging on the wall fell to the floor in a shredded mass of canvas, wood, and nails. Another snap and a suit of armour was reduced to quivering soup cans. Marguerite grabbed the forearm of the knight holding her, broke the bone, and tore the arm out of the socket, throwing it at Victoria and forcing her to dodge—her first move since the fight had begun. She then ripped the throat out of the knight, armour and all, so that the bits of vocal cord and gristle clinked with metal when she threw them onto the ruined floor.

His arm and leg useless, the decay spreading into his lungs and slowly up his neck towards his brain, Byron pulled his good hand off the stickiness of his left, retrieved the gun from his holster, and tried to take aim at Victoria.

"The bishops!" he grunted, his voice withering away even as his black, bony crown grew taller, so that his head drooped forwards with the weight.

Marietta quickly dispatched the rest of the pawns surrounding her and ran, legs full of energy and agile muscle, and flipped through the air. She flew over the bishops' heads and landed next to Victoria's throne. She lashed the whip out, wrapping it around the rusty cross of one of the bishops, and pulled backwards, yanking the guard towards her. Marguerite slid across the floor, gathering floating bones in a maelstrom of power around her and firing them towards the other bishop. He broke his protective stance and started deflecting the projectiles with his cross until his decayed arms couldn't keep up with the speed. One hit him in the side of the face and took his head off, leaving Victoria exposed.

Marietta moved to punch her in the stomach with the brass knuckles—then froze, her arm poised to deliver a perfect left hook, just as Marguerite, teeth bared, stopped just short of tearing Victoria limb from limb. Byron felt an empty space in his bones where his control over the two women had been.

"What are you doing?" he rasped. The ladies stepped in front of Victoria, blocking the sights of his gun. "Get out of the way!" He coughed and something purplish, covered in black goo, slipped between his lips and dribbled onto the floor. He wasn't going to be able to keep his gun steady for much longer.

"They are mine now," Victoria said, her voice ringing majestically through the halls. "My subjects." Her smile was wicked in the dim light of the flickering candles.

"'It is better to be alone, madam, than in bad company,'" Byron tried his best to quip between the internal organs slowly coming up his oesophagus. Victoria staggered and a small amount of control crept back in through his feet. He seized her moment of distraction and began draining the two ladies of their energy. "'Liberty, when it begins to take root, is a plant of rapid growth.'" His arm began to feel better, his right leg to stitch itself back together.

"What?" Victoria demanded. "What is happening?"

"George Washington, madam!" Byron cried, raising his left hand in the air as green flesh dripped onto the floor. "When I was a lad and my father thought that I was interested in the American Revolution, given my fascination with dumping his tea into the river, he was so glad that I had shown an interest in something other than the morbidity of my mother's situation that he subscribed me to the Young Yankee Yarners, a fan club for the affiliates of George Washington and all things related to the flowering of democracy. In order not to disappoint my father, I memorised every single quotation of Washington's ever written down and passed through the fine filter of history. Do you feel the burning in your Divine Right? Is your grip on your throne slipping with the sweat of egalitarianism? Is the cushion beneath your bottom prickling with representation? Because I have, loaded in this gun," he said, levelling the flintlock between her eyes, "bullets made of leafy green vegetables—"

"A common myth perpetuated by none other than myself, to undermine the futile struggle against Star-Crossing kind!" Victoria spat.

"—graveyard dirt—"

"Better than silk sheets to me!"

"—and the pulped wooden teeth of Mr. Washington himself, which I received by correspondence for being such a loyal member of the Yarners. Even got myself the title of secretary by the time I was seven. 'Real men despise battle, but will never run from it,'" he quoted as he fired.

The bullet drove into her skull, sending her neck splitting backwards, and she fell in a crumpled heap on the throne, as dead as her leadership had been the past thirty years.

Marguerite rushed to the throne and began devouring the previous Queen's prone body as Victoria's green skin lightened to a normal paleness and her white bony crown drifted back into her skull. Byron, exhausted, still draining energy from both of the women—Marietta mostly—to repair his decay, looked around for his companion to congratulate them on their victory. He turned at the familiar crackle of the electric arc to find Marietta holding a large chunk of rock that he had previously seen the young Spittle carrying at the Archduke's ball. His puzzled face fell as whatever repairs he had made now drained out of him and into Marietta. Her cheeks became plump and rosy, her lips regained their coral pinkness, her body filled out, and her red hair shone with health as his own body grew sallow and empty. His right leg buckled and he collapsed onto the floor, forcing him to rear his head back in order to watch what was happening.

"What? What are you doing?" he croaked. She thrust the device forwards and he felt its current surge into him, filling every crevice he had ever known about himself with pure energy. One of his eyes went dark completely, and when the brightness finally faded, the air around him was clogged with pink, green, and yellow spots. He looked at his arms to find them skinny and grey-tinged; his cheeks were sunken and his hair was greasy and flat. He recognised himself from years ago, from before he had met Marietta for the second time and decided to start eating human flesh.

For the first time in his entire life, the dark part of himself that had been Star-Crossed from birth was gone.

"You…you shocked me back into life," he growled. He blinked, coughed, sneezed, and then blinked again, trying to orient himself. He couldn't tell if everything was different because of the ordeal or because of the harrowing experience of being completely, absolutely, irresolutely normal. "Like those blasted Trucklers did to the young cabbie! How, how could you do this? When we had everything? When I had everything? Do you know what you've done?"

"No." Marietta pushed her luscious red hair behind her and sauntered forwards, completely human once again as well. "You had everything. You were so distracted by regaining your inheritance, by creating your Star-Crosser Queen, by making your life perfect and magnificent, that you were too busy to notice that Spittle and I had come to an agreement. In trade for saving his life after the Mephistopheles Market, he gave me this." She held up the large rock, whose surface held a rainbow gloss that shone strangely in the light. "Something you would well recognise if you had paid any attention to anyone other than yourself. It's the meteorite that hit Marguerite after you turned her into an abomination. A chunk of the Homunculus Star, whose wonderful properties include restoring life to anyone who has been Star-Crossed. When it hit Marguerite, it cured her instead of killing her—much the same fate, to your decayed psyche. She wore it for years until your Uncle adopted Spittle. Once he saw it around her neck, he thought it must be valuable, so he stole it. That is why she came out of hiding; she thought that you had finally found her secret, not realising it was her son all along. After the boxcar, when I went chasing after Spittle, we struck a deal: the rock for his life and his freedom. I've carried it in a lead box to block its power until just now, when it restored me.

"But," she said, walking around Byron, picking at his clothes and turning her nose up at his appearance, "I knew that what had happened to her might again happen to me. I needed a more permanent solution. And that's when I remembered this little thing." She held up her hand to admire the electrical device. "I knew if I could force all of the death we shared into you by using the Homunculus Star, then I could use the electricity to bring you back to life. You would be cured, thus curing me. And it worked! It worked!" she yelled, her voice bouncing off the rafters and around the remnants of the battlefield as Marguerite continued to devour the corpse of Victoria.

More soldiers, having finally woken up to the cacophony in the throne room, marched in with guns and swords drawn to look upon the carnage.

"Just a midnight snack, gentlemen," Marietta responded, gesturing at Marguerite and the now indiscernible Victoria. "Nothing to see here." Confused, they looked at each other and then slowly stepped out of the room, lest the well-known appetite of Victoria spill over onto them. "Now, Queen Marguerite," she said, approaching the feasting woman, "I believe there's the small matter of Byron's boon. You will return his inheritance in exchange for his information about the Star-Crossers. And I, as his common-law wife, will be the arbiter of his estate, as he is not going to last even the afternoon." She turned back to Byron. "I have been waiting for the day when I could kill you for years now. I have been dreaming of it, savouring it, rolling it in my mouth, trying to figure out the most painful, awful, despicable way to die, and I think I've finally found it."

Byron, whose wits were slowly returning just in time to realise that his life—the plebeian human life he now had—was in immediate danger, tried to think fast.

"Does it involve that unfortunately disgusting coffee beverage, an upturned and vaguely raggedy parasol, a slightly used but still sturdy corset lace, and a short piece of pipe? I've heard that the combination of those four elements produces the most horrific death known to mankind. And Crosser-kind as well. Which is saying something, given that it took some research and time to get that many Crossers to agree. So you know the results are hardy."

"I—" Marietta stumbled in her slow march towards Byron, her hands outstretched, holding a rusty spoon that she had retrieved from somewhere upon her person. "Do you really think so? Now I have to give this a little bit more thought. I mean, no death but the most grotesque will do, and I thought I had it, but you might be onto something there with the corset lace."

While Marietta was debating with herself, Byron looked towards Marguerite, the once-love of his life, then back to Marietta, the even more recent once-love of his life, and sighed. Her Majesty Queen Marguerite, by the Grace of God, by the swell of the Great Sailor, of the United Kingdom of Great Britain and Ireland, Defender of the Faith, Empress of India, Protector from the Star-Crossed, waggled her eyebrows at Byron in what he believed to be a very unqueenly manner until he realised that she was urging him to escape. Whatever their love had meant, it was worth one more waggled eyebrow. Yet embedded in that eyebrow was also a warning: This is it. After this moment, she would be done with him and everything he had ever meant to her.

As Marietta continued to debate his brutal death, Byron found one of the corpses that had been wearing a bowler hat and propped it up in a rakish manner that could be construed as him if one were to squint sideways and rant about the most horrible way to kill someone.

He had just made it to the hallway when he realised that the fingernail on his middle finger was black and slightly cracked.

"No," he said, stopping to look at his hand from every different angle. "No, no, no, no, no. What's the point? What is the point in living on this earth, even as a disgustingly normal human, if I can't be immaculate? No! This is impossible! This isn't happening!"

It was then that he heard Marietta running after him, having realised his switch after his voice had echoed down the hallway. He would have plenty of time to contemplate his ugliness at a later date if only he would survive for such a postponement. He slipped into one of the many rooms under construction and continued his egress inside of the walls.

"The Queen is dead," Marietta panted, left far behind. "Long live the Queen. But you'll wish you had never even been dead in the first place, Byron!"

In Which There is an Epilogue, Or: Ashes to Ashes, Bust to Bust

"…and so I held her rather plump body in my arms as she died, feeling the last dredges of her pulse as it shot out of the horrible wound on her throat, caused by the most revolting monster known to mankind, and comforted her as the light slowly faded from her royal eyes."

"So you're saying that the Queen we have now isn't really Victoria, but some ginger who took her place without anyone noticing?" the serving wench said, sitting in his lap and idly playing with his hair. He put a hand up to stop her, realising too late that it was his left and therefore his ugly one.

"What do you think about this fingernail?" He held it up in the light, nervously fiddling with it. "Does it make me roguishly handsome, or just an abomination unto the Great Sailor? Be truthful now; I despise lies in all forms."

"What's this about fingernails?" another server said as she set down a shot of whiskey in a dirty glass. Byron promptly threw it into the back of his throat, cringing at the taste. "Dirty fingernails are always a turn-off, as far as I'm concerned."

"I was afraid of that." Byron cursed the damnable Marietta for the umpteenth time for making his fingernail, and therefore the rest of him, a hideous monster. He didn't even care that he was human and that there was an assassin of the highest order after him, or even that his inheritance was further out of his reach now than it had ever been—but the fact that Marietta had ruined him burned more than the ditchwater whiskey served at The Ornery Owl. "But! Nevertheless! Now this disgusting creature, this six-foot, snaggle-toothed, bandy-legged, cracker-mouthed, dry-skinned, hairy-toed harpy has been trying for many years to kill me, never knowing how precisely to do it. Should she wrap me up in ball of furious bees so that the vibration of their bodies cook me internally, leaving my body nothing more than a roguishly handsome fried crisp? Or should she peel my skin back, stuff tea inside all of my muscles, then boil me in hot water and turn my fingers into crumpets and my feet into scones and serve me for breakfast like some common fare at Tantalus's table? Or should she brew a concoction that makes me dream of being killed time after time, eternally waking up only to find myself in yet another death-dream, interminably, while she works on my sleeping body and kills me over the course of fifteen years? Or, and this just came to me—"

"Please, Mr. Ll-llwe—" one of the wenches began before Byron cut her off.

"My Christian name is most acceptable, my dear kumquat."

"I was just going to say that this is a most unacceptable conversation for stomachs, especially those already filled with our whiskey. But if she's so horrible, why hasn't she found you by now?"

"Because," he said, leaning forwards and beckoning her with his pristine finger so she had to bend over in order to hear him, "she is secretly in love with me, and though she proposes all of these scenarios, she'd rather another different type of proposal happen, if you're finding my driftwood."

"None of that here!" the other wench said, slapping him lightly on the arm. "There's rooms in the back if that's what you're after!"

"But I swear, I will get my inheritance back, I will prove that there is an imposter on the throne, and I will get that hellion before she kills me. I've been tracking another rogue, a small boy—well, almost a man now—by the name of Jebediah Hiram Blackmore, or the more-fitting moniker Spittle, and I believe he can help me.

I've even tracked him to the nearby town and think him to be a frequenter of this very same establishment. See, I have a plan to turn myself into a Star-Crosser—"

"How will that help at all?"

"Shush, my dear, no one likes a talking kumquat. Not just any Star-Crosser, but one that can—"

The door swung open. Marietta's silhouette grew across the tables until its head lined up perfectly against Byron's table. The shadow of an axe-blade crossed over the three empty shot glasses and bottle of cheap whiskey and stopped at his throat.

THE END, OR: IS IT?

Acknowledgments

First and foremost, I'd like to thank Jessica Eidsness, without whom this novel might never have been made. Back in 2010, she sat me down at a coffee shop and told me to write and to write now. Under such an egregious spotlight, my mind came up with a simple idea: a magician pulling a rabbit out of his hat. From there, this story was born.

To my wonderful husband, Adam, who has put up with more of my imposter syndrome outbursts than anyone else, and who is frequently the subject of my funnier tweets. You have him to thank for allowing me to see the writer within instead of the little girl pretending.

For my glorious editors Ale Fresch and Julie Rodriguez, who took a rough, wordy, bawdy, and sometimes incoherent manuscript and turned it into the polished stone you see today. They are both perseverant and intrepid in their pursuit of taking my terrible sentences and making them readable.

Thanks so much to Stevie, who created the gorgeous cover art and is an all-around amazeballs artist. All of my blue hairs are a dedication to her talent.

To Big Beth, Little Beth, Bess, Chantal, Kathleen, Pattimiss Chau, Sam-Sam, Suguna, Natalie, Shoko, and Clara-mara. For being there at the beginning and for still being there today. Many of them read early, early drafts of novels that should never see the light of day and they still love me. At least one of them still has a floppy disk with an early vampire novel on it. That's dedication. (And total blackmail material.)

To my beta readers: Vanessa Lane-Miller, Vega Brhely, James Swayze, Tegan Bolton, Sarah Wright, Ryan Breuer, Michael Baswell, Lisa Northrup, Pete Laffin, Madison Shoemaker, Michelle Sauer,

Milythael, Morgan Glass, TJ Thorp, and John Andreula. You guys came through at the end and really made sure this thing all came together.

Lastly, to the semi-colon. Eff you, period.

About the Author

MK Sauer lives in Boulder, Colorado where she owns a coffee shop and spends entirely too many hours of the day caffeinated. She received a degree in Russian Literature from the University of Colorado at Boulder. Believing that everyone should have at least one party trick, she has finally decided that hers is talking about Stalin for three hours straight. Her favorite RPG character trope is the wily thief who looks like a cross between Indiana Jones and Xena and is somehow afraid of looking up. She developed an obsession with vampires at the age of nine because of her mother's flat-out refusal to allow her to watch Interview with a Vampire. At the tender age of 13, when she was exposed to Russian Literature—mainly Dostoevsky, Gogol, and Bulgakov—her fate was sealed, the sunflower oil was spilled, and her destiny was revealed. High-brow horror was created in the rumblings of her pre-pubescent brain. Nowadays, she tries not to put too many pop culture references in her historical novels. Most of the time, she fails.

You can find her, musing poetically and posting pictures of oatmeal and udon noodles, on Twitter, @MK_Sauer and also on the internetosphere, where she infrequently blogs at mksauer.com